CW01084814

Feather

Tales of Isolation and Descent

Feather

Publication Date: September 2011

Copyright David Rix 2011.

Cover Art, Interior Design and Photography by David Rix

ISBN: 978-1-908125-07-1

The Magpies first appeared in *Strange Tales II* edited by Rosalie Parker, Tartarus Press 2007

The Book of Tides first appeared in *Blind Swimmer*, Eibonvale press 2010

www.eibonvalepress.co.uk

Acknowledgements

As all writers must have discovered (with varying degrees of shock), no one works alone – many people contribute ideas and advice. In this case, special degrees of eternal gratitude go to Aleksandra Furlan, Nina Allan and Douglas Thompson for their comments and advice and support at various points during the 7 plus years that this book has been slowly growing. Also to Abigail Ingram, who caused *The Magpies* to come into being and to Marina Savva, in discussion with whom the idea for *Touch Wood* first came to me. I could go on – a whole life comes together to build up these things. Last mention though goes to the endlessly inspiring and remarkable Jasmin Topalusic, who has graciously fallen asleep to my quiet readings of these stories on more than one occasion.

Author Biography

I spent most of my life so far in the small seaside town of Whitstable, which has left me with an enduring love of seafood and shingle. I spent three years attending something very like a certain Archers College, studying things that were not quite closest to my heart – leaving the really important stuff entirely self-taught, with the help of six bookcases full of remarkable literature. Time after that found me moving abroad to the sunny side of the alps, spending a year in Slovenia, overwintering in the remote mountains then oversummering in melancholy Ljubljana and enjoying the company of the pretty Eastern European girls – with all aspects of the trip leaving an impression that will probably linger in my writing permanently.

My stories have appeared in the anthologies *Strange Tales 1, 2* and *3* from Tartarus Press, *Blind Swimmer* from Eibonvale Press and most recently, in *The Monster Book for Girls* from Exaggerated Press. The surreal art-fable *What the Giants Were Saying* – the first appearance of the wandering girl Feather – was published by Eibonvale Press back in 2005, receiving comparisons with Clive Barker and J. G. Ballard.

Contents:

Mysterious Worlds: An Introduction

By Alexander Zelenyj

I first met Feather many years ago. She went by a different, much more commonplace name then. She was an adolescent force of nature: ruggedly beautiful and spontaneous, playful and exuberant and wilder than any of the boys I knew could ever hope to be. She threw caution to the wind and seized days like armies sacked cities. I grew to know her well, and thought I'd nearly solved her many mysteries.

Bad things awaited her in her 20s, though: a spiralling decade of hard living and bad luck that ended in a prison in a foreign country. It's a long story, fraught with sadness and poor choices, and bound in a harsh reality completely at odds with her once seemingly dream-like powers, perhaps now faded forever.

Then, only a few years later, I met Feather again. This time her hair was longer and lighter (a dirty blonde), her eyes gentler (though no less mischievous under certain moons), and her outlook on life much like my own. A romantic at heart, with a healthy dose of carnal inquisitiveness, she turned the worlds of those in her orbit upside down and right-side up and all points between. Some called her an old soul, others a hippie misplaced in a future decade, but most didn't know what to make of her so settled on giving her the title which would remain with her throughout the years and into the present: *Weird.*

Again, this Weird dream came to its end, though much less fitfully than before, and I still catch glimpses of this incarnation of her from time to time, drifting like a Dayglo daydream through a summer afternoon, across a sleety wintry night's glacial streets.

* * *

I met Feather all over again many years after: this time she was elemental!! A raging tempest of unbridled joy! A whirlwind of laughter! A thing of Amazonian beauty encasing the most pure and virtuous of hearts. Here was the power of windmill-energy and the universe circling above in a cloudless sky: celestial, divine, wild and untamed! A Goddess walketh among us! A tome need be written to make a respectable attempt to define her though it could never hope to come close!

I'm still fortunate enough to see her these days, and still she's lost none of her magic (daily, nightly, yearly it grows, even!!). Oh, what a treasure she is, the rarest jewel ever sculpted.

A year ago I encountered her yet again: this time she was younger and hid her alchemical secrets deeply within her wondrous self, like a turtle retreated into its ornate shell. Still and still I seek to unravel her, and still and still is my breath taken away by the briefest glimpses she allows me into her secret world. Coaxing her from her shell is a difficult but bountifully rewarding magic! Her smile, her eyes, her penchant for wearing long chains with their stones hanging low in the valley between her breasts, her uncanny way of speaking to me without the hindrance of words: these are reasons to climb out of bed and fight the new day! To *beat* the new day! To revel in its joys and triumphs and sink its woes and villainies like dark ships into the deep green sea!

The magic wielded by a beautiful girl is a blindingly divine light to try to behold…

It was only recently that I met the enigmatic Feather yet again, only this time in a wholly unexpected place. I found her on the printed page, in sentences that described her exploits and in stories that carried her as much as she held them aloft, too. The first book in which I encountered her was entitled *What The Giants Were Saying*, and the second book –

which you are now holding in your hands – was entitled simply *Feather* (though the book's genesis saw it under several different titles, such as *The Whispering Girl* and *The Book Of Tides*). Of course, I'd encountered a wide variety of interesting and captivating women in literature before, time and again, and been swept up in their exploits and visions of their worlds like so many other readers. But this was different. This time it felt...personal. This time it felt... *unusually* personal.

Here were tiny pieces of those elemental girls and goddesses and sprite-like presences that have haunted me since childhood days, all woven together into a single fictional character, with suggestions of other wildly divergent personalities and characteristics living there too, some familiar and others wholly and engrossingly unfamiliar.

All of which begged the question: who was her author – who was he *really?* – who has documented the secret folds of the secret worlds I'd stumbled on in my day to day wanderings way back when, and how has he been documenting these things from the other side of the world (he resides in the United Kingdom; I live in Canada)? Who was this writer who so adeptly succeeded in melding into a single creature what I'd always deemed the most personal – the most private – emotions revolving around these disparate characters I've known for so many years of my life, and made her somehow a universal force, though entirely his own, with yet more mysterious twists and turns in her story than I'd even considered might exist?

David Rix is a busy man. This busy-ness stems from another fact about him: he is also a man of many talents and interests. He is an artist. He is a musician. He edits texts. He publishes the work of authors he admires. He collects and polishes strange and beautiful stones.

He also writes. And, like any author with a passion for his work, he has a muse which has allowed him to infuse his writing with a highly personal quality – the muse herself – and through whom he is able to convey universal themes and ideas. And there she is again...

Feather is innocence and freedom, wildness and purity, and occasionally something darker, even succubus-like. Often she is a wandering spirit, ever-curious and sprite-like, while sometimes she provides the starkness of reason in a world that is unintelligible, and difficult to navigate. She is an observer and a secret. She is the liberty of isolation from the world and its impure evils. She is an outcast from a world in which she does not quite fit. She is a thread of romance mapping out difficult steps through difficult terrain. She is many things, and different worlds to different characters.

A pervasive sense of isolation marks the stories of *Feather*, as if they exist in the shadows of the everyday worlds we each inhabit: far off the beaten path and among the densest trees; at the secret end of the narrow little-frequented alley and then only behind a tiny window looking into…what? Where Recorder-Players play the cries of magpies on their instruments like gateways between the planes of life and death. Interestingly, this sense of concealment is woven throughout the collection amid myriad genre forays which, in and of themselves, often represent completely antithetical leanings: the post-apocalyptic overtones of “Yellow Eyes”; the Lovecraftian worlds-within-worlds motifs of “The Angels”; the mad science of “Touch Wood”; The British mysticism of “The Magpies”, in the tradition of Blackwood and Machen; the hints of disaster story in The Book of Tides; the classic ghost story style of “To Call The Sea”, the hysteria-infused bastard cousin to the quiet respectability of M.R. James’ ghostly tales; and of course, the very subtly vampire-tinged cityscape of The Whispering Girl.

Yes, here lies a colourful hodgepodge of literary inspiration: you’ll catch glimpses of Lewis Carroll’s surreal run-amok imagination, in the throes of which you might always expect the unexpected. You might spy J.G. Ballard’s and Clive Barker’s penchants for grounding the fantastic in realms of the gritty and grotesque; and, perhaps most striking of all, you will find the subtle nuances of Haruki Murakami’s patient, painstaking atmosphere-building, in which the very fabric of these stories’ reality is imbued with that most delicious temptation of all: the great unknown that is mystery itself. Here also crawls the unsettling cinematic spirit of David Lynch, where things brim with tension and a sense that anything might happen, and at any moment, and it might very well be an unsavoury happening so one would be wise to devote one’s fullest attention to the weirdness unfolding before them.

When you explore these stories you will find that the unfamiliar is somehow made familiar, and that the everyday has about it a curious otherness, a surreal character embedded deeply within its recognizable fabric. The universal lurks within the hidden nooks and surreal folds of these dream-like tales, like the snatches of reality which ground our dreams in their dual context of believability and fantasy.

Not every dream and dream-moment here is pretty though: far from it. The grotesque lurks everywhere, waiting to ambush the unwary with visions of corpses spat up by the sea, and a World Cage containing the darkest of stories, and the deeply-embedded scars wrought by coil upon coil of copper wire. There is horror here, and beauty, woven throughout and tying together all of the dream-like strangeness as tightly as such storms can be held. These ingredients and more litter these pages, and among it all you will recognize her, running, weaving her way through the wild forests and windswept beach landscapes on display everywhere.

That is the inexplicable, frightening and beautiful secret of this book: I know Feather, and although I may never quite solve the puzzle of her I certainly feel her mystery, which is the world's mystery. And you feel it, too.

- Alexander Zelenyj
Windsor, Ontario, Canada, July 2011

Foreword

The Tiny Window on River Street

I see a woman in a room.

No . . .

She sits alone in a small bare room where . . .

No way. This is no good. I am not used to this. What am I doing?

My sister peered in and I glanced at her gloomily.

"How do I tell this?" I begged.

"Hmm?"

She gave a shrug, acknowledging that I had opened my mouth, but that was about all. She wasn't very interested in this – why should she be?

Gawd I hate creating stuff.

"What is it? Where are we?" she murmured.

"Those buildings down by the river," I said. "You remember? You know – near the bridge." I struggled for something else. I could see an image in my head very clearly – of dark walls and old bricks – crumbling urban decay. The arse ends of the small run-down apartments – the off-licence – the tiny general shop – the kebab house – those that clustered on River Street. The path runs between them and the water through a strip of rough, wild land, full of odd hidden corners between buildings and scruffy city trees. At that time of night, it is a dark, dirty city path and I was always a little afraid of meeting people there. This path seemed to be a place full of privacy – and, every time I walk along it, I am violating that privacy. At every turn, I expect to see something I really shouldn't. Some event or person that would really resent me seeing it. That's the thing about living in a larger town. I am still not really used to it . . .

I think the above. I see, smell, taste, touch, feel the above – but I don't write it down.

I always feel drawn to water though, that's the thing. That's why I still walk there. My sister doesn't like to go out much, but if there is any water around, I will find it sooner or later and make it mine. My ideal would be to live by the sea – my ideal job would be a lighthouse keeper (if that job even existed any more). But those are all dreams, just like most things are dreams, and the river here is a good second best. That murky old river has been a good friend to me in its own way – as I sit by its side and watch it travelling past. Watch the occasional waterbird or floating debris on the move. It always seemed heavy and slow – no matter how fat it was with recent rain. No matter how the little whirlpools and eddies appeared and vanished . . .

No matter how many hearts it stole each year . . .

It was a thundery evening. Not stormy yet – just electric. The sort of weather I always rather liked. Always made me feel a bit wired and hysterical, knowing that there was an explosion coming. At one place, as you walk along downriver, there is a road bridge overhead – where River Street crosses the river. Now that place is DARK, in spite of the standing street lamps either side. The path follows the river under into the echoing concrete, but before that there is a small open space and a patch of buildings that always puzzled me a bit. Here the buildings rise up in sheer ugly walls of blank concrete and brick, forming two sides of a sort of square courtyard of wasteland – the third side being the rising road deck. And in that whole huge expanse of plastered wall, there was just a single window – a tiny thing of frosted glass on the ground floor, just a foot square. That never made sense. Why just one tiny window? Why should this square wall, encompassing at least two buildings, be so blank? Who knows? Maybe something was here before, but ruined in the long ago war – pulled down, leaving just this blank empty space behind. A blank empty space with just a single tiny pane of frosted glass that could neither be opened nor seen through. As long as I could remember, it had been dark. I wasn't even sure what was on the other side of these walls. Apartments? Office space? A cellar? Something totally forgotten and ruined?

Not quite apparently, because tonight I saw that the light was on in the room beyond it. That was interesting enough for me to pause and look – wondering again what the hell that little glass pane was for. The stormy weather was making me feel wild and rather careless, so no doubt that's why I stepped up to the blurred glass and tried to look in. This was a quiet place after all – screened by a few of those rough city-type trees. Now – the glass was frosted and inlayed with a fine square wire mesh. It looked thick and tough, but it had still broken and cobwebbed in one place. In the centre of that star, a thin shell-shaped piece of glass had fallen out, not making a hole but taking enough frosting with it so that I could actually see in indistinctly.

Not that I was particularly expecting much. A squalid apartment perhaps. A fed up cleaner going over some small office?

Inside though was a small room almost totally without furnishing. In fact, I think the only thing in there was the chair under the seated figure. There was not even a light shade – just a bare bulb suspended . . .

Sorry yes – there was a figure in there. That took me by surprise. I might have expected someone in their apartment watching TV – but this sight of a youngish woman sitting quietly in a bare room was something new – and I stared in some astonishment. She didn't seem to be doing anything – just sitting and waiting uncomfortably.

Oh yes – and she didn't look well at all. She sat as though in pain – her expression rather twisted and unhappy – and she occasionally shifted her position, leaning forward and breathing hard . . .

There you have it. It's like a painting. Perhaps I am doing this wrong. I shouldn't write, I should be telling this thing with a brush or a pencil.

I sighed and yawned and leaned back in my chair. "Of course," I said. "She's wearing a quite large white dress that is actually quite loose and abstract – doesn't show much of her. That's why I haven't spotted what's wrong with her yet. Haven't spotted the bulging stomach. She has brown hair. It's untidy. Her eyes look very dark in this low light. I would call her pretty in a harrowed sort of way – but what does that mean to anyone else?"

"Hmm?"

"I need to paint this picture. Descriptive stuff. I need to make people aware of her there. The way she looks. Her face with prominent features – sharp nose, long straight hair, slightly foreign looking though I am not sure where from . . . dammit, it's important . . ."

I broke off, suddenly annoyed by my own voice yapping on. Maybe one should just stop talking. Stop telling people stuff. Giving advice. Asking about things. What's wrong with silence? Why were people so afraid of it?

Maybe it's what we are best at.

I sighed, feeling suddenly miserable – thinking about where all this was coming from. The real story behind it. The person – the old friend who I suppose was lurking behind this – had never liked silence. I remembered that vividly.

When friends can fall out like estranged lovers, you know something is not right, somewhere.

"I cannot be your muse," she had said, and that startled me for a moment before I realised that it was just something to say that filled a hole somewhere in her head. Muse? I wish she was. But she was hardly that. This was happening in the green rolling hills of the West Country with the roar of the ocean in the distance. "Mr Rix," she said, over the course of several minutes, "You are cruel and you are a fool. You are not worth knowing and you care nothing about me."

"You are not my muse," I said at last, feeling slightly dazed. This felt like a strange alternate reality coming from her lips – a second view of the world that seemed utterly unfamiliar. Maybe you gave birth to it though, I thought. To her. Right now. Right here. After all – what is creation if not a sort of parasite drinking from all experience? And you are certainly giving me some fucking experience now, aren't you! I thought that but couldn't be bothered to explain it. Or maybe I was just afraid.

She didn't answer me. Just carried on telling me everything that was wrong with me. I finally interrupted her.

"Ah," I said with a wistful smile, as though contemplating an image much nicer than that of the present, "if you were my muse . . ."

Wrong thing to say. I never saw her again. "I want to close this," she said later, by email. "I would love to think we could go on talking and perhaps arrive at some solution – but . . ."

I gave a dry smile that wasn't very humorous. Talking? I wasn't aware that we had been talking . . .

But somehow it didn't matter. Let her go. I was shocked by it but I just couldn't be bothered to argue. Perhaps she's right. Who says

I am a nice man? If I was a nice man, I might not be writing this at all. And in a way it was true: whatever birth she left deep in my head – whatever muse she helped create – is done, is mine, and can never be taken back.

The woman in the room – in the white dress – whoever she is – looked in a terrible state. Her head turning and turning, left, right, left, right. And the expression on her face . . .

Pain, that's all. The body in pain moves in certain ways. It's a movement that actors can't replicate, so in a world where we are surrounded by fake violence and where real pain is hastily shoved under a cloth, people have almost forgotten the dance of real pain. Until they are suddenly reminded, anyway. She was bleeding as well. There was a trickle of blood staining her clothes. Real, undramatic, unartistic blood. She was sitting in a small puddle of it and it was soaking her dress, making the fabric hang differently . . . which somehow was serving to highlight the large bulge of her stomach a bit more . . .

And at last allowing me to realise what was going on. I realised it with a strange chill that I didn't try and analyse.

Looking through the cobwebbed glass created a blurred and distorted image. As though these were fish in there, struggling in a murky tank. But I could see her – and see that she wasn't alone now. Someone was helping her. I think. He had come in at some point, but I couldn't make out much of him. Dark clothes. No visible face. It was just a dance of blurred shapes, but he seemed to be looking after her as best he could. There was something solicitous in his motions, anyway. He seemed to be trying to get her into some sort of squatting position, but she was too exhausted to hold it and just ended up on her back on the floor. I could see her – that red and white dress hauled up out of the way. I could see red. Red and white. Red and white that thrashed about . . .

Perhaps I should have done something useful right about now. There was still a world out there somewhere. A world supposedly able to help in bad situations. I had my phone. But I had the feeling that I was watching something that was most distinctly private. Something – how can I put it? Something taking place between the cracks of the world. As though two people had, for reasons known only to them, met up in this hidden empty room, so she could give birth completely divorced from the life going on above. So the thought never even entered my mind. Perhaps I should have done something – called someone. Perhaps I shouldn't. Who can tell? Certainly not you, reading this.

Then, somehow, it was over. Things were stiller and I could dimly hear a sound coming from inside. Not a pleasant noise, a baby crying, is it? He seemed to be holding the small figure and examining it carefully. That's all. More interested in it than her. She seemed to be reaching out an arm to its small figure, but he ignored that, I remember, and reversed out of reach. She seemed totally exhausted. Totally broken. But still – she looked intense, through that shell-shaped spot of clear glass – and she yelled some insult at him, I think tears were streaming down her face. Then she gave this – sort of – cough and collapsed. And with the cough – well . . .

It was small – just a few inches across. It wasn't very bright. Just a small moving ball of light. Like ball lightning. As I said, the air was electric and very heavy. So I suppose . . .

But I don't understand how she ended up almost spitting it out like that. He, whoever he was, didn't look too surprised or bothered by it. Just stepped aside and waved at it as though it was a passing moth. I saw him pick up the small figure – then he was just gone. Leaving her alone. The light remained though – it carried on drifting – crossing towards the window. Towards me. While I stared at it spellbound. Like – I dunno. I couldn't move much.

Then it hit the glass.

There was a shockingly loud bang and a small but vivid flash. I remember that. The glass didn't shatter, but that cobweb in it did expand to fill the pane. I was still staring through it so I got that full in the face and in huge detail. The flash of energy lit up the world round my eyes and rang in my skull and I jolted away in complete shock. Every muscle seemed to want to move of its own accord and it sent me staggering over into a heap on the ground. I might even have blacked out for a few moments – time is blurred at this point. At any rate, the next thing I can remember was lying on my back with the pattering of rain in my eyes.

I eventually hauled myself up and stood, arm against a tree, breathing heavily in the dark, the lights of invisible passing cars playing through the tree branches above. Obviously I looked at the window – but it was dark now. The room seemed empty. As I said, time was blurred. I wasn't keen to investigate further – all I wanted was to go home and to bed, to still the aching pandemonium behind my eyes. In the distance, thunder was muttering. I walked slowly – but it seemed only a moment before I was opening my door – my mind was so full of images and feelings that I lost track of the time.

And then what? Well – there is little left to tell really of this story. I did go back to the window the next day – I hoped in daylight to be able to find out a bit more. But I found that it was boarded up on the inside. I remember – I stood there for a while – just staring at it. At the cracks radiating across it like a spider web. At the curiously fused and melted looking smear in the centre.

I started several letters to her, wherever she was. That friend of mine. But all got deleted of course. It seems I could at least give her the credit of knowing what she wanted. When one wants to go, one must go and there is little point trying to fight it. I have seen enough of striving against the inevitable. People struggling to keep dead or dying relationships going – hoping that the other would be able to change to match your expectations or hoping that you could change yourself to keep the other happy and prevent strife ever happening again. But that itself only leads to desperation and falsehood – putting on a performance. Being trapped in negativity.

I feel strangely blurred though. Filled with the sense of something missing and of the effect of what vanished or dead people had left behind. My head aches slightly and I can still hear that nasty crack as the light exploded in my face. Maybe I have this all wrong. Maybe this woman in the room is not the key. Just something better forgotten like many things are. Just a lost and lonely tragedy now past.

Perhaps it is the new that matters. Maybe it is me running away into the night with that small bundle. Maybe I was watching myself. I am writing this story, after all – so why not?

And something new is what I desperately need right now.

"Are you still moping?" my sister asked, not unkindly. I gave her a rather melancholy look. "You should get in touch with her," she said.

I sagged against the wall, feeling a sudden ache at the thought.

"No," I said on autopilot, for I had already thought this through too many times now. So many times that I had almost forgotten the arguments. "It's better not to. She proved that very clearly."

She leaned over my shoulder and stared at the computer screen curiously. I followed her eyes. It's funny but when someone else is reading what you have written, everything seems different. And much more confusing. What had I set myself up with here? What had happened? What had I . . . created? I was feeling a creeping sense of uncertainty. Somewhere I was already on the move, I realised – running fast with something that was vitally important.

There were stories to tell.

What do the definitions of reality and story matter? Where is the difference? Who cares if I am sitting here telling you about reality or dream? Or both.

I sighed, turned to the computer, opened a new document and casually tapped out a word.

"Hey," I called after my vanished sister. "What do you think of Feather?"

"What's that about a feather?" she asked, peering round the door.

I smiled, my eyes suddenly prickling with tiredness. "Her name is Feather," I said.

"Who is?" my sister asked. "The woman you . . ?"

I shrugged and shook my head.

"No. Not her."

She gave me a puzzled look.

*   *   *

I did read something later though. In the paper. Just a tiny article. About the body of an unidentified woman that had been fished out of the river a little way downstream. It's probably nothing relevant. I never heard anything more, so maybe they never worked out who she was. Another Jane Doe that we were never meant to know. It might be nothing – but I did feel an odd prickle when I read that. Especially what it said about her long white dress . . .

Who wears long dresses these days?

Yellow Eyes

Here on the beach imagine small white shells glint on the white sand. Straightsmooth greysky – a quiet breeze shakes the coarse grass that grows off there above the high tide. Cold. A vastness of sky all round as the land fades to the strangeworld of dimdistant mist behind. There is sea all round as I walk slowly along – land back me, seabeach before me – a large peninsula of black of grey. A black mess of tumbled rocks in the greysea connected to the land by myself this beach of small shells. Behind this myself something strange.

Feather walks.

In the dreamtime seabirds cry in the vastness. Dreamsong – the white of white on grey. The rocks mess – blackrocks – approaches – the skymists – me. A quiet thing of sorrow in all noisy stillness – silence –

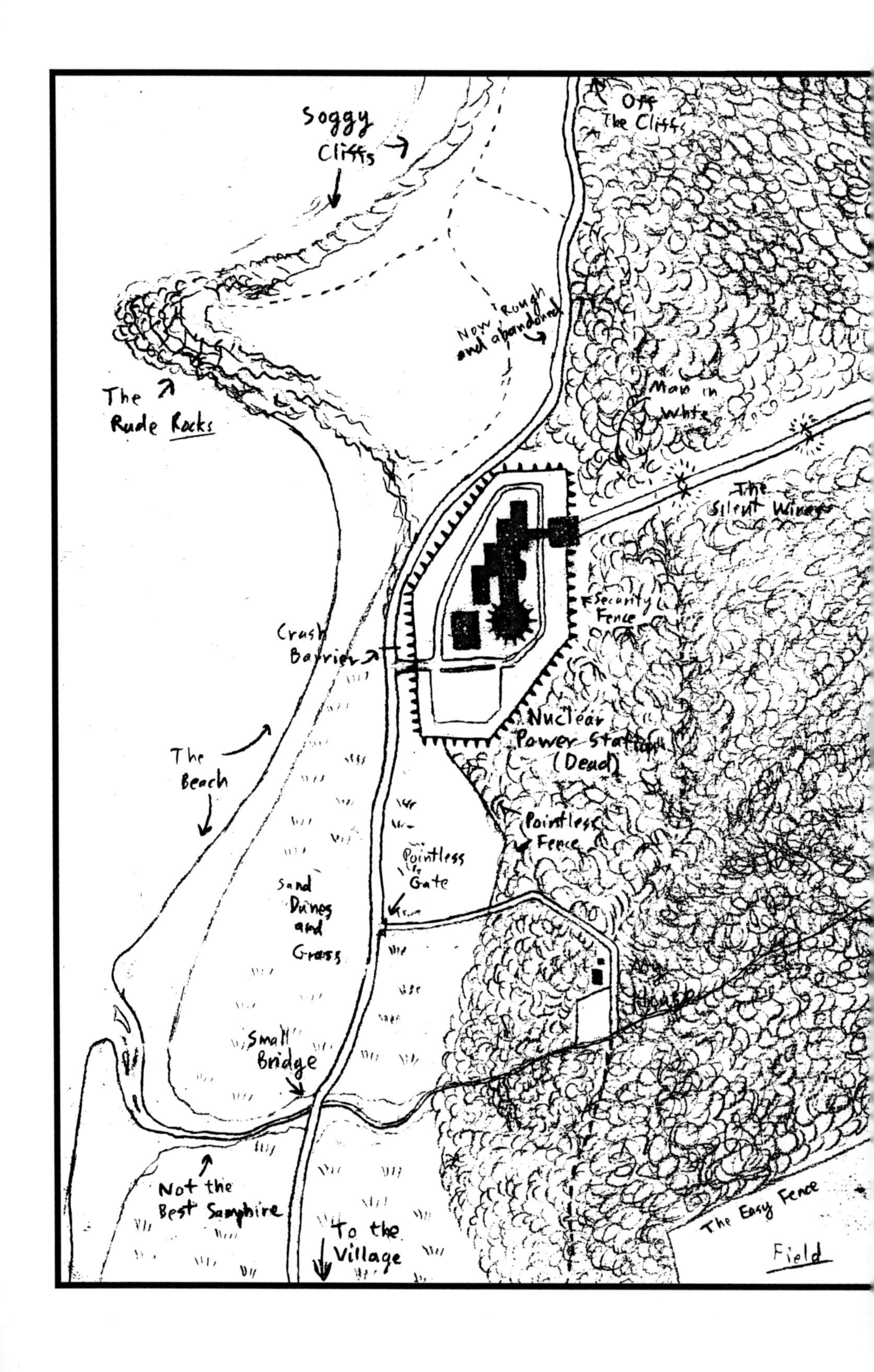

Soggy Cliffs
Off The Cliffs
Now rough and abandoned
The Rude Rocks
Man in White
The Silent Winery
Security Fence
Crash Barrier
Nuclear Power Station (Dead)
The Beach
Pointless Fence
Pointless Gate
Sand Dunes and Grass
Small Bridge
Not the Best Samphire
To the Village
The Easy Fence
Field

Morning came creeping through the trees. It crawled across the leaf litter and woke up Feather, lying wrapped tight among the bushes. She stirred and turned over awkwardly, peering up at the branches overhead. In the middle of the dawn chorus, she blinked painfully and stared without much pleasure at the morning around her. A thrush sat on a branch nearby, its beak agape – and, close to, the singing sounded less like singing, more like ear-splittingly loud screaming. Feather slung a handful of twigs and acorns at it and it flew away.

Heavily she pulled herself up into a sitting position, brushing leaves from her hair. She felt bitter from lack of sleep and there was a chill in the air now that the year was fading towards winter. She rubbed at her side and stretched. The woodland ground was not so uncomfortable. The soft leaf litter moulded around her quite agreeably. But she had been so sleepy the previous night that she had forgotten to clear away some of the twigs and they had dug in cruelly.

Overhead the clouds were grey and hazy. No sun to shine through to her – to cut through the morning sea-mist that was still creeping around. There was no point remaining lying here now though. She knew she would not sleep again. So she pulled herself up, hoisted her bag on her shoulders and made her way through the trees, tugging and shaking at her clothes to loosen them where they were rucked all round her. She was hungry, as she had run out last night without any food since a rather dreary mid-day dinner of vegetable stew.

Arriving at the edge of the trees, she emerged into the area of rough ground that stretched between the woods and the fence of the old nuclear power station. Its towers stood rearing up through the mist like standing stones – the warning lights on the towers and around the buildings still shining. As always, it was totally silent. As long as she had been here, she could not remember seeing one figure on the other side of that fence. Nobody went in – nobody came out. But even so, thin plumes of steam rose up from some places and the warning lights twinkled constantly. Maybe the place really was deserted, she thought. Just abandoned and remaining in some dwindling half life.

She had tried to research power stations on the internet once, in the library of the nearby village, but she hadn't really found much. A few basic guides to what they did. And a lot of people hating them, of course, and ascribing improbable sounding dangers to them. That puzzled her a little as she could never remember it doing her any harm.

She could not remember her father ever talking about it.

Her hunger was not going to let her speculate too much now though. Instead, she peered round the wasteland hopefully. She longed to slip off home, but not just yet. Even flavourless leftover stew would be sort of welcome now – but not just yet. Instead she went foraging.

Following the edge of the woods and skirting the big security fence, she found a few things. Wild chickweed – goose grass – tough sulphur polypore growing on an old tree trunk . . . she stared at them without much enthusiasm. How much did it take to remain wild here completely? How much to break the ties and stay out here forever? Here with the grey towers watching over her like sleeping guardians – but guarding her from within, or without?

More than this dismal salad, that was certain.

With a shiver against the cold, she caught herself wishing for the long departed summer – or perhaps the not so distant berry-autumn when the bushes had been laden with blackberries and hawberries and sloes, now shrivelling to nothing.

Gloomily she chewed on the fibrous goose grass. It was bitter and rough in her mouth and, like all leaves, it did little to ease her hunger. The sulphur polypore was more substantial but as tough as fibrous leather and she groaned mentally, wishing it was fresh cooked meat in her mouth. Her father was a man full of curious and intense beliefs and ways of doing things – which inevitably applied to the rest of the world as well as him and which needed neither explaining nor challenging in order to be valid. One of them was to not have any meat anywhere near him. It was not something remotely productive to argue with. Meat was just an evil. Thinking of it now though, Feather felt an uncharacteristic flicker of anger. Her back was hurting and she was cold and she felt tired of it all. Of everything. She wanted more. Out here there was only what could be scavenged – or maybe dug for, like earthworms. Or perhaps what she could find down at the sea below the power station, where she could pick for shellfish buried in the mud. Sometimes, when the tide was out, there would be cockles or clams waiting for her scrabbling fingers – or some clumps of mussels attached to the rocks on the outcrop. She could occasionally lay her hands on other food – in the nearby village for example. Hot food – meat, sausages, pies or, best of all, the delicious hot kippers served at the fish market. But all that was hard to get.

You needed money for that.

Usually.

She liked the village – she wished she could go there forever . . .

Tramping through the woods, picking her own path as she went, she passed under the silent wires that ran from the power station through the trees in a weed-ridden causeway of their own. Here there were a few more things to eat, but it was not till she was back among the trees that she finally stumbled on something more interesting. Possibly. A clump of white mushrooms were dotted about in the litter under a patch of beech trees. There was nothing dramatic about them. Indeed, they looked a little scruffy and misshapen. Just . . . mushrooms.

But she peered at them suspiciously. What were they? She liked mushrooms a lot – but these didn't look good. Living the way she did, she was very good at knowing which were good to eat and which weren't. She could recognise the families of the Boletes and the Field Mushrooms – the parasols, tree ears and the many other delicious ones that grew around. She had not seen these before, but her instincts and identification were whispering warnings. And when she dug into the ground around them they seemed to be justified, for they possessed the floppy bag (*volva*) and the miniskirt ring round the stalk that signified the poisonous amanitas and agarics. That was enough to send a snap of tension through her body and a frown across her face. These things were scary in the effect they could have on you – but, more than just poison, they were always associated in her mind with broken glass and cut flesh. After all, it had been an amanita – the bright red Fly Agaric with the white spots – that her father had eaten once as an experiment – talking about druids and pathways – mazes and eyes – twisting copper wire around his wrists before he had attacked her and thin white scarred her with glass in an incident that she had never understood.

These were white, not red, but Feather sighed and sat down against a tree, unwelcome memories and long-ignored questions flickering in her mind. She fingered one of the mushrooms – though even to touch them felt a bit discomforting, as though she was prodding at a taboo that she hardly knew she had. Whatever these were, they were not edible, but she picked them anyway, precisely because they made her nervous. Her face was tense as she stashed them quickly in her bag, before heading onwards down towards the coast. Maybe these Amanitas could answer some questions, even if they couldn't provide her with a meal. It was about time.

Finally she reached the road. Out here, on the far side of the old power station, it seemed abandoned, blocked off with heavy concrete crash barriers. Certainly she had never seen anyone else on it. It just continued along the top of the low clay and rock cliffs, its surface torn and wrinkled with the attentions of nature. Tree roots had made the surface ripple like the sea below. Horsetails had muscled up through the solid tarmac and, after they had ripped it, the grass soon followed. Even a few baby trees were growing there now. A mile or two further on, the road gave up completely, finally losing the battle and running over the edge of the cliff in a jutting overhang, ending in a tangle of sodden lumps on the sandy mud below.

The wind came in off the sea here, tearing through the rough bushes and grass and into the trees that flanked the other side of the road. Here the woods were at their loudest as the unnumberable leaves swirled and talked – a sound that seemed full of half heard things and hints of something that might have been recognizable. Feather strolled slowly back down the road towards home, her hair blowing around her face. Soon she arrived back at the power station's fence again and here also the cliffs finally gave way, jutting into the sea in one last rude gesture – a tumbled outcrop of black rocks strewn out into the white waves – before collapsing into a rough world of sand, dunes and grass.

She followed the road through the concrete barrier and as it passed the big wire gates, always closed and locked, and from here the road was in better condition. The sand-dusted surface bore the marks of vehicles and very occasionally she would see some person out here, enjoying the sea or wandering aimlessly through the dunes. They didn't bother her though. They had never done anything except ignore her. She remembered her father though, the one time she had been out here with him when a car had driven in from the distance. He had flinched like an animal and hurried her off as fast as they could walk. He had never explained why.

Now though, the dunelands were deserted – just the continual high-pitched hiss as the wind blew the sand grains through wilderness. In the hollows, grass sometimes managed to find a foothold – and when it did, tiny gardens would form of delicate sea flowers and small snail shells, white with black bands or delicate brown mottling – *Cernuella virgata* and *Theba pisana* she had identified them as during one of her trips to the village. These hollows, sheltered from the wind, were comfortable resting places. She could lie in the soft sand and enjoy the sun. Occasionally she would even strip off and lie there naked, enjoying the feeling of the sun on her skin – on all of it (which was important) – and the warm sand beneath her.

Sunbathing days were over now though, as the year turned towards its dark side.

Finally she arrived at the gate to the barely visible track that led home. It was a pointless gate because there was no fence for it to let you through and she simply walked around it, tight locked and chained though it was. The sand had flooded the track in places, but she could find her way these days even in the pitch dark and she crossed it easily, kicking it up with her shoes. It led across the dunes and back into the trees – the old familiar woods that had surrounded her like a blanket for as long as she could remember.

Home consisted of a small cottage-type building that looked as though it had been built in the woods for some special purpose a long time ago and then been forgotten about. Basically it was nothing more than a shelter – three rooms, no plumbing that functioned and a stove that worked off a gas canister. There were taps, but no water flowing from them. There was no heating except for that provided by the stove and an open fireplace. The only electricity came from a small generator system, wired up to power the fridge and provide a few lights to the rooms. Aside from the kitchen, her father lived and painted in one room. The remaining one was hers, when she chose to sleep in it. Outside there was a battered old car under a tarpaulin in which her father would regularly go off for supplies, and a small area of ground that they cultivated, growing vegetables and a few herbs. There was also a stream running nearby, which provided water that was drinkable after filtering and boiling.

At nearly seventeen years old and having lived here for as long as she could remember, Feather was pretty much used to life here and she barely gave it a thought. At least she hadn't until recently. Sometimes lately she had begun wondering why her father had settled out here into such a life, instead of everything else that the world offered. That was another thing he had never really explained in any way that made sense. But here he was free to paint and sink slowly into whatever kind of spartan esoteric haze he was looking for – and that was enough for him.

After a few minutes of walking she arrived, unlocked the door and slipped into the kitchen. She was hoping it would contain food somewhere in the oddly scented cupboards, but she didn't get far.

"Feather?" the voice came rolling through. She stopped sharply and frowned. Something about the voice sent a prickle of unease and annoyance down her back. For a moment she wanted to run out again, but instead she dropped her bag and coat, pushed open the door of his studio and peered in.

He glanced at her, rubbed his eyes and put down his pallet.

"Oh Feather," he said with a sigh. "Come here," he said.

She stepped gloomily into the studio. This was a room that she didn't much like to enter at any time because it was his room – in a very real sense. It smelt of him. His murky surrealist paintings hung around, suspended from nails on copper wire. It was thick with the smell of smoke and the ghosts of older smokes of many different kinds – of strange designs painted on the walls and door – which might have been charms and symbols – hippie paraphernalia and books and figurines from what Feather had identified as several different religions. In spite of the profusion of content though, the place was kept neat almost to the point of obsession. Even his artist's materials were in perfect order. She was used to it well enough, but it still made her feel alien and misfitting – and about as far from her familiar forest and from things that made sense to her as she could imagine.

He sleepily pushed his easel to the side of the room and peered at her.

"Where have you been?" he demanded petulantly.

She glanced round the room expressionlessly. "Just in the woods," she said. That was the truth.

He gave a deep sigh and looked at her piercingly. "Hmm," he said. "Now, do I believe you?"

Feather gave him an impatient look and said nothing. No particular point arguing.

"You spend half your life away from here. What can you find to do in the woods for all that time?"

She said nothing. Eat and sleep, she thought. What else was there to do in life? But she didn't say it.

"Why do I sense betrayal in this house?" he demanded.

"What do you mean?"

Her father peered at her. He was a tall and thin man, his hair grown long and untidy. His home-sewn clothes, mostly made of rough and undyed fabric, dressed him like the dingy old hippie he was, hanging over a loose and scrawny frame, his skin stretched tight over his muscles without any body fat to smooth him out. Around his neck hung numerous things – wood, a crystal or stone of some kind, various symbols that she had never really understood in spite of his attempts to explain them – suspended on more copper wire. Copper indeed was a dominant theme here. He tied back his hair with it. He wove it through his clothes. It surrounded him in his obsessively neat but smoky room.

"You've been to the village," he said grimly.

"What? No."

"There are fingers of change whispering through this house. Fingers of investigation – of Measuring. I can feel them. And they are all centring around you."

Feather stared at him blankly. His way of talking was familiar enough, but the meaning left her completely out of her depth. What was he on about?

"Why did I have to let an idiot into my house?" he growled, his eyes gleaming. "I should have left you behind for them – for . . . for them to tear to pieces. For the Measuring Men. What do I have to do to make you see?" he cried. "You are a fugitive, Feather. And what sort of fugitive goes strolling out under the eyes of her hunters?"

He caught her by the front of her shirt and she was hauled almost off her feet.

"An idiot fugitive," he cried, his eyes glinting. "A fugitive with a mind stuffed full of wet cotton. A fugitive who has forgotten everything and thinks of nothing."

He fingered her shirt front and kept her there, pulled in close, her body limp and unprotesting.

"But why am I a fugitive?" she demanded shrilly.

"Everyone is. If they know it or not. We, at least, know it – and have no choice."

Feather felt a stab of fury at that.

"Answer me properly," she shouted suddenly, trying to jerk away. "You never explain anything. Never tell me anything . . ."

"Feather," he whispered lyrically. "I am confused. I am bewildered. I don't understand you any more. So – what? Shall I follow the simple equation and hurt you if it will make you remember what can end us all?" he whispered. Feather gazed at him, realising what was coming and her fury doubled. "The Measuring Man," he said. "In his evil he found worse punishments than anything I can do – punishments that buckled and cracked the entire world. And so he laughed and danced . . . Is that really where you want to end up?"

"What are you – talking about?" she stammered. Still holding her tight, he stared almost forlornly over her shoulder and across the room.

"All that is important is that here we are safe from him," he said. "So long as we don't do anything stupid. To him . . . he has forgotten me – doesn't even know you exist and shouldn't know you exist. I worked hard to achieve that."

Feather closed her eyes and leaned her head on her shoulder. "But why?" she almost whispered.

"You must understand. If you go out – parading yourself under his eyes – the Measuring Man will see you and when he sees you he will say to himself 'now who's that?' And when he realizes that he doesn't know, then your life will be over. I wanted you to be free from that evil – from . . . all that pain. How many times do I have to say it to make you believe it? How much do I have to hurt you now to make you remember it?"

Feather was hardly listening. What could you say to that tone of voice? It was the slightly high-pitched, constant tone of one who speaks words without thinking about them any more because they have become so familiar – a ten ton truck voice that barges its load through everything that stands in its way. Most of what her father said over the years was vaguely the same. The Measuring Man was an old bogey. A familiar spectre that she had been afraid of once – but now tended to ignore. If she had pictured him at all it was as some humourless old man in a white coat, carrying an old wooden ruler and a notebook. What he measured with that ruler had never been explained. Something physical? All her searches on the internet had turned up no reference at all and when it came to choosing which to trust – the village library and the small museum in the converted windmill or her Father's ramblings – she was starting to make her choice.

"I didn't go to the village," she muttered.

"What did you say?"

Feather clenched her fists, driven to another small flare of anger by this so-close but wrong accusation. Of course she had been to the village. It was a much more interesting place than here. But not now. Not this time. And that made this an injustice.

"I said I didn't go to the village," she replied a little louder, trying to pull away again. He gave her a look that puzzled her and silenced her – almost gentle.

"Don't lie, Feather," he said. "Lie to the Measuring Man yes but not to me."

"I'm not . . ."

This was another thing that infused the atmosphere of this room, as pungently as the leaf-smoke. The occasional sensation of pain. He even had a special home-made implement for it. It was an old belt end, about a foot and a half long, but the leather had been wound round and round and sewn through with fine copper wire. That had made it flexible but inflexible – cold but burning – and as confusing as everything else here. Whenever he punished her he would get this look on his face almost of disgust at what he was having to do. The sort of look a person might wear when he has to clean up a small but unpleasant mess. And Feather just took it quietly for it was always limited and finite. Like the thunderstorms, it came and passed quickly.

At least – she had always taken it quietly in the past . . .

But why? Feather was angry. Things were changing and progressing in this house. There were indeed fingers of change. And maybe investigation and measuring was high overdue. A painful morning, an empty stomach and white mushrooms with a sharp reminder of earlier incidents had left her in a destructive mood.

She gave a violent jerk and finally broke free, backing away sharply across the room. It didn't last long though.

"Don't fight me," he shouted, catching her and jerking her back again. "Never fight me."

Feather tried to break away a second time, but couldn't. He may be skinny and twig-like but she realised he was strong enough to hold her. Strong enough to twist her round and pin her tight. Then he proceeded to lash her hard with the copperbelt. He always went for her arse – attacking it with a measured rhythm and formality – not out to achieve anything fancy, just controlled pain. Trying to research that in the library had set off some kind of security system and her browsing there had ground to a halt.

Feather struggled, feeling incandescent with fury. Had she ever fought this properly before? She must have. It made no sense not to. But anyway – now that she did, it felt electrifying. Like a cleansing wave – to let rip and let it all out. He seemed taken aback by the ferocity of her fighting – but he didn't let go and, after a few minutes of achieving nothing, Feather snapped completely.

"Why don't you talk to me?" she yelled. "Explain – and then – instead of . . . I only want to understand why. The village doesn't talk in riddles . . . doesn't have a head filled with drugged cotton. Give us a bit of measurement if it will help clear things up."

She shut up quickly, realizing that that was an admission. But the words had escaped. And she stared at the wall in dismay, feeling her father pause a moment.

"I ought to throw you out," he said, his voice different to anything she could remember hearing. "And I would if you wouldn't just bring them all back here. I ought to toss you outside where you belong – go and sit at his feet . . . suck his cock . . . perhaps?"

She landed on the floor with a bump, but still couldn't get away. The copperbelt landed again, though he seemed to have lost all control or measurement now. He had also snapped, in fact. Feather had always known that there was a lot of rage hidden inside him – and now it seemed to be unrestrained. She screamed at the assault. This was something more than she had ever experienced before. She yelled and struggled but had no choice but to lie there until he had finished, leaving her welted, twitching and out of breath.

"Right," he said, panting. "You don't leave the house again – you understand me?"

"What?" she gasped.

"If I have to lock you up in the shed. You are sixteen years old," he growled, "we have been here for nearly sixteen years – and I don't intend to let you land me in it now and break everything I have worked so hard to build."

She staggered onto her knees, then to her feet, staring at him in disbelief. She opened her mouth – but some instinct of self-preservation jammed it closed again.

"You understand me?" he repeated.

She actually gave him a small nod – which hurt almost as much as her body did – before backing clumsily away towards the door. She wriggled out like a dancer, trying not to touch anything with her burning arse and hurried through to the kitchen. Then she sagged against the table, letting her fists impact with a bang and trying to work out what to do with the rage in her, which was thrashing about like a cat trying to find its way out of a bag. Finally she lowered her head and closed her eyes, willing her heart to calm down.

Why? Alright, let's ask the question for once. Why? Why everything?

On the stove, a covered pot was simmering, filling the air with the smell of mushrooms. Slowly she crossed over to it, lifted the lid and peered in. The mushrooms – from the smell of it, a wild cep or two that he must have brought back – didn't seem to be adding much to her father's cooking. It looked watery and dull and she glared at it. That gloomy pot-full, devoid of any particular culinary creativity, seemed to conjure up her father perfectly. She knew he could be creative – he was a painter after all. But he chose, for no reason that made sense to her, to decline all hint of that when it came to food. As if it was somehow bad to find ways to make food taste good or to eat delicious things. It annoyed her. Words like 'Spartan' and 'Self-Denial' had cropped up occasionally in her reading – and they always made her clench her fist in exasperation. There was no shortage of herbs in the garden or the woods – but he rarely seemed to touch them for food. Just used them for medicine and scenting his room out with odd smokes.

Feather stared into the gently roiling liquid, remembering images she had seen online of creamy mushroom soup with delicious looking chunks of Cep or Horns of Plenty . . .

The Cep especially – *Boletus edulis* – she could smell their wonderful scent in here and catch a glimpse of their chestnut caps. The word wanted here was 'waste'.

A temptation to throw the contents of the pot out of the door into the garden weeds was restrained sharply. Never before could she remember being so angry and afraid – and what boiled inside her almost felt like hate. The accumulated weight of confusion and fury about the present and confusion and fury against the past burned and the thought of having to stay here indoors was just not possible to fit in the head.

"Why?" she demanded aloud.

Her bag caught her eye and her heart sank suddenly even further. It didn't take long for her mind to turn from one trouble to another one, much older and much harder to grasp. She opened it and was greeted by a waft of a sickly smell that made her flinch away. The memories these ghostly white mushrooms brought back were doubly unwelcome now. She drew a deep breath and let her fist hammer repeatedly but quietly on the table. She still didn't know quite what these mushrooms were or what had happened when her father had tried 'using' the old Fly Agarics. All she knew was that they were both Amanitas of some kind. Amanita meant Death Cap – Fly Agaric – Panther Cap – meant danger basically. Danger of upset stomachs. Hallucinations. Slow death perhaps. But most of all, amanitas represented the red of blood and the crystal flash of glass.

Many were the times when she wondered what would have happened if his experiment years ago with Fly Agarics – the Druid

Mushroom – had lead to more than just the hallucination that had subsequently hit him so hard. The contradiction of taking poison was a puzzling one in itself. As it was, he had tangled her in copper wire and attacked her with broken glass from the midst of his hallucinations, lacerating her arse and between her legs, leaving scars that were still very visible as faint white lines. What could you make of something like that? Which was to blame? The hallucinogen for putting things in his head – or the head for having such things there just waiting to be revealed? He had grabbed her almost with hate – perhaps not for her but for the concept she represented. And what was that? She had escaped quickly enough – he had been so incoherent that he hadn't been able to hold her for long. Filled with bewilderment, she had lashed out, catching him a square punch in the face. In his stoned state he had no chance at all to avoid that and he went over with a crash and stayed down – and feather fled, scrabbling the copper wire from around her and crying in confusion.

There it was. That was the story.

Reading later in the library internet portal, Feather realised that she had been quite lucky not to have bled to death. She remembered feeling dizzy and faint, forcing herself to stay awake and crying tears of pain while she fixed herself, using various herbs and white cotton – dealing with this just like any other injury. The cuts had been long and some quite deep. This had been one of the times the internet couldn't help her. Nothing she read answered any questions. Even other people who had been attacked in some way had nothing useful to say. Attack victims all over the world seemed to be covered in a pall of ignorance and a reluctance to ask questions.

She had also tried to find some accounts from the attackers. That might have been more help. But she had failed.

Nobody seemed to have asked them anything.

She stared grimly at the stew.

"Oh yes," she said. "You have a lot of explaining to do."

Though perhaps even he didn't know the answers.

Nevertheless.

Almost acting on autopilot she tumbled the white mushrooms out onto the chopping board. The knife slammed into them. Don't you dare, she thought, her mouth turning down at the corners . . . Don't you dare – over and over. A helpless and furious mantra. Don't you dare. Treat me like this. Keep me here. Blah blah. Don't you dare . . .

As the knife slipped through the soft white flesh, she had the weird impression that the white mushrooms were screaming at her. She screwed her eyes shut for a moment, wishing she wasn't so hungry. There was usually no time for such nonsensical thoughts. Living wild was no place for strange fancies, like she sometimes read about in books or online. Irrational fears, likes or dislikes. She could see that quite clearly. The books were from a different world – a luxurious world where people could do what they wanted – feel what they wanted. Be afraid of what they wanted. But now she was crumbling. The fungi guide she had read in the library described mushrooms as fruiting bodies – little more than berries and flowers were to a plant – but somehow this handful of white mushrooms seemed to her to be individual entities – a handful of small white corpses.

With a swish, she swept the mushroom slices into the bubbling pot, where they bobbed and shifted. A few minutes and they would have sunk – would look just like the overcooked field mushrooms and ceps already in there. Feather quickly washed down the chopping board and returned it to the dish rack, hoping he wouldn't notice anything in spite of his obsessive neatness. Then she added a good extra dash of pepper and a shake of salt. Let him have a well-seasoned meal for once.

As she stared into the stew, all her instincts were yelling at her. Danger. But that was what this was about. Maybe he would cut himself this time instead. Find your hallucination again, please, she thought. Only this time I will not be here to be a part of it – and I hope you learn something. And then you will tell me about it. Oh yes you will.

Finally she subsided away and opened the cupboard door. She was hungry and, however little stuff there usually was in there, she would take what she could. But before she could reach in, there was the sound of a movement.

"Feather?" her father called.

She paused. The studio door opened.

She jumped alert – a clash of eyes – then she bolted. Food would have to wait. Instead she charged out the back way, across the garden, straight through the last of the vegetables, and ran for the trees.

Her father's exasperated shout faded behind her.

*   *   *

For the next few days, Feather just wandered.

At first her body was still hurting – mostly her arse and back – but that was fading. Her dwindling anger faded away quicker than that though. It was replaced by emotions she could never remember really experiencing before. There was a shocking sense that she had broken something that could not be put together again – and with that, a sense of fragility and helplessness. The realisation that she was just an insignificant small thing on the surface of the world. The feeling that nobody knew that she existed or cared. The feeling that she was as alone as it was possible to be.

She had been making for the village originally, following the coast road through mile after mile of empty coastline – sometimes sandy, muddy beaches, sometimes rolling sea out of reach below low soft clay cliffs. She had left the wood behind soon enough and here the land was flat and bleak, save for a few patches of trees spared from the geometry of the fields that dominated the ground here. The wind crossed it without obstruction – a continuous presence in her hair and ears.

She arrived at the bridge, where a small river flowed under the road and sprawled out in a tangle of channels and muddy spits, and she stopped, unable to go on. The salt marsh here was covered in crisp and salty Marsh Samphire and she wanted to pick it to try and fill her stomach. She liked Samphire, but gathering it was a messy business that left you covered from head to foot in the rich mud. Normally she would have stripped off naked and gone in there like that. Half wading, half crawling through the deep mud was strangely pleasant – and that followed by a plunge into the sea or the river to wash clean again. But now, scarred and miserable, she found she couldn't face the salt-sting, the dirt or the red-marked nakedness. In the distance, the stationary sails of the windmill museum could be seen above the landscape. That was a familiar landmark for her – the first sight of the village. The old converted windmill where she often liked to sit and rest in the warm. She wanted to be there . . .

Soon, if she kept on, she would approach the first buildings. There would be tire marks on the dusty surface – places where feet had trampled the vegetation. Occasional discarded drinks cans and water bottles – food wrappers and odd unidentifiable pieces of metal. Just plain human dirt, in fact. Then the sea wall started – a long concrete construction that travelled right along the seaward side of the road, right through the village and beyond. And, to her mind, this was where civilization began. The land looked more constrained. The beach was a separated world. And there was less around that was edible.

There were tears in her eyes now as she stood on the bridge. Tears of terror and misery. The tears of anyone confronted with imminent change. Feather wanted to keep walking towards that distant sailed tower – if for nothing else then for the possibility of finding something to eat – somehow. But she felt afraid. Instead she scrambled over the fence and began to follow the river inland, trying not to give way to shivering.

This way, there was nothing but fields and marshes for miles.

What was happening at home? Had he eaten? What would her father do? What was going to happen now? Would he even be capable of killing her, she wondered, if he thought she had failed too completely?

Anything might be possible. But whatever it was, she realised that she had driven a knife deep between the past and the future.

For hour after hour she tramped through the countryside, sticking to the marsh paths to start with, then cutting across country. She knew enough to stick to the paths or the open woods out here to avoid attracting attention. She avoided getting too close to the town or to any roads or buildings – but at the same time she found herself reluctant to venture too far away from it, so she ended up moving in a vague sort of orbit round the village. When the night closed in she found a small patch of trees, curled up in a secluded place and lay there, feeling the cold trying to get through her clothes and the material she had dragged over her as cover. But she slept only to dream of mushrooms and windmills – red and white – which grew very large and suffocating and had her waking up in the grey dawn feeling as though frost had penetrated, crystallising her bones.

What do you have to do to get rid of memories? You couldn't forget them – that didn't seem to be happening. But why wouldn't it leave her alone? The red mushrooms – looking more like a decoration than a food. They were too perfect and improbable. The white mushrooms looked too insignificant.

A haunting memory like this, Feather decided, was a sign of something you yourself had done wrong – not in the incident itself but in dealing with it. Somewhere Feather had failed. She had been so good at taking care of her body when it got hurt or damaged – why had she failed with her mind? But then – what attention had she paid to her mind until recently? She had been a child – unquestioning and accepting everything.

Why?

Why a lot of things?

She sat up and peered around the trees that surrounded her. Young birches and chestnuts. With a sigh, she brushed the leaves from her clothes and started walking again – continuing her orbit. But it was not comfortable. There was nothing to eat out here. It was as simple as that. The wheat and oats that grew in the fields around her were useless. Monocultures they called it on the internet. It didn't sound a nice word. Oh, there were some plants growing by the roadside – clumps of dusty chickweed or deadnettle, even an escaped broccoli plant going to seed in a hedgerow. But they all seemed to taste bitter now – and none of it did much to fill the hole inside her or stop the cold shivering that was starting to creep through her body. Her head felt stuffy and achy, as though a cold was on the way, and even her eyesight seemed to be blurring sometimes.

Eventually she slept again, welcoming mushrooms that billowed and marched like pillows. Then she woke up again and just sat there, time passing slowly. She realised that days and days of subsisting on a few leaves and her father's unfulfilling food, were finally catching up with her in this cold. She felt ill and frozen to her centre and she stared around at the grey dawn bitterly. This was living wild, she thought, and gave a tiny laugh. A few of the books and articles she had read had spoken wistfully of 'living wild' – 'getting back to nature' – living directly alongside nature, just you and it – but now she thought that any little comfort of civilization would be more than welcome. Why was her father not living in a small comfortable house somewhere with hot water and plenty of food easy to hand – instead of out here in the middle of nowhere trying to put on some illusion of self-sufficiency and hiding?

It was all a lie anyway. Most of his food and supplies were bought, she knew that much. Bought on chuntering excursions in the battered and muddy old car that sat by the house.

Finally, driven by desperation, she scrambled to her feet and turned towards where the sails of the Windmill Museum still showed above the trees, silhouetted against the quiet morning sun. The old landmark seemed doubly appealing now. She couldn't handle this any longer. What could she do? The library with its internet and information, where she could perhaps work out what was going on? Then go off and steal a meal somewhere? Maybe. Or maybe just the comfortable chairs in the museum. Perhaps the young man who often minded the place wouldn't mind if she fell asleep there . . .

The Museum was a sweet and strange old building. The round brick tower sprouted out of a clump of small red and rippling-tiled buildings like a dumpy mushroom with small neat windows and balconies picked out in white wood. At the top, the four great white sails still hung – but they were nothing more than frames now and they could never spin again. The wings of this place had been clipped and only the bare bones remained. Feather knew that, but still it was a place that affected her somehow. The museum of local history and local natural history was mostly arranged, tall and thin, inside the old windmill tower, the displays nestling among a wonderland of huge cogs and beams. It was cluttered, sometimes cramped and it smelt of wood – but it was comfortable and impressive. The huge old machinery somehow far more directly moving than the technological bulk of the silent power station near her home.

Feather had practically learned the exhibits by heart now, especially the natural ones, but it was still a nice quiet place to sit. The atmosphere was peaceful and calm – totally different to her homely trees but this time in a very nice way. Sometimes she could read the leaflets or any book or magazine she might have managed to acquire with her light fingers. Now she had nothing but it didn't matter. She felt too tired to read. All she wanted was a soft chair – perhaps the one on the quiet third floor, nestled between a case of stuffed birds and a display of seashore pickings. Here it was warm and here there was never any pressure to move on or be doing something. That was what made it precious.

She stepped in, feeling the warmth with relief. There were a couple of other people in there looking at the exhibits and some glanced at her curiously. She hesitated, desperately not wanting their stares now, and trying to find the courage to venture further. Normally she at least tried to look smart and unobtrusive when she came here, but now she was aware of her clothes and hair, stained and tangled from sleeping rough in them. She nodded casually to the young man sitting behind the desk in the entranceway. He was one of the museum keepers and a familiar sight, though she didn't know his name – or indeed had ever really spoken to him. Somewhat chubby and with an untidy mop of hair, he was usually buried in a book and today was no exception. He glanced up at her with a nod and a small smile as she slipped in. There was an uneaten sandwich on his desk, and she felt a gnawing pain at the sight. Food was starting to occupy her mind in an almost continuous litany. But there was not much she could do about that now.

Unless she could steal something.

. . . her practised hands clumsily knocking three apples from their display crate – and replacing two of them with an embarrassed grin at no-one.

Munching with great satisfaction on down the road . . .

Why not? She had done it before.

Or maybe she could go back to that patch of mushrooms and have some herself. Even that was tempting now. What did they taste like, she wondered. Were they just like an ordinary mushroom? Or did the body know? Did they taste like what they were?

Sometimes – and now in particular – it almost seemed to Feather that it was worth the risk of poisoning, just to find out the answers to such questions. Just what were they like? What did the Death Caps and Agarics taste like? What exactly were the lethally sweet berries of the Deadly Nightshade like? Who knows what extraordinary eating sensations were there for the taking in some improbable last meal? If you wanted it.

What were they?

She stared speculatively at the young man. She was pining for some rest, but instead of heading upstairs and looking for her chair, she paused. Why not? Throughout her life, Feather had almost never spoken to anyone aside from her father – but, why not? She approached the desk.

"Excuse me," she asked politely, trying not to betray her tiredness. "But have you ever heard of the Amanita mushroom?"

He looked up at her again. "The what?"

"The Amanita mushroom."

He got it then, and nodded enquiringly. Feather was panicking already. She felt so unused to talking that the words struggled to form in her mouth, but she pushed herself. "Please. Is it dangerous? – if you eat some – what can you . . .?"

He hesitated, frowning. "Yes it is. Well – I mean I suppose it depends which one it is. But anyway – I suppose one should just get oneself to a doctor as fast as one can," he said. Then he looked at her sharply. "Why?" he asked. "You think you . . ?"

Feather jumped. Her heart was racing and her instincts were telling her to run. "I? What?"

"You think you ate some?"

She shook her head urgently and he looked slightly relieved, though still puzzled.

"Oh I am sure they can fix it," he said. "Stomach pumps maybe – or something. You would have to ask at the library perhaps. They might have a book on it somewhere." He hesitated a moment, remembering something. "Actually, if you hang on a moment . . ."

He broke off and hurried into the back room. Feather drew a deep breath and tried to calm herself down. She told herself it was stupid to be so disturbed at talking like this. It didn't help. She was uncomfortably aware of the tension in her body betraying itself in her stance and movement. She was even trembling slightly.

After a moment, he returned with a book. "Perhaps I can help you after all," he said, opening it with a smile. It was a fungi guide and she leaned over to look.

"Ok – amanita – amanita . . . which amanita are you interested in? Or is it all of them?"

"I don't know," Feather said. "It is the white one – I . . . I am . . ."

He handed her the book.

"*Amanita phalloides*? *Amanita virosa*? *Amanita citrina*?"

She spotted it straight away.

"That," she said, pointing.

'*Amanita virosa,*' she read. 'The Destroying Angel. August to November. Sometimes encountered in deciduous woodland, often at higher altitudes. Deadly poisonous.'

She scanned the page quickly.

> *Symptoms*:
> Amanita virosa is one of the few mushrooms to come close to the Death Cap in terms of potency, containing highly dangerous amatoxin poisons. This fungus has been responsible for many cases of severe poisoning and death. There is normally a delay of approximately eight to twenty-four hours after consumption before onset of the first symptoms – violent vomiting, persistent diarrhoea and severe pains to the stomach. Following this there may cruelly be a period of apparent improvement before the second effects of the poisoning occurs a few days later – a deterioration of both the liver and the kidneys resulting in a yellowing or discoloration of the whites of the eyes and skin. Thus, it is crucial to get treatment as fast as possible in the early stages.

She stared at it blankly and her body began to loose control even more. She felt herself twitch. What did she look like, she wondered. She felt the centre point of a hundred watching eyes now, not just his mild blue ones that rested on her uneasily. This was a nightmare. A complete nightmare.

"Are you ok?" he asked, and she almost jumped back a step.

"Thankyou," she said hastily, handing back the book. "Yes, I am fine. Thankyou."

Feather slowly backed away, bumping into the stair-rail and staggering clumsily. Her headache was getting worse now, her chest was tight and her heartbeat almost painful.

"Are you sure you're ok?" he asked with a worried frown and she flinched sharply. "Are you sick?"

"Thankyou," she managed. "I am fine." She turned to go, but before she could control herself she had wobbled sharply on her feet. Tiredness and hunger were sweeping over her like a wave and she straightened up with a sigh.

He looked puzzled.

"You sure?" he asked. "What is all this about poisonous mushrooms? You haven't been tripping, have you?"

"Yes – no – thankyou I am fine."

Feather wasn't sure what tripping meant, but from the tone of voice it didn't sound good. He was looking at her with increasing intenseness.

"When did you last eat?" he asked at last.

"Mmm,"

"Come on – when did you last eat?"

"This morning," she stammered, "But I am . . . so hungry."

It had slipped out. She hadn't meant to say that. "It's ok," she managed, turning hastily to the exit. "I am fine." She was aware of him staring after her as she hurried miserably out again into the fresh air. She quickly dragged herself round a corner into a small side road and there she collapsed again, against the wall, feeling a bitter twinge of disappointment. She had hoped to have a long rest in the warm – but now she had ruined it. She buried her head in her hands again. The late-morning air seemed even colder now and it beat down on her through her top and ate up through her jeans, tormenting the fading welts on her arse. It dawned on Feather then that she had probably never felt so miserable before. Her stomach and head were hurting and her home was in ruins . . .

As she sat, she stared up at the tower of the windmill museum – and, for the first time that she could remember, the huge windmill sails seemed to be turning.

* * *

Half way home – at the edge of the estuary – she finally collapsed to her knees, digging into the mud. She found marsh snails and lug worms and she washed them and swallowed them, trying not to choke on the brine. Ignoring her clothes, which were instantly soaked and freezing, she just lay there scrabbling for something to eat. In the leaf litter a bit further on were some more snails and a Great Grey Slug. It helped.

Finally, covered with sand and shivering uncontrollably, she began to cry for the first time . . .

In her dream, the Windmill Museum was still there, but it was transformed into a giant spinning machine weaving cloth out of copper wire. The same copper wire that her father used everywhere. But the cloth it was weaving was shaped into the figures of people – an endless production line of them, who marched away into the distance. She was still trying to recognise them when she woke up into a bright evening under a chill blue sky.

It had been a long sleep and she felt a little refreshed. Around her was the familiar home woods and they seemed a comforting presence, though she could hardly remember how she had got here. Her body felt filthy and colder even than the food she had gorged herself on earlier. Her clothes clung to her in tangled, damp twists and she heavily sat up and began to peel them off, flinging them away in disgust. Once naked, she actually felt a little warmer, if anything. A few beams of evening sun were cutting through the trees and she drank them up eagerly, trying to relax and let her skin breath.

The pain in her stomach had faded a bit now and she was feeling more alive, though still cold to the point of agony. Waking herself and getting warm was vital, so she got up and began pacing around, jumping up and down. Eager to keep moving, in spite of her complaining flesh, she headed towards the open ground by the security fence and when she got there she was glad she had. To her delight, the faint sun was shining down stronger – a luminous haze that was almost pink in the morning mist. Here, there was a little to eat as well and she went to it rapidly. Then she leaned her white body against the wire mesh fence and peered through, her fingers and toes curling through the links. The power plant was silent as always – the same ghostly buildings and wires. As long as she had been here, Feather had never been on the other side of this fence – though there were a few holes in places. Even to collect the food that grew there. She hadn't needed her father's warning about that one. She had always had a faint feeling that if she actually stepped through, then the sleeping complex might suddenly awaken again.

Then two things happened that turned her world upside down. It suddenly hit her that something was different. In the cracked and worn car park, there were two vehicles parked. Feather slowly dropped from the fence and stared intently at them. Just ordinary cars. Then, without any fanfare, there were three figures there dressed in coloured baggy suits, their faces hidden by helmets. Blue, white and green. Like something out of her father's paintings. It was such an unexpected sight that Feather just stared at them for a while, unsure how to react. The power station was always deserted. As long as she could remember. That was the way things were. Her mouth turned down at the corners, shocked more than she quite understood.

They were just walking across from one building in the direction of another – that's all. From one door to another. But instead, they stopped sharply and stared at her. Feather had forgotten for the moment how conspicuous she was, leaning against the fence.

"Hey," the one in blue called sharply, waving at her. They stared at her for a moment then hurried towards her.

It was her instinct that started her off. Not any kind of understanding or thought. She dropped from the fence and bolted back into the trees, trying to remember where she had put her clothes and thankful for the falling dusk. Surely it wouldn't be difficult to slip away in this low light?

After a few minutes she burst out into the causeway where the silent wires ran. The pylons were like surreal metal trees themselves – and the lines they carried, she knew, were the big power cables that carried away the electricity from the power station. But she wasn't sure. The wires hung inert and silent so perhaps they were as dead as the rest of the building. This was no place to be naked though. Brambles twined thicker here in the open and the place was filled with young birch trees, whose thin branches whipped at her or flurried in her face. But she ploughed through as best she could and dived into the woods again. She ran for a minute more, darting through the leaf litter now with barely a scratch, but then her foot caught in a hidden branch and she went flying into a small dip in the ground. There was a blast of pain from her ankle and she rolled in the leaves with a gasp, then froze, listening.

Even in the approaching winter, the woods always made some sound. The wind rustled the dying leaves. Occasionally something would fall to the ground with a thud. Or something would shift somewhere. Feather lay back slowly and shut her eyes, flexing her foot cautiously and tasting the pain there. Slowly her breathing calmed. Ears were better than eyes here. These woods were so familiar that any wrong note in it would stand out like a trumpet call. And the wrong note was certainly there. She listened to it for a moment – tramping feet getting closer – then she jumped up, only to fall over again with a grunt. Her foot was hurting, though not cripplingly, and she staggered up onto all fours, trying to move away to cover.

"Hey," a voice called. "Wait a minute. Steady on – what's the matter with you?"

She blinked round at him and hesitated. It was the white man. There was only one of them now at least. He had also taken off his helmet and didn't look so surreal any more. He was just a short-haired young man with a rather heavy face and dark eyebrows. Feather shrank back down into the leaves warily.

He came to a stop staring down at her. "Hey – I am not going to hurt you or anything. But what the hell are you doing here?" he demanded. "It isn't safe."

Feather said nothing. He regarded her with a puzzled and uncertain look on his face.

"Why are you naked?" he asked. "Are you ok? Has anything happened?" She just looked at him for a moment, then rolled over and scrambled clumsily to her feet, favouring her foot. She heard him give a startled hiss.

"What the hell happened to you?" he demanded. It took her a few moments to work out what he was talking about, then she realised that he had seen her arse and back – the fading welts there.

"What's that?" he demanded uneasily. "Are you ok?"

She nodded briefly, but he came forward anyway. She felt herself tensing as he approached, still wondering whether to dash off and escape – but instead she stood there and let him come.

"Are you sure?" he asked. She felt him turn her round and examine her – felt him wriggle an arm out of the suit – felt his hand on her buttocks.

"Steady. Are you sure you are ok?" he asked, an odd expression on his face. "What are you doing naked in the woods? You lost or just playing at something? Looking for something?"

She gave him a questioning stare. Looking for something?

He drew a deep breath and touched her again – a bit more intently this time. Then he shrugged.

"Well I'll be buggered," he muttered, shaking his head. "I thought this was going to be a strange day – but I never thought it would be this strange."

He turned her round and touched her chest, gave a short laugh. "Heh – nothing much here yet, but down here –"

His hand wandered lower.

"– already fully grown. Interesting. Do you know you are a woman, I wonder?"

Feather stared at him expressionlessly as his hand tugged at the small tuft of hair between her legs.

"Take it easy," he murmured. "I just need to have a look at you – make sure you are ok. You really shouldn't be here. This is not a safe place to be . . ."

She allowed herself to be leant back and her legs to be spread. She felt tense and nervous – from the simple presence of a stranger who really shouldn't have been there in such familiar surroundings. He was scrambling out of his suit, and then out of the formless undergarment that was beneath it.

Feather began to realise what might be happening.

"Perhaps you've got the right idea," he said. "It's fucking hot in this thing."

His body was pale and pasty, running with stretch marks and odd spots.

"Yeah," he muttered. "Now tell me I am ugly. But hey – looks ain't everything."

She stared in real surprise, peering through the fading light, for the man possessed two penises and she couldn't recall encountering any creature like that before, either in books or anywhere else. They were positioned one above the other, looking faintly absurd.

He gave another chuckle. "Who says there are no surprises left in the world," he said. "Take your pick, my dear – or maybe you would prefer both?"

Feather's instincts were gone now. She didn't know how to react to this at all. She was still trying to decide whether or not to jump and try to run when she found herself underneath him. She clutched a handful of leaves, feeling his weight with a wince of discomfort. Then, after a spit for lubrication, she was penetrated.

It felt bitterly uncomfortable and she wanted to struggle out of his grip. She could, she felt. In a moment. This was not violence. Not like the hysterical stories on the internet where people were tied down and immobilised and then – what was the word? Raped? Instead, for all her confusion, she lay back for a moment, trying to understand the weird sensation of having something inside her body. She was unsure if this should be something profound or alarming or just nothing much at all. But, before she could make up her mind about anything, he was gone out of her again.

She felt herself turned over – and the man hissed again in shock.

"What the fuck?" he gasped, running his eyes over her. Now what? she thought. It took her a moment to realize that he must be looking at the other marks there. Scars. Older ones – that lined over her vagina and perineum like paths on a map. She felt a twinge of an unexpected misery at being reminded of that.

"What happened to you?" he demanded.

She was silent and he swore to himself. She lay there half on her hands and knees waiting for whatever was coming next – but he just withdrew and started nervously getting dressed again.

"Hey," the man said uneasily, pulling on his suite. "You know these woods?"

Feather nodded, picking herself up.

"Then you know a way through these trees . . . without going back to the plant? How do you get to the town from here?"

She raised her eyebrows. The question was asked casually, but there was a lingering tremor in his voice.

"Without . . . going back . . ." he stammered. "I've got a fucking bad feeling about this."

Feather shook her head and shrugged, glancing back at the distant lights. They shone through the woods, illuminating the mist in a great halo – the red of them almost lost in the white. He stared at them and sighed, defeated.

"Nothing?"

Feather shrugged again.

"Well – I suppose someone has to do this job. Should get a bloody medal for it though."

With his head drooping slightly he began to walk. Unsure of what else to do, Feather accompanied him as the light increased. Where had she left her clothes?

Somewhere – perhaps even from underground – there was a faint grind of machinery. He paused, looking around, and hastily fumbled his helmet back on, his face lined with unease.

"No way," he said turning. "What are they doing?" They stared at each other for a moment as the rumble faded away. The lights of the plant flickered once – blanking the woods in darkness for the blink of an eye – before flooding out again.

He muttered something Feather couldn't catch and hurried onwards – then paused.

"Listen," he said. "You get somewhere away from here tonight. The place is closing down. They are decommissioning reactor 3, it's already a god-awful mess."

Feather stared at him with blank eyes. He gripped his helmet tightly, her eyes and muteness seeming to get under his skin. "Damn," he muttered, turning again. "Do what you want then." He hurried away, fumbling for the phone in his belt and dialling.

Feather stood for a moment staring out at the lights, then she slowly turned and headed back into the trees.

* * *

It was dark now. She walked along the beach with the eerie glow of the power plant trailing behind her. She was dressed again now – reluctantly putting her still damp clothes on. Her tatty shoes were not much use here in the sand though, so she impatiently kicked them away and left them behind. She was still a little un-nerved – mostly from the simple sight of figures in the power station. They also signalled a change of some kind. Everything was full of changes now.

Between her legs felt uncomfortable – as though bruised slightly – but she tried to ignore that and tramped on heavily, her feet sinking into the sand. She wanted to find somewhere quiet to sit and think about what had just happened to her – to swallow the significance of it properly and place it in the right shaped receptacle in the deep places of her mind. But there were too many other things to worry about, so that would have to wait.

The wind was strong and, beside her, the dark sea tumbled wildly against the sand and shingle – plunging in like tongues and tossing the fine polished tellin shells backwards and forwards. The coarse grass that grew in tufts, imprisoning the sand into miniature dunes and hollows, flurried violently, the wind hissing through it, laden with sand. It lashed against her trousers as she pushed through. It was colder and the wind was like knives in her hair, but she ignored it and pressed on, her face blank and expressionless.

As the light faded behind her, it almost seemed as though the sea itself was beginning to glow – a faint phosphorescence picking out each wave as it curled and crashed in. Overhead the sky was as black as ink, heavy clouds blotting out the stars. Feather knew her way well enough though. She knew these dunes with the knowledge of one who has grown up in them, and eventually she tramped up the beach and inland across the scrub and low bushes that grew there. Here the wind was less, though it still fluttered through the plants, making them toss and sway.

She pushed on until she finally reached the rough track that lead to her home. She scrambled into it and began to march grimly. Anyone who met her on that walk – if there was ever anyone on this remote and abandoned trail – might have been startled at the expression on her face. The corners of her mouth were turned down, her lips pressed tight – and her eyes were almost hidden under frowning eyebrows and lowered head.

What was going on at home?

The first thing she noticed when she arrived home was the smell.

"Feather?" he called from his bedroom. She hurried in and paused, staring at the scene. He looked ghastly – as though he had physically shrunken, and his always skinny body now almost skin and bones. He was sallow and dirty – his chin unshaven and his hair trailing in damp ropes. The bed too looked wet and clammy. Feather stared in, cringing.

"Where have you been?" he asked feebly. He didn't sound particularly angry – just sad and regretful.

"Just – out," she stammered. "In the woods. I am sorry – what is the matter?"

He shrugged. "Sick," he said. "Something I ate I imagine."

"What happened?"

"It's ok – I am feeling a little better," he said. "I think I will be fine. It just goes to show – no matter how careful you are you can still make mistakes. Even the Measuring Man sometimes makes mistakes and brings some small mercies to the world."

"What mistake did you make?" Feather asked.

"I don't know."

"Perhaps you should call for help," Feather said hopefully. "Shall I run to the village?"

"No." He shook his head urgently. "You mustn't do that. I will be fine."

She looked at him closer. His eyes were as yellow as amber, she realized, feeling cold. They sat in his discoloured skin like dirty precious stones . . .

In the distance, through the dark and with nothing to announce it or prepare for it, came the cry of a siren. It was the first time she could remember that a human sound from outside had reached as far as this house and they both listened to it in deep silence. It seemed like a signal sent directly to them – though of what she wasn't sure. Some sort of ending? Whatever it was, it unnerved her – and seemingly her father as well, for he clutched the bedclothes tightly.

The rising and falling sound tailed off into the distance and eventually faded out.

He murmured something to himself. She wasn't sure, but it sounded like "end." Feather drew a deep breath, trying to calm her fear.

"Why are we here?" she asked.

"Hmm?"

"You have never explained. You never told me. Why do we live out here, always hiding away?"

He gave a tiny smile. "I told you . . . times – many times," he said. "Remember?"

She gave him a blank look.

"And when the first man was cast in despair out of the city," he said, his voice going singsong and rhythmic, "the king Measuring Man said unto his people to watch him, for even out in the wilderness he shall not be free from our measuring eyes. The king signed his name on a piece of paper and tied it to the running man's back where he couldn't reach – and the king booted him in the arse and said to the running man to start running. And so the running man ran – ran for days and days and weeks and weeks. But always the measuring eyes were on him and always he was not alone."

He sighed miserably, while Feather stared down at him, feeling very cold. His babbling, singsong voice was familiar enough, but now, stripped down and eyes as yellow as a dying buttercup, she seemed to sense something in the story she had not heard before. Surely he was talking about himself.

"Why?" she murmured. But he was muttering to himself – almost inaudibly.

"Wandering the woods, he ate of the wild leaves and was guided uneasily . . . alone and afraid . . . didn't want to . . . In a world of stone pillars he was forced to fight and kill – the maze of reaching hands and gleaming red lights . . . each about a centimetre and 1 foot 4 inches above the ground. The fight – lasted many days – and both parties were broken men when it was over . . . the running man lost and kept running amid a storm of paper chaff. And the measuring eyes said to him . . . "

"Father," she called, shaking at him. He gave a moan and shifted in his bed – seeming to glance at her for a moment. "Please – talk to me straight."

He stared at her dumbly and she let him drop. She shrugged slightly. Normally she said as little as she could to him, but now she felt a terrible pressure and panic – there was so much she needed to know.

"I brought you here," he said, "Nobody comes here. They don't like that old power plant much. And those that do come out here – well, ordinary people are very good at minding their own business. I did my best to keep you safe," he murmured. "I didn't want you to be a part of . . ." He drew a deep breath. "Feather," he said urgently. "Never let the world catch you, you have to remember that," before subsiding into muttering again. The measuring eyes. A metal forest. And something about a hat that she couldn't understand.

"But why?" she said again – an almost wailing note in her voice.

She got no more out of him, though, so she eventually left the room and tramped into the kitchen, where the pot of mushroom stew still sat on the stove, ornamented with small tufts of mould. She stared round but couldn't face eating anything here again – as if the whole room had been infused with poison. As if it was dripping from the damp walls – staining through the cupboards like slime.

"Feather?" he called through to her after a moment.

"Yes?" she managed.

"Would you get me some water?"

She stared round the kitchen – but the big jug that normally contained it was empty.

"There's none left," she said, putting her head round the door of his room. "I'll have to get some."

He nodded silently and she withdrew. Saucepan in hand she went outside, across the garden and down to the small stream. It flowed over rocks with a gentle trickling and she quickly filled the saucepan, her face expressionless. Then she hurried it home and put it on the stove to boil. Then the gas faded out and, with a weary sigh, she ran out, a second time, to the shed to fetch a replacement canister.

This is what self-denial gets you, she thought gloomily as she connected it up. Then she stared dumbly into the pot. Hot water wasn't really that refreshing.

Thoughtfully she tossed in a sprig of dried mint and stirred.

When it was boiled and cooled a little, she brought him a tankard-full and then slipped out again without a word, entering her own room and collapsing onto the bed, staring at the ceiling.

Why?

That was the key. What happened – what you did – what other people did – did to you – wasn't the important thing now. You had to know why before you could know anything about the what.

Perhaps that was the way to exorcise memories as well, since most bad memories seemed to be questions. It was the only way that could possibly succeed.

Find out why.

The Measuring Man looked at her formally.

"What do you want to measure?" she asked, trying not to show her fear. The thing in his hand was looking less and less like a ruler – more like some complex surgical instrument.

"Feather," he said, with all the professional friendliness of a doctor, "You are a simple girl, aren't you . . ."

Feather shut her eyes and rolled over onto her face.

What were the questions . . ?
Why were we here?
Why rage and hate?
Why glass?
Why Measuring Man?

*   *   *

Next day she tried again.

"I need to know," Feather said grimly, trying to ignore those yellow eyes that seemed so alien now.

He sighed and shifted.

"The path to knowing things is never as simple as you think," he said faintly. It was a meaningless statement and Feather clenched a fist behind her back, her face lined with worry.

"And the path to doing things is even more complex," he murmured dully. "The path – up up and over – through the clouds to where we can understand what . . . you . . . I mean . . ."

"What path? Please," Feather begged. "Why did you . . ?"

He reached out and touched her hand, gently uncurling her fingers from the nervous fist she was holding. It was an unexpectedly affectionate gesture that made her flinch.

"Water?" he murmured. Feather sighed and ran to get some.

"Thank you," he said, and drank.

Perhaps that had been a mistake though, for he subsided in exhaustion and shut his eyes.

"What's wrong with me," he murmured. "I have never felt quite so ill before. I am finding it a little hard to breathe . . ."

"Let me get some help then," she said.

He shook his head.

"Why not? You can't stay out here alone for ever."

"I have to," he said. "It's ok. I am recovering slowly."

She stared at him in silence.

"I don't want to stay out here alone," she said woodenly.

"Don't lie to me," he said with a sigh. "You've been wandering everywhere. I've always known it. It drives me nuts, but I suppose it was inevitable. I should have realised that years ago."

She gave a discomforted sigh.

"I'm not answering any more questions," he said wearily.

"But I have to know. Why shouldn't I know?" she said tensely.

"You think I am just making up stories?" he spluttered suddenly, trying and failing to sit up. He flapped a hand at her feebly. "The

Measurers are out there, Feather. And maybe they'll find you one day. And when they do – you will be pining for this quiet hidden little place you hate so much."

He sighed miserably and rolled over.

". . . out into the wilderness," she caught faintly. "It was great. At last . . . out of . . . somehow. She was gone – so far away. She didn't care. And . . . Measuring man . . . her to . . . Running Man's death . . . thought. I . . . You don't exist, Feather – you . . . kept you safe and hidden. The world doesn't know you exist – even she doesn't know you exist – now . . . and it is better to . . ."

"She?"

He sighed. "The world is a terrible place," he said more distinctly. "You must never let yourself be caught by the world. Whatever you do – you mustn't be caught. It's too horrible . . ."

"But why?" she demanded. "What's the point of hiding if you don't know what you are hiding from? Tell me . . ."

He gave a long groan. "I feel sick," he muttered. "Please clear off and let me sleep."

Still murmuring something about a hat and red lights, he faded to silence. That was the last coherent thing he said, no matter how much Feather shrieked at him and poured water down his throat. And two days later he died.

She stood and stared down at him, feeling icy, her mind wandering. Was he even really her father? This deranged old hippie? Even that didn't make much sense. She could see no resemblance, either physically or mentally.

Too late to ask now, though. His deep yellow eyes stared at the ceiling. The stench filled the room – a stench she had never encountered before. A sickly sweetish smell that stuck in her throat and she could almost taste.

Aimlessly she roved around his studio, trying to look at the paintings rather than the figure in the bed. They were stacked in slanting heaps and hung on the walls and she flipped through them. She had seen most before of course, but she had not looked at them quite like this.

The paintings were like him. Cryptic and surreal. Filled with labyrinths and mazes, vast autophobic spaces and tiny cracks and passageways. Obviously these surreal landscapes meant something, but the dictionary was missing. The connection to his rambling about The Measuring Man and the weird world of that story was obvious, though there were few actual figures in them and no recurring characters who could help elaborate this. The Measuring Man was obviously a deity that should not be depicted.

Eventually she moved on from the paintings and began going through the contents of his drawers. In here was everything. Oddments, paraphernalia – everything. There were packets of herbs and a scattering of stones and crystals – some very beautiful, including a large green and pink natural tourmaline. There were coils of copper wire, which she held with a twinge of unease. There were artistic materials, a few books, pens, paper, a craft knife, pastels and charcoal. Then she came upon a sketch pad and took it out with interest. But all it contained was more of the eerie landscapes and images that filled his paintings. She skimmed through it, but it offered nothing that she hadn't seen already – until, near the back she saw something that brought her up sharp.

It was her.

She peered at the page, her skin prickling. She just stood there in rough but expressive soft pencil lines – an ordinary girl in her scruffy clothes, hands clasped behind her back, a casual and cute half smile on her face.

When had he drawn this? It couldn't have been done from life. She couldn't remember anything like that ever happening. He had just sat down one day and produced this picture of her. Where had she been at the time? Out in the woods? Wandered off to the village?

What had he been thinking about at the time?

Something glimmered in her head and she dropped the notebook back in the drawer.

Maybe the Measuring Man had been right when he had described her as a simple girl.

Something had blurred though. Something that had been simple had suddenly become less so. Feather found herself remembering things with a different kind of confusion.

She dropped the pad back in the drawer and floated from the room.

So . . . why?

Feather accepted then that she had doomed herself. She couldn't ask why anything now . . .

She would never know. That was the crime. There were no more whys. The question had lost meaning. She was left sitting in the corner of the kitchen trying to think, the angle of the walls cold against her back and the tiled floor colder against her arse. What was there to think about though? All she felt was a blank emptiness. Perhaps that was why this simple corner was so comforting.

And now what?

The Measuring Man was outside. The Measuring Man was looking for her . . .

What did that mean?

It meant that she knew nothing – she had learned nothing. The realisation was agonising.

The world was supposed to be a simple place. You lived – you ate – you reproduced – eventually you died. And it was over. That was what everything she could see around her had told her. What she knew of the world and the crazy stories of The Measuring Man just didn't fit together. As a child she had frowningly pictured him formally measuring the length of her nose and shaking his head in severe disappointment. Then, when she had grown up a bit, it was her vagina that was being measured. And the shake of the head was only more severe now. But it had just been a story – even though it was a story that ruled his life. That was what hurt. And from what she read in the news it seemed that everyone out there was just as under the thrall of stories as he had been. Stories were powerful things, she thought – and they were something she knew almost nothing about.

The world was full of incomprehensibilities; she knew that from her reading in the library. People, groups, authorities, countries – all danced a dance of death – a waltz of killers just like her. The small things made her uneasy. The big things made no sense at all and made her chuckle until she forced herself to remember that it was actually true and tried to picture herself caught up in them. And it was all because of stories. Every atom of it. So how did this fall out? Were the killers all Feathers, wandering out there lost and trying not to be caught by the world? Was that how they escaped the stories? Were they the ones who had fallen out of the stories, making victims of those who still clung there? And were the jailors all measuring men? Measuring you until what you had done in your life reached a certain length – and then all over with a clang? Was that what happened when you died? When they came for you and killed you? You just ran out of length? No more. Good bye.

That was what was outside, she realised. That storm of a world. Waiting for her. That was the sound that was approaching. She could hear it – as she sat huddled in panic, unable to imagine what to do next. It was a sound she knew – but one that should never have happened here. The sound of an unfamiliar car coming to a stop and switching off. That was what was banging and crashing on the door, howling for admittance.

Feather, the Measuring Man bawled. You have been measured and you are too long. The story no longer holds you.

Don't you dare, she begged silently.

If she just stayed quiet, perhaps he would go away.

No luck. There was a painful sound of splitting wood and the door opened sharply, sending a savage bar of light right across her. She flung a hand to her face to shield it.

"What the hell?" a voice cried. "This is supposed to be empty. Who are you?"

She could never remember feeling any more terrified than she did now. So terrified that paradoxically she felt beyond panic. There were four figures scrambling through the door – Black Suit, White Suit, Red Suit, Green Suit. She stared at them dumbly – but then one at least suddenly jumped into unexpected familiarity.

White Suit – a vivid memory of him in the woods. She wondered for a moment if they all had two penises – or all had duplicates of whatever anatomy they had, she corrected, for two of them, Black and Green, were women.

White was staring at her, eyebrows up – and for some reason he looked almost as shocked as she felt. Why?

The familiarity and the glimpse of his fear woke her up a bit. These were people, she realised – and a bit of reality came crashing back, delirious thoughts of her father's King Measuring Man fading sharply. No doubt they meant her harm – but . . .

Instinct kicked in.

"My father is dead," Feather said expressionlessly.

"What?"

She gestured to the next room.

"How? Are you ok?"

Her eyes glittered. What to say now? She was used enough to lying to her father – that was second nature. But this was a stranger, and she still wasn't used to strangers. Everything she had learned told her that these people were her enemies.

"I don't know," she said. "He got sick. Something he ate."

That should be enough.

"Why didn't you tell someone?" Red Suit demanded, while Green and Black ran through to the next room.

"Wouldn't let me," she said.

Why wouldn't these people just go? That was all she wanted. She knew it wouldn't happen, of course. Everything was turning very bad indeed.

"Stay here," Red said to White, "while I check over." He ran out and Feather and White were left staring at each other. White looked very uncomfortable.

"Hey," he murmured softly, sitting down by her side. "Er – you ok?"

She didn't quite understand why he seemed afraid of her and she gave him an expressionless stare – then touched his hand – a small touch with a question in it. His flesh felt just as soft and insubstantial as she remembered. It was a gesture she hardly understood herself. Red came running in again then, talking into his phone – followed by Green from the other direction. She gave Red a confused look. "I don't know," she was saying. "We haven't time. Someone else will have to deal with this. Just get the girl out of here."

"I don't understand," she murmured. The corner was comforting – the tiled floor cold against her jeans.

"There has been a small release of contaminated water," White explained. "This area must be sealed off while they dismantle reactor 3 at the power station. Please go and pack whatever essentials you will need."

Feather stared at him dumbly. Essentials? She felt a creeping terror running through her. They were going to take her away – take her into a world she didn't exist in. That was what her father had said. She didn't exist. The world is a terrible place, he had said. You must never let yourself be caught by the world.

"Please hurry," Red snapped, and Feather darted through to the other room, ignoring Green's call of protest. Her father still lay on the bed, yellow eyes staring at nothing and she watched him, trembling. What had he been protecting her from? What was going to happen now? She felt full of confusion and terror – a terror that was formless and unsure, but nevertheless made her chest tighten.

Then her eyes went to his paintings arranged round the room, and she suddenly felt an overwhelming sense of misery. It was a curious paranoid storm of creativity – but it was creativity nonetheless.

"Oh my god," she murmured.

She stared round the room.

"You can't just abandon the paintings here?" she called as White peered round the door.

"I am sorry," White said, joining her, "but there is nothing we can do about that now. The situation is too urgent." Green touched White on the shoulder. "Take her out to the car and get her into town. Report everything. We will carry on . . ."

Feather backed away.

"Don't be frightened," White called. "It will be alright."

Feather shrugged, her brain working fast. Quickly she picked up her bag from the corner and waved at the doorway. "I have to just . . ." she called, running outside.

White called something after her – something about not going far. But that was ok – the story was being told now. Feather simply darted across to the shed and noisily opened the door, waving her bag urgently. Simple though it was, White seemed satisfied and hurried back inside.

This was storytelling? It felt kind of good. But there was no point thinking about this now. Her brain was not equipped to know the answers. Instead, with a prickling sensation up and down her spine, she relaxed and let her instincts take over. Instincts that seemed to know better than she did that fact and fiction were one and the same thing. She glanced quickly round, then ran for the woods. She ran faster than she could ever recall running before – faster even than when her father had been chasing her. She dashed into the trees and carried on, scrambling through branches and around the dense patches of undergrowth. She thought she heard a voice calling behind her, but she ignored it and plunged on in a blast of pure energy.

Suddenly, far sooner than she expected, the security fence came at her from among the trees and she ran into the wire with a clang, clutching at the mesh and panting – wondering which way to go from here. The atmosphere felt electric – as though a storm was on its way. Or perhaps that was just her racing heart.

In front of her, the power station bustled and glowed, lighting up the sky and the mist – floodlights streamed across the scene, sweeping illumination right down across the distant beach and touching the edges of the restless waves with shining white. Vehicles moved and suited people hurried, and a small, insignificant plume of smoke was rising from somewhere. She watched the water crash in beyond it – pounding the sand and tossing shells that sparkled like stars. Then she looked away, longingly back into the dark woods that pressed about her. She had the feeling that those woods were more of a home to her than anywhere else. More than the house she had left, certainly. The feel of the bark pressing against her skin still glowed on her.

"Never let the world catch you." Those words had been beaten into her and they shone in the darkness now. That was the one thing her father had said that she found herself believing and she didn't linger long. She turned and plunged back into the trees.

The Angels

If he hadn't been drunk on cheap Shiraz, Jimmy Ward would never have spoken to the ragged girl on the beach. She was sitting in the shingle, hunched in the shelter of a slipway, her clothes stained with dried mud and sand, a tattered bag by her side.

This was a classic seaside town beach. Shingle and gravel sloped down to a dark grey sea under a dark grey sky – the strand line littered with seaweed and shells, bits of rubbish and fragments of wood. Breakwaters cut the beach into segments and the path wove its way between them and the varied shapes of the wooden sheds, boat houses and homes that clustered eagerly for a sea view. There was always noise here of some kind. The wind blew through the rigging of the boats hauled up and secured out of reach of the tide – ropes and cables flapping against masts with an almost musical percussion. The sea rolled in – waves sloshing through stones and shells with a crisp rattling sound. Even now, as the evening closed in, there was an occasional screech or peep from sea birds and the occasional engine from the harbour in the middle distance.

The air was filled with the scent of the sea as well – of seaweed and salt – of cooking shellfish from the harbour and fish scraps slung back to the sea again from the occasional restaurant. It was a smell that Jimmy rather liked though. That and the cold helped clear his head, which was foggy and unreal. In his head, the snow-threatening clouds seemed to boil like mud and the sea seemed slick, like the mucus of a snail. It was all just a surface skin for something else.

The pounding of the waves rolled like a drum as he tramped unsteadily through the softly moving shingle. When on stones, walking becomes something different, with every step causing it to move and sink. The first twinkling lights of the harbour and out at sea were shining, and they also seemed unreal. Seemed to move and change like constellations of stars seen from unimaginable vantage points.

He paused a moment and stared round, blinking, and that was when he saw the figure, seated with her back against the slipway – the steep wooden road down into the sea for launching boats. He stared at her for a moment, puzzled. In his current haze she looked the most unreal element of all, her white face almost glowing in the shadow of the weathered wood. She looked like something out of a story, he decided. Something imagined there.

Perhaps that was why he sat down next to her in a slew of shingle instead of just walking unsteadily on home. She looked at him sharply. It was a small relief to stop moving on that unstable surface though and he sighed.

"Things that can be seen on a beach," he said after a moment. He stared around. "Cockle shells, periwinkle shells. Seaweed – one, two, three, four kinds. Small stones bored into by piddocks," he said, picking one up and showing it to her. "Breakwaters, boats, sea holly – now dying to a crisp. A length of chain that might have held a leviathan. A car tire."

He leaned his head back against the wood, which felt comfortingly hard and permanent.

"It's all about observation," he said dizzily. "Sorry – I am drunk."

"What are you looking for?" she asked at last.

He gave a brief laugh. "Nothing," he said. "I have seen it all before."

There was a silence of almost a minute, while the light faded visibly and the boats and beach receded into shadow.

"What are you doing here?" he asked. "Why are you sitting under a slipway?"

She sighed.

"Because there is nowhere else in the world?" he suggested.

He could smell her a little, he realised. The stale smell of clothes that have been worn too long, of a body that hasn't been washed for too long and of a mind that had given up caring.

"Things that can be seen on the human body," he continued at last, shifting round to look at her and trying to drive away the drunkenness. "Hair – damp and windblown for a long time. Legs. Arse – somewhere – too used to being sat upon. Trousers – holey and covered with sand.

Jacket – thick and stained from sleeping in it. Shoes that have been worn for a long time continuously."

She made no response.

"It's been a while since you were indoors, hasn't it?"

She nodded reluctantly.

There was a silence.

"It's going to be a cold night," he said, glancing up at the heavy sky.

"I don't mind the cold," she murmured.

"I do," he grunted. "Might I suggest you come with me? I don't want to go home and dream of you under this slipway."

She stared at him. He hauled himself unsteadily to his feet.

"I do guarantee at this point," he said, raising his hand, "that I am not plotting anything nor planning anything. Not – not trying to to to pick you up or put you down. Nothing unmentionable is in my head – there isn't room, believe me."

She looked at him, puzzled.

"So come with me and get out of this wind. Do I look dangerous?"

She gave a microscopic smile.

"Do I?" she countered.

He was still a little surprised when she scrambled to her feet after him. She wobbled slightly and he caught her arm.

The fifteen minute tramp back through the town was slow and awkward – both of them rather unsteady on their feet and occasionally leaning on each other. No one paid them any attention, except to keep at a careful distance. Jimmy was used to that though. He was not that badly dressed. He had enough interest left to keep himself as smart as possible. His clothes were usually missing a button or ripped somewhere, but he kept them as neat as he could with his sewing kit. Even so – he knew that his face gave him away. Especially the look in his eyes. That was what people avoided, as though they would catch something of him themselves.

Finally though, they arrived back at the small block of apartments where he lived and they fumbled their way in, ignoring the glance of a neighbour whose name he had never known, passing them in the hall.

Once inside his three-room apartment, she was good for nothing. Her jacket came off and fell to the floor, but that was all. She glanced round the room.

"Copper wire?" she murmured, eyes fixing briefly on his World Cage.

"Hmm?"

"I don't . . ."

But she couldn't talk. She was almost asleep on her feet, he realised, so he just guided her to the bed, letting her sag onto it with a grunt. She groaned and sprawled there, seeming to pass out almost instantly. He stared at her in some surprise – a little puzzlement managing to creep into his head. She wasn't drunk – wasn't stoned. Wasn't anything. Worn down by nothing except exhaustion and chill. He tried to work out how old she was, but he wasn't sure of that either. Perhaps early 20s he guessed. It was hard to tell though. Her worn face might have been aged prematurely. In spite of that, he realised irrelevantly, she was a sharply beautiful person, in a ragged, pointy sort of way.

He rolled her over and tugged the duvet out from under her, sand and gravel rattling everywhere from her trousers and shoes. He brushed that away as best he could, then covered her up, checked round the room a moment, then slipped quietly through to the kitchen.

Not that she seemed likely to wake in a hurry.

He gave a wobbly smile and helped himself to a glass of Red.

When you are sober, a stranger could die in front of you before you will talk to them. Perhaps it was an English thing.

So three cheers for the Red.

I was born in a small town by the sea whose name I forget – and whether there was anything unusual about my birth – anything that could have pointed out the life that was to follow – I don't know.

I remember that I used to dream of light – always –probably from the very day I was born. Wonderful dreams actually, and not a bit frightening for their strangeness. I felt – how shall I say – quite privileged to dream them – and, as the other children raced up and down, backwards and forwards, frenetically, through the compartments of their lives, I was content, as far back as I know, to just sit back and enjoy the larger vistas that I felt that I alone could see. Shutting my ears to their crying, I would doze, drifting gently through oceans of whiteness – a whiteness that was made of myriad upon myriad tiny, floating, luminous particles. Sometimes there would be hints of wondrous, strange colours shot through it – and sometimes odd moving shapes might become visible – only as vague shadow shapes – moving amid the sparkling chaos. And how I yearned to join them. I yearned to just enter my dream totally – forget the real world – and be absorbed into that magical light. Sometimes in my dream I seemed to be flying – and then I would vision huge flocks of beautiful bird-like creatures soaring – with me among them – and then at others I might be aware of a ground under my feet – but the ground was strange. It had a softness and yet a hardness that was totally alien to me. And always – always there was coolness – blissful magical coolness – almost an ecstasy to feel after the sweltering heat of the nightmare summers of the real world. Through all this I simply drifted – letting it take me where it would – there was nothing more that I desired to do – just drift – drift until I would find myself – reluctantly – back in my young body again.

And so I sat quietly and dreamed while the other children stormed about me – and as the years passed, I grew stranger and more remote. I found that I hated the world about me and used to spend my time alone in strange and private places – and the world hated me back – shunning me as an outcast. I was not strong – but I was never bullied – for, in some strange way, I seemed to frighten them. Not by scaring them into keeping a distance – but, instead of bullying me, it seemed almost as if they were afraid to touch me – as if there was something repulsive about me. I didn't care. I still don't, now – on darker streets when childhood seems nothing more than another dream –

And now it was morning.

Jimmy woke up fully clothed and uncomfortable on the sofa, blankets on the floor, leaving him cold and exposed. Not nice.

It took him a moment to remember why he was on the sofa at all, then it came back and he glanced at the bed and the small figure lying there.

Ah yes – he had a guest. A stranger guest, in fact.

It was some minutes before he eventually managed to get up. But not many, as his back was grumbling at him like an annoyed neighbour. That was a symptom of being separated from the old familiar bed his body was used to. That must also be why his head felt filled with old rags and his mouth tasted as though he had been chewing pennies in his sleep. But what could you do? Some things were inevitable – and hospitality was one of them. He stepped heavily across the room and stared blearily down at his visitor, sprawled flat out under the duvet. For a moment he felt a touch of annoyance. At her for being there and at himself for starting this. What was she was going to do now? Bringing home strange people with nothing else in the world – would she ever leave again? What had she to leave to?

At last he made himself get into motion and tramped out of the room, letting the quasi-routine of the morning take over. He left his apartment in a brief foray down the hall to the mail box. There was mail there but nothing interesting. A catalogue selling useful and innovative devices and appliances (if he had anywhere to put them) – a formal letter in an anonymous windowed envelope, which no doubt wanted money from him – a magazine about cycling and a free newspaper. He tramped through to the kitchen half of the apartment, again glancing quickly back to where the sleeping figure lay. He flung the lot on the table. A few normal small-town news items stared up at him hopefully, but he didn't pay much attention. A charity concert. People protesting about a new cycle path. A dog walker's wallet pinched. It seemed an unwelcome intrusion of something that really shouldn't be a part of life. Too ordinary for comfort, almost. He wanted to set the whole heap on fire in his sink – the bill on top – and reduce them all to ashes. He had tried that once though. A bonfire of mail – but all it had done was set the fire alarm off and leave a scorch mark on the metal that he had never managed to remove properly.

Instead he just slung them in the recycling sack in the corner and filled the kettle, then settled down in a chair and gazed sadly out of the window at the street outside. There had been a shake of snow in the night, he saw appreciatively. But it was now turning to slush on the paths and walls – and the world beneath it was showing through again. It was just a narrow road with pavements after all – double yellow lines flowed past, stating the obvious. Blunt, flat terraced apartment buildings that frowned gardenlessly down. The only green in view was a few wintry window boxes.

Gloomy.

The kettle boiled.

As he bustled around making coffee, he intentionally rattled the cups and banged the cupboard door in the hope that she would take the hint and wake up. He shook his head and stretched his shoulders and poured – small espresso cups for this stuff was strong and black – stirring in a little honey. He muttered something under his breath and glanced hopefully into the bedroom.

She was precisely as he had left her the night before, sprawled out amid the covers, one leg hanging out and her mouth open. The smell of her was stronger now in the enclosed space and with a sigh he put the cups of coffee down on the bedside table and opened the window a crack, brushing the slush onto the pavement below. It was ok though. Human beings had the right to smell.

Then he drank his coffee.

Tiredness was creeping over him again though, in spite of that. Staring down at her and drifting off into some kind of sleepy trance, he found himself going blank for a moment.

Things that can be seen in a Ghost Writer's bedroom:

- Books – second hand paperbacks. Lovecraft. Ballard.
- Bedside cabinet slash desk slash storage unit with the front of one drawer missing, unwelcomely visible in spite of the elegant blue and gold cloth that draped over it.
- Gap. Where the wardrobe door wouldn't close because the damn magnetic clasp was missing.
- Small clothes airer – in the way as usual.
- Carpet – slight worn area c. 30cm^2 near the doorway.
- One thunderegg – Black Rock Desert, USA – there for ornamentation and for the comfort given by a lump of stone.
- Small desktop computer. Box, screen, old looking printer and speakers. Modem.
- The World Cage.
- Clothes on floor.

All that old familiar . . .
He sighed.

- One ragged girl sound asleep, one leg hanging out of bed . . .

He yawned hugely.

Aaaahh those times – those strange slow times. You sit in your house wondering what to do. But you can't settle down to anything. You are reluctant to go out (What is there outside?) but you can't find anything to do indoors either except watch the clock and let your mind run loose. While your guest still sleeps.

Wake up, visitor mine. The coffee I made you is cold. Don't you care? My dear pretty-in-a-wild-and-feral-looking-sort-of-way guest – and already Jimmy Ward has downed a glass of red. Well – you have to, to pass the time. What else is there?

Outside it is grey and snowy – the day well advanced. You stand and stare down at her. Nice. Nice to have someone else there. Nice even though it is a stranger you have never met and know nothing about. Is she burned out on drugs perhaps? Brain rewired. That's what it does. Frightening stuff really. Heh – another glass of red to salute that thought. Nice – nice and smooth tasting. Not a bitter tannin in it – this Australian Shiraz Petit Verdot. It slips down the throat like sweet blood – just as smooth and as deep.

And how old was she, he wondered again. He wasn't even sure of that. Could even be as young as late teens. Could be in her twenties. How much of her was her and how much was her looking older than her years? Worn down by too much sitting under slipways.

Things that can be seen on a sleeping girl:

- Face – the pure expression when all other expressions are resting. As still and as smooth as a dream. Was there any honour greater than seeing someone asleep? Forget the porn mags with their spread cunts – that was nothing. It was sleep that was the greatest revelation – the greatest exposure . . . the greatest thing you could show someone.
- Nose – breathing slowly. A very slight sniff in there. Lingering remains of the cold sea air?
- One eye – smooth shut with no frown.
- Tangled brown hair that trailed over the pillow like seaweed. But hey – can't seaweed actually feel kind of nice when you stroke it.
- A hint of the back of the neck – smooth skin disappearing under a
- Stained collar and back of shirt. Old fabric – impregnated with body and sand.
- Body mound. Rises and falls slowly. She's alive. She really is. She's not a dream.
- Leg. Singular. It ain't the twig of a girl named Ana (heh). It is slender – of one who does not get all they would like to eat – but Miss Ana is a long way

away. Ana was a luxury after all in a way – and there seemed little luxury here. The leg is clad in

- Tatty jeans – beautiful, functional garments that they are.

You're braver than I am, Jimmy thought, looking at her – sitting back comfortably in the chair beside the bed. He laughed. Yes – what did it matter? Sleep on my dear visitor. Sleep on and be refreshed. Sleep through the day if you need to. In the mean time I'll – I'll – just sit here. No different to any other morning really, is it? And when you wake up – what then? Will you go? Will you stay? Will you repay me my hospitality? Somehow? Will you . . . feed me something?

I am so hungry . . .

Will you tell me a story?

He was almost asleep again himself when she finally stirred. She twitched and he jerked up – she appeared to shift seamlessly from sleep to waking, sitting up in a moment and staring round her, as though refreshing her memory of how she had come to be there. Her eyes went round the room, settling first on the World Cage, then on him.

"Morning," he said. She smiled uncertainly.

"Your bed is full of sand," she said sadly. "Sorry. I would like to clean myself. Can I?"

He thoughtfully added the information 'non-smoker' to the list of facts he was building up. Very clean voice. But what a strange way of talking she had? Hesitant. She sounded like a foreigner, but with no trace of accent. Was she just unused to talking?

"Of course," he stammered, pointing. "And I will take care of the sand while you have a shower."

She swung out of bed and he watched her nervously. He pointed her in the direction of the tiny bathroom and she slipped out. He yawned hugely and rubbed his eyes, which felt as full of sand and gravel as the bed was. He stared after her as she entered the room, leaving the door open, and listened as the sound of flowing water came, then he turned his attention to the bed. That at least was a quick job. He peeled off the sandy sheet and dumped it in the kitchen sink, ready for later transfer to the bathroom for a wash. When it wasn't occupied. He gave the doorway a quizzical look, then hurried to get a clean sheet as the water stopped flowing.

Tuck tuck tuck – why was replacing sheets such a complicated job? Especially after a glass of red. They never seemed to fit right. Always too much hanging over one side, then too little on the other and the whole damn thing coming off in uncomfortable rucks as you lay on it. Then she stepped back into the room and the sheet suddenly didn't matter so much. She was rubbing at herself with his towel and he made a dismayed noise for aside from that she was stark naked. What what what was this?

"Don't do this to me," he groaned, rubbing his eyes. "It's too early."

She gave him a questioning look and he flung his bathrobe at her. She quietly put it on, draping it round her shoulder and doing up the waistband.

"Thank you," she said. "It is a little cold."

"Yes yes," he said with a sigh. "It is – isn't it just."

She sat down on the stripped bed. "I feel better," she said.

"Good," he said uneasily. She certainly smelled better. "Now hang on a moment and I will warm up your coffee – I I I mean get you some fresh. You hungry?"

She gave a nod, and Jimmy had a feeling that that nod was an understatement of considerable proportions. Ok, he thought. "Ok – I will cook something up. Now what would you like? I have –" he hesitated. "I have bacon and eggs – and . . . bacon . . . and eggs. There's a little goats' yoghurt. There's some oranges . . . errr . . ."

He rubbed at his hair in embarrassment.

"Sorry – not a lot if you don't like bacon and eggs. I – er – haven't been shopping for a while . . . Wasn't expecting guests and . . ."

"I should love bacon and eggs," she said with feeling. Jimmy Ward became just that little bit happier.

Later, a dressed and dried guest made hungry eyes at the plate-full of nicely-cooked bacon, eggs, sausages etc etc and all the other etcs that he had been able to find in the fridge, which he placed in front of her – and it was gone in barely more than a minute.

"Is there any more?" she asked shyly.

Jimmy smiled and returned to the cooker.

Four eggs, six bacon rashers and eight sausages later – as well as almost half a loaf of bread, an orange and a handful of nuts – she had to stop because the food was used up. The fridge was almost bare.

Jimmy was watching her with cloudy admiration.

"I say, old chap," he said, standing up. "I am acknowledging your appetite with respect and admiration."

She gave him the happiest grin he had seen from her yet, and he felt himself warming even more. Hey, he thought. I have a guest!

"My name is James Ward," he paraphrased, closing his eyes and declaiming. "I'm a Ghost Writer. And from earliest childhood I have been a dreamer and a visionary. Poor and isolated from any commercial life, and temperamentally unfitted for the formal studies and social recreation of my acquaintances, I have dwelt ever in realms apart from the visible world; spending my youth and adolescence in ancient and little known books, and in roaming the fields and groves of the region near this hoary old . . ." He hesitated. "Little harbour town." He gave her a crooked grin. "I hope you can stand my crazy little home while you are here."

"Thank you," she murmured, giving him a curious look.

"What's your name?"

"Feather, she said. "What's a Ghost Writer?"

"A writer who was – but is now no more. A writer who has died. Just Feather?"

She nodded.

He gave her a happy smile and extended his hand.

"Pleased to meet you."

However, I eventually discovered that there was one among the throng that did not fear me – did not hate me – and that person was the beautiful girl Feather. She did not hate me – because she also was an outcast. And so, while around me the others lived their life full of classic human contempt and annoyance, we became inseparable. Wherever I went, Feather was by my side – and where she went, so was I. Feather, with her wild hair and dancing eyes. Always dirty she was, always chaotic – and I loved her. Even in my dreams did she follow me – she, naked and wonderful in her wild-girl's body, drifting by my side in the sparkling chaos. But somehow I would sense that she was here in this place of light only because of me – that I was dreaming her in. By herself, she had no access to this wonderful dreamworld. This dreamworld was mine and mine alone – and for some reason that thought haunted me with triumph and poignancy. Then sometimes she would turn to look at me – her eyes huge – reflecting the light of a million tiny flashes. And she would reach out to me and touch my skin – causing strange electrical thrills to run through me – and sending flashes of colour for the first time through the whiteness – flashes of a deep and wonderful red. And then, for a long while, her eyes and mine would be locked together – but never for long enough. Always when this stage was reached – always the mystery would dissolve before any answers were given to it all – and she would be gone. The Dream would fade. Though sometimes it seemed as if, as the final shreds of the dream dissolved, I would catch the echo of her voice –

"– your eyes are glowing."

– echoing with hunger.

And I would wake, my body drenched with sweat in the dark of the night – and then out of the window I would see the North Star, shining brightly – like some magical eye watching me and me alone. And then, when I was unable to sleep again, I would gaze out at it from my bed – unblinking and scarcely breathing – as if it alone could answer my mysteries.

It was as tall as a person . . . it was a person in a way. It was a mannequin – a figure. A figurative sculpture. It was a suit of clothes suspended on a stand that supported it roughly in the shape of a man. A suite of inside out clothes. Everything totally inverted. Even the inside out undergarments were there – but the layering was also inverted and they hung on the outside looking slightly grotesque. There was even a pair of shoes positioned upside down on the floor at the base. This whole construction was wound with a tight looping cage of gleaming wire – copper wire – which shone a rich orange in the low light. At the top though, in place of a head, there was just an empty hole of a collar – in which nothing could be seen but darkness.

"What's this?" she asked, staring at it with her hands on her hips.

Jimmy had been waiting for this – and also trying to work out what to say about it. She had hardly been able to take her eyes off it since she had first come in. That wasn't surprising though – it was the centrepiece of the bedroom after all. It loomed in the corner looking rather too grand and significant for this rather ordinary apartment. He had to admit that. But what did that matter? Her glance would follow the coils of copper wire as they gleamed and bound – would stare thoughtfully as though trying to see right through to the inside and the secrets hidden within.

"That is my World Cage," he said obliquely, sitting down on the bed and briefly assuming a slightly pantomime mysterious expression.

Feather gave him a blank look. He laughed and sipped his drink.

"Yup," he said. "Why did I make it?"

"Yes?"

"Oh there's all sorts of things I could say. I made it to keep my stories away from me. I made it because I hate the world and everything in it. Because I would love to see the whole fucking thing fall into ruin. But above all because I wish more than anything that it was at a safe distance and somewhere far away from me. Where it can no longer fuss me around."

"I don't understand," she murmured, her finger following the wire slowly.

Jimmy gulped wine and shifted uncomfortably. Why was it always so hard to explain things? Things that made perfect sense in the head always came out sounding ridiculous when cast out into the cold, unsupported air. Was there anything harder than conveying a thought? A fear? A pain?

"Think about it," he managed. "It's a simple inversion. World. Me," he said, waving his hands vaguely to illustrate. "Now turn it around. Inside out, I mean. Turn me inside out. Me. World. Here we are somewhere even they cannot venture. Inside my clothes. I have caught the whole world in there, with that simple trick. Caught it and trapped it where it can't do any more harm. Only you and I are safe – inside," he said. "I don't have many guests here – so welcome."

There was a moment of silence, both staring at the sombre figure. The world cage, he wanted to say, was a talisman – a spell cast by one who did not believe in spells. It was a desperate and pointless gesture – a comforting doodle not actually that important. Only it was. That was the thing – that was what was so hard to convey. And a request to please take this seriously and give me the credit that I am trying to say something significant and don't dismiss it because it doesn't make sense.

He gave a grunt. "Ok," he said a little miserably, "so maybe you have to be drunk to really get the most out of it. But then," he prattled on, "you could probably say the same about a lot of art. And compared to some of the things in this world, I am perfectly entitled to call this art. Would you like some wine? This Shiraz Petit Verdot is really rather good."

Feather smiled vaguely and leaned closer to the cage, while Jimmy watched her almost desperately.

"What's in there?" she asked, peering in between the buttons of the shirt. Inside all was darkness.

"Secrets," he said, suddenly more uneasy. "The world. The last of my writing? That's all. Careful Feather. Don't let it in. That's why you should never take off your clothes. Otherwise they will get you. You have to keep somewhere safe from them."

She gave him a brief uncomprehending glance.

"Yes," he said. "Even screw fully clothed. It's safest."

She was silent – still staring at the wire. It was just a simple strand of copper, extracted from an electrical cable. Stiff but flexible, and wound round the clothes, forming the last line of defence. Jimmy watched her curiously as she continued stroking the metal with a finger.

"If you put your ear to it," she said, "can you hear the crying?"

"Sometimes," he admitted. "Though I think that may be the Red." He sighed again. "Perhaps I am too cynical for these rituals to actually work."

Without any fuss or ceremony, she added her own clothes to it. Jimmy blinked at her as she stripped herself down to nothing and each item she inverted and pulled on the sculpture, outside the wire. Her top was easy – but the trousers were more awkward. He watched blankly as she fiddled them onto the mannequins legs, struggling with the too-small garment. But they were in place eventually, and she quickly finished it off with her worn underwear.

"That was . . . creepily intimate," he said uncertainly, and she glanced at him with a half smile. "I am not used to naked girls in my apartment."

She wasn't paying attention though. She knelt down in front of it and put her ear to the thing's chest. Somewhere in the distance voices raised in a violent clash for a moment. A yell and a burst of swearing.

Footsteps passed.

"Trapped," she said softly and with a hint of satisfaction. "And we are safe?"

"Safe," he murmured, shuffling over comfortably. "You add your stories to mine? I hope you know what you are doing. One day, I shall burn that thing – and when I do . . ." he gave a hollow menacing laugh. ". . . then the world shall know apocalypse."

It was already getting dark and, in the gloom, she stood out like a white afterimage. He allowed himself to look at her properly, falling silent again – and he was a little surprised to find that, after a moment, the fact that she was naked was not even very important any more. Why not?

She seemed to be taking this more seriously and solemnly than he was.

"I feel like a child again right now," he said at last, his voice unexpectedly soft. "Things are very simple then. Perhaps I never really grew up. You are wonderfully innocent, Feather."

"Am I?"

"Yes. Which means you are the strongest of all."

Feather slipped onto the bed, climbing over him and squeezing her body between him and the wall. He gave her a startled look.

"Trapped," Feather muttered again.

"Wine can't get me addicted, but maybe the red blood can. The rent collectors can't break my bones, but maybe the stray dogs can. The job centre can't fill me with despair, but maybe the blue skies can." Jimmy muttered the litany quietly, then he suddenly slipped his arms round her and hugged her tight and warm. She hugged him back.

"Trapped," she said again with satisfaction.

"Tentacles in the lake don't scare me, only being chased down from above. Other people do not scare me – but accountants most certainly can . . ."

"What secrets?" she asked. He gave a tipsy laugh.

"Secrets? Secrets?"

"In the cage?"

"Only ones I can't tell."

"I thought you were a writer?"

"A Ghost Writer," he corrected, and gave a dramatic smile. "The living dead, in fact," he growled. "There must be thousands of us around the country," he murmured more seriously. "The world kills more artists than it saves, and whether we survive or not is certainly not a measure of how good we are. So who knows what wonders are left rotting away in mind-fucking jobs or sprawled out homeless and lost? Unable to do anything, let alone tell a story."

He subsided with a sigh and rested his face in his arms, staring at her speculatively.

"The stories are long dead," he said at last. "And that is best. I don't want to tell secrets, I just want to lie here and hug you."

She smiled.

"Feather," he murmured. "I'm so hungry."

Feather sighed. "Was it good?"

"Was what which?"

"Telling stories."

"Well – yeah. I suppose."

"Is that what is in the cage? Your stories?"

He nodded.

"Are you keeping them in or out?"

He sighed, looking confused. "Sort of," he said. "Out. Yes – I mean. But – oh, I don't know. Sod that."

"Very well," she said with a shrug and a tiny smile. "Let's hug instead if it feels good. I am not used to it . . ."

"Hmmm . . ?"

"But it's nice."

The sweltering heat of summer faded into the cool of the autumn of that magical year with Feather at my side – and then winter was here – magical season. As every year, we would romp out of doors together, loving the new cold in the air, and soon divesting ourselves of any stifling extra clothing we had put on. We would play together in private and mysterious places, while the snow lay upon the earth, stripped down sometimes even to our underwear. We rubbed our bare skin in the snow, while the exhilaration crackled through us. The cold was exquisite. Sometimes, while the snow was falling about us, the endless flakes swirling and shifting in a thousand strange shapes, we would be reminded of our dream, and I would half expect to find ourselves surrounded by birds. And sometimes when I was particularly excited I would catch her looking strangely towards me, a look in her eyes that I could not place.

There were changes in the air that magical winter – I could feel them with every particle of my body. Sometimes I seem to see myself transparent and glowing with a wonderful light – a light that shone through the whirling snow like a beacon, bathing Feather's bare skin in glory as she gazed at me wide eyed. And there were times when it seemed as if I could float – drifting upwards through worlds of flying flakes, arms spread wide. I would grasp Feather by the hand and draw her with me, and together we would soar through space, our eyes fixed on where, behind the snow clouds, the invisible North Star gleamed – the star that seemed to pull at us like a magnet – always – always –

– but then we would merely collapse in an ungainly heap together in the snow, laughing breathlessly.

Feather was also changing that winter – her body was different – more wonderful. There was a new quality to her skin – she moved like a creature newborn and fresh. Even her smells were different – and as the Winter moved towards its climax, I began to be aware that a certain kind of expectation had taken root within me – a restless knowledge of something about to happen – something looming on the horizon of my life like a great cloud. It grew and grew – welling up and pulsating within me and spreading its tendrils from horizon to horizon.

Outside, the dark was already falling, heavy as the snow.

She stared down at him. His eyes were closed now and he didn't move. She watched his face for a moment, trying to analyse the distortion accumulated over the years. The down-turned mouth – the frown lines above his eyes – and trying to picture what he had been like as a boy. The entire process of life becomes like a story – a story written on a body that came into the world in some sort of purity. Then lines get etched into the skin – expressions get fixed and thus meaningless. Fear. Suspicion. Pain. Isolation. They all leave traces. What sort of story is that? A story that wasn't fiction? Perhaps the sleeping face was the closest you could get to that old original. It looked boyish and innocent now. Different to the sealed and rather ridged surface he had when he was awake. Perhaps he was right when he told her he had never really grown up.

But then – did anyone?

Finally she gave up on him and stepped back to the World Cage. Carefully she opened up a few buttons on the front of the shirt. That was a tricky job when they were inside out, but she managed it, feeling the presence of something heavy inside. Stories . . . but what kind?

There was just a big role of papers wrapped in what looked like clear plastic food wrap. She carefully extracted it and turned it over, trying to see what was written on them. She opened it, but all that happened was that a strew of scraps slid to the floor through her fingers in a paper waterfall.

Feather quickly went down on her knees, gathering them up and flipping through them. These scraps were all sorts of odd clips and cut-outs. Short articles from newspapers – brief scribbled notes – snippets of information . . . all confusing.

- A young man sentenced to death by stoning for a kiss. The girl given two hundred lashes. Where? Why?
- An American woman arrested for going nude in her garden.

- The personal account of a parental punishment in Lima – a sanmartin whip on a girl's bare buttocks splashed with cold water.
- A teacher sacked for letting her pupils look at classic nude sculpture on an outing to a popular museum.
- The suicide of a writer in Miami.
- The suicide of another writer in Croatia.
- A page of housing adds from a newspaper.
- Accounts of horrors in Croatia and Bosnia. Holes in the ground filled with writhing masses of arms and legs.
- The blog of a fluffy, pink-obsessed teen girl in Switzerland. My glitterkitten =^;^= , lovely boys who's not men but BOYS :-D :-D . . . And dying of brain damage. Drugs.
- The suicide (or mutual murder) of a cult in America.

Feather sat down on the floor, legs crossed. She was only aware of relief that this was trapped safely in the World Cage – nothing here made any sense. She stared bleakly at the figure, thinking that that was the place for fictions like this. And, as she stared, the fabric of her own clothes seemed to be undulating gently – as through from some slow-moving liquid contents. She stared at it without moving – and began to feel a creeping sense of unease at what she had done. But, before putting it all back, there was more to see in this bundle. There were different papers – white standard A4 sheets – and she pulled them out. On some, thick and heavy and crinkled, were the faces of women – thousands of them, cut from catalogues, photos, news reports, porn mags – all of them just pasted on the paper in a thick jumble, piling on top of each other until some were completely obliterated. There was page after page of them. To her, almost all of them looked identical, alien and unreal – hidden deep under layers of makeup and style. Why were these locked up inside the world?

Well – why not? They were fictions too. Fictions that they themselves seemed only too happy to embrace.

On other pages were drawings, and this was the biggest shock.

The art was beautifully created – all drawings in pencil. But some of these were gruesome and made Feather's chest tighten even more. Torture and pain and cruelty. A thousand victims – a thousand screams of immolation. Feather stared at them. Of course – it wasn't real either. It was all the product of stories impacting the world. Unreal beliefs and the feelings they create. But even so, this eerie mass of paper was making something rise in her chest – something complex. Even making tears prick at her eyes. It wasn't horror or shock exactly. Perhaps it was just a sense of unending pain. Not even personal pain – just the pain of the world. This was – Feather wasn't sure, but it felt familiar. She turned to look at the sleeping Jimmy with an uncertain expression on her face – only to find a pair of eyes quietly looking back at her.

Feather jumped. A thousand sad deaths and mangled fictions strewed the floor again. "Yeah," he murmured hazily. "You had to, didn't you." He shook his head. "Bless your curiosity, Feather," he murmured. "I love you for it. But fuck you for poking into things." He gave an angry growl, leaned off the bed and picked up the papers – gathering them into a heap. "I didn't want anyone to see that. They think I am crazy enough anyway."

"I don't understand," she said. He glanced at her curiously, trying to understand the tone of her voice and the expression on her face. There was a gleam in her eyes that caught his attention and held it for a moment. A gleam that almost looked hungry, not critical.

"I had to put it somewhere. It deserves to be in chains. Put it back," he begged. "It's all I have left. Even paper is sick now."

"The Measuring Men?" she murmured.

"Pardon?"

"Is this why you gave up writing?" she asked. "Because of the horror of what stories can do?"

He stared at her blankly for a moment, then took a drink.

"I . . . . . . what?"

"Because that is what has made the world what it is? Because that is why we lost what we were and became something imaginary?" She sighed. "Why do you . . ?"

"Feather," he wailed abruptly. "I don't want to think. Thinking hurts."

The expression on her face made him turn to the wall again. He gave a deep breath like a repressed sob.

"Go away if you don't like it," he muttered.

Instead, she just came back to the bed and slipped her arms round him again, resting her chin on his shoulder. It was a slightly uncertain hug. The hug of one who perceives pain but doesn't know how to respond to it. Jimmy flinched, then cautiously rested a hand over hers. She didn't say anything else.

"There is something in you that I have lost," he said at last. "I wish I could find it again. Stories make their own worlds. Worlds of red and white – where we can fly where we want – do what we want. Feed on what we want. Away from that which screams and storms outside."

They both lay close together, his arms wrapped tight. It was suddenly a very simple affection – almost childlike. She hugged back. They were both children again. The two of them together, curled up against the night that screamed and sucked.

Perhaps you never lost that – and there was always so much to curl up against. Outside howled and rattled. The Cage shuddered in rhythm to it. It seemed to be outlined in a soft sickly radiance.

Snow fell.

Feather moaned . . .

In my dreams, the beautiful Feather still haunted me in her changing body – always naked. We still drifted together arm in arm through our chaos – but even the surrounding chaos was changing now – It was turning red. Everything gleamed ruddy – even Feather's bare skin and her uncut triangle of hair were the colour of blood. It was beautiful – terrible – wonderful. Her naked body seemed to be blossoming and opening – changing even as I watched. I felt frightened – I felt exhilarated – and above all I felt alive. My own body glowed almost continuously now – shedding its light for miles around as we sported in the snow – and it seemed at times as if Feather just couldn't take her eyes off me. My whole body seemed to be building up for some kind of spectacular event – something stunning and unimaginable – but I didn't know what.

And then one night, as I lay spent from tumbling in the snow-blanketed grass – and with the expectation throbbing with a new sense of imminence – Feather came to me close. She put her hands on my chest and looked into my eyes – eyes that blazed a vivid red from her sharing of my dreams.

"There is something in you," she said, "like a great light." She was silent for a moment, then: "it is in you – but it is not in me. It is wonderful." She stroked my chest, and then, with a new gleam in her eyes that I had not seen before, she whispered: "I want it."

I looked at her – but she said no more words – Just rolled away, settling on her back in the snow – her eyes on me. Then she reached down, and, as I gazed in silence, finally removed the last scrap of clothing that clung between her and the night. Now she was naked in the snow.

So I went to her in delight. I pressed my lips to hers and she began to drink from me – exchanging our breaths – she inhaling my breath even as it left my mouth – and when she breathed out again I felt her entering deep into my body in its warm gust and absorbing and absorbing more and yet more, only to draw it out at my next exhale. I saw her red eyes flicker – and then begin to glow a beautiful golden – which brightened and brightened up until it was almost dazzling. The luminosity had woken – but still she wouldn't stop sucking and sucking at me. Soon we were equal. I tried to wriggle away now – but she clung to me, arms and legs wrapped round me inextricably. Still she sucked – I felt myself draining – emptied – I tried to cry out to her to stop. But I couldn't – and she just went on sucking at my mouth and gasping with the pleasure of it at the same time – no matter how much I struggled.

And then she let go.

I tumbled away, crying, into the snow, clutching at myself – my precious light – and curling up into a tight ball – but it had gone. She had drunk it all – she had robbed me of every last glimmer.

Things that can be seen on the human body – part 2, revised and expanded:

- Skin – someone else's – a stranger. Smooth but tough. Skin that has seen a lot – done a lot. For the sense of touch.
- Legs – plural. Two of them. Giving you the feeling of muscles that are not your own, pulling – and pulling.
- Arse – soft and round and bare. Two round masses of flesh all too often sat upon and forgotten. Good to be reminded.
- Mouth – open and breathing. A gust of air on your face. She's alive. She really is. She's not a dream.
- Vagina – yes, all got one. Well – half of us have. The human flower. Soft and warm and hungry. As parts of the anatomy goes, it is really really quite fun.
- The list goes on.

Finally I uncurled slightly and looked up at her. She stood there like a flame – beautiful – terrible – almost unbearable to look at. Feather – my love – she did not look at me – just stood there radiant from head to foot with power – and gazing up at the sky. I had no trouble following her gaze. The snow had stopped now and the sky was clear – and there, icily gleaming, like an eye that now watched her alone, was the North Star. Like an eye – gazing at my humiliation – but an eye that was far from human – and Feather simply gazed back.

And it was then that I finally saw it – saw what she had robbed me of – and the sight of it happening to another after all this was almost too much to bear. Feather had fallen to her knees and was beginning to moan softly – writhing strangely in the snow. Her skin was moving – changing – I realised as I gazed numbly at her – she was changing shape as she writhed and writhed, gasping and straining – something seemed to be growing on her back – It was swelling and rippling all over –

– and then her skin split - a rent right down her spine out of which a trickle of gleaming fluid ran. With that her struggles only increased - and the split lengthened – ran over her shoulder – down across her buttocks. She clawed at it – pulling it free of her – light spilling everywhere – and at last I caught a glimpse of what lay under her skin – the magic she had robbed me of – and at that I began to cry properly – for it seemed that there emerged from the strange swelling on her back, two shapes – two huge wings – beautiful – terrible. Light poured everywhere as she struggled out of her old skin – emerging from its collapsing folds fresh and new. She dragged her arms free from their casing – dragged it away from her face, actually pulling it out of her mouth and from around her eyes – then pushed it down her legs and stepped out as though she were stepping out from a pair of trousers.

And then she was free.

She stood there, her skin glowing, her wings spread – and then for the first time she looked at me – but the expression that glided across her face then was more than I could read. I seemed to see both triumph and sadness there at the same time, plus other things even more complex – but then her eyes turned again northward to where the North Star still gleamed – and she forgot me. Slowly she stretched her mighty wings – shook them once or twice – and then with a movement that blasted the ground clear of snow for several yards around, she took off.

I watched that wonderful form climb into the sky – wheel around a few times – and then plunge away northward – but I didn't move. Her shining light dwindled in the distance as she moved towards the North Star – Polaris – and the world of red chaos – like a star herself for a while – and then she vanished. I just sat there – empty – like some kind of dried husk of what I had been. Presently the sky began to cloud over – and even the North Star was hidden from me. Then it began to snow again – I was naked – and I found I was shivering.

Feather stared round the room. Outside there was a glimmer of grey light. Day was here.

Finally she stood up, testing her muscles uncertainly for a moment. She felt stiff and tired, as though there was a tension that needed to be drained off and blown away. She stared down rather forlornly at the dozing figure on the bed. He lay there with his mouth open, Red-dregged glass on the floor beside him. She could smell him faintly – a dreary stale smell pickled in alcohol. But why not? Human beings had a right to smell.

Are you going to wake up? No, she thought. Don't. Sleep on. Sleep and find something refreshing.

Then she turned away and stepped to the window. Outside, the snow still flurried from a dawn as dark as a stone, but she ignored it. Her clothes were hanging on the World Cage and, after a moment's hesitation, she left them there. Whatever was trapped in there – whatever stories it contained – were best left undisturbed. She helped herself instead to a few garments from his hangers and drawers and put them on.

"Goodbye," she murmured into his dreams. "Don't miss me when you wake up . . ."

Lastly there was her bag. It was a little tatty but still intact and she quickly shouldered it. Then, with a last glance at him and at the shabby clothes stand and gleaming wire, she slipped out of the room.

Horse Hospital
Antiques
SHOP
TO LET
EXIT

Touch Wood

For Marina

"Alice? What do you recommend for a broken heart?"

The waitress looked thoughtful. "Ooohh I dunno – we are not allowed to sell anything genuinely magical here." She smiled apologetically at the red haired man leaning over the bar and he gave a small sigh in return. "There's a few remedies I can think of – I suppose," she continued, slowly filling a tiny glass with something brown and strong looking. "But none of them involve drinks."

Richard Jarvis sighed again, still with a roguish twinkle in his eye that made Mark nervous. "Anything you can provide?" he asked. "On or under the counter?"

She shook her head. "Not even in the back room," she said with a sly grin.

"Ok," he said with an expansive gesture. "Must have something to toast away heartache though. So – ok. A bottle of Shiraz, a plate of your hard pecorino sheep's cheese, pršut, artichokes etc etc, please, and –"

He paused.

"Mark? Anything else?"

Mark stared round the quiet interior of The Yellow King feeling uncertain and depressed. It was pleasantly gentle and relaxing in here, compared with the shimmering bustle of Camden Town outside, but that wasn't helping much.

"Mezcal," he said abruptly, careless of wrecking the central European mood of the order. "Just that. Can I?"

Alice nodded. "Noooo problem," she said. "And if it's broken hearts, I can at least change the music."

He nodded. "Thanks."

Richard leaned back against the bar and surveyed the room. Mark followed his eyes for a moment. Low and relaxing light from various nooks and crannies – bizarre yellow and black furnishings – sprays of knot-willow branches adorning the wall.

"Her favourite drink was cider," Mark said glumly.

"Hmm," Richard murmured. "Cider. . . . What are we to make of that?"

"Make?"

Richard nodded seriously. Mark shrugged.

"I dunno – she never tasted enough to really have much of an opinion. It was always cider or beer. Liked cider – hated red wine. That's about all I know. But . . . make of it? Well hmm. I make of it that I will try this Shiraz with pleasure. Just to spite her."

Richard chuckled. "Absolutely," he said, looking far too relaxed – long suited legs extended and his untidy red hair trailing back. There was a curious mix of antique and boyish in his appearance – his hair marked with hints of grey and his skin heading towards wrinkling, but with an eager and very sharp gleam in his eyes. His suit looked old-fashioned, but with a few startling touches of ornamentation that were almost post-modernist. "What do you make of my little hidey-hole The Yellow King then?" he asked.

Mark nodded without much interest. At the moment, this quiet cocktail bar was nothing more than a set of absences – absence of noise, absence of bustle and movement, absence of certain people. Pleasant absences certainly, but the place itself was barely registering. "It's nice," he said. "Nice and quiet – if I can relax here for a moment for a bit of peace then it gets my love."

"That's what we are here for," Richard said brightly.

Then the door opened, letting in an unwelcome moment of Camden Town.

"Aha," Richard murmured, straightening up and eyeing the figure that had caused the breach. "Excuse me a moment – Matherson?" he called sharply. The figure waved and hurried over. Mark wasn't best pleased to have a stranger join them, but he said nothing. The newcomer was a large man dressed in a smart coat – longish hair going grey and a rather off-putting slimy smile.

"Hi," he said. "Phweeeuuu – Richard, I hoped I would find you here. I have something for you."

Richard gave a happy grin. "Good," he said. "Will you join us at our table for some wine? This Shiraz is quite exceptional I think. Just the right touch of mellowness and warm wood-chocolaty undertaste."

Matherson grinned. "Yeah?"

"Indeed."

"Well, each to their own," he said with a twist to his face. "Personally I don't much care. Wine?" he asked. "It is all just a few certain combinations of liquid molecules, after all. Water. Alcohol. A few sugars and acids. At that level it all looks pretty much the same, so I fear I rather lost my taste for it."

Richard gave him a theatrical stare, head on one side.

"Then you go in deeper – then what? Carbon, hydrogen, oxygen, some nitrogen and whatever else. Just like our own bodies – Just like this bar top . . . it's all the same."

"Hmm?" Richard said dubiously. "So, um, is that a yes or a no?"

"Alice, my dear," Matherson called across to her. "Get me a gin and lemon would you." He smiled. "Citric acid always wins against Tartaric – any day."

"If you say so," Richard murmured, still looking very dubious. "Shall we sit down?"

They tramped back across the room to a table, stepping through the low yellow and black chairs. As they did so, the quiet background music cut out and was replaced by something cold and crystalline and modernist on two pianos. Mark glanced round in surprise and Alice gave him a nod. And it was right, he realised. It wasn't sad music, but the frostiness of it fitted his mood perfectly. Matherson plumped down into a chair with a grunt, while Richard folded himself up beside him. Mark gingerly slid his arse into a chair on the opposite side of the table and wondered what to do next. Was he supposed to make small talk? Just chatter away? He wasn't feeling very much like small-talk.

"Then pull those atoms apart and even matter itself suddenly seems uniform," Matherson was saying. "Just a few particles existing in nothingness. How do you like that?"

"Well let me put it this way," Richard said. "My taste buds know *nothing* about advanced physics – and are quite happy knowing the difference between a Merlot and a Shiraz, thank you very much. But anyway Matherson – you are intruding on a broken heart – so I am going to have to hurry you along . . ."

Mark winced.

"It's ok," he said, almost under his breath, and Matherson regarded him curiously. He twisted his lips with what he hoped was humour and wished he had never accepted Richard's invitation for a quiet drink.

"Broken hearts haven't studied advanced physics either, I believe," Matherson said gloomily.

"Right right," Mark grunted. "But I'm fine, really."

Matherson dismissed the subject and hoisted his bag onto the table. "This time I managed to get six bottles," he said. "The bloke who makes it was a bit shitty about it – so much work. But here you are. This should keep you going for a while."

Mark watched curiously as Matherson plonked a small bottle on the table. It was little larger than a wine miniature or a large perfume bottle, but it was filled with a richly dark brown liquid. There was no label.

"Ah, thank you," Richard said. "Yes – I have a few people waiting. So I will definitely be able to pass these on."

"What is it?" Mark demanded curiously. Richard smiled as Matherson counted more bottles out onto the table, hastily and almost furtively slipping them into his bag.

"Let's just say that . . . maybe there is a little magic in the world after all."

"Really? Can I try some?"

Richard chuckled. "Not that sort of magic, I'm afraid. I don't think this is good for broken hearts."

Mark stared suspiciously at the last bottle as it disappeared into Richard's elegant leather shoulder bag. "Have I just sat in on some sort of drug deal?" he asked.

"Yes. Precisely," Richard said placidly, and Matherson gave a snort of laughter. "Matherson," Richard said, "you will find your bank account subtly larger tomorrow. Though I wish I could convince you to try for something other than cash!"

Matherson grinned. "Cash is too useful," he said. "Can you give me anything I can't buy?"

"You'd be surprised," Richard said dryly.

Matherson grinned. "Well – maybe next time. I need to buy a new Isopycnic centrifuge now, so this will be very welcome."

"Ach," Mark groaned comically. "So much for my relaxing drink. Am I now going to be arrested for drug dealing without even any of the benefits?"

Before Richard could respond to that, Alice was behind him with a tray, making his neck prickle with the unexpected presence. She leaned over the table and deposited a plate of sliced meat and cheese – crisp, crumbly and strong – served with a few dips and some bread. Then two wine glasses were laid out.

"Allow me," she said, pouring the Shiraz neatly. "Do you have a broken heart, Mr Jarvis?" she asked, leaning over him.

He smiled.

"Not me," he said. "My heart has been quiet for a long time. Broken or not. But nevertheless, broken heart medicine is needed, I think."

Alice put the lightly golden mezcal on the table, then the gin and lemon. "Well," she said as she withdrew, "what magic is mine to offer – is yours for the taking."

"My heart is not broken," Mark muttered.

"No?"

"You know – this ain't that important."

"I disagree, as a matter of fact," Richard said, sniffing the wine appreciatively. "Why shouldn't it be important? Why shouldn't one make a fuss? What happened to the grand old days of tragedy and lost love?"

"Long dead," Matherson said bluntly.

"I know I know. You're not supposed to care these days," Richard said darkly. "If they think you care, you are just throwing a tantrum. Right?" He put his glass down with a bump. "No one takes it seriously any more – and they wonder why everything is so fucked up. They deserve it."

"Deserve . . ?"

"A life of loneliness and woe," he cried dramatically. "We shall toast that as well later. But in the meantime, let us raise our glasses in contempt . . ."

"But . . ."

"Contempt of one specific bloody fool who hasn't exactly displayed much of human empathy, intelligence and respect. Am I right?"

Mark gave a wry smile.

"You seem more upset than I am," he said, picking up his glass of wine.

"Yes – and that is worrying me somewhat. Why haven't you torn your shirt open yet? Why haven't you cut off your ear and posted it to her registered?"

Mark blushed slightly. "Ok ok," he cried. "A toast, if you want. Yeah."

"Solemnly?"

"Solemnly. A toast in – in all contempt, yes. That that that useless . . . bitch. Gawd – that feels sort of good."

"A toast in appreciation of the doom and gloom she will soon be experiencing."

"Will she? Well ok – touch wood." His hand reached out and found the wooden surface of the table almost without conscious thought. Matherson gave him a curious glance but before he could analyse that, the toast was interrupted by another presence behind him. Two presences in fact. Two more figures invading this space. Richard gave a wave with his glass and Mark flinched, glancing round with a frown of annoyance. This 'relaxing drink' was getting less relaxing by the minute. "Hi Feather," he said to the first figure with a feeble grin and she sat down softly with a smile. He liked Feather, ever since Richard had first introduced her to him, but it was the other figure that caught his attention this time. A continental looking girl with high and prominent cheekbones, sparkling eyes and a flare of long brown hair above them. It took a few moments of scrambled analysis of memories before he remembered who she was. She was one of those who hovered about in the background of Richard Jarvis, like a small moon around a planetary gas giant, at least to his perception. She was dressed in scruffy jeans and an elegant black top complete with a necklace of what looked like petrified wood beads.

Impatiently he picked up his glass of mezcal and downed it in a couple of sips.

"Who are you toasting?" she asked, her accent hard-edged and almost harsh, but very engaging.

Richard gave a dark chuckle. "Just the demon of a broken heart," he said. "Toasting not to forget her but to put her in her place – to offer moral support. Sit down and I will order you a rakija and you can join us." Richard swivelled round in his chair. "Matherson – this is Željka, from Serbia. With her usual sense of timing, she is what you might call a customer for your merchandise. And you know Feather, don't you? The remarkable girl who has settled with me for a little while?"

"I do indeed," he said with a smile. "And how is my favourite vagrant?"

Mark winced at that, but Feather just gave a quiet grin. "I am enjoying the city life," she said softly. "It is very alien – you would not believe how alien."

Željka sat down in the empty chair between Mark and Matherson. Richard signalled quickly to Alice. He pointed to Željka and mimed a small pouring gesture, jabbed the air in her direction twice more, winked humorously, then shrugged.

Alice seemed to understand.

"Thank you," Željka murmured, making herself comfortable. "But who am I toasting to destruction?"

"Mark?" Richard murmured, and Mark drew a deep breath of exasperation. His face felt as though it was blazing crimson and he was acutely aware of Feather staring at him with frank curiosity. Why was this going so far? This was stupid. "She is Princess," Mark explained wearily – but even as he did so he was interrupted yet again as Alice came over like a bird and deposited a small glass of ever so slightly yellow liquid in front of the new arrival – with a pungent smell that made his nose prickle. Feather was given an empty glass as well and Richard quickly poured some of the wine for her. She gave it a curious sniff, holding it in both hands and looking startlingly childlike. "Far far away," he continued. "And . . . casual as fuck, I think. And I sort of wish she wasn't – to both. Certainly doesn't care what anyone else thinks or feels. As worms in the ground to her are we mere mortals. And of course, the company of sexy immature jerks is always so much more exciting than . . ." He sighed. "Than that of this rather less sexy jerk here. That's all. Richard seems determined to make it into an opera of some kind though. And here I am singing the introductory aria. La la la la laaaa la laa la laaa."

Željka grinned and picked up her glass. "I'll toast this thing very happily," she said.

"What has happened to you?" Feather asked curiously.

"Love," Richard barked, and Feather flinched. "That's the word. Unrequited love lacks any sympathy for a person's faults and that is what we are doing here. We enumerate her many faults to try and make Mark feel better. The relief is transitory but welcome nonetheless."

"Wow," she said.

"Now," Richard cried, startlingly loud. "Now – toast. Toast so that electricity crackles in the air. To Princess – may her royal self bite herself in the arse one day – preferably soon."

Five glasses rose.

"Eyes, Mark. Eyes."

He hastily glanced round for some eyes to meet. They flashed across Richard Jarvis and Feather, who was staring into her glass of wine, avoided Matherson and then settled on Željka. She gave him a small smile as she slowly downed a long sip of that clear liquid – whatever it was. He stared back – caught for a moment by those twin brown pools.

"To Princess," he murmured vaguely. "I . . . I expel her. I cast her out of my head – and, ahem, anywhere else she may reside. She shall trouble me no more. Touch wood."

Željka's smile twitched and broadened slightly and she allowed him to hold her gaze a moment longer – even as he touched the table again, running one hand along the polished surface.

"Nazdravlje," she murmured.

"They say," Matherson said, cutting through the atmosphere the toast had created like a wet cloth in the face, "that one way to take control of your dreams is to make a habit of trying to put your hand through something solid."

Mark flinched and blinked at him, shaken sharply out of his reverie. It took him a moment to work out what he was even referring to and he glanced vaguely at his finger.

"You have to work it so that you really expect your hand to pass right into the solid matter. So that it becomes an almost subconscious habit. So that when, one day, it does pass right in, you will realise that you are dreaming and can take control."

"But I'm not trying to put my hand into the wood," Mark protested. "I just want to touch it."

Matherson frowned. "Why?"

He hesitated. "I dunno. It's just . . . an old good luck thing. I have always done it."

Matherson grinned and raised his eyebrows. "I see," he murmured, drinking another sip of gin. "Yeah? A little superstition? So why wood? How is that significant?"

"I dunno," Mark said helplessly.

"What would happen if you touched stone – or glass?"

The Shiraz wine was fine and strong. Rich and woody and smooth. The sip he had swallowed said hello to the mezcal already in residence and immediately began making itself at home. He could feel it in the front of his brain. "Maybe the world would end," he said, suddenly with the eloquence of the tipsy. "No meaning anymore. Maybe it is just about reassuring yourself that the world is real."

Matherson gave a dark grin. "Or maybe just the opposite," he said with mock drama. "Maybe you seek support for a great lie. Reassurance that it is not all just a storm of identical particles that have never even heard of humanity? Not all just a mass of carbon, hydrogen, oxygen, nitrogen that we can never really understand. That it is not all basically nothing . . ."

"Oh gawd," Mark wailed. "Isn't it bad enough to be sitting here trying to swallow away some careless Princess without this on my back as well?"

Željka touched his arm, making him jump.

"Hmmm, ignore him," she said dryly. "Music is just air . . . atoms, molecules moving – vibrating about – but that does not make Richard's opera any less grand. We rather like those molecules I think – yes?"

He gave her a curious look, surprised at her seriousness. Matherson shrugged and grinned.

"Well, I hope so," Mark muttered. "Touch wood." He jabbed the tabletop with his finger and gave Matherson a defiant look. Touch wood was an odd old comfort, even if he had no analysis concerning why that should be.

"The fact remains though," Matherson continued in his college professor voice, "that the further you look, the more it becomes clear that it doesn't matter a damn whether you touch wood or glass or whatever or don't touch anything – it's all the same, or all almost nothing. Just an empty void. And why not?"

Mark sighed and looked at him with barely concealed annoyance. Any thought of a quiet relaxing drink was finally fading away forever. Feather gave a shrill giggle, also looking slightly tipsy, even after her few mouthfuls of wine.

"Then we might as well make up our own superstitions," she murmured.

"Absolutely," Matherson cried. "When you think about what the world really is – down at the deepest levels – well, I dunno. Everything seems very simple then somehow. As though all our complexes and emotional tangles – our hang-ups and our ideologies are so far out of the equation as to be nothing but ghosts. Just one tiny slice within an infinity of other tiny slices. The world is the world however we see it. And I really believe that we can only be enriched by knowing more and more about how it works."

"I'll buy that," Richard said approvingly, finishing his wine and nabbing a slice of cheese. Mark wasn't sure what it was, but it looked strong. His slight tipsieness focussed on that plate and he reached out and shoved it across the table, almost knocking over Matheson's glass. "Would you like some Pecorino?" he offered, with a flicker in his eyebrows. "Or does it matter, if it is all just a void? Perhaps you would rather a slice of this wooden table instead? I am sure Alice would oblige if we asked her very nicely."

Matherson laughed, taking some cheese. "Fortunately my taste buds also haven't heard of modern physics. What we don't know, can't hurt us, yes?"

Mark subsided over his wine and stared at nothing. Thoughts of Princess came and went with varying degrees of importance. Any use of the term 'meaningless' seemed threatening in the face of all that. He didn't want meaningless – not through people's carelessness and not through Matherson and his particle physics either. That was just another part of the great war that must be fought here. Yourself who knows, against all the ranks out there who didn't – and didn't care. Maybe it was true what Richard had said, and it made Mark smile appreciatively. The thought of standing up and screaming was very appealing sometimes. Tearing his hair, breaking things – just celebrating pain with an outburst that was worthy of it. But . . . well . . . you couldn't, could you?

He glared at the table top. It was made of polished planks rather than artificial plastic and he quietly rested his hand on it. The solidity of it was comforting.

Then there was a movement that roused him out of his daze. Željka was standing up.

"Thank you for the Rakija," she said with a smile. "And the toast. But I have to be moving. Richard – do you have anything for me? Any merchandise?"

"I do," he said quickly. "Here."

He fumbled in his bag and produced one of the bottles.

Mark acted abruptly. A quick comparative analysis of Željka and Matherson revealed who would be the best company.

"Actually, I should also be going," he said, rising to his feet and trying not to sound flustered.

Richard gave him a sharp look – a look that read his mind easily and saw his exasperation. But he said nothing. Željka took the bottle, opened it and sniffed.

"Ah yes," she said. "Thank you. You are the best one for finding things."

Richard nodded and grinned. "One small transaction closed. Usual payment terms?"

"Of course."

"Mark? I hope you feel a little better for our toast? Even if we couldn't find any magic for you."

"Thank you," he murmured. "Yes I do. I will be fine. Sod her – she really isn't worth fretting about. Just a selfish bitch."

"Good," Matherson said amiably. "I hope so – touch glass."

He tapped the wine glass with a ringing sound and grinned. Mark sighed, trying not to be riled.

"Stop ridiculing other people's belief systems," Richard said, smiling.

"You're a fine one to talk," Matherson grunted. "I didn't think you had any belief systems."

"I try not to."

"This is not a belief system," Mark yelled, waving his arms. "It's just a – a – thing, that's all. Just a thing."

"Yeah? Well have a good evening – touch emulsion . . ."

Matherson touched the painted wall this time and Mark gave an exaggerated sigh and spun away towards the door. It dawned on him as he went that he hadn't offered to pay anything – but then, nor had Željka, who was following just behind him.

By then it was too late.

They ended up outside in the bustling Camden evening and he drew a deep breath. Now he was on his feet and walking, he actually felt slightly drunk. That was ok though – he rather welcomed that. There was something soothing about it, especially when surrounded by the faintly hallucinatory bustle of Camden Town. He glanced at Željka and she gave him a small and somehow sympathetic grin in return. That brought his thought processes to a halt sharply. She knew. She could read him. Read that he was cross and scrambled – and why. It felt strange. He was not used to being read.

"Would you like to stroll through the market?" she asked.

"I should love to," he murmured eagerly, and they began to move down the road – defiantly refusing to let the swarming crowd of people rush them. Camden always seemed to be busy. Thronging people hurrying this way and that. Slightly dirty and informal London, always unsure whether it was quaint and exciting or just drear and messy. Mark was used to it now of course, though less used to the London streets in company. Željka's presence was adding a small glow to the clustering buildings and narrow streets.

"This Matherson is a . . . menace," she said. "A useful menace sometimes – but yes, still . . ."

"Mmm," he said. "Quantum particles of nothing – I don't like it! And that bottle? Dare I ask?"

Željka smiled dryly.

"Yes?"

"I mean – he was handing it out like a drug deal."

She laughed, stopped walking a moment, plucked it out and opened it.

"Here," she murmured. "Smell."

He leaned over and took a deep breath – too deep perhaps because the violent blast that entered his nose made him cough and back away sharply. It was a smell totally beyond analysis save for the one unavoidable factor of alcohol, which hit him in the nose like a hammerblow. There were sweet herby scents, and hard bitter medicinal scents and even a hint of woodsmoke about it. It smelled nothing like any drink he had ever encountered before.

She gave a grin at the expression on his face, then carried on walking. He remained a moment staring after her, then followed.

"Hey," she murmured. "There was . . . there are some drinks in the world that are a bit more wild than what you buy in the shops. With import licensing labels and official . . . systems. Absinth – that was unjustly banned but it was bad additives rather than the absinth itself that caused problems. There is the Slovenian Salamander Brandy – with a drowned poisonous salamander in it . . . it is supposed to make you want to, to make love to trees. And this – this is the same sort of thing. I had a bottle once before. I don't know what's in it – but I can tell you that it's absolutely fucking amazing. For those few . . . special occasions when you really need it. Richard calls it the Ghost in the Bottle," she said. "He is good at finding things for people – though not usually in return for money, these days." She sighed. "The thing he insists on in return . . . that man is also a menace."

"What things?" he asked uneasily.

She shook her head awkwardly. "Well – nothing is quite as bad as money," she said, rather obliquely. "I will say that much."

"Yes but – what is it?"

Željka gave a wry look.

"Would you be unhappy if I say I don't know?"

"Um . . ."

"I am told that there is nothing illegal in it – that good enough?"

"Not really, no," he cried.

She shook her head. "I think you will have to ask Richard – though I dunno if even he knows for sure."

She took a deep sniff herself, and drew an ecstatic breath, tossing her head back theatrically and letting her brown hair tumble. Then she quickly sealed it and bagged it again. By this time they were approaching the railway bridge and the cobbled turning into the market, and Željka gave a little satisfied sigh, looking as though she was about to dive into a warm pool and swim. But the conversation had halted and he was unsure what to say next, the silence extending uncomfortably. He paused and stared around at the bustling people – endlessly varied like a microcosm of most of the world, all jumbled together into one great mass. Pink died hair, blacks under dreads – black leather and shabby street clothes. Gothic prancing or post-anime cosplay toned down just enough for street use.

"You know," he murmured, as much for conversation as anything, "I have been here so many times – but every time still feels as though I am arriving here for the first time."

Željka gave him a half smile over her shoulder.

"Yes, I always find this place very comfortable," she said. "It's a bustling crazy . . . muddle but somehow – I dunno. Very relaxing."

He looked at her hesitantly, wondering what she was really thinking. She stood there looking serene and totally at home – not a trace of self-consciousness about her. Did she really care at all that he had joined her here, in this strange centre of London? Or was he of no significance at all?

After a moment, she pressed further into the bustle and he followed her, passing stalls filled with strange and lurid clothes and curious oddments. DVDs and posters clamoured in one direction – exotic looking carpets in another – ersatz African statues in a third. Giggling anime girls and formidable mannequins – sloganned underwear and tee-shirts that he would love to wear if he dared trumpet those messages out into the world. And over everything loomed the grim architecture of the railways. Built among a knot of elevated tracks held up by Victorian brick arches, Camden market was a counter-culture blob in the heart of a cold-hearted city that even the posturing Goths couldn't entirely make pretentious. Something here glowed with an unearthly aura – something not seen in many places in the beleaguered British Isles. It was a genuine place. A place where clamouring voices suddenly seemed like music of some kind and where you could almost convince yourself that the small-minded world had been left at a distance for once. Chinese hovered over huge woks serving steaming food. Ultraviolet light glimmered from some of the shops. And mysterious signs that might have meant anything but which seemed to be aimed at him personally sprung out at odd moments.

He trailed after Željka feeling strangely content, watching her back view that fitted in here so perfectly. Better than him. But she hadn't completely forgotten him because she glanced over her shoulder, then waited for him to catch up.

"So how are you feeling now?" she asked?

"Fine," he said with a smile. "I think there is more magic in this marketplace than any of Richard's elegant drinks."

"Or perhaps in combination," she said with a twinkling grin. "Let us sit down for a bit. I like to just sit here – and watch."

He eagerly followed her to a picnic table strewn with abandoned foil food trays and settled down beside her. Maybe he should have sat opposite – he wasn't sure. What was the etiquette here? He didn't know and etiquette was stupid anyway. Nothing mattered in Camden Market. It was a place where curious and unusual and outrageous things could happen with ease. He stared around, half expecting to see someone appear naked or jump into the air and fly.

He wondered whether to convey that fancy to the girl beside him, but decided against it. He glanced sideways at her, taking in her face where it glowed in the coloured lights. She looked piercing and strong and somehow very real and there. Unlike Princess, he thought. Richard was right, he thought. Princess really was nothing.

"Princess," he said abruptly.

"Hmm?"

"You want to know what she is?"

"Uhuh?"

"She's an illusion," he said. "A ghost. She doesn't exist. She's nothing more than a lump of artificial meat substitute hiding under layers and layers of illusion. Layers of makeup and glamour and civilization. Somehow in the brain as well as on the body." He paused and frowned, feeling drunker than ever. "How can you wear makeup in the brain?" he muttered. "I dunno – but she managed it somehow."

Željka gave a mischievous laugh. "Yes – I know people like that. It creates – raises a question though. If there's nothing there, then what is it that you love?"

He gave a humorous grunt.

"Good question. Princess the princess. She didn't touch the ground, you know."

She raised an eyebrow enquiringly.

"Nope – she floated a few inches above it – always. She only ate dew from the morning leaves – and when she went to the toilet, all she could produce was flower petals."

Željka laughed gratifyingly loud at that one and he grinned happily. Željka's sharp nose and shining eyes – her thin lips twitching in a tiny smile at nothing – she was achingly beautiful, he realised. A magnetic thereness that pulled at him with education and revelation.

He rubbed at his temples.

"Funny thing is," she said, "I know exactly what you mean."

"I don't think you shit flower petals," he said before he could stop himself.

She gave him a strange look, eyebrows up.

"I mean," he stammered – then gave up. He pulled a face of confusion. "That was a compliment . . . sort of."

"I should hope I don't," she said dryly, and chuckled to herself.

Darkness was falling now and Camden Market was becoming illuminated with thousands of lights. Stalls and shops glowed invitingly.

"Hey," she murmured. "Are you ok? I like to just sit here – I can sit here for hours. If you are bored . . ."

"No no," he said urgently. "I like it – sitting here. It is a great place to be."

She nodded. She almost seemed lost in a reverie now.

"This place," she said at last, looking almost sad and hardly seeming to address him at all, "this is what people . . . are. Yes?"

"Um . . ."

"I mean – you read the news – all the stupid things that happen in the world . . . the stupid things that people think – do. It's all – wrong. Unreal. In a place like this, somehow the whole world is a microcosm. Without countries. Without governments . . . am I making any sense?"

"I think so," he said uncertainly.

"If all the world finally comes together into one great mass – without countries or borders. If everyone went outside and fucked their neighbour until we were all just one colour . . . it might be something like this. This one aspect of London. All these markets . . . the whole world is there. This is what people are about."

He smiled uncertainly and she gave him a sharp glance, perhaps worried that she was saying too much. He gave her what he hoped was a reassuring look. Her only response though was a long sigh.

"I should be moving," she said. "If not, I will sit here all night."

"So – what now?" he asked nervously. "Do you want to come back to my place or something? We could . . . have another drink. I have a bottle there – and . . . and . . ."

Even as he said it though, he felt foolish and as transparent as a polythene bag. What the hell was coming out of his lips? Željka gave him an enigmatic look.

"Heeeyyyy," she murmured.

He blinked at her helplessly and she leaned comfortably over the table.

"You know – I have another dream, Mark," she said with a smile. "I dream of a world where people be direct and say what they mean. I think the world would make more sense then." She reached out and touched him on the nose with a small grin. "And it would be the end of princes and princesses as well. I appreciate honesty. You should just say 'hey, there's magic in the air. I really fancy a comforting screw'. Nothing is more gloomy than playing games and –"

She suddenly stood up and twirled herself round on one foot, arms raised.

"– dancing the dance."

"I didn't mean . . ."

"Yes yes," she murmured. She gave him a shrug and a smile. "Hey Mark, don't think I don't appreciate the compliment, but – well . . . no."

"Yeah yeah," he agreed hastily. "Ok – I mean – I didn't mean . . . I was only . . ."

She gave him one of her sharp grins and sat down again, fingering her petrified wood necklace.

"But let me give you something to make up for it."

She reached out for an abandoned paper cup on the table and then, before he quite knew what she was doing, she had the little bottle in her hands again. Open.

"This can help to . . . granting wishes," she said. "And I think, I think he can get more. My services – well – they can be duplicated. So my gift – to you."

She slung away the dregs in the cup and slowly poured in a trickle of the brown liquid. About a third of the bottle. "Hey," she said. "Be careful what you wish for. Wish for someone to come out of the night to you that will make you forget princesses forever. Wish for something else entirely. You choose."

She slid the cup across to him, touched his cheek gently and stood up. "Take care," she murmured as she strolled away. "And enjoy. This stuff is precious."

He stared after her feeling a little stunned – following her neat figure through the market until she was lost in the crowd. Then he suddenly buried his face in his hands with an exasperated grunt. He sat for a while trying to decide if she had been making assumptions or not. Her remarks assumed that he had known precisely why he was issuing the invitation, and he wasn't so sure about that. But maybe she was right. There was no sense denying it. You couldn't deny what was at the back of the brain, no matter how much the world tried to pretend you should. It was hard to analyse the feelings that were running through him now, like a jittery old tape reel through an old-fashioned computer. But somewhere in there was a large dose of disillusionment – with himself. That was the way it went. The body still goes rampaging on. It knows precisely what it wants – even if it doesn't make sense to the mind. And who's to say which is best. Mind games? Flesh games? What can you do? The mind hates the flesh. But the flesh doesn't care, you know that? And which of the two has the upper hand?

According to Matheson, everything was nothing anyway. If so, what did any of this matter? What was all this? Flesh? Love?

Red desire? All the same nothing. He was no different to the wood underneath him.

A few people glanced at him as they passed – enough to make him realise that he must be wearing an expression on his face – that he had cracked just a little. But not many. Don't meet eyes, they think. Just walk on – and don't meet eyes. Below him, he tried to understand the feel of that cold wood – strangely profound in some ways. Almost too rough for comfort now, covered with ridges and textures making their unidentified tactile presences felt. It was hard. Like stone but not stone. It also felt insubstantial. Caught up in the world of Mark's head. Dizzy.

Rock hard nothing, amid the hallucinatory shimmer of Camden Town.

His phone rang then, cutting through his thoughts like an intruding drill and jolting him out of his reverie. He read the name, glanced wearily in the direction Željka had taken and sighed.

"Hello?" he managed blearily, startled by how drunk his voice sounded. Mezcal and red wine and embarrassed sadness were an odd mix it seemed.

The familiar voice came down the phone line. "Mark? Are you ok?"

"I think I have to drown my sorrows, Richard," he said. "A cheap *cabernet sauvignon* no less. I have it at home. And no one to share it with. Which means only one thing."

"Let me guess?"

"All the more for me," he said. "Touch wood," he muttered, fumbling for the wooden fence behind him.

It didn't feel very substantial.

"Hey," he muttered. "Why did you call?"

"Because Željka came back to the Yellow King," Richard Jarvis said with a chuckle.

"Did she?" he said, feeling glassy. He tried to work out what that meant and failed. In this world of subatomic nothing, exact meaning also became inevitably compromised.

"She's currently arguing with Matherson about sound waves and the sense of aesthetics. The strange thing is, they seem to agree on all salient points – but they are still arguing. And poor Feather seems completely overwhelmed by all this talk."

"Damn that man," Mark muttered. "I don't want to think about that shit right now. Quantum blankness. Parallel Universes. M Theory. Bleeeehhh. Everything is nothing and we all don't exist – it isn't very fucking comforting."

"Are you sure about that?"

"Well – where does that leave me? I don't want this to be meaningless. You were right of course, my dear English Gentleman. Everyone has done their bit to make human desire seem trite – can't the scientists mind their own fucking business?"

"Unrequited love nothing more than a few elementary particles in the wrong place?" Richard asked. "A few gluons too few for the successful fusion of matter and antimatter? Leading to the creation of a mini black hole somewhere in your stomach that feels as though it could destroy the world? Perhaps you should come back here? Don't underestimate Alice's magic."

"I am not in love," Mark snarled emphatically. "I am fine."

"Mm? Really? That's interesting."

"What should one wish for?" he demanded. "For something to actually work out once in a while – or to just fade away and lose all this forever? Damn," he muttered again.

"Are you ok?" Richard asked sharply. "Maybe you should come back here. Matherson is no use but maybe you can talk to Feather. She has this wonderfully simple and direct outlook on things."

"Feather?" he murmured, imaging her small figure in his mind. And for a moment he was tempted. But no. Željka was there.

"My head is spinning," he said. "I'm sorry," he stammered. "I didn't mean to spew that all over you. I am talking absolute fucking rubbish."

"Think nothing of it," Richard said. "You go right on talking rubbish. Everyone has the right to be sad and miserable when they need to. And talking rubbish is usually the key to it." He paused. "You know – I am supposed to be good at finding things for people. I might be able to help here."

Mark blinked at the phone, as what that meant sank in.

"Richard, no," he cried. "I'm ok. I don't need . . ."

A low laugh came down the phone line.

"Not important? Have you decided to fade away then? You should come back here. Really."

His realised that he was staring at the cup containing the portion of liquid that Željka had left him and he picked it up uncertainly, then sniffed it. The smell of alcohol made his sinuses prickle. What to do? Drink it? All of it? He peered into the cup again dubiously, then put it to his lips. Tossed it back and swallowed. Bad idea. It was so strong that his body didn't want to accept it. He coughed sharply, spraying droplets over the phone in his hand. It had a cringing planty smoky sweet taste that made him choke and he spluttered more droplets, trying to swallow it away. He gulped – and then again – then coughed.

"What are you doing?" Richard demanded.

"Oh you idiot," he groaned.

"Huh?"

"Not you – I just – oh fuck it. Hang on."

He put the phone down and coughed again violently, leaning over, heedless of the startled glances from the throng milling around the market. He swallowed a few more times and finally brought the flavour down to something manageable.

"Hi," he said to the phone again. "Sorry – I have to go. I . . ."

"Yeah? Yes – I had better go and break those two up. Before the first blows are struck."

"I'll be in touch . . ."

He shut off the phone quickly and glanced at the cup. It was empty. Its entire contents had vanished – somewhere. He could feel it burning in his mouth – warming up his throat. A herby, smoky blast. He sighed. The hallucinatory market seemed to be blurring slightly even now and he buried his face in his hands.

"Ok," he said aloud into his elbow. "Make a wish, right? I wish . . ."

He hesitated, then shrugged mentally.

"I wish that you would come back. Touch wood."

He jabbed the table half-heartedly and sighed, feeling wrung with a sudden bolt of misery for a moment. The market came and went for a while – the eternal crowd of London – a beast with a vague consciousness and sentience all of its own. Camden Town was a clockwork toy that never needed winding. It wittered and jittered onwards in the background, lights turning and processing. A zoetrope that never actually repeated but never really changed either. Faces – bodies – mannequins – models – ghosts – all wandering past. Leaving him as the still point. The centre of a spinning disk.

For some reason Feather was back in his head and he nodded. She was a curious character. Where Richard had found her, he had no idea but she was often around and he seemed to be taking a great delight in showing her the city. She was quiet but once you got to know her she could start to get under your skin with a curious and unexpected fascination. Maybe he should have gone back after all. Or maybe he should have wished for her to join him rather than that tall brown-haired Serbian.

And as Željka invaded his mind again, there was a sound behind him and he looked up sharply. Instantly there was a flash of colour in his eyes and a small but specific pain in his head – and he felt a chill at the back of his neck, feeling as though something very alien was happening.

"Hi," he murmured.

"Richard said something weird was going on," Željka said tolerantly. "Oh, Mark, what are we going to do with you?"

She glanced at the empty cup and he stared up at her dumbly.

"That stuff is precious and you went and . . . and swallowed it like whiskey? Now you are going to go totally . . . round the bend. I had better get you out of here before you are on the national news."

"Um – yeah, ok," he said as she pulled him to his feet. "But look – I'm ok. It doesn't matter . . ."

He wasn't sure about that though. The colours flashed again when he stood up. Hints of red and green in the world around him. He stared round dreamily. For all the bustle of people, there was a curious quietness in the world and it took a moment to realise why: he couldn't hear any cars. The nearby Chalk Farm Road seemed to have fallen silent and he wondered why. He frowned.

"What the hell was that stuff?" he muttered, feeling a tinge of anger through his spinning brain. She gave a wan smile.

"The ghost in the bottle?" she said. "What did you wish for?"

"Well," he said as they began to walk – then he paused, suddenly no longer sure. "Who knows," he said.

"Hmm?"

"Where does a wish stop being a wish? When it is not spoken aloud? When it is not a part of the top level of the conscious mind?"

She gave him a curious look.

"Or suppose you wish for one thing with the conscious mind – and something else entirely with the unconscious – which wish gets granted? Hmm? So I have no answer for your question. You see, Miss I-Have-A-Dream – I also have philosophy."

"Bravo," she said with a smile.

"When I am sober again, of course, I won't call it a philosophy any more – but who cares?"

They arrived at the back gate to the market – the rather formidable metal monstrosity guarding Chalk Farm Road from any strange emanations from this place. He paused, realising then why he could hear no cars. There weren't any. Chalk Farm Road was vehicle-less. Pedestrians thronged. A few cyclists pedalled past. But beyond that, nothing. Nothing was even parked. Someone had lit a bonfire in the middle of the road – a flickering glow of orange surrounded by shadow figures.

This was decidedly strange.

"Wait," he cried, stopping sharply and jerking her to a halt at the end of his arm. "There is something in the air here," he said.

"Yeah," she murmured, watching as a huge bluish fish lazily immerged from a side street and swam quietly overhead into the market.

"Let's go back," he said eagerly, turning and making off after it.

"Mark," she began in exasperation – but he was already hurrying away. She gave a wry sigh and followed him back into the shifting theatricals of stalls and shops and food counters, as the fish slowly drifted on. They watched as the Thai cooks neatly reached out their blades and whipped slices of flesh out of its flanks – the only response being a flick of annoyance and a quick dart away. The fish slices went into the steaming woks and the scent of frying filled the air.

"Yes, my friends?" the Thai girl said, noticing them watching. "Would you like some Tom Yum?"

"We haven't any money," Željka said with an unhappy shrug.

"You don't need money on such a night as this," the girl cried, holding out two foil plates, on which perfectly cooked soup steamed scent into the darkness. "On this night – you smell the air. Everyone is dancing . . ."

Mark followed her gesture with his eyes, taking in the seething crowd. And they were dancing, he realised – circles and pulsations to music that was far older and more powerful than anything normally played here. He drew a deep breath in amazement.

They gratefully took the plates and strolled on, relishing the soft fish, which had something of the flavour of sea bass, but was still subtly different. Then there was a fence in front of them barring their way – beyond it the railway lines gleamed in the dark. Railway lines that spoke of journeying to other places. Željka didn't pause for long.

"On such a night as this," she murmured dreamily, "fences feel embarrassed, realising their ultimate pointlessness – and they make way for lovers with deference." And it was true. He held up a hand to the wire and it actually pulled aside for them like a curtain, allowing them to step through and climb down onto the shifting ballast.

"Lovers?" he managed.

"Yes?" she said with a smile. "That's what you meant, wasn't it?" She leaned forward then and kissed him. He froze slightly at the sensation of soft flesh with a touch of moisture – then he found her hand nervously.

After a long moment of silence they started strolling down the railway line, hand in hand, while the market buzzed on in the middle distance. The few trains that passed them on this hot night looked almost empty and they waved cheerily to the drivers, who flashed their lights in return. They walked on through the arse ends of buildings and dark urban railway architecture. Massive brick walls that seemed to rise up into the night to infinity, or dark square tunnels where the city had grown over the tracks like some weird fungus. And the eyes followed the threads of the rails, imagining them travelling off to places unknown.

Eventually Željka sat down in the narrow wedge of grass where the tracks split – two massive train routes passing off into the night. She sat almost formally, knees up, facing the junction – the perfect arrow of turf passing under her, between her legs, and penetrating the tangle of metal points and ballast. She gently pulled him down as well, seating him in front of her intimately and holding him gently with legs and arms, and together they sat and watched the trains passing either side. Small passenger trains. Screaming InterCitys. Slow and formidable freight trains. They looked like living things, with personalities and facial expressions, and as they passed, they shook the ground with a profound vibration and left wakes of colour glimmering uncertainly behind them.

Then she hugged him. "Still fancy that comforting screw?" She murmured in his ear. Mark gave a quiet smile. That really was the most natural thing to say in the world.

They rolled over and somehow, with a few gestures their clothes had vanished, seemingly far easier than physically possible – and they lay between the tracks languorously with the shaking ground and rolling wheels all that they needed. Željka was soft and hard, smooth or unexpectedly interrupted – and startlingly strong. And her brown eyes flashed with red and green, seeming to spin and churn gently.

It was a long time before they separated again and sat up, while a massive intercity train accelerated past with engines at full power. They scrambled to their feet and walked as though in a dream across the tracks and climbed up out of this world of trains, hauling themselves over a low wall and through another fence. To his surprise they were still in the market – still surrounded by the same buzz and activity. These stalls and shops seemed to go on forever – and maybe that was true. Maybe, if they had jumped on one of those passing trains, it would just have taken them miles away, only to drop them where the same food scented the air and the same lights twinkled and the same crowd thronged.

"Of course," he said, "I know I am dreaming. None of this is real – but that's fine. One day, the whole world will be like this – as you . . . as you said."

She nodded. "I hope so." She looked dreamy and distant again now, staring round at the eternal bustle. "When there are no more borders and lines on the map," she said in a sing-song voice.

"Yeah," he said. Then added "Touch wood," out of habit, jabbing at a passing fence. When his finger went straight into the wood with barely any resistance, he could only stand there and stare dumbly.

"Touch wood, I said," he yelled, staring stupidly at his embedded hand. The shock of this was somehow profound – an instant feeling of nakedness and helplessness without his familiar good luck gesture that prickled down his back and all over his skin. And instantly the market seemed to have changed slightly to match his shock – gone darker – more subtly menacing.

I'm asleep, he thought dizzily. This means I am dreaming. Of course I am bloody dreaming. *Take control of your dreams,* Matherson had said. Mark didn't feel in control at all though. "Željka," he cried looking round sharply. "What is . . ."

But she wasn't there. She had vanished. He stared round in a complete circle feeling a shock of loneliness. Everywhere he looked there was just market – market that now seemed filled with colours that he had never seen before. The flaring lights and bustling people made his head hurt. He reached out to steady himself – but his hand sank into the wall beside him and he jerked away, feeling a prickle of terror. He jabbed feebly at the railway-arch brick again, but the result was the same. His whole hand disappeared into it. He couldn't see it, but he could still feel it – the feel of cold stone that offered no resistance. Trying not to shiver, he waved his hand back and fourth in the wall as though swirling up a pond.

Then he urgently juggled with his phone and somehow got it out of his pocket. Fumbling fingers found buttons in an agony of terror that this also would just fade away into the insubstantial. He could have called Richard of course. Or anybody. But his fingers found the only possible number in his directory without any conscious thought.

"Mark?"

"Željka?" he cried down the phone. "Where did you go?"

"I – what's that?"

He back-tracked hastily.

"I mean – I mean, that's fine. Go if you want. It's ok, I don't . . . it's just – I mean . . ." He stumbled to a halt, then the words came bursting out in shrill terror: "For god's sake what's going on here please help me . . ."

The phone slipped out of his grasp. There was a clatter on the cobbles somewhere below him – but it might as well have fallen into an ocean.

"This is just a dream," he reassured himself, while 360 degrees of market continued to swarm around him. "Just a dream just a dream just a dream. Just a dream just a dream – will wake up again and the world would be just as it should be. Just keep remembering that. Just a dream just a dream just a . . . What the hell had he done? A ghost in a bottle? Something to grant wishes? If so, that still begged the question . . .

What had he wished for?

There was something about this insubstantiality that seemed very appropriate.

He tried to slap himself – but even that impact felt muffled. Numb. A residual sense of caution made him try not to act too unusual in case anybody cared about that sort of thing, though in this dreamland it hardly seemed to matter. He realised that he had to get out of this market – though he wasn't sure of the way. There was something unmappable about Camden Market. It seemed to exist in more dimensions than the usual and he wasn't sure where he was or which direction to take. He started moving anyway though, slipping through the crowd, trying not to touch anything and following the avenue he happened to be in. All that happened though was that it spat him out into a small open area where huge statues reared up. They were gatekeepers – figures of men on horses – but all he could see beyond them were more avenues going off in all directions with very little regard for geometry. He gave the statues uneasy glances, half expecting them to suddenly bring fists or hooves crashing down on him if he tried to pass, but they didn't move – they let him through and he continued. In the confusion, scantily clad heroines with pink hair battled with huge metal men, sending shrapnel flying. Light blazed and flashed from somewhere and he backed away, only to find himself suddenly smothered by fabric as insubstantial as gas – oceans of it in every bright colour you could imagine that his hands and body just passed straight through. He gave a choked wail and stumbled free of them, bolting down a side avenue, surrounded by shimmering fire.

And he was right, he realised. There was no way out of this place. Reaching the end only brought more avenues and more random junctions – nothing but the eternal noise of voices all trying to be heard, music and the distant rattle of trains on the elevated tracks overhead or down below. Finally he came to a stop, feeling exhausted – just standing still in the middle of the path while people swarmed around him. Then he staggered into an open area that contained some benches. It looked like the place where he and Željka had sat together, but it couldn't be. He must have walked at least a half mile since then. He experimentally tried to touch one, only to fail as before. He didn't dare sit down – he would just fall straight through – so he just stood, staring around vaguely.

He was about to give himself up as doomed when there was a sudden intrusion of red into his world – red that tugged at him. He stared with huge eyes at Richard Jarvis in the middle distance, then waved sharply. "Hey," he called and tried to run in their direction. There were four figures – Željka's beautiful brown hair was there as well, contrasting sharply with Richard's red explosion, Matherson looking a little fed up and Feather staring round like a wary small mammal in a very alien place indeed. He didn't seem to be making much progress towards them though – and they paid no attention to him, even as he called out.

"Where the hell is he?" he heard Richard mutter, eyes darting round the thronging crowds. "Are you sure?"

"But I'm right here," he cried dizzily.

Željka shrugged. "I think so – it sounded like the market . . . in the background."

Richard nodded. "Oh boy – what a place to have to find someone." He shrugged and turned away – the group making to move off, Feather clinging close to him and staring around nervously.

"Wait," Mark cried urgently. He reached out and clutched – his arms feeling more like prosthetic extensions than an actual part of him. "What are you doing? Don't just leave me here." He grabbed at Željka's shoulder, but his hand just went right through and into her flesh – unexpectedly warm with a body's warmth. That was a startling flash of intimacy that sent a tingle into his stomach.

"Željka," he yelled shrilly. She was staring around the benches with a very curious and uncomfortable expression on her face, one that Mark could hardly even begin to understand. Her lip twitched and pressed tight. He tried one last time to reach her – jabbing his hand right through her eyes and into her brain.

She flinched and came to a halt.

"Željka?" Richard called back impatiently.

She stared after him blinking.

"Of course," she muttered. "I'm coming."

He followed them in an absurd progression, still calling their names, keeping pace as best he could and frantically trying to grab her. Always failing. Then they stopped again. Mark made an instinctive movement to avoid running into Željka's back, only remembering that it didn't matter when he staggered face first though her in a brief flash of complete blackness and warmth – a tiny hint of red glow. He jerked away in shock, flapping his hands.

"Weird," Matherson muttered. "Are you sure he didn't say anything else?"

Željka shook her head and shrugged, but Mark realised that Richard was staring at her intently.

"You ok?" he asked.

"Yeah," she muttered.

He gave her a piercing look.

"Ummmmmmmm," he said. "You – er – didn't by any chance . . . give him some of . . . did you?"

She flinched.

"Oh no," Željka said hastily. "No – I – I mean . . . Ne – mislim – ovaj . . ." she sighed, looking into the impossible eyes of Richard Jarvis. What was the point of lying when he already seemed to know the answer? "Yes," she said. "I – I did give him a small . . . taste."

Richard rubbed his nose with a wince.

"And . . . . you explained . . . ?"

Mark watched in fascination as Željka fiddled with her shirt front, suddenly looking like a naughty child in trouble. She glanced furiously at Matherson, who was watching with a delighted grin on his face.

"I told him it could grant wishes," she said.

Richard sighed. "Željka, may at least three government employees take you over their knees and spank you till you are forced to ride the tube standing even off peak simply because you can't sit down. And may Alice start importing her Rakija from a demented Croatian bootlegger who lost his wife to Serbian atrocities. That stuff is dangerous."

"I thought it might help," she muttered.

Richard drew a deep breath.

"Ok," he said. "I could be wrong – but I think we ought to find him. Matherson? Would you check as far as his house? Željka?"

"Yes?"

"You bloody search the market with us, ok?"

"Yes – yes . . ."

"If you find him, get him home for gawd's sake . . . and phone me," he added as he hurried off.

"Wait," Mark wailed. They were all playing games. Predictable – almost inevitable games. Again he reminded himself that this was just a dream. Just a dream that he would wake up from any time and be absolutely fine. You always just wake up again . . .

He watched Željka as she stood staring around forlornly, then she gave an angry snort and turned away. He made a last scrabbling clutch at her, but the result was the same and he opened his mouth in a wail, on the point of giving up. Why fight this? This unsubstantial world – this invisibility – was what he had wished for after all. He glanced down at the ground then, that particular aspect of this only now occurring to him. And almost as though to oblige him, his feet had sunk a little way into the pavement. He flung up his hands and trod around, trying to find something solid. But there was nothing.

"You did it on purpose, didn't you," he cried, reaching after her retreating figure and sinking lower as he did so. "All I wanted was . . . you didn't have to . . ."

He sighed and let himself fall – the bizarre sensation of a slowly sinking perspective of the chaos around him. Would he be able to breathe, he wondered. When the cold cobbles closed over his head. Would he be able to see anything? Or would it just be absolute blackness until he suffocated? He was a little surprised to find that he hardly felt afraid at all now – as though there was little sense panicking about the inevitable. After all – he was home now. All hopes and dreams over – all wishes granted . . .

Then there was a touch – a hand fastened on his jacket.

That sense of something substantial came as such a shock that he almost screamed – and it changed everything in a violent implosion. Instantly he was no longer sinking. He was yanked back to the surface again and found himself lying on uncomfortable stones – shockingly cold. Blankets were all over him, suffocatingly heavy and he scrabbled at them, pushing them aside until there was a flash of light – suspended bulbs mundanely glowing against a dark sky. He stared at them dreamily, the sight washing all other thoughts from his mind for a moment. They were just light bulbs – just ordinary dirty glass with incandescent filaments glowing inside. But right now those bulbs seemed like home.

Finally he stared round very slowly, looking for what had touched him. What it was that still had a hold of his shoulder. There was a pair of brown eyes staring at him quietly – and untidy hair. For a long moment, he tried to translate that face into Željka's continental features, but then it clicked and he drew a deep breath.

"Feather?" he murmured.

"I just pretended all this was trees," she said, rather obliquely, waving at the swarming people and market stalls. "And you were the one item of food I was hunting for – to catch and kill. It was the only way I could get this place to make sense."

Mark stared blankly at her and she grinned shyly, an interested gleam in her eyes. In a few stammering phrases, he tried to tell her what he had seen, but soon gave up, unable to find the words. He looked round – still moving in slow motion. A few other figures were staring down at him anxiously – passers-by and stall owners – but as before most were ignoring him. Don't meet eyes – don't meet eyes.

Then she was gently tugging him to his feet. "I think we should get home, yes?" she murmured.

He nodded and smiled gratefully.

"Um," he managed. "Yes. Thanks. Um – I have a bottle at home. A cheap Cabernet – would you like a glass?"

"Yes," she said simply. "Then you can tell me all about it. It looks as though you have been somewhere interesting."

The Magpies

For Abigail

On the 18th March, 2007, news came through to Elizabeth Ise that her brother Jacob had died while travelling in Europe. Accident. No one seemed to know how or why.

On what must have been the same day, two other things happened. One of the pair of magpies nesting in a tall tree outside her house was found dead on her garden path. No obvious injury. Two lines – one angle. A vertex.

And Elizabeth Ise, musician and composer, put down her Celtic harp and couldn't pick it up again.

Part 1

The Bird Caller

A faint white light from a white Dartmoor dawn. It shone into the room, crawling around the corners of her vision and illuminating the bed dimly. Elizabeth lay on her back, her eyes open and gazing out of the window. From where she lay in bed, her view was wide and luxurious. The low hills of the moors above her. Patches of trees. Crawling areas of mist that gathered in the low places. The trees in her own wild garden, with their branches standing out jet black against a pale sky streaked with a few tiny wisps of horizontal cloud. But now, both the light and the view were unwelcome, for they only underlined the fact that she was still awake. That her eyes were prickling and her sight was blurry with absent sleep.

These days, she was used to the complete moorland darkness and silence that you got during the night and she found that there was something comfortable about it. In the city, there had always been some noise somewhere. Some light radiating. The sound of traffic somewhere in the distance. People passing. Voices. The light of street lamps and their reflected glow off the clouds. Out here though, the night was how the night should be.

It was good for sleeping in.

She watched as the room around her gradually became more and more visible – as the light transformed the shapes into recognisable objects. It stole across an electric keyboard standing large in the corner at the foot of the bed. It reflected dully off the screen of a computer next to it, wired in with an uncomfortable nest of cables. A tall standing mirror gleamed softly. Papers returned from the darkness to litter the floor and books clustered again on the dark shelves. The light hurt. It seemed heavy. Just as the quilt she was under seemed heavy. Perhaps they were the same thing. A unified world of brittle white full of the cold and the damp. The one pressing down on wet grass, the other on her own skin.

At last she shivered. She moved her hand and forced herself to turn over – to stare at something other than the window. Her body felt heavy and stiff and she tossed her straggling hair out of her face, closed her eyes and wearily tried again to fall sleep.

But then the silence was also cut, just like the darkness – and by a sound that was much less pleasant than the night.

The first birds began to sing.

A long clear note rang out from somewhere in the far distance. It rose and fell about a semitone, then faded out.

Elizabeth clutched at her quilt and breathed deeply.

You have received an online message from ***Feather***

Do you wish to add Feather to your contacts, to be notified when he/she comes online?

Add!

Feather says: Hello?

Feather says: Hello? Elizabeth Ise by any chance?

MissEyes says: Whos this?

Feather says: Remember me? It's been a while since we talked -

MissEyes says: Aaah Feather? Hi!!! I didn't expect tp hear from you like this? I thought you were out somewhere sleeping under a hedge.

Feather says: I am not often near a computer!

Feather says: How are you?

MissEyes says: well - not bad. A Bit hauinted right now. How did you find me?

*You have added **Feather** to your online contact list.*

Feather says: I just tried a few versions of your performing name - Elizabeth Eyes - just on the off-chance. I thought you wouldn't abandon it. And there you were.

Feather says: Haunted? What's wrong?

MissEyes says: Oh - it's nothing really.

MissEyes says: Just suffering from composers block a bit. I cant compose anyting at the moment. Or play -much.

Feather says: Your brain is trying to tell you something.

Feather says: I am staying with Richard for a few days at the moment. So I am borrowing his computer. I never used this program before.

Feather says: Richard Jarvis? Remember him? I was wandering for ages, staying with friends or wherever - and now I am here. He's a collector of all sorts of stuff. It is interesting. I can't stop here long now - dinner is awaiting me downstairs. But I will try and get online again.

MissEyes says: Vaguely yes. You will have to bear with me - I am abit isolated here - cut off from the world. Yes - look for me online. It would be good to talk more.

Feather says: One thing he collects is food and drink - from all over the world. Cheese, wine, liqueurs, meat. And I am sure some of it is illegal. ☺

MissEyes says: Illegal food? Interesting! Such as?

Feather says: Well . . .

Feather says: He had a cheese with maggots in that he smuggled in from Sardinia. And a bottle of unbelievably cruel brandy with a slow-drowned poisonous salamander in it from Slovenia . . .

MissEyes says: Wow!

Feather says: He says it makes you - what is the word? Horny? I dunno though! But I am putting on weight right now.

MissEyes says: :-)

Feather says: Which is good. Storing it all up for the future, you know.

Feather says: I am feeling the cold even less now, I think.

MissEyes says: Heh! I wish I was as relaxed about that!!

Feather says: So I will be in touch yes?

MissEyes says: Absolutely - and enjoy your meal! ☺ Whatever it is!

Feather says: ✋

And now something had been at her bird table.

Something . . .

She wrapped a white knitted shawl around her shoulders and tramped wearily out into her garden. As she did so, the last of the magpies flashed away, a glimpse in the bushes. Elizabeth Ise had always thought of it as the female, though perhaps that was more to do with personal identification than scientific certainty. Elizabeth stared after it forlornly. Wasn't very trusting, was she? No matter how much food she left out, she still would not linger around when anyone was outside.

But never mind that now.

The old chop bones she had left out here were completely gone – no surprise. They were often carried off. But something had pulled the chicken carcass into fragments and left it scattered around the rough lawn. Even snapping a few bones. This didn't make sense. What was there out here in the middle of Dartmoor that would be big enough and interested enough to do that? She stared at the bones feeling puzzled and uneasy, then glanced round at the surrounding bushes. There were no traces that made any sense to her though. No patterns apparent here.

This wasn't comforting.

But anyway – there was little left out here that was edible. That at least was certain. Time for a refill obviously. With a sigh she stepped back into her kitchen and opened her freezer. A moment's thought and she selected two lamb chops, took them out and tossed them on the table. They steamed slightly in the cool air.

It really wouldn't do to lose the second magpie.

She glanced quickly round her garden and the flat landscape of Dartmoor, looking for the familiar black and white shape, but there was no sign of it. She shut the door behind her sharply and locked it, then tramped out of her garden and across the road. She was feeling bitter and grim – and alone. And that meant that the moors would be good company. In its intense wild isolation, Dartmoor could make any human emotion seem small and needless.

There was no one about at all as she hopped over a gate onto the moors and followed the narrow stream of the river Dart. But that was not unusual. It seemed that no matter how much people loved the moors – how many tourists it attracted – it still managed to produce that feeling of being far bigger than anything human. And of being as empty as another planet. At this time in the late afternoon, the only company she seemed to have out here were the birds, which she listened to uneasily. The familiar chattering call of the magpie came from somewhere and she jumped. But it was just the magpie – no doubt bewildered by the rock-hard frozen food she had left out. The sounds that surrounded her were just the birds. And yet, she was feeling less and less certain.

Why did it sometimes seem as though there was something else in the air? Something unreal and almost musical . . .

Rhythms, structures – rondos and canons . . .

She had never heard that before.

Haunted, was the word she had used earlier, almost without thinking. But it fitted. Elizabeth Ise was haunted by music. This was starting to sound crazy – she knew that. Perhaps it was time to do something drastic here? Perhaps Elisabeth Ise and her cool and calculating thought processes were starting to break down? And yet – what could you do? Patterns were patterns. The mind followed the patterns in the world and drew conclusions from them – and when new data arrived, new theories were written. It was that simple.

The Dart was just a low and rocky slash here, passing through the gentle marshy hills. And up ahead, the smudge of a small patch of trees huddled.

"One for sorrow, two for joy," she murmured. "One for sorrow, two for joy?" She gave a weary grunt. What did that meaningless magpie doggerel have to do with anything? One for sorrow, two for joy – all the basic urges of life summed up in one inane sentence? Two for joy? Now no longer. Not for her – and not for a black and white bird, said to be an omen of death and misfortune but who had now only suffered them itself in direct parallel to her. One for sorrow? Indeed and absolutely. Severance and loneliness. Was it worth a dumb rhyme to say something so simple? She sighed and scrambled over a stile over a low stone wall, and now at least there was something to prove that she wasn't the only person left alive. A single person was walking along the path that crowned the hill nearby. All she could make out was a black and bulky figure, head down and somehow shapeless, with fabric billowing out in the wind.

So what? No doubt just another wandering tourist, carefully sticking to the paths and without a clue as to what lay just a few metres away in the trees she was heading for.

"Three for a funeral, four for a birth," she muttered. "Five for heaven, six for hell. Seven's the Devel, his own sel'."

Elizabeth disliked superstitions and traditions, in spite of the lines and angles that were forming in her own head. It was just a bird – clever and resourceful and efficient, but still a bird. And besides, how could anyone even begin to take a rhyme or a superstition seriously when the different versions could mean so many different things? According to her admittedly sparse research, three magpies could mean a wedding or a funeral. Six could equal poverty, gold or hell itself. This was not a very convincing degree of accuracy. And Elizabeth liked accuracy.

The woods were closer now, covered in mist. There were fewer birds out here as well, and that was comforting. These trees were Wistman's Wood – just a small patch of dwarf oaks on the side of the valley some way from the road – and some way from the normal tracks of the tourists. But the trees were low and twisted almost into unreality and hung with treebeards and lichen. The rocks that strewed the ground between them were covered in some of the deepest moss she had ever seen. Inches of it and as soft as a pillow. Mushrooms grew everywhere in their season – tiny, colourful studs on the branches or in the leaf litter. Sometimes this place felt more like her own personal garden than just another moorland reserve and these soft rocks were a perfect destination for her feet. Out here you didn't have to think so much. The silence was intense and default – just the distant Dart flowing quietly. Nothing moved. The mist cancelled out the distance. And all there was in this fairytale was her and these twisted shapes.

It was a relief to quickly slip off the path and disappear amongst them.

Jacob had never been like her – content to stay at home quietly and get on with things. In fact, it sometimes seemed as though he hadn't a home at all. All their lives, he had been pulling outwards and she had been pulling inwards. It had usually been a comfortable sort of tension though, because they each went their own way, content in the knowledge that the other was out there somewhere and they would eventually come together again. But even so, it wasn't really so surprising that he should end up vanishing – and vanishing not into the familiar green of England but into a limestone forest somewhere in the high Slovenian mountains. Elizabeth didn't know anything about the Slovenian mountains. She didn't even know for certain where they were. But the Alps were vast and lonely – and somewhere in them was a huddled form. That was all the information amounted to. An accidental death.

Two accidental deaths.

She sighed. The pattern was connected. Two lines – but just one angle.

And her own line an intersection of both . . .

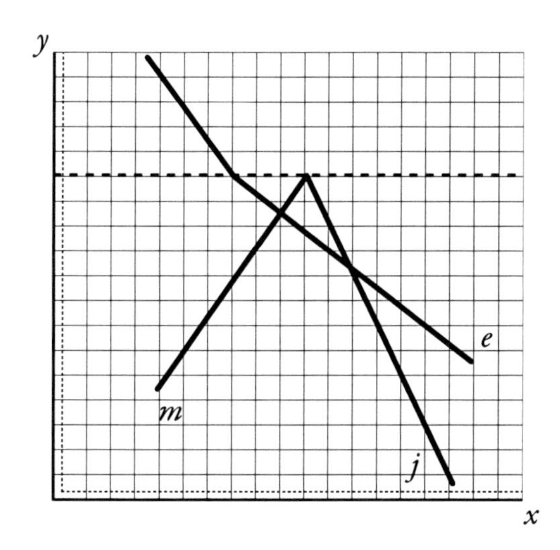

Why should a bird and a man be connected? Maybe they weren't. Maybe it was simply the pattern itself that made it significant. But you can't argue with a simple relationship between lines and angles. The lines of life, the angle of death. Why not?

How beautiful was that? Everything humanity wanted to believe was just an expression of lines and angles. Forget credulity and superstition and religion. It was just maths.

At least, it was to her.

* * *

Feather has signed in

Feather says: Hello Elizabeth. How's the music?

MissEyes says: Music isnt. alas . . . All I can find under my fingers at the momen t are chords I hate. Nasty jarring intervsala.

MissEyes says: Intervals.

MissEyes says: like tritones. I cant compose with that!! I cant get them to resolve anywhere for some reason,

Feather says: err – no?

Feather says: Why not?

Feather says: What is a tritone?

MissEyes says: Ooohh **. . .** *diabolus in musica*. Heheh. The devil's chord. It all just feels wrong. These are patterns that don't mean anything comforttable.

Feather says: The devil?

MissEyes says: No no – It just sounds like isolation and things that do not frit together.

MissEyes says: Fit together.

MissEyes says: Do not connect. I cant get the two harmonicv lines of the tritone tp meet so they are left very lonely.

MissEyes says: And I really don't want that now.

MissEyes says: Sorry – I am too fast a typer, I know.

Feather says: Why not? I thought you were feeling alone? Perhaps that is what you have to do next.

MissEyes says: :-(:-(:-(:-(

Feather says: You never did explain what all this was about? I sense there is something going on?

MissEyes says: Just a silly fancy which I wont goi into here. Everythng is starting to sound like music. There's music on the moors. I really need to get writing it again – I am starting to go crazzy.

Feather says: ?

MissEyes says: Feather – I am a composer and a bit of a mathematician. Its the patterns that are getting my attention, that's all. The maths. Is it so strange to watch the patterns and see where they lead? That's what its all about. I'm not loosing it. You have to find your own conclusions. And if they dopnt match everyone elsezs then tough for them.

Feather says: What patterns are these?

MissEyes says: The angle that exists between my brother and this magpie – and perhaps what's happening now.

MissEyes says: That angle is my only comfort. That speaks so clearly, that there is a pattern in this. And it might be one that I can understand one day.

Feather says: What is this thing you are talking about? I don't really understand.

Feather says: I think you may be thinking too much though. The world is not a complicated place.

MissEyes says: I don't KNOW what is happening. Maybe I am just dreaming.

MissEyes says: the world is full of patterns. Everywhere. The way things grow. The way things relate. So why not the way things die?

Feather says: Die?

MissEyes says: My Brother.

Feather says: Your brother is dead?

MissEyes says: And I was . . . very fond of my brother. I mmiss him terribly. Is that a crime?

MissEyes says: Jacob should be here . . . somewhere. Perhaps he his.

MissEyes says: Do you believe in ghosts?

MissEyes says: In any form?

MissEyes says: Maybe ghosts can exist mathermatically.

Feather says: I am sorry to hear that – and I begin to understand your mood! You sound confused though. Tell me your address. I might be able to send you something that might help. Just a little.

Feather says: I will ask Richard. He has a few curious things here that maybe . . .

MissEyes says: I am not drinking any Salamander brandy!!!

Feather says: No no – not that. But there's something I think. I'm not sure . . .

Feather says: He is an expert at finding curious things like this . . .

MissEyes says: Thankyou – I appreciate! You can find my address in my profile – click on the picture of me.

Feather says: Ok . . .

Feather says: Got it. I will see what I can do.

* * *

The end of night time. Cold. Dark and wet. The same white dawn.

"Jacob?" she murmured, stunned and fully aware that this was impossible.

Most of him was missing. Only his face seemed intact, for some reason. She watched him wearily hold out his arm and immediately there was a black and white flash as a magpie darted down and yanked out a morsel, before settling on his shoulder to swallow it. She felt herself freezing inside at the sight – what was going on here? Jacob's fading flesh as bird food?

She struggled to maintain her analytical mind against the image, but it didn't seem to help her much.

From where he sat perched on Jacob's shoulder, the magpie looked almost like a guide. An usher. Certainly not an enemy. Was that how it worked? She realised that Jacob's eyes were as dull and lifeless as ancient egg white – so perhaps there lay the reason. She winced at the thought. No wonder everyone associated the magpie with death. Jacob didn't look particularly troubled though. There was no sign of pain in his face. He just looked forlorn and ruined. He opened his mouth and tried to speak, but there was no breath or throat to speak with and she could only stare helplessly. What could she do? The magpie also stared at her, a shred of meat still hanging from its beak. The bird couldn't speak to her either. The pair were dumb and helpless. So what were they doing here? What did they want? Why should Jacob want to say anything to her?

Finally they seemed to give up. The bird guide jumped into the air and urgently indicated movement. Wearily Jacob turned and walked away obediently, stumbling unsteadily through the grass. The bird kept close in front though, and he followed it faithfully.

She remained watching until they had faded to a tiny dot in the distance.

And then they were gone.

The dream or half-dream – or brief image – was over, so she opened her eyes and stared at the grey dawn outside. She felt full to the brim with water. Far more than it would ever be possible to cry out of her. Her Celtic harp was standing by the bed and she brushed at the strings, mostly to chase away the thoughts in her head. The instrument was getting out of tune now though and she winced. It had been such a long time since she had been able to play it. Her music felt totally dead. The lines and patterns of her harp strings felt completely out of reach. And what did they mean? Here there were no intersections or angles whatsoever. Just dead ends.

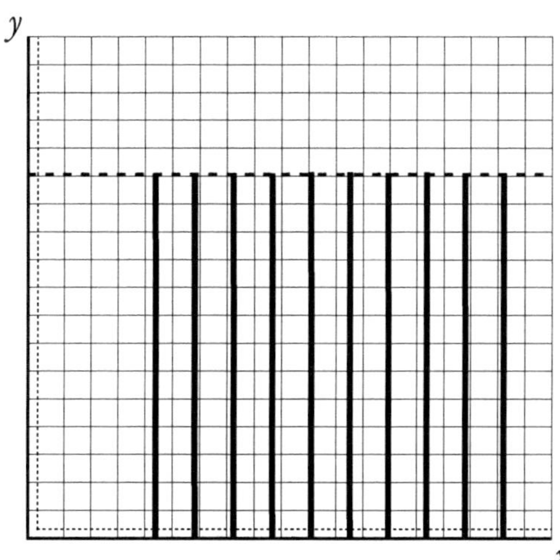

Music seemed to be everywhere these days, anyway, so what need was there for her? She could hear it on the moors. As she slept. In the birdsong. Somewhere in the shadowy space behind her brain. Ghost music. Even now, the birds were calling and even now, music was playing. Why not? A simple rhythm was pounding through it all. As though someone somewhere was playing a giant drum or bell with a rhythm so slow it only came once every five heartbeats, and so low it was more felt than heard. And was there a hint of a melody or melodies as well? Harmony – counterpoint. A tuning system and even a temperament. Something you shouldn't hear with birds. She could hear the magpie laughing wildly occasionally, as usual – and even that was a part of this symphony of sound.

Of course it was.

What was going on?

It was all patterns. She shut her eyes and listened to the sound. There was a long, keening note coming in from the distance, which rose and fell, each call lasting almost a minute. Sometimes it would change pitch, each call like the notes in an impossibly stretched out melody. And the birds followed it, creating measured music. The drum ushered onwards a whole chorus of pipers, wailing and whining in microtonal random noise, feathers shaking, eyes gleaming – in some sort of grotesque processional.

Elizabeth suddenly felt a shock of pain at the image and she opened her eyes quickly, begging the world to return to normalcy. It sounded like an execution parade or funeral march.

What the hell was making that keening noise?

Maybe this could be her next CD . . . *Funeral March of the Magpies*. Could she ever express this? Music was only another form of language, after all – and therefore as proficient as the person speaking with it – and as the person listening to it. In spite of her block, music still flew through her head in an endless swirl. Rhythms and melodies, all tangled together into a babbling chaos. But that was no use. The impossible part was letting it out, carefully and controlled, and making it say what she wanted it to say. She had to spin the chaos inside her out into written or recorded musical compositions – she had to create an order out of it. But now the tap was closed. Jammed. And what was she going to do about it? Life seemed to have come to a standstill. That happened sometimes when you worked in something as fragile as creativity – but soon another month's rent would be due and she wasn't even sure if she had enough money to cover it.

Impatiently she kicked the bedclothes onto the floor and squirmed round till her feet were on her pillow. The air on her skin was suddenly cold, but also refreshing and she reached out and touched her keyboard now, gently playing a silent chord.

A, E♭ – the tritone. It was a strange sound. It sounded different to most of what she regarded as familiar. It was not such a big deal – but right now, all she wanted to do was play that one jarring chord over and over again, repeating it like that keening call and the drum. Thump thump thump. And where was the music in that?

Before this is over, I'll be in a council cupboard in Exeter, she thought bitterly – and on that thought she scrambled off the bed and hauled on her clothes. Better to move than to lie here and keep thinking. Before heading outside into the cold morning air of the moors, she went into the kitchen, selected a small but sharp knife and hid it in her pocket. Why? Who knows. There was nothing dangerous about the moors – at least not in her experience. But even so, the blade was comforting somehow in these haunting days and she hardly bothered analysing it – hardly had any image of what the blade was intended to penetrate and defend her from.

Then she hurried out.

Instead of her usual destination of Wistman's Wood, she headed the other way this time, following the road up over the low hills. But even the lines and angles of these roads had developed a symbolism . . . Sometimes it almost seemed that there were too many patterns in the world for comfort, in spite of the rigidity they gave things. Even just walking up the road was making her feel a bit uncomfortable right now as it made her feel that it was a life she was walking along, which was true enough, she supposed. It made her realise that she also was heading towards some sort of meeting of lines – a vertex – off in the distance. And she didn't like to think what she might find there. What else would share that vertex? Would she have her own magpie waiting for her?

There was a flash of black and white fleeing and she flinched with familiarity. Talk of the devil, she thought with a sharp grin. Then she noticed something else, a huddled shape on the road ahead. Something brown and furry, a foot or two long and her heart sank. It was not until she approached it that she realised that it was a cat. Obviously young – a rough tortoiseshell.

"No no no," she said aloud to the now invisible magpie. "Keep away from the road. It's not safe."

Everyone drove fast here – in spite of the road's narrowness. She stared down at the furry corpse and hesitantly touched it with her shoe. Its head was crushed and its back was twisted and must be broken. It looked quite fresh though. Just a few hours dead.

The sound of a car approaching in the distance decided her. She stepped aside, trying to look casual until it passed her and vanished over the hill, then she crouched down and gathered up the cat, frowning uncomfortably. She put it in her bag, wincing at the mess, then heavily shouldered it. There were safer places than this for her last magpie to feed and she made for home as fast as she could.

There was no sign of the bird now though, but it must be there. It was no doubt following her, puzzled and irritated – wondering what she was doing with its nice fresh corpse. It kept pace with her and watched her warily as she dumped the furry mass onto her bird table alongside the one remaining chop.

Birds everywhere . . . and why did they always have to make such a noise?

"There, you ungrateful bitch," she muttered, rubbing her hands on her trousers. She withdrew, feeling a little resentful because she knew she had to get out of the way before the magpie would come. She wished the bird would trust her more. She lingered for a while, watching, but nothing happened. No black and white bird picking over the new and gruesome offering, so she wandered heavily to her garden bench and sat down, dropping her face into her hands. The corpse of the first magpie was still where she had left it by the path in front of her and she looked at it mournfully. Was this little bundle of feathers the only connection she had to a double tragedy?

Why?

Where was the rest of all this?

Off in the distance, she seemed to hear a faint sound. It moved to a different pitch – then again. It really did seem close to a melody now, but its language seemed different to anything she had experienced before. What it was, she couldn't imagine, but anything close to music was starting to seem mocking. It was all out of control. It was all escaping her. Leaving her redundant and impotent. Abruptly she sat up and tried to sing back. Elizabeth had a nice clear voice, which she purposely kept clear of vibrato, pop-style crooning or any other trained human inflections. She preferred that simplicity and she occasionally used it in her compositions. But now it hardly functioned. She couldn't even find the note and ended up sliding all over and giving up with a cough.

Somewhere in the distance, the magpie laughed.

She gave a sudden grating cry and jumped to her feet.

"Fuck you," she screamed out across the moors, aimed at everything out there that was making a noise. Then she stamped furiously on the small corpse in front of her. It was too far-gone to bleed much – but the soft crunch of it under her shoe made her grit her teeth and stamp again – and again.

"You bitch," she snarled at it. Then she staggered indoors again, treading slimy footprints, and slumped in front of her computer.

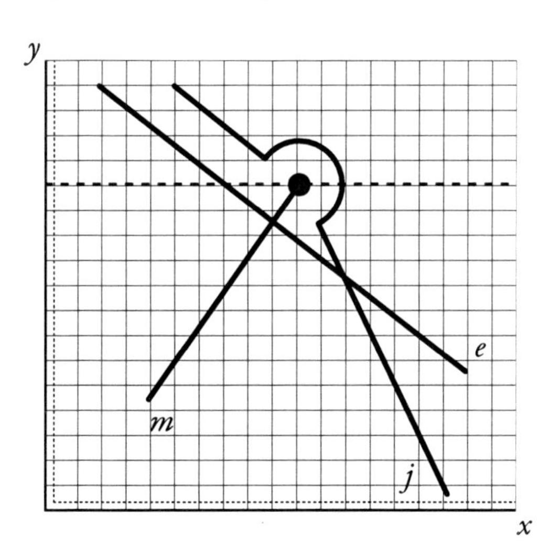

Why not? That's what it should have been . . .

Feather **is offline**

MissEyes says: Hello?

MissEyes says: Are you there?

MissEyes says: I don't know what to do. I don't know what's going on. I am getting scared of this – and I don't know why.

MissEyes says: :-(

A small parcel arrived the next day, which took her by surprise as she never received unexpected packages. It was compact and heavy – and opening it revealed a small bottle, filled with a thin dark brown, translucent liquid. It was filled so full that there wasn't even a bubble of air. Perhaps that was to make the packet silent. Or was she just being paranoid?

There was a torn slip of paper in the box as well.

> *Richard is a collector and very good at finding things – that's all. Remember, this is not magic. But it is a shock. If there are ghosts it will make them talk. If there aren't it will make them vanish.*
>
> *Even mathematical ones, I hope.*
>
> *Shocks can be good.*
>
> *Feather.*

She stared blankly at the bottle and shook it. It was label-less and logo-less. Just a simple clear glass bottle with an anonymous metal screw-top lid.

She opened it and sniffed, then recoiled at the strong scent of alcohol that punched her full in the nose. It was mixed with a sweet and herby smell that she couldn't recognize at all.

She stared in bewilderment, unsure what to think about this. The temptation was there to frown unhappily. Getting drunk wouldn't help and it was obscurely disappointing that Feather should think it would. She didn't even like alcohol much – it tended to interfere with her thought processes too much to be comfortable.

But she curiously took a sip anyway.

The shock was intense. She coughed as a wash of complex and very bitter-sweet flavours flared up in her mouth. Herbs she couldn't recognise, a sweet hint of honey and spice – and something almost like woodsmoke. Whatever it was, it was very strong. It had the punch of navy strength gin. She could feel it burning its way down her throat and seeding a warm glow inside her and she thumped her chest hard. Within just a few moments, she could feel a faint cloudy feeling behind her eyes – like the spinning of a gyroscope. And in her mouth the taste of the bitter herbs lingered.

Making a mental note to ask Feather what was in it, she closed the bottle with an uncertain sigh and pocketed it. The knife promptly gave her a prick on her leg to remind her of its existence and she paused, then tramped outside determinedly. With any luck she would never find her reason for carrying that thing.

Her bird table was now slimed with carrion and small bones, filling the air with an unpleasant sickly smell. The cat was in pieces now. The gruesome mess was visible from the road and, for the first time, she wondered whether she should feel embarrassed about this. Fortunately it was heading towards being unrecognisable fast. The body had been dismembered. All four legs were completely gone – somehow – and the rest was sinking into furry anonymity.

What would happen if the cat's owner had managed to spot it? That was not a nice thought, but the magpie seemed to like it – and if this was what the magpie wanted, then she was going to be happy.

Songbirds were singing noisily but she tried not to listen to them as she tramped to the bottom of her garden, across the road and onto the moors. She didn't want to know what music they were playing. The cool air hit hard and brittle, but that only served to highlight the fact that she was still glowing with warmth inside. That effect at least was quite pleasant, so she paused a moment to take another swig from the little bottle. The bitter blast it gave her was like a slap from a friend. Painful, but somehow invigorating and she hurried on with new energy.

A few minutes walking brought her back to the old familiar Wistman's Wood and, once inside and among the trees, she stopped and sat down on a mossy boulder, bracing herself against the cold wind and trying to relax and empty her head.

It seemed that her magpie had followed her though, for almost immediately she heard a familiar chattering call somewhere off in the bushes. Then she spotted a black and white flicker. She sighed miserably. Why couldn't everything communicate with each other? It would all make so much more sense then.

The magpie called again.

"Hi Miss Magpie," she called back quietly. "So sorry to hear about your loss – damn shame and all that. Lets get together over a drink one day and try some female bonding."

Damn Feather and damn thinking too much. The fact that Jacob was gone and no longer existed was final enough. If he had a ghost, then surely it was haunting the southern European mountains, not gentle wild Dartmoor.

Wouldn't it be rather nice if his ghost was still around – somewhere?

She wasn't sure, actually.

Then, completely unexpectedly, there came an answering magpie call, from a different direction – somewhere among the twisted trees nearby. It came almost like a blow and she felt every inch of her skin prickling in a huge swell of shock. Two? Back? How? But surely . . . She thought the words almost in a scream. The magpie in front of her was also startled and she responded with a furious calling, jumping from branch to branch, tail flicking furiously. But Elizabeth wasn't listening to her. Instead she jumped up and pushed through the bushes towards the source of the new call. There was a flash of black . . .

But instead of finding what she was looking for, she came face to face with a figure and stopped sharply, exchanging a startled glance.

"What the hell?" she stammered.

He looked bulky, both tall and fat, and completely unreal. He looked slightly grotesque in a tatty black open raincoat over a white shirt – and he held an instrument in his hand. It looked vaguely like a black recorder, but her blinking and confused eyes couldn't settle on any one detail for long enough to really see it. He gave her a brief shy smile underneath intensely burning eyes, then put the pipe to his lips – and to her amazement the magpie call rang out again. How was that possible?

The cloudiness behind her eyes had suddenly increased now, adding to the sense of unreality. Where were her familiar moors and trees now? The figure actually seemed to flicker and blur slightly in front of her, moving in and out of focus and visibility. Staring into those black eyes sent two bolts of electricity through her body to wallow in her stomach, but at the same time his expression seemed disconcertingly ordinary – almost embarrassed by her staring, if anything. He quietly slipped the instrument into his pocket and hopped backwards a step. Then a blast of pain hit her head, causing the woods to flash a vivid, improbable green at the edges, and the figure was swallowed up, vanishing in a black flash that trailed away among the trees.

Stunned quite beyond coherence in either mind or body by the encounter, she staggered to a rock and sat down, massaging her aching head. It was a few minutes before she could make herself move her legs and walk home.

Feather **is offline**

Elizabeth flopped out on her bed and buried her face in the pillow, trying to stop crying. Somewhere in the distance, that same long note sounded. Music? Some animal? Something else entirely? But memories of a worn black flute played by a black and white flautist floated in her mind and confounded everything now. She just picked up a smooth smoky quartz palmstone and turned it over and over in her hand. Anything to stop thinking.

The moon was shining fitfully in a patchwork of clouds and stars. Its pale light picked out the gleaming bones on the bird table – now here, then gone, then here again, then gone again. Aside from that occasional gleam, the night was at its full Dartmoor darkness. Barely a prick of light from the few other houses within view. An empty road. It was dark enough for the imagination to run wild. To imagine a moving figure in the rough land next to her garden. A shadow on the grass – large and flowing. A flutter as of wings. The sound of wet bones rattling against each other. The crunch of gristle. The sound of breathing.

Elizabeth lay in bed, eyes wide. She felt blank. It was hard to find any emotion now, here at this time of the night. Perhaps it didn't matter. Perhaps it was just the Magpie – accepting her food from her. Well – it was the least she could do.

Feed the birds . . .

Outside, the sounds were withdrawing. Bushes rustled heavily. Elizabeth sighed. The moon still came and went, but it showed nothing of any use. Then the call also came and went. It coiled through the dark and there were times when she wondered if it was all just inside her own head. Sometimes it transformed into a bird-like singing. Sometimes it was just those same long keening notes. Sometimes the magpie would chatter in the darkness.

Could nobody else hear this?

Was there anyone else to hear it, for that matter?

A thin, single line of noise – now here – now gone – now here again – now gone again – in the Dartmoor wind.

Part 2
Ringing the Carrion Bell

Corpses.

One day old: Greenish-blue spreading from the face and neck over the rest of the skin. Beginning to smell.

Three days old: Bloating and blistering. Fluids leak from all body openings.

Three weeks old: Flesh cracks and splits. Hair and nails falling out. Flesh sagging and disintegrating, becoming shapeless.

Elizabeth stared round her uneasily. Everywhere, as far as she could see along the low slopes of the moors, were dead people. It was nearly dark – evening dark – but not yet the total moorland darkness that she was becoming familiar with. It was light enough for her to see the procession of decay that was laid out in the wet grass around her with almost scientific precision. She stepped between them, counting up the days and watching the rot and disintegration setting in, corpse after corpse. What was the reason behind all this? They didn't look pained or massacred. This wasn't a picture of a war grave. They were just – dead.

Dead and increasingly dissoluted.

She tried to work out the smell that she was perceiving, which only increased and changed as she walked. But that was a lie surely? In this dream, whatever she could smell must be a fiction. What did a decaying human body smell like? She had no idea – but she was sure that any conceptions that she may have based on too-old chicken breasts or the smell of chop bones forgotten on her bird table would not be very real.

So smell was ruled out. How about touch? Would the touch be real? She reached out, then caught herself and drew her hand away quickly from the soft clammy flesh – but too late. It felt just like normal human skin would – if it was taut and ice cold and wet and slimy.

She rubbed her hand urgently on her trousers and stared determinedly at the horizon.

This was death. This was carrion. This was . . .

She sighed.

This didn't matter. These weren't people any more. Let the magpies feed. It was all you were good for when you were dead.

Besides, this progression wasn't helping her yet. She was still only a few weeks into it so far. She was in the wrong place. Jacob had been dead longer than that now, so she stepped onwards, treading carefully as the grass became ever damper and boggier. But now recognition was fading – everything was fading. It didn't take long for a face to become unrecognisable, but even so, something would linger for a while at least. But now it had been over a month. Now there was not much left here for her to see except bones. The remains lay there in a slimy anonymity that could only be cracked by the unwelcome prying of forensics. Flesh had simply sagged or trickled off them. Or been eaten. Large bones in a heap mixed with sticks and leaves. Tiny bones – out of the ear or toes – lost into the soil. It was all starting to look more like the earth – and in a way that was comforting. A release from identity. What use was identity after you were dead?

So this was it? Nothing much even for a Magpie to feed on now. With the logic of a dream, Elizabeth realised what that meant. Jacob had nothing left to bargain with. So where did that leave things? The grotesque image of Jacob feeding his bird with his own flesh was still vivid in her mind – but now it also seemed completely false. A magpie guide? A bargain cemented with your own carrion?

That pattern didn't work.

The concept of one of these strewn heaps coming back and wandering the moors to look for her, as he had in her earlier dream, seemed laughable, even with a magpie guide. That wasn't how it worked.

As if in answer, over the sopping field, the manic chattering call sounded. Elizabeth jerked round, coming face to face with a black and white figure. He gave her a blank look out of huge round black eyes, head on one side, then put his pipe to his lips and screeched again. Then pranced off, hopping agilely over the bodies. She stared after him dumbly. He even moved like a bird, with long, darting steps and sharp movements of his head. He poked about till he found something that still had a little flesh on it. Then he grabbed up a bone and chomped.

Elizabeth winced. This image of the Magpie really seemed to be living up to its superstitions. The bird of sorrow. The omen of death. But this wasn't a horror movie – in spite of the low mist, the sopping wet moorland grass and the increasing darkness. And Elizabeth was not superstitions. So please keep a hold of that cool reasoning, ok? This was just a carrion eater doing what it always does. She forced herself to keep calm as he deftly cracked the bone and sucked . . .

Just a cat on a bird table . . . just a magpie . . .

What did the horror movies know about death anyway?

It was hard though – because she suddenly seemed to see the face of Jacob everywhere. Every one of these corpses might have been . . .

And with that, the feeling that it all seemed pointless and patternless came in a crashing flood. Just a life that had come to an end. A road that ran off the edge of a cliff.

It was in the bone structure – the line of the chin, the shape of the jaw . . .

It could be.

"Jacob?" she managed aloud in a painful voice.

How was she to know? What did this mean?

She found herself shivering. She couldn't help it. She landed abruptly on her knees, which were instantly soaked with icy cold fluid. She drew a deep breath and almost choked, for the smell suddenly seemed much more real. Everything was real – and a horrible reality. But how does this work mathematically? Why should the magpie be here in this strange new form, while Jacob lay in a heap of bones? What the fuck were these patterns indicating? She was starting to feel desperate. All there seemed to be in this body-strewn marsh was a straightforward progression of facts, and one black and white piper.

The patterns had to mean something . . .

"Who are you?" she wailed, and the figure glanced at her bleakly.

Almost deliberately, Elizabeth woke herself up then, fingernails digging in her face, and stared blankly at the dawn-lit window, desperately trying to recapture the patterns that she could see.

Feather has signed in

MissEyes says: Ity doesn't make senser!!!!!!

Feather says: what?

MissEyes says: I mean . . . sorry – I am a bit confused. Hang on – brb . . .

MissEyes says:

Feather says: ok

Feather says: are you alright? I have just had a nip of that Salamander brandy – Richard told me to watch out for any urges to have sex with trees. But you sound as though you need something stronger. Did my bottle arrive?

MissEyes says: yeah – sorry. I mean it doesn't make sense what I have seen. What's happening. I don tg know if I'm haunted. of just going madx. What thed hell have yo9ou givem me? Is it a halluycinogen? Is it legal?

MissEyes says: I feel as though I am living in an Arthur Machen story . . .

Feather says: It's no hallucinogen . . . (I think)

Feather says: A what? Who?

MissEyes says: i juswt met the magpie – at last after alol this time. Here'shere.

Feather says: ?

MissEyes says: He's here.

MissEyes says: I mean . . . ?

MissEyes says: I don't know. I met some nthing onvthe moors . . .

MissEyes says: But it sounded like . . .

MissEyes says: I mean, when you think about it, it makes sence. I used to think that this strange stuff had something to do with Jacob. But Jacob is somewhere lost in the allps hes gone. A long wa away. I would have to go down there to find him. But the magpie was here It's the magpie thyat came back to me. . .

MissEyes says: It's the magpie that has completed the vertex

MissEyes says: or perhaps the two together in some way I fdont understand . . . The patterns could suggest it

MissEyes says: Aaahahhhh

MissEyes says: The patterns – the lines are . . .

MissEyes says: What the hell is t5yhat drink you sent?????????????? It went t5o my HEAD I THINK I ONLY HAD A FEW mouthfuls

MissEyes says: fuck

MissEyes says: Caps lock key sorry

MissEyes says: Brrr – Feather the corrupter.

MissEyes says: And that Inhstriument – cant sdound like that. It's not real!!!!!!!!!!!!!!! There is something gojng on.

Feather says: Elizabeth . . .

MissEyes says: You cant have a polyhedral vertex with just two lines. Nothing in this world is two dimensional. There must be more lines – shooting off from the flat plane of the familier into xsomething else. Some other plane. but I never imagined . . .

MissEyes says: What?

Feather says: :-S

MissEyes says: Whatg?

Feather says: I don't get this at all. Are you ok?

MissEyes says: What?

Feather says: You never explained what you were talking about - but why are you obsessed with patterns? Sure there are patterns - and sure there are sometimes not. Not in this way. Surely sometimes things just happen? No pattern or regularity in that sense. Is that such a strange concept?

Feather says: And also that a magpie is just a magpie.

MissEyes says: But it isnt any morte. A Magpie seems to have turtned intro somethikng else complete different. something that plays music and eats cats . . .

Feather says: ?

MissEyes says: That's not my doing - I am not making this up. It's just what I can see. i can't help what I can see. The patterns are real.

Feather says: So what do the patterns look like? Are you talking about how all creatures interrelate? How everything eats and kills something else in order to live, creating a great web? I can understand those patterns.

MissEyes says: :-(

MissEyes says: Just lines - and intersewcvftions

MissEyes says: sorry - intersections.

MissEyes says: that's all.

MissEyes says: but its klike a complex polyhedron. There is nothing random about it. things just grow and develop from other things in stellations and truncations - lines meet at vertices. Vertices are sliced off by more lines, but make more vertexes in the process. That's the important thing. And the lines HAVE to meet at these vertices, otherwisde nothing would function right. THE shape would be randiom and it wouldn't be solid and wouldn't be a real shape. And if it isn't a real dhape – it wouldn't be real at all.

MissEyes says: The world IS solid and real – therefore . . .

MissEyes says: I cant help it

MissEyes says: If you don't like the way my worl works – then by all means go and live your own way. I don't want to be evangelical

MissEyes says: Are you still there?

MissEyes says: Feather?

MissEyes says: I remember you. You were always the practical and pragmatic. That was great. But I don't think that is much use to me here and now.

MissEyes says: . . .

Feather says: Yes – still here. Sorry -I am feeling a bit drunk and was just looking up stellation etc on the internet . . .

Feather says: Well – I am drawing a blank with what you say. But that drink is powerful stuff. If this is real, talk to him then. That's what that drink is for. Richard calls it the ghost in the bottle. He doesn't know what's in it, but it's made by some English guy in London. So cant be too exotic. Not many people know about it though. I don't believe in ghosts – but I do believe in communication. I hope the communication make sense.

Feather says: I am off now – Richard must do something on his computer. Some mysterious thing that I cant imagine . . . Probably ordering a komodo dragon fillet or a bottle of snake wine with opium.

MissEyes says: I will try

Feather says: 👋

Great Stellated Dodecahedron.

Fourth Mainline Stellation of the Strombic Icositetrahedron.

19th Mainline Stellation of the Snub Dodecahedron.

Great Inverted Retrosnub Icosidodecahedron.

These were polyhedra. Polyhedral forms were beautiful, as well as mathematically perfect. Elegant interactions of regular shapes in regular ways, eventually building up the most complex objects you could imagine – in fact, far beyond what you could imagine. Vast stars of spires and pinnacles – vertices in fact – of meeting flat faces. But for all their sometime complexity, the formulas were too simple. They didn't express far enough down the road to the world out there. The stellation process especially. To stellate a solid form consisting of flat faces, you simply extend each face until it meets another extended face and so you formed a new solid form – perhaps star-shaped. Then you did it again. Eventually you could go no further without the faces shooting off to infinity – and that last solid form before infinity was the final stellation. The Great Stellation. But this was not how the world she was walking through worked. She sensed that there were wholly different worlds of regularity out there. Whole different meanings for the word regular, in fact. Things that went far beyond these simple geometrical constructs – far beyond triangles, squares and pentagrams. But somewhere, somehow, it was similar. The patterns of the world were not so different to the patterns that come together to form these polyhedral constructs.

Somewhere – somehow. Far beyond the simple world of what you could see. Far beyond anything you could ever mark out on a map.

This was Wistman's Wood again. Early afternoon. It was quiet and misty. Not even an isolated walker to be seen tramping the moors this time. She pressed into the centre of the small copse, clambering over steep mossy boulders and among the twisted trunks. Mushrooms, ferns and huge hanging treebeards keeping her company. The cold was only increasing and she shivered. There was a distinct temptation to turn to the bottle that was still in her jacket pocket. She remembered the warming effect of that drink and that was appealing. Alcohol didn't help logical thinking, she knew. Less still whatever was in this strange liqueur. But at the same time, it would be invigorating – so why not?

Finally she sat down on a soft rock – softer to her arse than any armchair – took out the bottle, opened it and drank a whole mouthful.

It was so strong her throat almost refused to swallow it, but it went down with a cough and a shiver. It really did taste of woodsmoke –

somewhere in there among the flavours. And it was certainly warming. For a few minutes she sat there without moving, enjoying the feeling, then she took another gulp, in spite of warning herself severely to ration it. It wasn't a large bottle.

This was Alice in Wonderland now – not Arthur Machen. And this wood was the place for it. It was better than any wonderland. This bottle was labelled 'Drink me' and she glanced about, wondering what would happen if she suddenly started shrinking. Anything seemed possible here. Then Wistman's Wood would become incredible. Moss and lichen stretching up like jungles and the myriad tiny mushrooms like pagodas. Dartmoor would become something out of a misty surrealist painting. And somewhere below this, there was a polyhedron beyond anything – waiting for her.

The strange thing was that everything was making more sense now. Magpies? Carrion-eating shadows? Marching processions of birds? Ghosts in the patterns? What of it? She decided that her reasoning made perfect sense at one level at least. Jacob wasn't here – at least not as such. If she wanted to find Jacob himself, she would have to travel down to where he was – to the mountains of Slovenia. But the connection was still there – the pattern was intact, in a glittering hot-wire across the surface of the world. That was proved by everything that was coiling round her on the moors. Every sound and every encounter.

No way was this polyhedron constrained by mere distance.

This polyhedron was beyond even the concept of distance.

She smiled and jumped to her feet, her head already starting to spin slightly.

"Helloooooooooooooo?" she called as loud as she could, singing it triumphantly in two tones – no idea who she was calling, but it felt good. Someone somewhere to answer some questions.

"Hellllllooooooooooooooooooooooooo. Come heeeeeeeeee-eeerrrrrrrrrrrr."

She gave a brittle laugh, wondering what she would do if anyone answered her. Perhaps she was sending out the wrong messages though, so she cupped her hands to her face and let fly with a cackling imitation of a magpie calling. It wasn't a very good imitation, but it felt good and she didn't care.

Then another mouthful of the liqueur went down, giving her a crescendo in the cloudiness behind her eyes and she sat down again heavily, then abruptly twisted over onto her front and draped herself over the rock, enjoying the softness of the moss. It was like hugging a soft furry animal and she wriggled against it happily. Hanging over this rock, arse-up, felt strangely good. Almost sexy, and she gave a sharp giggle. Maybe her arse offered more hope and sense in all this than her head did. That seemed very possible right now. Maybe her arse was more able to extrapolate this geometry than her head was. Perhaps this was something that went rather beyond thinking . . .

She remained hanging there, kicking her legs in the air, until a sound disturbed her and she flinched. Something black and white . . .

Feeling a blade of ice freeze through her stomach, she jumped up and squirmed round, staring in shock at the figure that had appeared among the bushes. For a moment her brain refused to process the images properly and she twanged in confusion. Near and far weren't as they should be. Someone leaned down over her sharply with beady black eyes and she shrank backwards. There was a flutter of feathers and a shift . . . then he just gave her that familiar uncertain smile and shook his raincoat.

She blinked furiously.

"Hi," he murmured shyly. "Was that you calling?" His voice was as quiet and retiring as the rest of him, very light and high-pitched. A tenor – or even a countertenor. She could still only blink, though. This figure still seemed to be trying to be two things at once. Bird and man fought for space, but his unexpectedly gentle, plump face regarded her with a curiously open and innocent look. She stared blankly – trying to see what was moving behind it. Something that stalked and leaned forward with big gleaming eyes. Every so often, it would flicker into view for a moment, making her prickle, then vanish again.

Her head was starting to ache.

"Are you ok?" he asked.

In his hand he still held the jet black instrument, casually, like a stick. Now she had the chance to look closer, she realised that it really was a recorder. An ordinary-looking treble in F. Its joints were ringed with white and the wood was dull and aged. Old and worn ebony. He followed her eyes to it, twitched it uncertainly and lifted it up. Put it to his lips. But even before the magpie chattering came again, the bird came back into view. The recorder seemed to have merged with his mouth to form a grotesque bird's beak. His eyes blacked over and his whole posture changed.

Then the bird screeched.

That was a jolt and she was up and had the knife out of her pocket and in her hand in one quick scramble. It was a movement based completely on instinct. Magpie or no magpie, she felt frightened almost to incoherence now.

However, the figure only flinched away. The young man looked startled but she had seen enough.

"Who are you and what are you doing here?" she demanded shakily. "Are you looking for me? Are you really?"

"Me? Who? Oh well – yes – I mean . . . I'm – I'm just . . ."

He put the instrument to his lips again and blew an eerie little phrase. He shrugged helplessly, staring at her in bewilderment.

She stared back at him in silence. For all his size, he didn't look very imposing. Instead he seemed to shrink and crouch as though trying to compensate for himself. His round, amiable face just looked ordinary and inoffensive, framed by long and rather unkempt hair. He even had a tatty black rucksack on his back. But as she stared, the flickering increased again, matched by a throb of pain in her head.

Was this real?

"Ok," he murmured. "It doesn't matter. Sorry – I will go."

She flinched.

"No you won't," she said. "You came here to find me – so now you have, then what?"

"Find you?" he stammered, stepping back a step. "Yes – well, I just wanted to . . ."

"Who the hell are you?" she whispered. "Or should that be what are you?" She gave a shrill laugh.

"I'm just the Recorder Player," he said with an embarrassed smile.

Without warning, he put his pipe to his lips again and blew a screeching note. Elizabeth clutched at her head in pain at the sound and he blurred violently again, the whole woodland flashing in sudden vivid colour. His eyes glittered at her and he grinned – a thin grin, head lowered.

What was going on here?

And the wind was so cold.

Drink me . . .

Shakily she took out the bottle and drank another sip. The Recorder Player watched her curiously for a moment, then he swung away and hurried off through the twisted trees. His strides were long and stalking for all his size, and his black raincoat fluttered around him like wings. Elizabeth stared after him in bewildered panic. She was losing something important here. Something was escaping. Why the hell had she pulled out the knife?

"Wait," she called. "Don't go.

He ignored her and continued pacing off towards the edge of the copse.

"Fuck it," she shrieked, slashing the knife through the air. "Come back and talk to me."

He paused, put his recorder to his lips again and played a little melody. It was melody, not bird song, but that didn't make her feel any better. It was somehow mocking and not quite in any familiar key or mode. She had been trained in all the complexities of classical and modern composition, but this had jagged harmonic edges and a frosty brittleness that was totally new. Then he sheared it quickly into the familiar sneering sound of the magpie chatter again and she winced. He gave her a last bleak look before turning away and heading off through the trees, the mist quickly blurring him into a shadow.

How did he do it? She still couldn't see how a recorder could produce a noise like that. She shivered at the cold and stared after him. Follow? Her head was still cloudy from the liqueur – the gyroscope was still spinning – and she cursed herself and shoved the bottle furiously back into her pocket. What sort of time was this to get drunk? Grimly, she pushed herself into motion and stepped after him, trying to catch him up.

She pressed onwards in an unsteady walking-speed chase, following him through to the further edge of the wood and out into a new landscape. Here was a land of low hills rising up from the tiny stream that was the Dart – occasional stone walls and wet patches of marsh getting in the way. He tramped on ahead, glancing back occasionally, but keeping carefully out of reach – and looking strangely ragged and shapeless now in the misty air. He looked like nothing more than a moving bundle of cloth and she was no longer quite sure what was him and what was his coat and rucksack. He was also breathing heavily, she realised. He didn't seem very fit. His face was already damp with perspiration and his step looked painful. But she was not in much better shape herself. Her legs felt watery and uncertain and flashes of light still seemed to be discharging occasionally at the edge of her vision. It was as though she was dreaming again and it almost seemed to her as though the drumming sound was again sounding from somewhere, but faster this time. Every three heartbeats – or, disorientingly, it would occasionally come every four. And even though there were usually few birds out here in the wilds, she could still hear a high-pitched droning in the air marching her onwards.

After a good many minutes of tramping, and without being able to narrow the distance between them much, human traces were fading from the land. This was a wilder part of the moor than anything she was used to, but how was that possible? How long had they been walking? There were no paths here now, anyway. They were just following the banks of the trickling Dart upwards and the hills around them were getting lower and lower, the landscape flattening out more and more into the high moorland plateau. The ground by the stream was very wet now as well and the Dart was nothing more than a small, shallow slice littered with rocks that cut through the marsh that birthed it. The ground squelched and sucked at her feet, but sometimes there would be something else. Sometimes she would hit a patch of rippling turf – something she had heard walkers talk about but had never actually experienced before. That was an area of ground where a thick and solid mat of grass and sedge floated on top of something soft – so that when she stepped onto it, it would ripple like a waterbed below her. In her present state of dizziness she just sailed straight over these, oblivious to any thought of falling through or of what might be below.

The patterns of the world seemed to be coming back now. She was as sure as she could be that the land they were walking on was formed into vast concentric circles of regular shapes, as though surrounding a polyhedron vertex. Circles that literally spanned the moors like a surreal rippling splash in the ground. Every hill seemed to have its place on these circles and every valley was leading towards some new shape.

Here and there, large chunks of the grey, smooth Dartmoor granite lay in the marsh and these also marked out patterns. They accentuated the highest and lowest points – and perhaps they also marked lesser vertices. The secondary vertices of the giant polyhedron that underlay everything here. And as such, they must also be regular, though that regularity was not visible to her yet. It was the same regularity as that of the drum beat – though as it became clearer it was starting to sound more like a bell – very large and very deep. Deeper than any church bell or orchestral percussion. The bell made her think of death. It was tolling as a summons for all the dead things to come to this spot and find what other lines they met. All the corpses in her dream. A march of carrion to one central point.

She stared around her dizzily, feeling almost sick with the intensity of it all. But at the same time she was also feeling unusually clear and precise. Every sight and sensation was highlighted and known and memorised. The black figure, keeping carefully a little distance ahead. The shapes passing them and converging. The cold wind. Very cold.

Drink me . . .

Occasionally a bird would burst from the grass and streak away in a trail of black. Their harsh calling ringing and echoing round the faces in a rhythm that melded with the tolling and twisted her with a knot of discomfort. The light was fading slowly. The sun was low in the sky on their left, lighting up the clouds there in a white flare. It shed quiet colours across the ground – hints of blue and purple. Then flashes and streaks of gold and red that flickered across the pattern like electricity.

Heading north.

And the processional continued.

Ringing the carrion bell.

The Recorder Player had his pipe at his lips now and was blowing huge long notes on it that seemed to defy breathing. His raincoat was open and it fluttered in the wind revealing the white shirt beneath. The flaps of glossy black fabric really did look like wings. The magpie was coming to the fore more and more now in an increasingly unstable blend of bird and man. The magpie must be far too big to fly though, she thought. So big in fact that he looked faintly absurd and suddenly she found herself laughing. This was what he had become? A Magpie Man? It was crazy. It made no sense. The reason was beyond her. But it was somehow beautiful as well.

Could there be anything of Jacob in there after all? Why else bring a man's figure into this?

He glanced back at her suspiciously at that laugh, then finally paused, waiting for her to catch up.

"Why are you following me?" he demanded, when she staggered up.

She grabbed his arm, leaning heavily, and instantly there was a flutter. More birds erupted from the marsh all around her and she nearly collapsed. Suddenly they were everywhere, filling the sky with movement and making her uncertain which way was up. The recorder player, the biggest bird of them all, spread his wings in response and gave them an experimental flap. He gave her a quick open-mouth grin, which changed his face completely. She realised that his teeth were trailing with strands of slimy meat, and even some wet brown tortoiseshell fur.

"I'm going," he cried.

She took a hesitant step, but her legs were suddenly losing all control.

"Please no," she wailed. "I can't walk. We have to get on. Somewhere these lines come together . . ."

She took another step, but found herself standing on rippling turf again. It was too much. The whole moorland almost seemed to turn upside-down and she flung up her arms, gravity swinging like a compass needle. She looked down without enthusiasm at the sopping wet marsh vegetation she was about to fall into, but then she was caught. A claw had wrapped round her as casually and easily as though she was another of his musical instruments.

"We have to get on," she repeated, reeling. "We have to find the centre of this. Look at it all . . ."

She leaned against him dizzily, clutching and breathing rapidly. It was slowly getting through to her senses that something wasn't right. Something was hurting her. She could smell a strong rotten smell about him as well. Carrion. But of course, when that is what you eat . . .

She made a small noise of questioning, bewilderment and impatience. Trying to indicate what should have been obvious – that they should move on with all speed. But he just stood staring down at her analytically, and she felt a sudden wash of discomfort. How safe was this?

Of course – magpies were hunters as well as carrion eaters.

It was the first time that had occurred to her and again she felt that blade of ice inside her stomach. Perhaps she had this all wrong. He was a big figure – with a cold and unfriendly gaze. A hungry gleam.

"Hey," she managed. An image flashed through her mind of herself imitating her dream – left in a jumbled pile in the wet grass and looking too much like her own bird table for comfort. She made a choking sound that was supposed to be of protest – but it came out meaningless. She tried to pull away, but her legs weren't functioning.

It hurt . . .

Yes. She wasn't so much being supported, as held. The magpie adjusted his grip and clutched her painfully, claws digging into her skin, reaching from shoulder to arse with a pain that shone like burning manganese.

Where was her knife now?

"You followed me," he cried harshly. "I don't like company."

He flung her away. Literally. Tossing her through the air like a cloth. Elizabeth choked and wailed as she flew, then crashed face first into prickly sedges and slid into the stream. The water of the Dart was freezing cold, and for a moment she was horribly aware of that – of the cold round stones under her, then she floundered over and stared up.

The magpie came down on her in a huge black pounce, hitting her and the water with an impact that sent spray over a wide area. She screamed and bubbled in shock, going under again. Rocks one side – claws the other. And she realised that she was helpless. She couldn't even begin to get out of this.

Somewhere in the distance, the processional still sounded, but it seemed to be retreating. It was leaving her behind. The thought of that, and the feel of her heartbeat getting out of synch with it all as it raced in panic was agonising. The sound was nothing more than a mocking murmur now in the distant wind. The magpie's beak tore at her, reducing her clothes and skin to shreds in a moment. She struggled and splashed, but could no more do anything than a spider could in a normal size bird's beak. She stared dumbly at the river that surrounded her – at the streams of red that now drifted through it. Dumbly imagining her blood mixing with the water of the Dart and being carried – even down off the moors eventually, through Totnes and finally to Dartmouth. But then the magpie picked her up by the head and shook her violently, flapping her around like a rag. Blood and water sprayed everywhere and he tossed her away again into the grass, where she landed in a cracking of bones, her neck lolling at a crazy angle. All she could do now was stare up at the cold grey sky, paralysed and unmoving as the magpie came stalking over.

"I don't like company," he repeated, leaning over her.

He darted down and obliterated her face, turning her world black and sightless, blanking the patterns forever. And then the feel of herself losing flesh . . .

"Jacob?" she murmured miserably. "Where are you?"

Life? What was life? Sentience? Awareness? Who knows. In those terms, you are alive if you know you are. The converse was probably not true – but this at least seemed reliable. She felt too close to a vertex of the polyhedron – but not quite there yet. She still sat at the meeting of just two faces, the ridge of them sharp and precise under her arse.

The realisation came slowly, and she stirred with reluctance – not looking forward to what it would feel like to be awake. There was something very big waiting for her there, she could feel it. Much nicer to just lie here forever.

She had to open her eyes in the end though. The cold was pricking at her mercilessly. Evening was closing in properly now, she realised, but she could still see and she stared round dazedly, trying to focus into the growing dusk. She was lying in the ruins of an old medieval tinners hut, she realised – just a rough square of rocks almost lost in the grass. The ground was still very wet, but at least there was almost no mud in this marshy ground. Her head was aching painfully. The cold here was beyond living. Perhaps a drink of liqueur would warm her. She had to be warm.

But the bottle was no longer in her pocket.

Not a surprise, really.

The Recorder Player was sitting hunched a few metres away looking bleak and grim, his backpack on the ground beside him. She stared at him feeling a prickle of horror for a moment, but then she realised that the magpie part of him was not in evidence now. Except possibly in the presence of an old carcass of what must have been a sheep lying nearby. Just messy bones strewn about and a sprinkling of white fluff. She glanced down at herself then, still feeling the total bodily destruction that was the last thing she could remember. But it seemed that, while her clothes were in tatters, her body underneath them was still mostly undamaged. Bloody in places, but intact

Where on earth were they? The marsh was featureless and unchanging wherever she looked. Only the trickle of the stream gave her any hint of a connection to the outside.

She gave a long groan and he glanced round. There was blood on his face as well – a long and painful looking scratch.

"What happened?" she managed through a mouth that felt full of glue.

"I don't know," he said grimly. "I don't care." He paused and glanced at her. "I should have left you here."

She stared at him miserably and sat up.

"I dreamed . . ." she broke off with a shiver and a terrified laugh, then she swallowed heavily. "What happened? What's going on?"

"Why did you have to follow me out here?" he muttered grimly.

"I only wanted to find out what was going on," she cried. "Why is all this happening? Who are you?"

"What did you want to find out?" he said.

"You're the magpie," she stammered, hauling herself to her feet. You . . . came . . ."

"What? Well – yes – no – but . . ."

"Fuck it," she groaned. "Stop messing me around and tell me who you are," she cried. "Why are you here?"

"No reason," he said coldly. "I like the moors. It's lonely. Plenty to eat. So I came here."

The world flickered red at the corners of her eyes and the Recorder Player stood up abruptly.

"What are you on?" he cried suddenly. "Are you ill? I am a simple man. I am not a bird." He spread his hands angrily. "Birds are just birds for fuck's sake," he cried. "I play their music – but that doesn't mean I can talk to them. Doesn't make me one."

She scrambled up onto her knees and stared at him, trembling. The Recorder Player suddenly gave a shrill laugh, put his instrument to his lips and blew the magpie chatter at her again.

"Come on," he said. "Make music. That's much nicer than all this. Come on – you can. I have heard you."

"Heard me?" She drew a deep breath.

"Yes – I heard you playing I think. In that house. I liked it. That's why I was looking out for you."

"But that was ages ago . . ."

Her tongue shut down. Ages ago, she wanted to say. Before Jacob was even dead. Before this whole business had even started.

She stared at him blankly, feeling a throb of pain in her head. Did this figure really have nothing whatever to do with Jacob, magpies or anything else? Where did that leave her?

He grinned again and in the fading light she saw that his teeth were stained red. She flinched, shaking her aching head.

"How long have you been here, then? Where's my brother?"

He sat down again, his back to her.

"I don't know what you are talking about," he said blankly and dully. "I'm just a recorder player. Sometimes people tip me for it. Sometimes they don't. Not out here, certainly. But there's always enough food to live on if you know where to look."

Elizabeth didn't know what to say. The Recorder Player stared at her a moment, then turned away and put his instrument to his lips, playing a few seconds of soft melody. It was not magpie music – just a curiously sweet little passage that coiled all over the instrument's range like a worm.

She watched him. He wasn't flickering any more. He just looked like solid flesh. Just like a rather tatty young man in a long coat.

"I don't like talking," he said wearily. "I am not good at talking. I have no practice at it. That's why I came out here. I am a better player than talker." He smiled. "You called me a magpie? Perhaps I am more . . . like . . . that . . . perhaps I have to be."

"You are the magpie," she insisted, desperately.

He sighed and shrugged.

"I . . . don't understand," she muttered, a tear trickling down her cheek.

Elizabeth sat down abruptly in the coarse grass again, heedless of the wet. She had felt so close to something earlier, but now the feeling of patterns springing apart and unravelling inside her was almost a physical pain and she shut her eyes, trying to empty her head. Was this all really something she had spun completely inside herself? Disappointment tasted heavy in her mouth, but she wrestled with that. She must not slip. Coldness was everything. Everything is based on what you can see and what you can extrapolate from that. So when new data emerges – new theories are written. It's that simple.

"Hey," he murmured uneasily. "You are – a nice . . . musician. You shouldn't be sad."

He reached for his pack and opened it. From it he took something that looked familiar, though she gazed at it as though she had never seen it before.

"A harp?" she stammered, marvelling.

He nodded. It was a tiny harp, not more than one and a half feet long, and it looked worn and weather-beaten. Not like her own pristine and polished 34 string celtic harp at home. But the sound of it, when he plucked it, was sweet and rich.

"Let's both be Magpies," he said eagerly, handing it to her.

"But I – I can't . . ."

"Smell the flowers – don't try to talk to them," he said unexpectedly and with a sudden smile.

The Recorder Player screeched again twice, then, without waiting for her any longer, started to play. It was music unlike anything she had previously heard from him. He sheared the sound of the magpie chatter into a musical phrase – short, jagged and atonal. There seemed to be more than one note happening at once in that sound. It was harsh but it rang through this desolate space like a trumpet. Then he launched into a stream of sound that made her eyes widen. It was still a little like bird song, but now it had more of a musical structure – almost as if he was relishing having a human audience again. Even hints of melody in there

– and it went on and on and on with no form to indicate a beginning or an end. How anyone could make a recorder sound like that was totally beyond her understanding.

She plucked at the A string uncertainly. It sounded very small and high and feeble out here – but even so, something about it sent an unexpected shiver down her spine. The Recorder Player followed with a flurrying phrase – a quick reprise of the magpie sound, then he was off again. She plucked the string again. It may have been quiet – but this time the sound rang through her like an echo of a huge bell, and her eyes widened. Then again – and again. She tried adding a second note – hardly noticing that she had found the tritone again. But the sound came with a violent familiarity.

The Recorder Player gave a small, breathless grin and the music matched her notes – slowing and melding with it, and then they were marching again. That same march. As slow as a march of stones. The recorder fluttered overhead with birdsong and piped her onwards with droning glissandi, but she just continued tolling that chord over and over, high and clear. This was enough. Who needed more than that? Each ringing of the note was completely unique. Each note seemed like an entire symphony of sound. But it was a pattern – a perfect pattern. An echo of the polyhedron beneath them – the lines and angles and intersections that surrounded them. The message it conveyed was simple. So simple that it was almost painful. So simple that it went far beyond words.

She was crying now – but that didn't cause the music to crumple. At last the recorder faded out, but she just carried on ringing that bell while he sat staring at her, looking almost rapt. Then it ended abruptly as she collapsed again. She stopped uncertainly for a moment, then keeled over into the grass on her face and lay there without moving, staring blankly. She was dimly aware of the Recorder Player hastily turning her over onto her back, dabbing her face dry and rescuing his harp.

Then there was just shapes.

* * *

At last Elizabeth awoke.

The first thing she noticed was that she was freezing cold and very wet. Looking around she added a few more facts. She was naked, and she was in her own bedroom, sprawled out on top of the bed. And she was hurting all over. She felt that her entire body was one large bruise. Every muscle complaining – every joint aching. Her skin felt prickly and she glanced down at herself and flinched. She was covered with bits of grass and there was a liberal sprinkling of it on the floor as well. They were clinging to her, mostly to water, but her skin was also smeared red in a few places from cuts and grazes. Her hands and finger-nails were messed with it. Streaks ran up her arms and there were patches on her chest. Her face also felt wet and sticky and there was an unpleasant taste in her mouth. Her clothes were on the floor nearby – still wet and in tatters.

Someone had stripped her and put her to bed.

A well-chewed bone sat on the quilt beside her – looked like a chicken bone. She looked at that for a moment. There were more bones on the floor. There was a strange smell in the air as well, which she eventually recognised as a mix of human body smell – straight from her own crotch and armpit – and a hint of rotting flesh. Carrion.

Dimly she was aware that there was a lot of thinking to be done in the near future. But for now her brain was hardly responding. She hauled herself off the bed and through into the bathroom. She scrambled into the bath, turning the hot tap on as hard as it would go and gasping as the scalding water crept and sprayed over her. It was nice to wash that smell away – almost as much as the cold. Fragments of grass lifted off her and matted the surface of the water. She lay back with a sigh, idly tapping a complicated rhythm on the side of the bath – a rhythm that vanished as soon as she tried to listen to what she was doing. In her head, the sound of that bell was still ringing though – and she had to sing it to herself – A and E*b*. The two notes still sat together uneasily, almost without harmony, but somehow it didn't jar as much now. Somehow it was almost comforting. It was her music now – and music reminded her that there were still patterns in the world. And that geometrical and polyhedral structures were still valid.

She staggered out of the bath and dripped back through to her bedroom/workroom. She glanced nervously, first at her computer, then at her harp, but in the end, she touched neither. She settled on the bed by the window and peered out. Gazed down, almost puzzled, at the bones strewn on the bird table and the surrounding grass.

Coincidence?

What was it Feather had said?

If there are ghosts it will make them talk. If there aren't it will make them vanish.

What the hell did that mean here?

She finally looked away from the bird table and out across the moors, taking in that wide and luxurious view. It was a big and open expanse filled with an eerie bleakness and anything seemed possible there.

The patterns still existed.

Somewhere and somehow, this polyhedron was complete.

Her head felt less empty than ever now. She gave a sigh and lay down on her bed again, staring at the wall.

Five minutes later, a few tears trailed down her cheeks.

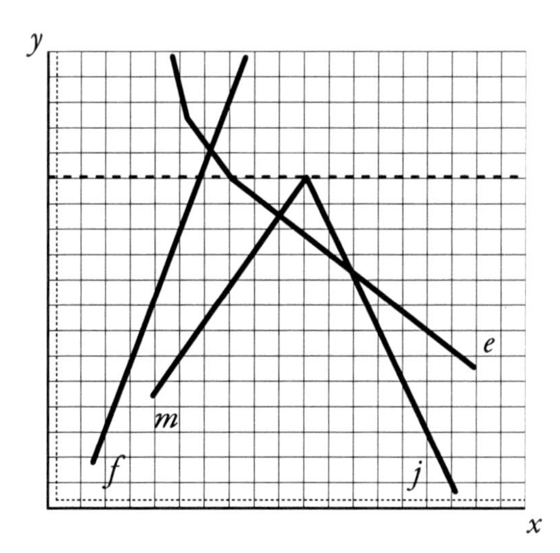

Feather is offline

MissEyes says: Hi Feather. I don't know when on earth you will next check online – but hopefully when you do, this will be waiting for you.

MissEyes says: Just wanted to say hi. And thanks for that weirtd drink. Whatever it was.

MissEyes says: Oh – and I have a new cd out soon. Well you can see it on my website. I will call it White Dartmoor – or possibly Ringing the Carrion Bell. I'm not sure. It's not quite like anything I have done before so I hope it wont upset people. It's based partly on the tritone – remember I was talking about it?

MissEyes says: I doubt it will make me much money – but I would guess it will be enough for a cheap plane ticket and a hotel. I am thinking of travelling as soon as I can manage it.

MissEyes says: Maybe out to Slovenia – you know.

MissEyes says: Mountains to climb . . .

MissEyes says: I like planes. They travel in streight lines.

MissEyes says: :-)

MissEyes says: Perhaps you can visit me out there. It's nice to have company when travelling.

MissEyes says: See you!

The Book of Tides

On this lonely Scottish beach, it was rare to see people of any kind and those few who did pass by were usually heavily loaded walker-type wanderers tramping through the hills – a certain breed of people distilled by the distance from anywhere populated. But now the ragged girl had been sitting there for three days and when he finally approached her, he realised that she looked different somehow. A different species of human. She seemed too lightly dressed for long walks in the wilderness.

He approached her, realising that he was treading softly though he wasn't sure why. She hadn't moved much since she had arrived – always just sitting or lying there in the sand looking dejected. She was curled up now in a tight human comma and she gave him no response as he approached, so he put down his bag and knelt beside her. She looked young – scarily younger than he was. Was she even alive? he wondered. She wasn't moving and, now that he was up close, he realised that her face was terribly pale – the sort of paleness that almost looks transparent and makes any skin blemish show up like a wound. This thing was never living, surely, he thought. She was an empty husk, the wind whipping sand over her and playing with her hair. He shuddered at the implications of a death on his doorstep. People would come – wanting to talk to him. The police would have to clear the mess up and his isolation would be shattered.

Maybe he could at least haul her down below high tide level or something, for the strong currents here to take away somewhere else.

He remained looking at her for a long time without reaching any conclusions and he realised that he was going to have to touch her instead – to see if there was any ghost of warmth or pulse in her flesh. As his fingers touched her neck, he realised that her skin was cold and wet – seemed as cold as the sand in which she lay. And he sighed.

But then she gave a sudden twitch and he flinched away, aware of two eyes staring at him. He felt a wash of panic and the immediate reaction was to leave right then. Just jump up and walk away. He had solved the riddle, after all – she was a living person. What more interest was there? But he hesitated, his brain ticking over.

“Ok,” he said reluctantly after a long pause, in which she just stared at him in motionless silence. “I had better take you home, hadn’t I? You – you need to be warm? Right?”

She made no sound.

“Um . . .”

She blinked.

He didn’t want to touch her again but there was no alternative. As though trying to work out how best to pick up something very exotic and unpredictable, he took her shoulder and gently shoved her into a sitting position. Her eyes were staring a question at him, he realised, which he didn’t know how to answer – so instead he just concentrated on what he was doing. He got an arm under her legs and the other round her back, then lifted her up bodily, dimly aware of her hand fastening onto his jacket. She looked lighter than she was and the reality of her weight surprised him. But even so, he was easily strong enough to get her up in the air and her arms went round his neck like an exhausted child. Up close, he could smell the reek of sea and the human body on her together – brine and cold sweat. It was a puzzling smell coming from someone unfamiliar.

Slowly he made his way towards his home, occasionally pausing to shift her weight and trying to ignore his racing thoughts, which chattered in panic at what he was doing. Trying to convince him that he should be far away from all this. His home was a lonely looking old building set a few metres above the sea. It sat there slightly surreally within a small walled off area, surrounded by wild brown hillside. It looked like a discarded toy that someone had thrown there, a simple square brick of a structure with a few outbuildings and a small boathouse down on the beach. There was no road to it as such, just a rough rutted track leading away inland. There was not even a car waiting in the drive. The only means of transport here were a battered old bicycle and his small boat, shut carefully away from the weather. The house really did look as though it had no right to be there. A few rather stunted trees kept him company, but most of this land was bare.

Even from a distance though, the strange forest of poles that surrounded it stood out. It was a forest of elegantly twisted driftwood and spars, raised upright and set in the ground, then festooned with oddments that the sea had cast up. Each one like a surreal tree. Choice artworks from the various tides he had read and recorded suspended there as mementoes – all given a uniform aesthetic by the processes of the sea. It was a strange patch of art in the wilderness that few people ever even saw.

Getting the door open and her through it was challenging but he managed it eventually and then she was sliding from his grasp onto the sofa in his impossibly cluttered front room. Her eyes were closed again now and he realised that she had begun to shiver. She hadn't been before, he registered. Her flesh still felt far too cold to be living. He stared down at her, his mind turning like clockwork, trying to compute all the things he would need to do now. And in which order. Kettle. Coal. Hot soup. Kindling. Drink. Newspaper for the fire. Perhaps she would want to get out of those freezing clothes. And if so, into what? If she showed any sign of moving at all, that is. He bent to the grate, hastily and clumsily shovelling the ashes out and rebuilding the fire. Balled up newspaper was shoved in there, followed by a scattering of kindling, and he lit it quickly. Then he just came to a confused stop, and continued staring at her as though, for all her stillness, she was putting on a performance for him.

As the fire began to take hold and radiate, she finally began to open up to it. Her shivering faded a little and she stretched out her hands towards it and gave a huge sigh.

"Is there anything I can get you?" he asked.

She shook her head.

"No – thank you," she managed in a low voice. "If I may – I will just go to sleep for a bit and warm up. This fire is amazing."

And that was her first verbal communication, her voice so quiet it was almost a whisper, yet light and clear.

"Of course," he whispered. "I won't be – I I mean, I will be here . . . if you . . . if you need anything . . ."

But she had already closed her eyes.

Looking at her, he still couldn't shake off the feeling that he was looking at a corpse. Now she was on his sofa, he could see her chest rising and falling, but her pale skin and lank hair still looked dead. However, a few minutes later, she was actually snoring quietly.

Outside, the day was progressing and he suddenly remembered the bag he had left on the beach. He gave a low laugh, realising just how much this unexpected visitor had thrown him into confusion. He hurried urgently outside again to fetch it, then settled down, idly going through the stacks of material it contained.

- Intact light bulb – clear glass – how gentle the sea could be if it chose
- A wooden ruler.
- A length of steel cable, snapped and with the strands trailing viciously at the end.
- Swimsuit bottom with a thread tied roughly to the waistband – that was a mystery.
- A battered old floppy disk.
- A fragment of some kind of dial containing a circle of measuring increments on a weathered metal face.
- A sodden pencil.
- A bird skull.
- A necklace of shell fragments, almost intact though with a few missing pieces. Taken from the sea. Constructed. Then back into the sea. And now washed up again for him.
- A piece of bright purple cloth – thin silk – maybe from a head scarf.

He laid them all out on the table and examined them, one by one. He tested the strength and flexibility of the metal cable, which was immense, then fingered the swimsuit thoughtfully, a frown on his face. Something about this went far beyond its simple appearance, he could tell that much. It was iridescent blue and small. Whoever had worn it had been quite willowy. It was also skimpy, just thin bands of material that would have shown a fair amount of arse. It was just a simple bikini bottom. But with a long chord attached to the waist in a neat knot and ending with a frayed twist.

Finally, he put it to his face, not sniffing it for that would have been little use after its time in the sea, but instead feeling it. Trying to read it.

And he winced and put it down sharply, shaking his head. It wasn't a violent pain he felt or a panicked pain, but a leaden one. A pain that clouded inside him like a cold mist. And he knew what that meant.

At last he crossed the room, sat down at his ancient looking beige computer and began to write.

> *The girl is in the water. She swims gently. The water glows faintly with phosphorescence. Behind her trails a thread and what she has tied to it. People like to judge in life and people like to judge in death. People said of her afterwards that she was selfish. Her mother never realised that she was a poet. Secret texts. Loneliness and helplessness. You can't change the world around you. Feelings of guilt and cowardice. The razor tied to her swimsuit. She stared up at the moon and stars and the distant lights of the shore with nothing clouding her eyes now. The night is beautiful. Warm air. Water that flickered faintly with phosphorescence. The falling tide. Floating gently on her back. Cuts wrists in a T shape. The first good, the second less so as her wounded hand trembled.*
>
> *What force lies behind this event?*

He sat back with a deep sigh, then glanced at his visitor again. He was not used to having someone with him when he worked but she was totally dead to the world on the sofa, mouth open, one leg flopped out onto the floor, still snoring gently. There was something unexpectedly cute and affecting about that snore that made him pause and stare at her with a small frown. Under the influence of the fire, her skin was already flushing and looking healthier and, under the ruined clothes and seaweed-like hair, she had a distinct sharp-edged beauty, which he couldn't help registering.

But even as he stared at her, she seemed to feel him for she shifted abruptly and opened her eyes.

"How are you feeling?" he asked awkwardly.

"Better . . . thank you," she said, her voice slightly less hollow than before. She sat up with an effort, holding her head, and turned towards the fire eagerly.

"So, who are you?" he asked at last.

"I am Feather," she said.

"Just Feather?"

She nodded and he accepted it with a smile.

"I didn't expect this," she said at last, gesturing vaguely at the window. "I'm not used to such wilderness. There's nothing to eat out here, except for a bit of shellfish. And it is all so exposed. I'm not surprised no one lives here."

The fire was at its hottest now – the coals a heap of glowing orange, and she stretched out her feet towards it luxuriantly.

"Yeah," he said. "Not many do. There are . . . well, it's a long way to anywhere from here. Where were you trying to get to?"

She shrugged, with a faint ironic grin. "I wanted wilderness," she said. "But I didn't expect it to be quite so inhospitable. Believe it or not I was in London before this."

"Right," he said. Words felt like alien things in his mouth and he struggled to think what to say next. But she spoke first.

"Do you mind if I take these clothes off? They stink."

"Of course not," he said. "I have a robe you can use. And – and I will get some dinner ready maybe?" A look of hunger came to her face. "What do you – like to eat?" he asked and she gave him a crooked smile over her shoulder.

"Anything – seriously. If it won't kill me or make me see green goblins then it is fine." She sighed. "And at the moment I might even take the goblins."

In spite of himself, he found himself grinning shyly. She leaned down and fumbled for her shoelaces.

"I am not sure I ought to do this near a naked flame," she murmured and he was surprised to see a flash of real humour on her face. "There might be some sort of explosion . . ."

"I'm sorry?"

"Been wearing these for rather a long time," she said, tugging off a shoe.

He caught a faint hint of the smell of it and she gave an awkward smile.

"Um," she murmured, "I await your instructions."

"Yeah," he murmured. "Just dump it all straight in the washing machine in the kitchen if you want – or rather, I will. Leave them here. I mean . . . and I will . . . do them . . . for you."

She nodded and kicked off her other shoe, followed by her socks. Then she began undoing her trouser belt and he hastily exited the room, vaguely aware of her dry glance following him.

"I sense things going on here," she said.

He quickly swallowed another mouthful of their simple dinner.

"I'm sorry?"

"You are a collector?"

"Sort of, yes," he muttered. "I'm a . . ."

He hesitated, then gave her a stubborn look.

"I'm a writer."

"So what do you write? Do you tell stories?"

He shrugged awkwardly. "I suppose."

He felt increasingly uncomfortable though. It was hard to answer this kind of question – partly because nobody had ever asked it before but also because it meant actually defining it – and defining things could sometimes be a sure way of killing them. He waved vaguely around at the room and the vast array of odds and ends it contained.

"Those," he said. "Every tide. Rubbish, I suppose. But if you look hard enough, you can read rubbish as clearly as any great literature. And . . . it all has stories to tell if you can find them."

He sighed uncomfortably. But Feather was staring at him curiously – a gleam of interest in her eyes. Finally she gave a small nod. "You tell the stories of the sea," she murmured, as though there was nothing strange about that.

"Of the tides," he said. "Of all the tides. Two stories every day."

"Wow," she murmured, staring round at the piles of materials. He followed her eyes, trying to read her expression. Feeling the prickling sensation you get when something familiar is being examined by someone else, leaving you with an unexpected sense of the alien.

"Every tide has a story to tell," he murmured at last. "Stories from somewhere, somebody. I just write them down."

"From the tidal debris?" she asked, wondering. He nodded and she continued examining with her eyes the seemingly endless array of rubbish that the sea had cast up. Finally she returned her attention to him. "And what about me?" she said with another flicker of that wry humour. "Am I now a part of this . . . rubbish?"

She sat back from her empty plate and he gave her a curious look. That aspect of things hadn't occurred to him.

"You picked me up on the beach after all," she said, grinning quietly. "What story did my tide tell? Is it about me?"

"I . . ." he hesitated. "I don't know. I don't think I read that tide yet. When was it? Three days ago? I – I will need to read properly." He hesitated a moment, realising where this was leading. He was reluctant because this was supposed to be something private, not through any conscious decision, but because that was the way it always was. He was reluctant because he already felt tense all over at the presence of another and how could you read like that? He felt reluctant because he didn't know what to do or what to say that could actually explain any of this. But Feather's eyes were gleaming with interest and there was a curious twist to the corner of her mouth that wasn't a smile – and he could find no reason not to continue. He gave a sigh, then stood up and crossed to his desk. He looked around vaguely for a second chair for her, which he knew wasn't there, but it didn't matter for she simply settled behind him, leaning comfortably on his. He quickly opened up *The Book of Tides* computer file and started skimming through it towards the present, while Feather stared at him and it curiously.

"All this?" she asked. He nodded. "It's huge," she murmured as page after page of small texts flashed passed on the screen.

"Each one is a separate story," he said. "And together they make up one . . . big . . . novel."

The file reached the end. She read briefly: *The girl is in the water. She swims gently. The water glows faintly with phosphorescence.* But he cut her off and backtracked a few pages until he reached an empty one. His eyes wandered over to the stacks of material, neatly arranged tide by tide – and picked out the pile he wanted.

"This is your tide," he said. "The tide you came in on three days ago."

- Military Jacket – shredded.
- Distress flares x 6.
- One male shoe.
- A fragment of cloth.
- A girl's hairband.
- A broken flower pot.
- A cardboard carton that had contained cheap wine.
- A length of rope with a knot in it.
- A worn plastic warning sign – explosive.
- A bulldog clip.

He picked up the shoe and held it thoughtfully. It had once been smart, made of black leather – very businesslike – but it was well worn even before it ended up in the sea. The leather was bulging and split and deep indentations had been left in the heel. It had also been burnt somehow – there was a certain charring to it. Had it just been discarded as a cast-off? Or was there something more lingering in this shoe? There was something about it that stirred him. He sniffed it curiously and flexed it in his hands. A sense of pain, though not quite like the swimsuit – and he felt his heart sinking. There was a scream somewhere – not a groan of despair, but a full throated scream.

Then the hairband came to hand – a sad piece of garish purple and black elastic cloth adorned with a small metal skull. When he unfolded it, he found the word 'fuck' hidden deep within its elastic folds – soon followed by 'the world'. It had been a young girl piece – the stroppy and rebellious goth with a score to settle with the world. He put that to his face as well and abruptly flinched away with a grunt.

"What is it?" Feather asked. He glanced at her, his heart beating heavily. He wondered for a moment how to put that hairband into spoken words, before immediately giving up. There was no way to express the almost bottomless rage it had contained, except by writing it down.

And then the length of rope. It appeared to have been cut and sealed to this short length, not frayed, and this also sent a little prickle down his back. He glanced up at Feather in silence. What the hell was all this stuff? He felt an uncomfortable sensation in his stomach and on his skin and gave Feather another heavy stare.

"What is it?" she demanded. "Why are you looking at me as though I murdered your first-born son?"

"I . . . don't . . ." He couldn't explain though. Spoken words were never much use. "The plant pot is corporate," he said, as much to fill the silence as anything. "No question. A pot that sat in an office or bank housing some plastic twigs. It reads dead to me."

"Is it?"

He nodded, and quickly typed a note to that effect.

"Cheap wine," he said. "And an explosive sign."

"Meaning?"

"A burnt shoe," he said, "and . . . and a lot of rage. Something has happened. Something more extreme. Are you angry, Feather?"

"Not really," she said blankly. "Are you really reading these things? Are you a fortune teller?"

"I am just trying to find the stories in them," he muttered, putting down the last items.

"What do you see in me then?" she asked.

"I . . ."

He paused.

"You read all those – what about me?"

"In you personally?" he asked, almost formally. She nodded. Trying to forget that this was a person, he reached out hesitantly and touched her shoulder, then leaned in close up against her robe, while she stared down in silence.

"Sorry," he said at last, "I must write it down. I – I cannot . . . talk."

He quickly turned to the computer.

Fugitive. On the run as a misfit. Never matched the normal units of measurement. Far from normal life. Physical pain and emotional misery and confusion. Wandering – always."

She stared at him with wide eyes. "Fugitive?" she stammered. He winced.

"I don't mean you committed a crime," he muttered urgently. She nodded slowly.

"Why did I come out here?" she murmured. "I wanted the wilderness – I wanted to escape . . ."

She drew a long heavy breath.

"And . . ."

She suddenly lifted up her robe, revealing her upper legs. He stared for a moment before picking out the faint network of white lines of scar tissue that traced there. He stared up at her – feeling some large emotion rolling inside him. Something he was completely unequipped to deal with or express. He could say nothing, but Feather didn't seem to mind. She let the robe fall again, then fixed the screen with a piercing look.

"That's about right," she whispered. "But – did you just deduce that . . . or?"

He swallowed. "I'm not sure," he said. "Let me carry on." He picked up the shoe and the hairband for a moment and gave a groan, shivering briefly at the intensity. "There is something really frightening in here," he said.

"Um . . ."

But he was already typing.

So much rage. But you have to know it from within. From without is blind and you see nothing. I see exhilaration. I see the misfit finally lashing out at what squashed her and tried to shape her world in ways it could not be shaped. The exhilaration of extremity and of the final escape.

"This is too easy," he said, trying not to catch her eyes. The expression on Feather's face was unnerving. "Ok," he said softly, "this is the story of your tide."

> *White light. No pain. Just a white oblivion that obliterates everything – both you and that which squashes you down. A room where many many people sat working, spinning the nets of lines and angles that are the world. They surrounded her, with eyes of glass and hands of wire. Until they realised what she was. She stared round the room, taking in the fleeing figures, and those cowering in corners, too scared even to move and attempt to get away. Their eyes were wide. Maybe this wasn't so futile after all, she thought. Maybe this would instigate some thought and questioning. But then she gave a sigh. Why? That had never happened before.*
>
> *"No politics," she whispered. "No religion. No race. No ideas. No stories. Just truth . . . and reality."*
>
> *White light. No pain. Just a white oblivion . . .*

* * *

He surfaced from that, becoming aware of Feather behind him, staring blankly.

"Are you saying I'm a . . . *suicide bomber?*" She shook her head. "I don't understand. What does this have to do with me?" she asked guardedly.

"That's the story," he murmured. There wasn't much else that he could say. He drew a deep breath and again pressed the hair band to his face. So much rage. Dull, helpless rage. Then he glanced at the text again, as though seeing it for the first time – wondering where it had come from.

"No stories?" he quoted, puzzled.

She gave a shiver. "I don't like stories."

He gave her a sharp look, feeling a touch of dismay at the words. There was a look in her face that frightened him. "Why not?"

She gave him a wan stare. "Maybe because they have too much power in people's minds – to start distorting reality."

"But . . ."

He broke off – his limited powers of speech deserting him completely. She finally stepped away, looking cloudy and unhappy.

"Is any part of this true or are you just telling tales?" she asked at last, sounding almost fierce. "Did some girl really blow up a building? It is just stories, isn't it?"

"What . . . part of a story isn't true?" he asked, feeling puzzled and helpless.

"Um – the part that is unreal?"

"I don't know what's real or unreal," he muttered. "It's all the same . . ."

"I . . ." Feather shook her head. "Stories have wrecked the world," she cried dramatically. "People thinking things that are not. Fucking fantasies."

He stared at her in amazement.

"You told me that physical pain and emotional misery and confusion were my foundation in my life – and I can thank stories for that. People telling stories and expecting me to just believe them. What to do. What to think. What fucking religion to believe in. Even what to eat. Singing fantasies at me. It's all stories. And my confusion when the world I saw had nothing whatever to do with any of that? What am I supposed to make of that?"

He was silent. Then Feather suddenly sagged and gave a smile, looking very tired. "Sorry," she said softly. "You scared me a little. For a moment there, I thought you really were trying to be a fortune teller. And I am still not quite my usual bonny self."

"Of course," he murmured uncertainly. *Really trying to be a fortune teller?* What the heck was the answer to that? "Don't worry. Just . . ." He gestured vaguely at the couch. "I think I need a rest as well," he muttered, glancing sourly at the materials beside him. His heart was still beating with frightening speed and when he rose to his feet, he was startled to find his legs week and trembly. He gave her a long look, aware of some form of pleading in his eyes, but unsure what he was pleading for. To make the world simple again? To not exist? To restore the isolation that was the basic tenet of his life? Feather sat down with a sigh, staring at the floor and he slowly began clearing away the remains of the dinner.

In the kitchen, he ran water with a sigh of relief and slowly washed up – enjoying the fact that he was alone again. He leisurely packed all the utensils away, then forced himself to re-enter the living room, only to find that she seemed to have fallen asleep now. Either that or she had simply curled up and shut her eyes to close herself off. He wasn't sure. After a moment, he slowly tramped upstairs and grabbed the quilt from his bed, then draped it over her, tucking it nervously around her face. She gave a sleepy murmur and squirmed into it gratefully. Finally, after a last long look, he stepped outside into the cold night wind and drew a deep breath. He could feel his face relaxing for the first time in several hours and he sighed, feeling the night air cutting into his cheeks. A mist had drifted in and was covering the hills but there was enough moonlight to see, and to make out the vague shapes of the land across the water. In the midst of that darkness there were just two lights showing – shining out from the scattered buildings. The stillness here was absolute and even the gentle wind in the heather and the soft sound of the waves on the beach couldn't break that. This really was a lonely place, he thought, and now he felt a sharp appreciation – Feather's presence had reminded him of that somehow.

Finally he stepped back inside, stood for another long moment staring down at her sleeping face, then finally tramped upstairs to find his own bed, trying to put images of his guest from his mind.

* * *

City. Night. London. Tall, cramped buildings clustering over narrow labyrinthine one-way streets. Shops of many kinds and many languages. Grim apartment blocks. People crowded together in a desperate attempt to exist within the shimmering stench of the city. Camden. Soho. Brick Lane. Anywhere where the roads were narrow and murky and where neon flashed and glimmered. It was silent, however. I see no cars or buses moving. Only Feather – running. Running. Head down. Exhausted. Casting dark glances round her. Cliffs of stone and glass and narrow cracks of sky. But even here, impossible to lose yourself in.

Then there are figures ahead and Feather darts to the side. Black and fluorescent yellow jackets that spoke of the official. Feather running down a corridor of low red lights against black. Obviously frightened. Gazing round with wide eyes.

"Stop telling stories about me," she screamed.

"Feather," I call, wanting to help but unsure how. She flinches and gazes at me with fear in her eyes. Why is she frightened of me?

Running again. Away from me down the corridor of red lights.

And I am running after her. I have to. Something here needs clearing up – I don't understand. But others are running after her as well, I realise. I finally see her pursuers and they all look like me. I am an older man after all – and she looks so young.

Then the lights suddenly end in a place where something big lurks. Gleaming metal and heat. Dead end. Feather stops in despair and the pursuers swarm over her. Feather down. Vanishing under hands. And mine are among them. My fingers are on her leg. Tearing fabric. My fingers pushing into her flesh, which parts for me like dough. There is a thin scream.

Then my hand on her face holding her down on the tarmac. No struggling. Then the knife going cleanly across . . .

He woke up with a jolt and a gasp, gazing into the faint dawn light of his bedroom with eyes that felt huge. His heart was throbbing and prickly cold ran all over his body, his leaden limbs barely able to move. For a long few minutes he just lay there, breathing deeply and slowly smoothing the nightmare away. The window was a dull grey square in the almost blackness of his room and he focussed on it, willing his mind to imagine the soothing wild shoreline outside. Trying to imagine the harsh pounding of the waves sweeping like tongues – tongues filled with stories. Of those stories, he could be the master. At that thought, his heart began to slow, the ache in his limbs fading. He quietly pursed his lips and produced a long whistle – just one note that continued until his breath died. Any desire for sleep seemed to have completely faded now. There seemed little point just turning over and closing his eyes, so instead he got up and tramped downstairs. Feather was an inert heap on the sofa and he found himself staring down at her, his eyes prickling with unexpected tears. She did indeed seem so very young somehow – though in reality she must surely be somewhere in her twenties. This was a mystery, he decided. The mystery of the stranger – the other person. A mystery that his brain seemed unequipped to fathom. Those were feelings that he had tried to escape from before when he first came out here, but now here they were back again.

After a while, Feather gave a small sleepy shift and sigh under the quilt and he turned away unhappily, heading for the door and the dull grey dawn. Now that he was up, he might as well catch the night tide. Sleep was over today and maybe there would be something interesting on the beach. Something to continue this bizarre novel.

The first thing he saw when he stepped onto the strand line stopped him in his tracks though. It was strewn with passports. He found sixteen of the sodden documents scattered along the beach, tangled up in seaweed. Still somewhat haunted by the feelings of his nightmare and by Feather herself, he felt a prickle of amazement. He thoughtfully added them to his bag – the foundation stone of the pattern of this tide – and began looking around for more debris that would give them context and help unlock their stories. But he felt an uncertainty that he had never felt before and he gave a sharp and rather humourless laugh. The turmoil Feather had induced in him, and which he could sense in her, seemed to be reflecting in nature. There was something unnerving about these passports and the sea seemed to be filled with tales of violence and suicide everywhere he looked. For the first time that he could remember, he felt reluctant to read what the sea was telling him.

Finally, his bag weighted down, he made for home again, scrambling over the rocks and grassy sand at the head of the beach. He tramped into his garden, through the forest of driftwood, then paused in the doorway just as the first hint of a pale sun appeared, cutting through the milky sky. There was a faint mist drifting over the ground now and the many flotsam-decked poles of his garden loomed out of it like surreal ceremonial objects. Like a pathway of totems. From here, he could see the whole of the remote sea inlet that he called home. The familiar pattern of hills that enclosed him. The familiar islands dotting the sea in the distance. This was where a mountain range fell into the sea, after all, he thought with a smile, and it did indeed seem a safe distance from anything human.

Then the stillness was cut by a sound behind him and he glanced round, realising with a slight flinch that he wasn't alone. Feather had joined him in the doorway, leaning against the frame, and he gave her a sleepy but welcoming look. She stared out at the garden.

"Good morning," she whispered.

He watched her. He was subtly proud of his show of marine debris here, even though there were few people to ever really see it. Just the occasional passing walker. And now the perfect melding of art and morning – sea and mist – somehow stifling any desire to speak. It was the sort of morning that reminded you of the power of silence and of the bleak magical inhumanity of the world.

"It is so quiet here," Feather said at last. "So far from any of the noises of life."

She paused for a moment and the silence came back.

"Funny," she said at last with a tiny giggle, "how we always associate sound with humanity."

"Hmm?"

"It isn't silent," she said. "And yet – it seems silent."

"What can you hear?" he asked and, though he still felt wary of her, he was pleased to find that the atmosphere between them was relaxed and comfortable.

She shrugged against him. "The sea on the beach," she said in a drowsy monotone. "I can hear it on the rocks and on the sand separately. I can hear the wind – calm, but its gently shaking the grass. I can hear it in the bushes and I can hear it in your stuff there. Your sea stuff. Things are moving. I can hear it on the roof and in the walls. And that's it. That's silence?"

He grinned. "That's one of the beauties of isolation," he said."

"What are the other beauties?"

"No one to see or hear you in return, perhaps," he said. "You can make a racket at any time and nobody cares. You can do what you please really. Be whatever you want."

She gave an enthusiastic smile.

"I like that," she said. "Yes. You can flop out naked on the beach and nobody will get scared. You can go running round screaming your head off and no one gives you any disapproving looks."

"Um – yeah," he said, unable to avoid smiling and finally moving to go indoors.

She glanced at the bag in his hand. "Another story?" she asked.

"Yes," he said briefly, shaking it. He stepped inside and spread the pieces out with practiced hands. "A very strange one," he murmured.

- Passports x 16.
- The stock from a shotgun.
- A black leather belt with metal-reinforced holes and a missing buckle.
- A mangled bird cage.
- A length of thin chord.
- Three non-matching children's shoes.
- A cracked plastic dinner plate.
- Thirteen wine bottle corks.
- A length of electrical cable with a standard three-pin plug.
- A hair band – pale blue and cute this time.
- A half of eggshell.
- Shreds of soft fabric – underwear-style maybe.

He stared at them for a while, then glanced over his shoulder at Feather, who was watching curiously.

"This is really an unusual tide," he said at last, announcing it almost formally. "I have never seen a horde quite like this – and . . ."

He spread his arms in a dramatic shrug.

"It's frightening. I'm not really sure . . ."

Feather made a questioning noise.

"I – I – I am not sure . . . what stories. What is . . ?"

It was, as usual, hard to articulate anything and he forced himself to shut up and concentrate. This was just another tide after all.

Just another story to be found and recorded. He grabbed the passports impatiently, examining them – feeling the small thrill that they sent through him. The sensation that these passports radiated was horrendous – stifling, chains, helplessness, ritual, random, the opposite of freedom. He tried to feel them in more detail, but subtleties seemed blocked by the default radiation that they emitted.

"Nationality," he murmured. "Nationality . . ."

He quickly counted them off, painfully aware of Feather's eyes on his back.

"All British," he said. "Nothing strange there. Except," he murmured, "yes. They are all young. Like students. Your sort of age." He put them down heavily with a sigh and reached for something else.

"Look," Feather said, coming up behind him. "I still don't really understand . . ."

He glanced up at her, feeling a twinge in his stomach. Please don't ask me to explain any more, he begged silently. To cover it, he quickly picked up item after item and felt them carefully.

How the hell could a birdcage make its way here? He shook it sharply. "Restraint," he said softly. "Prison."

"Or . . . cherishing – cherished pet? Protection?" He glanced at her, looking confused.

"Really?"

She shrugged. He quickly continued. "Look – shotgun stock. Leather belt. Electrical wire."

"Hunting for food – electric light – keeping your bloody trousers up . . ." she murmured, but he ignored her.

He picked up the tattered knicker fabric – just flaps of very soft cotton hanging on a thread of elastic. He fingered it and felt it carefully, briefly picked up the shattered eggshell, then sat back and clasped his hands behind his head. "Rape?" he wondered aloud. "There is violence everywhere."

"The sea is violent," she said softly.

"Yes . . . but . . ." He sat back and gave a huge sigh. "The world is a rotten place, isn't it," he said heavily. "I get the feeling that you er know that . . . well enough. Wherever you have come from. Yes?"

"I really don't understand," she said earnestly, sitting down on the sofa. "How does this work?"

"What?"

"I mean – what about everything else on the beach that you didn't pick up? What about other beaches?"

He spread his arms, suddenly trembling slightly. "I – don't really know. I just tell stories – like everyone else."

"Yeah?"

He drew a deep breath.

"Look – I know you don't like it," he stammered. "But – but . . . I have to . . ."

He shook his head and dropped the fabric.

"What is this," he said, painfully aware of the almost whining tone in his voice. He rose to his feet and glared at the latest piles, trembling. "What is there to read in this thing? It feels like there's a bloody war on," he muttered. "These things are fucking stifling."

"War?" she asked sharply.

"I can't stop trembling. And all this mess – it never used to be like this."

"Um . . ."

"There's just so much violence – so much . . ."

She jumped up and rested her hands on his shoulders, rubbing gently.

"Please relax," she said with a smile, but he tensed violently and pulled away with a gasp. Feather stared at him in dismay.

"Hey," she murmured. "What is it?"

"Sorry," he said. "I just – can't . . ." He drew a deep breath. "Look – um . . . would you mind leaving me to it for a few minutes. I can't really concentrate . . ."

Even as he said it, he hated himself for it, but there didn't seem to be any choice. All he felt was confusion.

"Um – sure," Feather said with a slight frown, backing away. "I'll go out for a bit."

"You don't need . . ."

She gave a sigh. "I think you've spent way too much time on your own," she said. "I am not an alien, you know."

"What?"

"Just a person. I may be younger than you – you may not have seen many of these things before – but I am just a person. You are looking at me as though I was another species."

"I know what you are," he said, trying force himself to calm down.

"Yeah," she muttered. "I know – you're the Fortune Teller."

"Look," he managed. "There's something very strange going on in all this stuff. In this novel. Something serious. And whether you like stories or not . . ."

She gave a little sound of discomfort at that. "Suddenly I am not sure what is real anymore," she muttered, rubbing urgently at one eyebrow. There was a moment's silence. "I am going out for a bit," she said at last. "You are making me nervous."

He stared after her in dismay as she slipped out with an uncomfortable half smile. Then, glancing back at the passports, he punched the wall hard, realising that any reading was now further away than ever. There was a savage knot of guilt inside him and a bitter wish that she hadn't gone at all. That was fundamentally surprising. It was ridiculous that he could possibly want her there, or anyone for that matter – and yet he stared after her with a small prickle of loneliness. Maybe even a brief wash of sexual interest. He cringed in despair, hunching his shoulders and sitting down heavily at the dinner table. The pile of this tide, which had made him think of war, almost seemed to grin at him from the desk – nothing more than a confusing mass of malevolence.

In the end, Feather wasn't gone long. Less than an hour later, she slipped back in with a curious look in her eyes that sent a prickle over his already nervous skin. She gave him a hesitant stare.

"How's it going?" she asked, sounding absently curious. He shrugged dismissively.

"Nothing . . . much," he stammered. She sat down and stared into space for a moment, while his heart felt heavier and heavier. Whatever was hanging in the air now was very bad indeed.

"Um," she said at last.

"Yes?"

"You, er – you were out searching earlier, weren't you?"

Why did she want to know that?

"Yes," he grunted. "Very early."

She hesitated. "Where did you go?"

"Not far."

"Then you haven't found the bodies yet?"

Whatever he had expected her to say, that wasn't it. He watched her in astonishment, trying to work out what she meant.

"The what?" he asked at last.

She sighed. "I had better show you," she murmured, rising to her feet. She shook her head blearily. "You're going to like this."

"Ok," he managed. He followed her to the door.

Outside, she set off on a quick wordless tramp along the head of the beach and, about ten minutes later, they scrambled over a small ridge of grass and rocks and he glimpsed a huddled form – then a second. And he finally realised that she had been speaking literally. He stared blankly at the two bodies, then hurried after her down to them. Both were young men, dressed in ordinary clothes – both had their hands tied behind their backs.

"There's another on the other side of those dunes," she said. "Come on."

He silently followed her and now a teenage girl was laying face down, legs half buried in sand.

"I have found five altogether," she said. "Scattered along the beach. Washed up here. Is this another part of your tide you were trying to read? Part of your war?"

He shook his head, not in negation. Feather looked genuinely stunned and confused now, her sense of reality given a severe shaking by these huddled figures. He, on the other hand, felt strangely serene at the discovery – as though it wasn't even so unexpected.

"Of course," she murmured, half to herself, "accidents happen. But . . ."

"Mmm," he said vaguely.

"I am going to search them," she said.

He gave her a startled look. "Why?" he asked stupidly.

"If there is anything interesting on them, you can put it in your novel," she said with a brittle sound to her voice. "Right?"

He winced uncomfortably as she crouched down beside the sodden form and began going through her clothes. Her zipped trouser pocket produced a wallet and she examined it quickly.

Sodden money. Business cards. Credit cards. Misc pieces of paper.

"Catherine Bennet," she said, reading a small piece of plastic she had found. She handed him the wallet and he took it reluctantly. There was a photo of a young man in one compartment, now almost obliterated by the sea.

Then Feather started going over her body, probing it, apparently looking for injuries. And eventually she found it – a single neat knife wound in the back of her neck. She stared at that, then sat back, her face seeming even paler than usual.

"Any ideas?" she asked, her voice thin. He shook his head dumbly. "You are the reader," she muttered. "Tell me what these are."

She was actually trembling slightly, he realised.

He sighed and tried to focus, trying to remember the feel of the items on his desk and reluctantly staring around the beach, hoping for more clues. Presumably this was all a part of the same story. But the detritus here also just seemed meaningless. Just fragments of rope, plastic and paper. He was seeing things through Feather's eyes, he realised. Just an old familiar pragmatic world where stories were an enemy. He turned his back on her and tried to recapture the sense of violence he had felt earlier – the radiating stench from the passports. The ropes used to bind . . . the sticks used to beat . . .

Then something unnaturally round caught his eye and he leaned over to investigate. It was a button – a large one. Just a plain brown disk with four holes and a ridge round the edge. The sort of button that might have been ripped off a very old and heavy coat. He picked it up and felt it curiously. There was a shred of cloth attached – just dull brown and rather coarse.

Something pricked at his mind. Memories. Previous tides. The young poet cutting her wrist. Feather's own tide – and Feather herself – the Running Girl.

"How old is she?" he asked. "Any idea?"

Feather glanced at the card she still held. "Seventeen," she said.

"And the rest?"

She shrugged miserably. "All the same I suppose. All as young as she is – I think. Can you read something?"

"Let me see that," he said, reaching out for the card. He fingered it uncertainly, trying to work out what it was for. It wasn't a credit card and didn't seem to be a travel or membership card. It was labelled *Youth ID* and bore the logo of the home office in all its deceptive innocence – but that was all. *Glasgow*, it said. *Building a safe, just and tolerant society.* On the back was a magnetic strip. He touched it to his face. There was a cloying and slightly stifling feeling about it that was not so different to the passports he had held earlier. He stared bleakly at Feather, suddenly feeling as though there was something very heavy inside his head.

"Is there a war going on?" he asked softly. "And . . . if so, then who is fighting who?"

He turned his attention back to the beach and stared at the sea, always so comfortingly inhuman, for all the stories it told. Feeling sentences coming together in his head.

> *The heart raced at the sheer impossibility of knowing what was happening coupled with the urgent need to understand it before it was too late. But it could never be understood, Catherine thought, her muscles taut against her bonds. There was nothing to understand. And everything anyone had ever said on the subject of humanity, life and death was wrong.*
>
> *So what should you do? With your life-time measured in seconds. What could you think about? Just a storm of memories, none of them relevant to the present.*
>
> *Outside came the distant sound of gunfire – just three shots – and the murmur of voices. The sound of a crowd. But she ignored it. Then there was a whimper and a twisted breath beside her as Steve fell forward on his face. Then the prickling awareness of someone behind her – her neck suddenly an agony of exposure. Someone had said something, but she wasn't sure what. She was shoved sharply.*
>
> *"Well?" the voice demanded.*

"I am not listening to you," she said dreamily. "You don't make sense."

For that, she found herself shoved forward onto her face and pinned down with a knee in the small of her back – the feel of something cold touching her neck.

"I wish there was a hundred like you," he said sharply, in a voice that would have been farcical if he wasn't the one carrying the knife. "Right here. Why do I have to work so effing hard at this? Have you no respect?"

She glanced round at him, just a dull and shabby man with an anonymous face behind her. The face of an older man, lined and set in a permanent sulk. Brown jacket – worn and torn and marked with blood spots.

"Yeah," she managed. It hurt and her breath was short, but even that didn't matter much now. "When I was young," she began hesitantly.

"You are still young," the voice muttered contemptuously. "Well?"

"When I was young, I used to escape into the fairy tales – where curious creatures lived under mushrooms and where stupid kings could be bested by cunning bards and the bards were the heroes. Where magic was possible and where you could fly with the clouds – where you could achieve things. And you know what? That makes perfect sense."

There was silence.

"That was real – somehow. You aren't real – you can't be."

The man gave a dismissive grunt and there was a needle-sharp pain at her neck, sending an electric shock sensation right through her entire body. Then paralysis and complete shutdown . . .

"That makes perfect sense," he echoed sadly, glancing at Feather. He wasn't sure what expression he was wearing, but she frowned uneasily.

"What does?" she asked carefully, kicking at the sand.

"Fairy tale," he said, then shook his head. He drew an intense sigh, realising again that there was far more that he wanted to express here than he ever could in words. "It's all we have," he said at last. Feather stared at him and suddenly he felt as though they were speaking different languages entirely. "You hate stories, yet without stories, none of it makes sense. Look at it," he said.

Feather was silent.

"Just a dull dreary horror? The world has – has . . . hiccoughed again and the sea is full of torture implements. Full of death . . ."

"Yes, but what is happening?" she demanded, a shrill edge to her voice.

"It is a war, yes," he said solemnly, trying to work out how best to explain something so momentous. "I was right. I can't – I mean, I have no more doubt. This story is about war. It is generations are fighting generations I think. After all . . . there's more difference between generations now than there are between countries. That's what it's all about . . ."

He felt strangely dreamy, almost hallucinatory for a moment. As though the beach that surrounded him might start rippling like the sea at any moment or reach out sandy tentacles for him. It felt strange for so many words to be coming out of his mouth, and he was not even totally sure that he understood or believed them all – but he didn't stop them.

"A war? Really?" Feather asked carefully. "Somehow broken out since I came out here into the wilderness? Do you really mean that? I mean – are you serious? The generations have always hated each other but surely you don't mean . . ."

He sighed and turned away. "Maybe I should have been writing fairy tales instead. They make more sense . . ."

"Huh?"

He glanced at her. Then Feather suddenly gave a grating growl. "Fuck it," she snapped. "It's ridiculous."

He flinched. She scrambled to her feet and stared at him with eyes huge.

"It's not possible," she cried shrilly. I don't believe you. Do you seriously mean that this country has suddenly declared war on itself in the few days since I wandered away from it? You're living in a fantasy land."

That silenced the words in a moment and he stared at her in silence, feeling frozen. But it's true, he wanted to cry. Of course it was true. But he knew that he could not speak again.

"It's a fucking story," she cried. "Can't you see that? These bodies – I don't know. Gang war – murder – who fucking knows? How can you just sit here, totally . . . you are isolated from every fucking thing and yet you are trying to tell me the fucking news? Why don't you go and see what's happening if you want to talk about it?"

She stared at him intensely, waiting for an answer, then pressed on – in a softer voice but still with an icy glimmer in her eyes.

"You live out here – you never have any contact with anyone or anything. You never hear much . . . what's going on – so you start making up your own. Right? And then you forget what's real and what's just make-believe. Right? You think you are a fucking fortune teller."

No, he wanted to say – but how could you ever explain? How could you ever formulate an argument containing everything that clamoured in your head? It was impossible. Instead he just stared out to sea.

"Right?" she repeated.

Then he exploded.

"What do you know about stories?" he shrieked at her, feeling every muscle in his face suddenly twisting. She stepped back sharply, then accidentally trod on the hand of the dead girl behind her and gave a wild flinch, loosing her balance and sprawling out in the sand on her back. "If you're so so so clever, you try and tell me what makes them. And where they come to an end. And . . . and what they have to do with reality? Do you know that?"

"Hey . . ."

"I just tell them," he whispered. "It's what I do."

Feather was silent – her eyes large.

"Please," he muttered at last, turning away. "I think you had better go."

"What?" she said, her voice unsteady.

"Please," he repeated. "I need this isolation. You'd do – be better off elsewhere. Back somewhere less wild and cold. Back in London. If you find me so insane."

He turned away and stalked towards the house, trying to stop shaking. Then he paused. Surely he should at least give her some food and drink for the journey. He glanced back, but she was already pulling herself to her feet. He watched her brush sand off herself, then she turned away, looking crestfallen and heavy. He wanted to call after her, but his tongue was tied again and, just a few moments later, she had scrambled over the rocks and vanished. She had come with nothing, and she left with nothing. He just stared at where she had been, then back at his distant house and its poles of sea debris, now all seeming sinister and foreboding. Then he glanced down at the body in the sand and shut his eyes in despair.

"The world is at war," he whispered aloud. "Who cares what happens now?"

* * *

- A round wood pole with the remains of white paint on it.
- A fragment of fishing line and the decaying seabird attached to it.
- A plastic bottle marked shampoo.
- A discarded plastic wallet containing a sodden rail ticket – destination obliterated.
- A fragment of tire rubber.
- A half-burned wooden plank.
- A plastic flower.
- A broken doll – naked.

The tide had been and gone again now – the old storyteller leaving one more chapter for him to read. As he tramped home along the beach with his heavy bag, still making himself pick up items that caught his eye, there was a dull roar and an arrow-shaped grey jet passed overhead through the dull and undramatic afternoon light. He paused and stared after it tensely. Even that was not such an unknown event, even out here in the wilderness, but now it was only another confirmation.

There was no doubt – no doubt at all . . .

As the train raced towards London, there was surprisingly little to see of the city. As suburbia was left behind, the rails passed through deep cuttings, behind high walls or in half-tunnels under buildings. The decrepit and grim railway architecture seemed just as usual and it wasn't until she was well into the centre, when the tracks emerged onto an elevated section, that she caught a glimpse of the smoke. It hung over London in a pall of dull haze, with a few rising columns on the skyline, rearing up over the buildings like serpents. Down below, the streets were unusually empty and many were strewn with debris. And Feather stared with a sinking heart – a sudden realisation . . .

He sat back in his chair and began skimming through *The Book of Tides*, wondering whether this novel was anywhere near finished yet. Or maybe it had only just started. Maybe everything so far had been building up to this epic conflict in the world outside, which he would now have to chronicle. He would need to concentrate, but it was hard. He had the feeling that Feather's name would be deeply woven into everything the sea had to tell him now. And in what roles? Feather the fugitive? Feather the outlaw? Feather the freedom fighter? Feather the terrorist? He closed his eyes, her form suddenly vivid and the memory of her presence – the presence of another – sending a tingle through him. A restlessness.

Quietly, he got up and inspected the sofa, where she had slept for the few days she had been there. After a bit of searching, he found what he was looking for. Three hairs – long and brown. He knew that it was the only trace of her that would remain here, but it was sufficient. He quickly twisted them together into a loop and tied them with a small scrap of white ribbon. Then he looked for her tide. As of now, he decided, he would have to name this one 'Feather's Tide' and it deserved something more than the eventual clearout that was the fate of most tides.

In a prime place in his garden, he dug a hole. Then he tramped to his shed and studied the stacks of wood that it contained – wood for the fire, and other wood. Driftwood. One of the largest pieces was dragged out into the grey evening. It was an impressive piece of branch, as tall as he was and splitting into two substantial stems with several twisted knots in various places. Barkless and cracked, it seemed to reach out, though he wasn't sure whether it was in agony or exultation. Maybe both. Dragging it back to the hole and setting it firmly upright was the work of a few minutes, but he spent the rest of the evening armed with twine and wire, slowly building the new flotsam tree. The single shoe was suspended, toe-downwards, at the bottom and the broken flowerpot nailed above it. The cloth and the rope were twined round loosely and fastened. Then the military jacket was added scarecrow style over all and, within that, the three hairs, were hidden, carefully nailed to the central junction where the branches divided. The distress flares and the warning sign studded the tree like fruit. It was a simple arrangement, but it didn't really need to be anything else. It was the objects that were important here and nothing should get in the way of that.

Finally he stepped back to study his work. The sun was long gone now and the grey was deepening. His world bordered by the familiar shapes of the hills and a stony sky – as comforting as always. As lonely as always.

It looked good.

Around him, people bustled. The endless stream of faces that was London. Glancing round, he seemed to be the only person who wasn't moving. He stood as a still point in a storm of people. Feeling horribly exposed.

"Well?" he cried out at last. The passers-by took no notice, carefully avoiding eye contact. Overhead, the roar of a jet made him look up anxiously, but it was just a 747 passing low overhead. Nothing more. And in a few moments it was gone, hidden above the buildings.

To Call the Sea

Somewhere in the wilderness a lone domino fell.
It was the last domino.
That's what it felt like.

The sound it made was just a tiny click in silence.

Nearly every evening when Kay came home, he would find a penny, just inside his room – as though it had been slid under his door. He had given up wondering about this by now and he kept them in a steadily growing pile in a jar on the shelf by his bed – perched next to his shaver and his old antique wooden flute. He thought he knew the inhabitants of Jade Halls pretty well by this time, but he could form no idea at all as to who it was slipping them to him. And no – he had never caught whoever it was in the act. Even on the days when he didn't go out, sometimes it would simply appear there during a moment of distraction or music – and when he hurried to the door and peered out, there was always nobody there.

He sat down on his un-made bed, fingering the latest offering with eyebrows raised. There was something about this that was almost comforting. As if no matter what he might think or feel, someone was watching him. And Kay liked the idea of being watched. It was an antidote to loneliness. He almost had enough now for a spin of the tumble dryer in the chaotic laundry room. Give it a few days and he could change it into a nice bright shining 50 pence piece – a curious request to the house warden or the local shop down the hill in Archers.

Or wasn't there some old shoplifters trick where you gave the unsuspecting sod on the till a sack of pennies to sort out to buy your few items – and while he or she was distracted and struggling to count them, your partner rifled the shelves?

But at any rate – that meant it had been going on for at least fifty days. That was a long time for someone to play games . . .

Here in the Brockden Centre, the lonely halls of residence at Archers College of Performing Arts, you either got used to things like that – or sank and died and vanished. And many had. But enough always remained so that the smell of a hundred different artistic outlooks permeated the corridors here like gas – students, sex, paranoia, whacky baccy, depression and enthusiasm. Bad art, saving the world and tortured theoretics. Naïve beyond years perhaps, blistering energy, thoughtlessness or even misery beyond imagining. Over the years, it had penetrated the dingy, badly painted walls bearing the scars of countless young people passing through and the messes left behind and it had transformed them into a dim tape recording that seemed to impart a faint glow to the building. Sometimes, in his better moods, Kay could feel it and it made him smile.

This time of year was especially difficult and the emotional cocktail in the air was especially heady – for now it was the dead end of the year – the academic year that is. Spring was in the air outside, but there was precious sign of it lately within doors. There, the grey clouds sat overhead with the threat of rain, sleet, snow and thunder. The stark form of the Brockden Centre seemed grim and oppressive against the clear sky and Kay sighed wearily as he peered out of the window. The year was almost over – the last of the college work had now been handed in with the usual good riddance but, instead of feeling celebratory, the mood was sombre and bad tempered. An oppressive cloud of gloom.

Outside, a solitary figure tramped heavily up the path to the door – the faintest of faint crunches of feet up the steps – and Kay shifted. Suddenly the penny in his hand seemed to fade and loose its significance and he peered down, lips twitching.

A key gleamed – a fumble. Entry. A clash of the door closing.

Somehow so so simple. Kay did not like that simplicity. He tuned his ears to the building and took in the sounds. Down the corridor, a beat of music pounded like a distant engine. There was always music somewhere here, no matter the hour. There was a clatter from the kitchen downstairs – a different music blending in and creating bizarre rhythms. An Ivesian Haze. Someone ran down a corridor. A TV full of voices somewhere at the other end. Then footsteps ascending the stairs. Count them. Up up up – brief silence of carpet. The door opens – a clank against the fire extinguisher. Soft padding footsteps now – carpeted. Eight or nine? He counted them. Three four five – getting closer. Seven, eight. Then stop. The grate of another key in a door – a small creak – then a sharp bang as it swung closed again. The painfully familiar sound of a Brockden Centre door closing on a student's room.

Kay sighed. All the rooms were alike. Small but manageable, with basic furniture, bed and washbasin. All were unimaginably different. As different indeed as the people who lived in them. The hundred artistic minds, with varying degrees of lunacy, let loose on a small space of not more than seven or eight square metres, a window and a bed.

He slipped the penny absently into the glass jar.

The sound it made was just a tiny click in silence.

In the spacious kitchen – a large square room with four cookers and a liberal scattering of fridges – Cal and Feather sat at the table, rather gloomily watching Bel eating macaroni cheese. The gloom was well-founded for the quivering plateful in front of her looked far from appetizing. Partially congealed, flecked with burnt milk and a vivid yellow in colour, the platefull wobbled like jelly as she dug in. The cheesy smell filled the room, almost drowning out the faint but pervasive scent from the piles of unwashed dishes and gently steaming cloths and sponges in the sink.

"Yellow food," Bel was protesting when Kay came in, "is the best. How can you dis that?"

"I can't off-hand think of a single yellow thing that is good to eat," Cal said dryly.

"Mango?" Feather suggested. He shrugged.

"Well yes ok," he said. "The exception that proves the rule. But I still say that the best things, the greatest flavours of all, are red . . . or pink," he added. "Don't you think so, Kay?" he demanded, suddenly dragging him into the conversation as though by the scruff of the neck. "Red like strawberries or wine – pink like prawns and ham?"

"Eh?" Kay said. "Red? Yeah perhaps."

Bel made a nasty noise of disagreement and mock-nausea. "Red is . . ." she sought for words and Kay grinned to himself. Everyone in Jade Halls knew that Bel never ate anything coloured red. Why that was had never really been explained – but it was a diet she stuck to with vehemence, eschewing everything from strawberries to red sweets. She also wouldn't touch meat, soft cheese, blue cheese, peanuts and a host of other things that Kay had long since given up trying to remember.

Not many people cooked for Bel or invited her to dinner.

"Well," Kay said with a smile, "I am on the browns today. I dunno. Maybe they are the best flavours of all. A nice steak. Nuts. Noodles. Soya sauce. Good sausages. Mushrooms . . ."

Bel hunched over her plateful and snorted. Feather grinned.

"Have you got all that for dinner?"

Kay shook his head. "I wish," he said. "I just have the mushrooms and the noodles. That'll have to do."

Cal leaned back in his chair with a happy sigh.

"Mmmmm," he murmured emphatically. "I wish you hadn't mentioned steak. I could use one right now."

"Sorry," Kay murmured.

"Nicely medium-rare – chargrilled and with lots of onions . . ."

Bel gave another snort and Feather jabbed Cal sharply in the shoulder.

"Shut up, Cal," she said with mock crossness. "You will get me going as well!" She jumped to her feet and hurried across to where Kay was busy fumbling for his dishes from amidst the tottering stacks by the sink. He swore under his breath and Feather grinned. "Any interesting life-forms in there yet?" she asked. "I live in hope." He dumped his saucepan in the one partially empty sink and began scrubbing it.

"There was a screaming flap in here the other day," he said. "Some girl thought she had seen a cockroach in the sink here."

"Really?"

"No not really," he grunted. "Everyone running up and down the corridors yelling their heads off. I exaggerate not. It was just a beetle – a cockchafer – sitting there covered with tea."

Feather gave a snort of laughter and twirled away down the side of the kitchen range, rolling herself along the edge of the work surface until she rolled off the end. Bel looked up from her plate. "Oooh, those dishes," she grunted. "Why the fuck can't people . . ."

"Fundamental law of life," Feather crowed. "Humans are not meant to be tidy, so in a place like this . . . what else could there be?"

"Yeah but it's looking like a pigsty."

"You know – pigs don't tend to use dishes . . ."

"Surely if we each do our bit . . . you know we should all handle our own stuff. That's the way it works. If we each do our bit then . . ."

"Then there'd still be that one dish that someone left till next morning and forgot about. Then there'd be another to keep it company. Then that strange saucepan that nobody identifies would join the party. Then . . ."

"Well yes but . . ."

Feather yawned and leaned against one of the three fridges.

"Interesting lesson in psychology," she said, nodding her head. "I was feeling quite like doing some until you spouted that 'if we each do our bit', stuff."

Bel gave a low noise of disapproval and once again subsided to her meal.

"What are you cooking?" Feather asked, returning to Kay's side and looking on hungrily.

"Don't get too excited," he said. "Just got these mushrooms to use up. I got a few ceps as well – I found out in the woods. Sorry Bel."

"You must be nuts," Bel said dryly. "With luck I will be out of here by the time you start to cook them. Are you sure they are safe?"

"I manage," he said. "I haven't made any Amanita stew yet. And you'd better eat up then." He dropped a chopping board on the table and followed it with a rolling pile of mushrooms. Bel gave them a sour look.

"Now," Feather said thoughtfully. "If I were to help you chop them – then I wonder if maybe . . ."

"If you may be able to bum a free meal?" Cal finished. "You are hopeless."

"Exactly," Feather crowed with a beaming grin.

Kay smiled. "Well," he said. "You can chop this onion if you want. I haven't much – but what's mine, is yours."

She grinned again.

Bel finished her macaroni, then ostentatiously washed up her plate and cutlery before carefully putting them back in her cupboard. It was a hopeful gesture. Hopeful that they would still be there tomorrow, that is. The unwashed dishes were a life-form that knew how to perpetuate their existence – and it was well known how, at night, people's crockery would develop legs and march across the kitchen to join the increasing army of mutineers by the sink. Bel gave one last look at the mushrooms that were coming apart under Kay's knife. "Totally minging," she said, waggling her eyebrows. Feather slung a chunk at her and she retreated with a growl into the corridor.

"That woman needs to visit a therapist," Cal said *sotto voce*.

Feather dumped the onions into the pan. "Do you want some ham in it?" she asked. "I have a scrap left."

"Please," Kay said rather formally. He was happy though. Feather was – well – always welcome. And he certainly didn't mind sharing a meal with her. It was hard not to feel good when Feather was around. When she had first arrived here, Kay had watched with interest as she nosed around the kitchen and the hallways like a nervous cat, hardly saying a word to anyone – as though trying to work out if everyone was a friend or an enemy. But she soon figured out the answer to that question and eventually revealed herself as a stridently confident and endlessly inventive character, full of a bizarre personal creativity unlike anything Kay had seen elsewhere. However, her initial wariness and intensity never quite vanished. Her energetic and excited ways were rather belied by her eyes, which were rich brown and filled with a haunting gleam that, once spotted, could never be quite lost again. Kay liked her for it. And also because she was one of the most original students here – totally different in foundation to almost everyone else and with a rigorous, experimental and questioning outlook – and, of course, a willingness or eagerness to get her hands dirty.

What Feather did on her degree here was rather hard to classify. It was not quite theatrical or performance art as one would expect from the genres. But he liked her events, which were like her – simple, direct, sharp, sensible and sometimes amiably didactic. Liked them more than most of the other performances he had seen actually, where students dressed a salad of their own depression, scars or insecurity and called it conceptual art. Serbian exchange student Senka's brooding but deceptively gentle Balkan War performances with their barely concealed nationalism – or Jenny managing to never once mention anorexia either on stage or in her documentation . . .

Sometimes Feather got extremely good grades – sometimes she would fail projects completely or just scrape a pass – but rarely anything in between.

Not that she seemed to care much.

She leaned over the pan where the ham and onions were simmering in a savoury gravy and then, before Kay realised what she was doing, she had tossed a small pinch of cinnamon in.

"Indulge me," she said with a smile.

"Anything for a free meal," Cal muttered comically in the background.

"Hey," Feather cried. "I'm working for it. I always work for my dinner."

Kay glanced at her. "Do you?" He coughed in embarrassment. "I mean – I didn't know you had a job? I mean . . ."

Feather gave him an enigmatic smile. "Yes?"

"I mean . . ."

He floundered slightly.

"Combine what they call work and what they call study?" she grunted. "No fucking thanks."

"Then how . . ?"

She gave him a friendly pat on his arm.

"You would be happier not knowing," she said.

He would have liked to press it but instead he shut himself up and carefully dumped the sliced mushrooms into the bubbling pan.

Feather stared after him and laughed softly. "That's what I like about you," she said. "Who else could I say that to and get away with it?"

Kay felt himself blushing slightly. In the saucepan, the mushrooms were taking shape nicely. The scent of cinnamon was coming through distinctly now, combining with the herbs, and he sniffed curiously, then tasted. Gave her a small grin of approval. He grabbed the noodles and tossed them to her. "Here," he said. "Cook these."

It was a simple meal, but by student standards it was almost palacial. Even if it did contain that great student synonym, pasta. Feather had produced some delicately spiced and pleasantly oiled noodles that steamed appetisingly in the pan and he sniffed them appreciatively. He dished Feather a decent plateful and turned uncertainly to Cal, who smiled and shook his head firmly.

"And what are you planning to do tonight?" Feather asked, tucking in with great enthusiasm. "Are you joining us all for our gold and silver happening?"

He pulled a face. "I am hiding," he said bluntly – and with a hint of mock gruffness. "I can't be bothered with this house and its damned parties."

Feather chuckled. "Awwwwwwww."

He grinned. "Predictable Hogarthian grotesqueries," he said, and Cal gave a delighted snigger. "Oh so inventive. Let's all dress up in gold and silver. After a few minutes of beer, weed and bad music, it won't matter what anyone is wearing."

"Gold and silver," Cal murmured. "I have to say – Kay dressed in gold and silver is something I should like to see."

"Are you going?"

"That question assumes I have a choice," Cal said, with a dry nod.

"Hey," Feather cried. "It might be fun. Kay – you are a . . . a . . . what is it? That person who spoils the fun?"

"Scrooge, I think you mean," he said, grinning over his mushrooms.

"Yeah – that's it."

Who else is going?" Kay asked.

"Probably pretty much everyone," she said.

He nodded with satisfaction. "Then it will give me a nice quiet Jade Halls to work in, then," he said. "No no – Feather please! I really don't want to. Let go of my arm and quit dancing. You know me. I am not a party animal . . ."

Feather waltzed away and Kay sat down again with a grunt.

"I think I will suddenly discover I have to be in town tonight or something," he muttered.

She laughed.

The door opened then and Elizabeth came in. Feather called out a cheery greeting, while Kay settled down over his dinner and fell silent. All conversation seemed to have been driven out of him in a moment. It had been like an invisible wave, he thought. A wave that had come crashing through the room, sweeping over him and washing away every last thing that he might have wanted to say, silencing him completely.

Another introduction here: Elizabeth – Elizabeth Ise – or Elizabeth Eyes as she sometimes had the conceit to sign herself when she was playing her Celtic Harp. Tall and serene with long light brown hair. One of the older students here. Almost adult in fact. A serious-minded composer and folk musician – one of the college's top composers in fact, as at home presenting elaborate serialist etudes on the piano as she was performing her uniquely brittle and raw interpretations of Welsh folk music.

Feather swallowed the last of her food and spun her chair round to face her, launching into a conversation liberally sprinkled with gold and silver – Feather twinklingly and Elizabeth seriously. She always did everything seriously – even a bit of fun like this. Kay felt a twinge of jealousy, but there wasn't much to do with that except swallow it. Instead, he allowed his eyes to follow her flowing hair down her back. Nice.

Except that it wasn't.

He quickly finished eating his own meal and hurried to the sink, grabbing Feather's plate as he passed. "Thanks Kay," she called after him, and he nodded as he quickly rinsed the plates and left them to drain in the rickety drainer beside the sink, he realised that it was time to go to his room. Time to get out of here.

"Great dinner," Feather called. "When I get some money again it will be my turn, OK?"

He smiled and nodded. Feather's cooking was well known here and well respected. "Great," he said. "I will look forward to that. I am just going to get on with some work – some practice."

"Sure," she said. "See you later."

"Have fun," Elizabeth called after him as well. He actually felt a prickle run down his back, but he nodded in what he hoped was a casual way and gave her a quick grin, before slipping out. However, just as he left, he happened to catch Cal's eye – and that was not so good. There was a wry speculative look on his face that was easy to read and Kay fought off a flinch.

That man was too fucking perceptive.

* * *

Brockden was just starting to bustle now as he sat in his room, staring without moving at the score on his music stand. Britten's *Six Metamorphoses after Ovid* for solo oboe. It was a gorgeous composition – especially that haunting first movement – but he couldn't put reed to lips. One thing about classical music, at least in Kay's experience. Even the saddest and most emotional music couldn't be played if you were feeling sad or emotional yourself. Instead, it seemed to demand that you feel strong, healthy and positive, otherwise the connection between yourself and the instrument and the piece just wouldn't form. That was one of the strange dichotomies of an art form that demanded such precision and concentration to get it exactly how it should be. Kay hadn't worked out if that was just his own quirk, but it was an unpleasant irony that, as actual depression and pain nibbled, there was less and less that could be done about it in terms of music. This sort of music anyway.

Besides, there was something about the title of the first movement that struck a sharp chord right now. *Pan, who played upon the reed pipe which was Syrinx, his beloved.* It was a poignant image of wrecked love and loneliness that put a knot of discomfort inside. Wrecked love and unrequited love were cousins who could communicate and chatter very easily.

Another law of life and art: You can't create from or understand love and desire when you are too close to it.

Putting down his oboe, he listened to the noise outside. Nearly 30 students lived in the two floors of Jade Halls – so there was almost always bustle and activity. But now the whole building was filling up with the sound of students getting ready for a bit of fun and it brought a twinge of humour. Footsteps came running upstairs, followed by a tremendous thumping on somebody's door. It was answered by a chorus of feminine shrieks and cries – "Ooh, look at you." "Sexy lady . . ."

It was impossible to resist and he stepped to the door and peered out.

"Hey Kay," Shirley cried, seeing him and giving a twirl. "How do I look?"

Kay laughed and shaded his eyes. She was gold and silver from top to toe – metallic silver trousers – very tight and outlining her somewhat less than pert backside with admirable confidence. Something that might have been called a boob-tube circling round her middle in vivid gold – hair full of silver glitter and a huge bow –

Introduction: Shirley was a young playwright specialising in bitter and grim social realism, which Kay did his best to like. Tales of man's injustice to women and women's injustice to themselves and the general crumbling mess of the world . . .

"Looking good," he commented cheerfully. She grinned and jiggled happily. "It's all quite crazy, you know," he said, smiling.

"I know, I know. Fantastic! Where is your gold and silver though? You are coming with us aren't you?"

He screwed up his face.

"I dunno . . ."

"Oh come on," she cried, grabbing his arm and tugging furiously. He fended her off and chuckled.

"Perhaps," he said without meaning it. "But I am not promising. I'm not sure if I can make it you know – I have to . . ."

She pouted slightly and giggled. "Hey – you have to. It's compulsory. You will not be allowed to just sit here! We'll carry you down there by force if we have to."

"Hey – pax!"

He fought her off laughing.

"Ok ok," she cried, "I have to go and find some shoes anyway. But see ya' later, Ok?"

"Have fun," he said after her, and was left staring at an empty corridor. He sighed/smiled lightly and tramped down to the kitchen again. Perhaps Feather and Elizabeth Eyes would still be there. However, the noise of that room radiated most of the way through the lower floor and when he got there, a scene of pandemonium greeted him. It was filled with a silver and gold storm. The TV was on but either silent or inaudible, while music blared out at full volume from the portable CD player. Several bottles of wine stood open on the tables and the air was heavy with smokes of various kinds. Everywhere, silver and gold met his eyes in a dazzling display as people swarmed round the room or sat fussing over each other and the clothes they were wearing. Bel seemed to be trying to wrap her middle with aluminium foil from a roll and laughing wildly, while Jim was wearing a necklace of teaspoons, which jangled like a tea trolley as he moved.

Feather jumped to his side, now dressed sexily in silk trousers and a shirt that was heavy with metalwork, with vicious looking metallic shoes to round it off. On each cheek, a swirl of gold glitter flowed, accentuating her cheekbones and the corners of her eyes, and on her forehead, two silver stars hung gleaming, one over each eyebrow. She gave his arm a quick squeeze and shook her head with a laugh.

"I think we've all gone mad," she cried laughing. "Look at us!"

"You look great though," he responded and she grinned and squirmed with mock-bashfulness, then spun round in a complete 360 degrees for his viewing pleasure.

"Why thank you! So – are you still not coming?"

"Yes – really," he said. "I hate that place. But I will see you off with pleasure and admiration."

"The Mousehole? Well – yes. I suppose. I am not sure I can disagree with you there."

Introduction: The Mousehole, of course, was the student bar up at the college – a small and dingy place that always seemed just a bit too small to accommodate the number of students trying to pile into it – and too small to be able to disperse the music that always permeated it like a large ship engine.

"I love the excitement in the air, though," he said, half to himself. "The whole building is just full – like electricity. All you girls running about, doing each others hair and wearing each other's shoes . . . This is much more fun than getting drunk in that place. Why don't we all just take off our clothes now and have a red and purple party – then a green and gold party. If we're lucky we will never make it to the bloody Mousehole."

She laughed. "Hey – I like it. But you know what students are. Pity you won't join us though – it's still kind of fun. Now I must get ready. I have to find a suitable belt from somewhere before I embarrass everybody."

"Gold?"

"Yes – any ideas?"

"Not at all," he said, shaking his head. "Unless you strip down some electrical wiring and use the copper."

She gave him an interested look.

"Where could I get electrical wiring from?"

He shrugged and grinned a wicked grin. "Pinch it from the TV?" he suggested, jerking a thumb to where the black box struggled vainly to make itself heard above the student racket. "You would do us all a favour."

Feather stared at it, wrinkling her nose. Then she gave him a quick slap on the shoulder and scurried off. Kay stared after her with a smile, then spun away towards the fridge – and came face to face with Elizabeth. The next partner in the dance of a crowded room. She had a glass of white wine in her hand and her neck and shoulders were draped with golden Celtic medallions, which clanged softly.

"Hi Kay," she said with a slightly tipsy smile, but as smooth and serene as ever. He jumped but collected himself quickly.

"Ah – good evening Miss Eyes," he said with a touch of the grandiose.

She nodded. "I see from your sumptuous costume that you are set for a wild evening," she said, not maliciously. Kay glanced down at his plain white shirt and grinned.

"Indeed," he said, looking her up and down. "More wild than you I suspect."

She had gone mostly for the silver look – a flowing silver dress with odd metal additions – even some narrow trailing chains – and a few shots of gold to complete things. She gave a short laugh and shook her hair. "How right you are," she said dramatically. "They call this running wild? I call this dumb escapism. My wildness will have to wait till tomorrow when I get back into the studio and raise the roof."

"What is it this time?"

"Aaaah," she said. "I just want to try out some new folk music settings. I have been looking at Dartmoor and working on a little set of pieces for piano. Using some sort of vague polytonality – you know. Two different scales at the same time. Wonderful patterns."

Kay knew what polytonality was, but he gave an interested flick of the eyebrows.

"It adds a nice touch of the strange and the wild," she said. "Should hopefully be quite mysterious – something for my liminality set, which is rather hopeful."

Kay wasn't so sure what liminality meant, but he nodded earnestly, trying to think of something intelligent to say. He took a sip of fruit juice.

"Sounds suitably unlike a usual folk music setting," he said lamely.

She shrugged. "Most ballad singers and so-called Celtic musicians should roast," she said darkly. "But I never really knew what I wanted this stuff to do instead. Now at last something seems to be forming. So yes – three cheers for liminality."

Liminality or not, Kay could picture it. Something brittle and slightly eerie – emotionally terse and almost frosty probably – but with ghosts of poignant melodies cutting through it in unexpected ways. He nodded.

"I can't wait. You out till late then?"

She nodded. "Oh yes – must take one's dumb relaxation where you can find it."

"It's getting on, people," Shirley cried. "Shall we make a move?" The roomful of gold and silver turned as one and thronged towards the door like some exotic flock of birds. Elizabeth grinned smoothly and finished her wine.

"Well, I wish you fun with your wildness."

She slipped away with a grin to join them. Feather gave him a wave and he grinned back half-heartedly, but it was Elizabeth he was watching – in her flowing silver dress. She linked arms with Jim affectionately and the two of them swept out with the throng like a leaf on the wind. The storm of noise faded almost suddenly into the distance, travelling first left, then right again. Whoops and high pitched calls sounding from outside – that particular high whirring, tongue-rolling cry, like some sort of demented bird, that some of the girls here always filled the air with. And then they too faded – into a silence that was almost shocking.

Kay stepped quietly to his fridge, his face falling a little and some sort of tension leaving his back. He took out a carton of fruit juice and drank a long drink. Imagining Elizabeth going away into her own world. Sweeping herself away into it all – into the still night that remained still no matter how many rowdy students passed through it.

Kay looked round the deserted kitchen, taking in the piles of antique washing up, the empty, wine-dregged mugs where dead cigarette ends and roll-ups floated forlornly. The cracked portable disco light and someone's forgotten weed, looking like crumbled rabbit droppings, sitting on an electric hob. A big moth had come in and was circling near the high ceiling. It looked like a Yellow Underwing of some kind – a large one – and he watched it for a moment. The TV was playing some program where couples sat in improbable armchairs and squabbled publicly at a low volume and he crossed to it and switched it off. Couples and couples arguing was not something he wanted to know about. Certainly not here, in the eerie quiet.

Eerie? The thought had entered his head without much significance, but now it was there, he realised it was quite appropriate. This building – this remote building full of students in the middle of the countryside – was indeed a slightly eerie place when empty. It was like a large railway station in the small hours of the night or a deserted supermarket – as though it should have been busy but, for some reason, wasn't. That emptiness seemed to fill it with a strange desolation – a sense of loss and hollowness that chilled him.

The stories that inevitably circulated about haunted rooms and the ghostly presences that walked the building seemed closer now. More understandable if not more believable. More alone.

Nothing to do with that thought except forget it. He opened his drawer and took out a bowl and spoon. Sweet crunchy cereal with freeze-dried fruit – the start of the 21st century would probably be remembered as the era of the freeze dried fruit, he thought. Genetically modified of course. They seemed to sum it up somehow. A slosh of nice full-cream milk and he sat down moodily to eat it. The sweet, wheaty stuff probably wouldn't do him much good. The heavy mix of sugar and grain could only add to a bad temper. But even so, one could not argue with the mighty pleasure of that sugar and he went to it, eating rapidly.

If only he had a little chocolate . . .

Feather was gone too, now. They were all gone. He was probably the only person left in the house, save perhaps for one or two other die-hards working in their rooms. That concept began to turn in his head

– turn like an animation of a galaxy revolving. There was a question in all this as well, if he could be bothered to find it – a why. Lots of whys. A whole list of whys. Like why was he sitting here while a bewildered and frightened moth danced on the ceiling? While the building frowned in emptiness? It was all an act of course. That gruff 'can't be bothered to party' attitude. Kay knew that and smiled to himself over it. It was the sort of act that you couldn't help putting on if you wanted to remain polite. In reality though, it was a matter of taste. Nothing more. And at least now, in this quiet, he didn't have to put on a performance. This was a college of performing arts, but Kay hated performing.

He tilted the bowl to his lips and drank the last of the milk – milk heavily sweetened and fruity from the cereal it had nursed – then put it aside. The moth still flew overhead, bashing itself every so often against the ceiling, and he wished for a moment that he could reach it to put it out. Buildings must be the most horrible deserts for insects. As alien as anything you could imagine in an SF movie. But of course, nobody cared about the moths . . .

The washed and still-wet bowl went back into the drawer. Leave it out to dry and somebody would use it, he knew that much. Well – someone would probably use it anyway – but what did it matter? What did it matter if the kitchen became a vast free-for-all? It was all part of the crazy physics of this place. Feather was right there. Then he restlessly headed back upstairs. In his room, he toyed briefly with his oboe, wondering weather to try and play something to calm himself. But he shoved that aside impatiently. He had already played a lot today and now he felt in the wrong mood to create anything – even to sit there and play Benjamin Britten.

So instead he turned to the only alternative that he could think of.

Kay had found this small wooden flute in one of the several little shops in Archers that sold antiques and junk and odds and ends, and he had been working to get it playable ever since. For some reason he couldn't begin to fathom, the mouthpiece had been completely stopped up with what looked like hard wax, which filled the entire head end of the instrument. It was an annoying puzzle and one that slightly offended his musician's sensibilities. It was almost as if it had been deliberately disabled, and why the hell do that to a musical instrument? Instruments were meant to be played.

It was a straight whistle, like a recorder, rather than a transverse flute, but everything about this instrument was strange, not just the sealed mouthpiece. Most whistles had six or seven holes in a line down its length, and maybe a thumbhole the other side. This flute had eleven holes in a line that twisted curiously – and two thumbholes, which was unlike any other wind instrument he had ever heard of. Positioning his hands on it, thumbs in place, it was just about possible to cover the first eight finger holes with only a little discomfort, though the position of them seemed to want some fingers to be longer than they were – but the remaining three were quite out of reach, trailing down towards the end of the tube. Kay was mystified as to their purpose. He was also curious about the tuning. A recorder has eight holes, and there are eight notes to the octave. With thirteen holes on this bizarre pipe, how did that function? It must have a very different tuning system to anything people were used to in the UK.

All these mysteries only made Kay more eager to get the thing playable. But each time he had tried – carving the wax out with needles or tiny tweezer blades – he had given up in despair and left it sitting in silence. The flute was constructed from a single slightly curved length of wood tube stopped up into a mouthpiece with a tightly wedged fipple. So there was no easy way to get in there and clear it.

Now though, Kay was loosing patience. The only way to get rid of wax is to melt it, he decided. So that was what he would do. The thought of cooking a musical instrument gave him an uncomfortable feeling – but what did it matter? It was little use as it was. Back in the kitchen, he fished in his cupboard, dragged out a small milk pan and filled it with water. He tossed the forgotten weed packet into the bin (cheerfully picturing in his mind the expression on the others' faces if they had seen that) and, with only a little hesitation, he put the flute on to simmer. Head immersed. Kill or cure.

A faint unpleasant scent soon began to haunt the air and he sniffed curiously. It made him think of salt, though he wasn't sure where the association came from as salt has no smell. It must be the sea, he decided. The scent of the sea. But the scent of the sea was a familiar one to him, as he had grown up close to it and smelt the smell all of his life. It was a nice smell – a fresh outdoors smell of seaweed on the strand and a sea breeze in the face. Here, there was an undertone that seemed less pleasant. It seemed to taste slightly salty as well, he discovered, when he put the whistle to his lips.

Finally, after twenty minutes of fiddling, near-boiling and blowing into it, the instrument announced itself with a sudden piercing squawk at his lips and he gave a satisfied smile. It was alive again! Quickly he ran it under the hot tap one last time, running water through the whistle and down the tube. Then he positioned his fingers carefully over the holes, wondering how to play it. Then the first actual note from it – a salty-tasting breathy but clear tone. He would probably never know if the hot water or the wax had affected it or not – but a playable instrument was better than an unplayable one. With a satisfied grin, he quickly dumped the waxy saucepan in the sink – if anyone wanted to use that, they were welcome to – and ran back upstairs to his room.

"Ok," he said aloud, sitting down. "Elizabeth – I dedicate this *etude* to you . . ."

. . . and pulled himself up sharp. He had never even played the instrument before and here he was giving a dedication?

As he produced the first few notes though, a waft of something new seemed to be filling the air and he found himself warming to it. It was affecting, for all his inexperience – for all its odd tuning. His oboe was a perfectly machined thing of precision and almost superhuman refinement that demanded skill and dedication – an instrument that made its player its slave. This, on the other hand, felt simple and primeval – a thing of rough wailing notes cast out into the wind and the darkness beyond the fireside – as though the merest unrehearsed touch could still create sounds with power and a weird twisted beauty. The sound, as he began to find his lips for it, was rough and filled with air, more like panpipes or shakuhachi than a recorder or a modern transverse flute. The note responded to his breath pressure, rising and falling in barely perceptible microtonal lifts and he happily went with it, letting the instrument shape the whole musical world rather than trying to force any familiar western traditions onto it. The tuning was slowly making more and more sense, the more he heard it. And as he played, he found himself unexpectedly filled with emotion that almost made him choke – made his breath control waver and tremble. His dedication had been a bitter joke, of course, but in reality Elizabeth sat at the heart of this music. That was a great inevitable.

Someone had once described this sort of love to him as like a child denied his yearned-for toy, a comment that had sent a jolt through him at the time. And maybe that was true. But if that was so, then all people were toys. Everyone. And the phrase meant nothing. Just a part of humanity's general and ignoble tendency to criticise the inevitable. What could you do about it, after all? You couldn't escape from this. You couldn't tell it to shut up or argue it out of your system. All you could do seemed to be to sit there and take the torture for as long as it chose to rip at you – and try desperately to minimise collateral damage. One day it would fade away – but how could there not be scars lingering forever? Surely you could never completely recover from a pain that burned like this? Kay just didn't know. The future was a blank, as always.

Did everyone feel this way? If so – how did the world manage to function?

Finally, he sat back, panting from the unusual breath control that the instrument demanded. Somewhere down the hall, some lingering fellow student not at the party was playing CD music – the usual background murmur of this building, consisting of a pulsing beat and some girl singing about something inaudible – but he hardly heard it. That plastic sound seemed utterly irrelevant to anything here and his mind just blanked it out.

Kay put the flute down on the bedside table and lay back on the bed, his tense shoulders beginning to loosen and his twisting face beginning to relax.

"Elizabeth," he whispered, smiling, "I hope you enjoyed that. I shall call it . . ."

He broke off. That music didn't have a name. It just came, and then was gone forever.

Sleep came quicker than usual – but the nightmares were exceptional.

It began with music echoing through space. A crash of polytonal piano music, and he gazed around sharply. They were surrounded by water – mud – the sea. A lonely piano sitting incongruously in marshland.

They = himself. Elizabeth. Each of her hands a different scale. Kay winced as the sound pulled in two directions at once and continued in a stream of blurred minimalist-repetitive sound. Water splashed and vibrated in response.

And the audience sat in ranks in the water and mud and watched quietly and critically. Heads on one side – eyebrows up. Familiar people sitting in accepting reception of a performance, just as they had for many others in this college. Even the image of an audience sitting in a salt marsh wasn't so strange here. This wasn't the first event that Archers had hosted in an incongruous location. Kay could recall flute players sitting in tree branches or suspended from ceilings and theatrical events in the local river. Mystical happenings out on the moors and brightly coloured clothes marching down wooded tracks with hippie paraphernalia. This was just the same – just another hopeful avant-garde performance, with that same sense of stylised and largely emotionless seriousness. And wet arses were a small price to pay for high art.

But as he glanced around, he realised that he wasn't watching. Out in front of everyone, he was hit by a wash of shock. He was on stage – and hadn't a clue what to do. Performances shouldn't be unfamiliar when you are the focus of all eyes.

There were other people here as well, he realised. All female – standing behind him in a curved line, looking formal and serried – dressed in trouser suits and white shirts. Immaculate makeup. Who were they? Familiar faces from around college, that's who. They carried manuscripts from which they read, but all he could really focus on were their eyes, which made him feel uneasy. They seemed fixed on him bleakly – rendered even more chilling by the formality of the situation.

They were a chorus.

The music played on – defining itself more and more, crystallizing almost, Elizabeth's strong arms blurring like a cartoon. It was a hypnotic haze of sound – simple but intense. And Kay shifted his attention back to her, dimly aware that he could read this music. It seemed very female – that was the key. Not simply because it was Elizabeth sitting there so proudly, hammering the keys, but because it was music with an agenda – a sense of something self-glorifyingly, fundamentally and even aggressively female. But maybe with little to say beyond its own femininity. This was also music that was setting itself up as his opponent with a belligerence that he didn't like. Words and phrases seemed to hammer in it, all of them accusatory. And what did that make him? What was his role? What was the audience, staring at him so earnestly, waiting for him to do?

Ladymusic, Kay thought, the word popping into his head fully formed like a gift.

Elizabeth just sat there, back arched forwards and head thrown back – an expression of self-satisfaction and glory on her face. She was not revealing anything yet – just prolonging this strange diffuse moment. But eventually the chorus behind him began to shift and change – joining the music with an accusing murmur. And the murmur spoke clearly enough. Aimed at him clearly enough. Be my victim, it cried. Accept the salt atonement for a world mad with who all needs to blame . . .

Blame?

Kay was the dancer here, he realised. Kay the soloist. In the end, his unease at the unexpected situation didn't stop his feet moving to the music in a prancing, jerking walk, as repetitive and unending and as lacking in progress as the music itself. Moving like a slowly shifting video loop that made something clench in his chest. It came and went, the phrases and steps churning and churning, whipping up the mud like boiling chocolate seasoned with salt. Kay strutted before the audience, twirling sharply yet moving nowhere, sending water everywhere but unable to escape from it. He gave the audience a snarl and spread his arms to them dramatically – bowed to them a formal bow, playing the pantomime villain, with a cape and top hat. He flashed his teeth and gestured sharply – beckoning almost obscenely, then spinning away. And hey – he was good. He knew it. The mud was like oil and the motions came easily and fluidly. Kay was still the puppet though – dangling helplessly on strings of sound. He jerked his hips. Even licked exaggeratedly at the air in an obscene gesture that felt totally alien.

It didn't last very long though. Scene two and the puppet villain was vanquished. The chorus moved suddenly. The music changed. Grabbed him and pulled him off balance in a sickening swirl and the feel of many hands – landing him in the shallow water, kicking up a huge splash. Hands that held him fast under a nest of staring eyes. He lay there, trying to shake the mud from his face, but able to do nothing.

No more than a specimen laid out for dissection, ankles together, knees apart. The hands were all as female as the chorus was – soft and sleek, bony and anorexic – just the basic hands of female college students. And yet somehow they all seemed like extensions of her hands. These were all nothing – just empty shells of girls – burned out long ago on drugs, phobias and too much dreamtime. Shells that had been taken over by their queen – Elizabeth. They were puppets as well – but dancing a different dance as the ladymusic played on and the piano settled lower in the mud.

Just that – just this little clump of people lost in a vast expanse of rippling flats and marsh grass.

Scene three. Naked. Elizabeth, white-naked now. Music decayed to an unending phrase of organum – a stream of parallel notes with neither form nor structure. An unending phrase that flowed like water – that sounded as though it had never started – would never stop. Sand and blood smeared the out-of-tune keys. The blood was trickling from her hands and from her face. She was bleeding from her eyes – red drops oozing like tears.

Chorus immobile – only holding him.

But nothing is permanent. Entropy was guiding organum with its iron hand. Slowing and simplifying it – eventually reducing to a single irregular clanging chord repeating over and over, which buckled and cracked and jangled as the piano disintegrated more and more. Wood becoming twisted and worn, like the wreck of a ship – the huge metal frame, barnacle-encrusted and rusted red. The piano and the sea merging. Then, finally, Elizabeth's hands left the filthy keys and silence descended. The lady-music immolated in salt.

Scene four. And then she came sweeping down off the ruin and added her own hands to the swarm – dismissing her puppets, who retreated almost deferentially. She clutched the struggling and mud-drenched Kay and dragged him easily through the oil-like mud to where the instrument lay, wires trailing out into the water. They tickled and tangled round them both and the audience stared in breathless interest. Kay struggled to speak, but his mouth was silenced with water.

Blood and salt.

Then, white sex against the sagging weight of the old piano. Two mud-drenched bodies continuing the dance. A flowing motion of thighs and hips. But Elizabeth Ise was squirming on top of him and fucking him like a porn star and Kay stared up in horror. Like a porn star, she looked plastic and artificial. Her mouth wider than it should have been. Riding up and down, in and out, tossing her hair violently. It felt like sticking his cock into a mushy fruit – full of pips and dribbling juice. Kay screamed sea water . . .

"All will to be look at you and know your crime," she gasped incoherently, while the chorus echoed her words in an equal babble. Shrieking – screaming – singing. Loud. "And your secrets shall be secrets to no more. You blackest of black is be food for ravens and crows and the sea shall wash us to me clean of for you criminal stain . . ."

It was true. This wasn't sex. There was nothing in her eyes except contempt and Kay felt himself sinking into the mud in the face of it. The only way out of this, downwards to where the worms lead much simpler lives. The chorus yelled, seemingly as excited as their queen was – as though they also were feeling the same in out in out in their own student vaginas. The audience just watched and evaluated-the same quietly serious look in their eyes. Kay stared at them glassily. Everyone was there of course – all the familiar faces. Even Feather's face – staring at him expressionlessly, eyebrows up. And here he was being punished and ruined before them, here on this mysterious sea shore. Paralysed by Elizabeth's weight, her arse planted on top of him – her body as white as the sky, save for its signs and letters of red.

"That's not what it is about," he choked.

A negative, scolding yell from the chorus. They didn't care. In out in out was enough for them. Their muddy trouser suits made a strange contrast with their lewd and extremely aroused movements, that threatened to turn the whole beach into an orgy, their immaculate makeup now smeared and trailed across skin. But there was a bitterness in there as well. The bitterness that sex takes on in a world filled with human agony and suffocation. The chorus was howling for blood and retribution for their own pain, even as they masturbated and he stared up at them feeling dead before all this sickness and utterly unable to say anything. Instead of speech, he felt something big begin to expand even bigger inside him. Something that seethed like boiling mercury. He struggled to sit up underneath Elizabeth's arse, clawing at the rough wood of the piano legs for leverage. He could feel his own eyes, huge and wide-skinned. And with the boiling mercury, was rage. Rage at this farce of a performance. What kind of event was this? This wasn't art – just some sickly outpouring of glorified illness. And what grade would this get? It deserved an F. Fail the ladymusic that had nothing in it except poisoned and dead ladies. Fail was all it deserved. The rage in him was humming as the mercury went pouring through an uncharted cave, resonating and booming among the vaulted spaces. He hauled himself along through the mud, physically dragging her along on top of him and leaving a trail of blood like a snail. Moving towards the front of the piano. It was hard, but after an eternity, he got there and hit the half-drowned keys with his fist.

The noise was painful – a jangling clang of flaccid strings. The calm water around them rippled and splashed in response in a thousand shimmering drops. But that crash cut through everything. It was only a cluster chord, but it added something new – something non-female – to the event. And Elizabeth froze at the sound.

"Stop it," he screamed. He clutched at her by the throat and sent her brutally sprawling among the sea grass. The chorus bayed at the assault on their queen. Bastard. How dare you fight back. You must accept your punishment . . .

"You," he yelled, ignoring them, sitting up and struggling to pin her down. She gave him a breathless and triumphant grin, as though he had proved a point for her perfectly. "I see," he panted incoherently. "Ok –" His nails dug into her flesh, his knuckles going white. It was the pointless, meaningless babbling of words, but it was all he could do. "Ok – enough. I shall never know you again – I don't want to know you – I don't want you to exist."

"Of course," she said, satisfied. "Oh how you hate."

"Shut up," he yelled.

Her face went under the water then – a stream of bubbles spluttering to the surface. He held her there coldly, her white legs thrashing, while the chorus yelled louder. Even the audience was getting restive. Beginning to murmur in confusion. Startled eyebrows up and uneasy glances exchanged.

"Idiots," he screamed at them.

In a white nova of flame, the figure of Elizabeth burned in his mind as it had burned for months. Burned like a white-hot ember. Burned like magnesium. Burned like the heart of a gamma ray burst.

Elizabeth – the target of this thing called love, so strong and so painful that it must surely leave the flesh charred forever. And now the climax had come. Now the pain was reaching catharsis. Elizabeth was going to be finally snuffed. Squashed out of existence even as the water played with her hair and her struggling legs kicked the shimmering mud into the sky. Elizabeth – smashed to a stain – ripped into chopped steak.

"*How dare you*!" he howled, so hysterically loud that his voice cracked and a sharp pain shot through his vocal chords.

And – the conclusion of this performance . . . even as his hands squeezed, the chorus finally came to the defence of their queen. And everything collapsed. The tonality of the scene was gone – there was just hands. Hands that tore him to pieces – ripping limbs from limbs, hauling organs apart from organs – fighting over torn shreds of meat like monkeys. Bits of him were tossed away into the stunned audience, who ducked and shrieked. Only Feather seemed largely unfazed, curiously examining some unidentifiable organ with a frown and sniffing . . .

Even as his face came to pieces – his eyes staring off in different directions as they were hauled from his head, he saw Elizabeth sitting up – flushed and satisfied – a ridiculous grin on her face. She sat legs apart, not caring about her cunt. It looked engorged and bloated – and she rubbed at it absently . . .

Hands – in his mouth. His tongue ripped out. Hands down his throat. Hands tearing at his genitals. Hands fumbling among his bowels . . .

Then a crack.

Swallow. The dream drunk down in a gulp. Fabric. Shouting voices. The fading scream of reddened mud. And he was jumping into violent wakefulness, a grating squawk somewhere around his lips. His bedclothes were wrapped around him in a horrible tangle and his body was soaked with sweat in the shocking, unutterable horror of silence and darkness. Trying to breathe with missing lungs and larynx and drawing huge gasps. Flesh dead and numb. Missing. Try and remember how to move muscles. Legs twitch. Buttocks clench. Blood streaming and flooding. The prisoning grasp of fabric. Gazing into the dark in immovable horror – blinking and blinking. Trying to find the marshy daylight again . . .

"Elizabeth –" he wailed under his breath, his shoulders shaking.

Then he was stumbling out of bed, still unsure of the ground beneath him –forcing his sluggish and reluctant muscles to obey and wriggling the bedclothes out from around him – ignoring the stiffness and pain – fumbling for the torch beside the bed – desperately in need of light to restore normalcy – and flicking it on, half expecting to see something wrong with the sights that met his eyes. Something in disarray, something broken or melted. But everything seemed normal. The brief islands of light just showed him his old familiar books and clothes, his oboe case sitting on the desk – the music stand – a bag of oranges – the old flute . . . He stepped across to the light switch and flicked it on – a comfort – then opened the door and peered out into the corridor into more darkness and silence. He had no idea at all what time it was. Either everyone was still at the Mousehole or this was the brief but impressive dead time of the night.

Kay stepped out of his room, trying to adjust his eyes again to pierce the darkness and gloom – and stopped sharply. Everything was silent and still but there was a weird smell in the air. That same dank and salty smell that made him think of the sea. The smell mated with his dream and fear crescendoed again – a sickening sensation of something wrong and out of place in these familiar surroundings. He coughed and looked around urgently, then reached for the hall light switch to extend this little island of illumination. His eyes found the door of Number 18 instantly of course – without conscious thought. Elizabeth – the complete and utter mystery that was another person. Puzzling images of her asleep in bed vanished though as he realised something strange. Realised that there was a huge spreading stain soaking the carpet outside her door.

Fingers of his dream seemed to be threatening to enclose him again – the scent of the sea crushing him. He leant against the wall for a moment to keep his feet – then hurried across. The stink was not excessively strong but, crouching down, he felt a wave of nausea from it. No way was this the fresh smell of the seaside – of drying seaweed and saltwater. There was something rank and rotten about it that spoke of slimy, polluted mud filled with dead things. He touched it – felt the dampness – the sodden fabric – the salty smell. For a dream-like moment, he half expected his finger to come away red – but it was unstained. Perhaps it was nothing. A flooded sink – leak in a pipe. A spilt bottle of something that was soaking under the door. The only thing that was certain was that he could not knock. Wake her? That was impossible. Listening, he could hear nothing – absolute silence from within.

Except what sounded like a dripping tap.

Finally he rose to his feet. He wanted to stay there – to curl up in that puddle and go to sleep, like a dog on guard. But instead he walked softly back to his room and shut the door behind him.

Sleep was frightening – the way it stripped the mind of its self-control and opened doors to everything. No doubt to horrible truths that he should be able to handle but which he really didn't want to know about right now. Instead, he lay there in bed for the rest of the night, light glowing painfully, gazing up at the ceiling.

Students, Kay knew, tended not to be early risers unless they had to be. And this morning they would be later than ever, if last night was anything to go by. Jade Halls was eerily quiet, without any sound of movement or activity. Slowly and still feeling a little shaken, he left his room and made his way down to the kitchen, hoping for some sound to indicate that someone was awake. His mind was buzzing.

And the sounds were there.

"Hey," Feather was saying emphatically as he entered. "You really haven't a clue, have you?"

"Ok ok," Cal said wryly, hands up, palms forward in a gesture of pacification. "Point taken, but . . ."

"Point nothing," Feather snapped – but Kay was relieved to see an amused and teasing grin on her face. "You are just a wasteful decadent."

Cal gave an expressive shrug. The argument seemed to be centred on a well picked over chicken carcass on a plate on the table between them. A near-by bag revealed it as having been purchased hot at one of the local supermarkets on a shopping trip, then no doubt taxied home as fast as humanly possible. Feather leaned over it and peered closer – then gave a tut. "Kay," she barked suddenly, making him jump. "This useless sod was just going to sling this in the bin. Not impressive, I think?" She aimed back at Cal again. "You call that finished?"

"I'm sorry?" Kay murmured. He still felt too shaken by a bad night's sleep to cope with Feather and her energy.

"I call it all I could comfortably get off with my knife and fork," Cal said. Feather gave an expressive snort.

"Aaah the luxury we live in," she said. She tapped the plate. "So – I take it you have finished with this then?"

Cal sat down comfortably and regarded her, as though waiting for a performance to start. "Sure sure," he said expansively. "It's all yours. I'll deal with the 'decadent sod' bit later when we are alone."

Feather grinned. "Then I will demonstrate."

She skipped off, washed her hands and grabbed a small bowl. Then she plumped down in a chair and got to work.

"Hi Kay," Cal said turning to him with another wry smile. "Good morning. Take a seat. Feather the Didact is about to perform."

She slung a chicken bone at him but he dodged quickly. Kay leaned over curiously to watch what she was up to. Her fingers were working over the chicken carcass with great familiarity, plucking off the remaining shreds of meat and tossing them into the bowl. She went everywhere, very dextrously, probing into the nooks and crannies. They caught trailing remnants of the thighs and plucked lingering shreds of breast meat. She flipped it over and quickly removed the small muscles of the bird's back and spine. Kay watched with interest – and some appreciation. Right then, Feather's hands seemed to shine through the dull haze of sleep as one of the most beautiful things he had ever seen. They were hands that knew what they were doing and were beautiful in that capability. Quite a substantial little pile of chicken was gathering in the bowl as well. Little shreds and filaments, but chicken nonetheless. Finally she sat back with a pleased grin, licked her fingers and surveyed the results.

"Mix a few things with that," she murmured, "and it will last you a day." She gave Kay a quick smile. "These decadents should have to live wild for a few days. That would be the end of finicky diets and wasteful habits . . ."

She broke off with a yelp as Cal slung the chicken bone back at her, catching her on the back of the neck.

"You are right of course," he said, rising to his feet. "I humbly concede. I abase myself before your indisputable reasoning with neither sarcasm nor exasperation."

He reached for the bowl, but Feather twitched it out of his reach.

"Oh no," she cried. "It's just what I need for supper. And, as you had finished with it . . . You can have this though." She shoved the plate of bones in his direction. "That will still make a good stock. Use it well."

She quickly covered the bowl with film and slung it into her fridge while Cal gazed expressively at the remains.

"Hey Kay," she called. "Glad you are up. I wanted to show you something."

"Oh?" he said sleepily. "Up? I thought I was up quite early – for today."

"Yes," she said. "I didn't stay out that late. It was fun for a while – but hey. It came clear that it wasn't going to do anything it wasn't doing already – so I came back."

She came spinning over and grabbed him by the arm.

"Come through to my room," she said. "Your idea worked a treat – though I almost missed the start of it all."

"Idea?" he asked, following her.

Her room was untidy, but not chaotically so. It was just the room of one who knows how far down the list of priorities neatness should fall.

Clothes on the floor – a strewing of books and papers. Odd trinkets picked up in the local shops or when out walking . . . pine cones, unusual stones, a clump of blue Copper Sulphate crystals . . .

"The copper wire," she said, leaning over her computer. "It was just bizarre enough to work." Indeed, there was a tangle of it by her bed, presumably where she had shed it on returning. She picked it up. "I always rather liked copper," she said dreamily, running her fingers over it. She handed it to him, then called up some images on her small computer. Pictures of her in full regalia and of the party in full swing. Gold and silver everywhere. Noise. Activity. Students. And there she was. Glittering – her waist swathed in coils of the stuff, woven through the belt-loops on her trousers. She looked great, he thought with a smile – looking both at the wire and the figure it encircled. He wondered who had taken these pictures. Whoever it was had liked what he had seen, for the images followed Feather lovingly – enjoying her silver trousers and flowing top. The wire added a touch of roughness that contrasted agreeably – not to mention accentuating her hips and buttocks.

"Kind of hard in the bathroom," she put in with a chuckle. "But worth it."

"Anyway," she said. "Have a look through. I just have to get changed quickly before I go out."

Kay sat down and began pressing the arrow key, while Feather unconcernedly stripped down to her knickers and began rummaging in her rickety student drawers for clothes. Kay gave her a brief startled glance – but now, after a year living in the same building, this was something one was used to. Feather wandering back from the shower, stark naked and with her towel slung over her shoulder. Feather answering the door straight from bed, blinking, white and messy-haired – and heedless of embarrassing anyone. And, not so long ago, Feather naked on stage before most of the college, which had taken people by surprise not because it had happened – it was not so rare to do that at this college, dedicated as it was to experimental art in various forms – but because it had been so simple and without any fuss or obvious agenda. Feather, the mischievously defiant naturist. Kay had hardly recognised her then. It was amazing how much of a person's visible identity is caught up in what they wear rather than what they really are. Just a smallish girl with pale skin. Nothing fancy or complicated. No make-up that he could see – and it only helped the feeling of simplicity that she never bothered with razorblades or the rigmarole of shaving, so she was naturally adorned with three defiant tufts of hair – crotch and armpits.

"Is this better?" Feather had asked afterwards, clothed again.

He had flinched. "What?"

"Come on," she said, grinning. "Quit the embarrassment. It's nice. You know as well as I do that we are all just flesh – nothing odd about that." She grabbed his arm and pinched him sharply. "I grew up in the countryside," she said. "I practically lived in the woods and on the beach – not a silly country farm-lass. I was a wild girl with seaweed in my hair. So I know what is real and artificial. You are artificial," she said, pinching him again. She flapped her still open shirt. "This is real. Get used to it."

That was her amiable didactic way of course, with no malice in her voice at all – but Kay had almost crumpled up under her assault. He had stammered and spluttered and tried to grin. But he had soon realised that she was right. Now, Kay just carried on looking through the rest of the pictures with a half smile, only vaguely and happily conscious of bare skin just behind him.

Unsorted. Blurred. Excited. Students fooling around. This was the Mousehole. As cramped, crowded and kinetic as any student bar. Studying these pictures made Kay feel like an unwelcome naturalist.

On one, there was a glimpse of Elizabeth – just standing there looking rather red in the face, plastic cup of white wine in her hand. He stared at that intently for a moment – but could find no clues in it.

And then there was Cal again. Slightly chubby, sleek, smart, mannered and unrufflable Calvin – his face unexpectedly delicately formed and elegant. In some ways, Cal was one of the most alarming students in Jade Halls. He was quiet, reserved and slightly superior. A notorious perfectionist when he got interested enough. He never said more than he had to, but gave the unnerving impression that there was a lot that he could say if he could be bothered to or decided to let himself. And some of it, you just might not like. He looked slightly out of place here in the partying Mousehole – not least because he was the only person in the frame not decked in gold and silver. At least so Kay thought. He was dressed in jet black – but closer inspection revealed his contribution. Two tiny broaches on his jacket – just plain disks of metal. One gold – one silver. That merited a small laugh. As always, he gave the impression that he was just there because he had been pulled there – but there was a twinkle in his eyes and a microscopic grin on his lips all the same.

One picture featured both her and Cal, she pulling a minxish grin and Cal trying not to laugh as she dragged him into the image, looking tolerantly at the camera that she had obviously held out at arm's length.

Feather the party girl?

Then she kissed him.

And that was something different.

She was up to something again – trying to prove a point of some kind. Wasn't she? Feather the experimenter? The Try Anything Do Anything girl? Kay looked at the picture nervously and put the wire down beside the bed again.

Why are you showing me that, he thought? I don't want to see that.

Can't you understand that? his mind added petulantly. Isn't that obvious?

He chased the thought away and quickly pressed the keyboard for the next picture – but the mood had changed a little. He glanced at Feather and round her room uneasily, suddenly feeling the prickling of tiredness. She had found and climbed into some neat striped trousers and a vest top and was now studying her untidy hair in the cracked mirror over the sink. He nodded through the last of the images, but they had become generic. There were a few more of Feather but most were just of other Jade Hall students or people he had never seen before – no doubt from other Halls. Finally, when he had gone through the set, he rose to his feet to find Feather behind him, waiting.

They just stepped out into the corridor again and made their way upstairs together, he towards his room.

Then Feather paused and glanced around.

"What on earth," she began, gazing at the stain outside Elizabeth's door – and Kay froze in shock. Then, with a casualness that brought Kay a pang of envy, she hurried over and banged smartly on the door.

"Elizabeth?" she called, and leant her head to listen.

Kay shook his head and tried to shrug.

"She might have told me she was going out," she said with tolerant crossness. She peered at the stain. "I wonder what that is – it must have been a heck of a spill. The warden will have a fit when she sees it!"

"Hmm," said Kay, and yawned. Feather looked at him.

"Hey," she said with a sudden look of concern. "Are you alright?"

He smiled uneasily. "Well – I didn't sleep very well."

She rubbed him sympathetically on the arm – a touch which she must have noticed made Kay jump slightly. "You look rather rough. You should go back to bed. And if anything is making you get up – sod them."

"I don't know," he said. "I dreamed – it was so horrible that I didn't want to sleep again." He laughed shortly. "I had to lie there with the light on – first time I ever had to do that in my life."

She made a sympathetic noise and together they walked back to his room.

"What was it about," she asked. "Or can't you remember?"

Kay climbed heavily into bed and she sat down by his feet.

"I – don't know –"

For a moment he actually wanted to tell her – to tell it all – to pour it all out at the feet of this amiable girl – try and talk it out of himself and find some sort of comfort in that. But he couldn't of course. He looked at Feather helplessly and she saw his reluctance quickly enough.

"It's ok," she said. "Never mind. But it's only a dream. Right?"

"Yeah – let me dream about something else," he said. "Something much more appealing."

Feather gave him a mischievous grin. "Anything spring to mind?"

"Give me something," he said lazily.

"Ok," she said, smiling. "Red cucumber."

"I beg your pardon?"

"A red cucumber and a fox's tail," she said, jumping up and twirling herself round. "I know you have a good imagination. Ok – get some sleep and have some dreams – you will feel a lot better."

She leaned over and gave him a brief, friendly hug, rubbing her hair under his chin. It came like a warm wave and left him staring at the ceiling blankly.

"I will bring you a cup of tea in an hour or so, shall I?"

He smiled. "That would be fantastic," he said, and she grinned and turned away.

"Where are all the lazy sods?" she asked as she made for the door. "All drunk out of their minds I suppose. They will come crawling out of the woodwork at midday groaning, grumbling and grousing about how rotten they all feel!"

"Yes."

She stepped out with a laugh. "Sleep well," she said over her shoulder. "And if I am in your dreams, I want to hear about it later."

And she was gone.

Kay snuggled down comfortably in bed with a smile and continued staring at the ceiling. Red cucumber and a fox's tail? It was a sneaky, almost naughty image – somehow – and he found himself grinning to himself. Bel the waif-like red-phobe was uppermost in his mind of course. Feather – bless her. Feather was lovely, he thought. Just generally a really nice person. He felt as though he was still glowing from her hug and he smiled again. He was a fool. A fool for getting into a panic about Elizabeth. A fool for a lot of things. Perhaps he would be able to sleep after all.

He slept heavily – and when he woke it was much later and any dreams he might have had were forgotten. He peered round doubtfully. The clock said 13 minutes past midday and he groaned. There was a penny gleaming softly by the door, but he hardly noticed it. Where was Feather and her cup of tea? By now she would have gone out, wouldn't she? he thought with a half-smile. She had failed him after all. Of course, she had simply not wanted to wake him – but he felt a vague sense of disappointment nonetheless, which he shoed away like an annoying insect.

Plodding out into the corridor, he stopped to stare at Elizabeth's room again as he passed. The stain looked faded and was beginning to dry – but the carpet was marked even then with an encrustation that might have been salt. And the smell was still there.

In fact it seemed to be spreading. It followed him all the way down the stairs before it faded out – as though he had trailed salty wax from that flute all the way up to his room. It was a smell that stuck in his throat, however faint it was.

In the kitchen he found Cal and Feather again, still there, along with Shirley and Senka the Serbian exchange student. He gave a quick nod to Feather, who swung to greet him.

"Hi," she called. "Feeling better?"

"Yes thank you," he said, swallowing the smell away. "Much."

He didn't quite like to speak to her properly though. Cal was making him feel nervous now. That man's sharp quiet eyes made him feel uncomfortable, and the memory of that picture lingered uneasily in his head as well. Instead, he just gave her a quick smile and busied himself getting a meal. Two potatoes went into the microwave to bake and he rummaged in the fridge for something to have on them. Some blue cheese caught his eye and he plucked it out.

"Must you eat cheese in front of me?" Shirley wailed abruptly. Kay flinched and stared at her blankly. Shirley was lactose intolerant – and the tone of her voice was joking. Just a joking complaint at being isolated from a food group that she obviously missed. But Kay hesitated and put the cheese back in the fridge. Shirley stared at him. "Hey," she said. "I didn't mean it."

"It's ok," he said uncomfortably, wishing he had stayed in his room.

"Kay, what are you doing?" Cal growled. "So many people here either can't eat or won't eat so much – you can't pay any attention to it. Look at Bel and her mushrooms and her red food. Look at Jenny. People who think that strawberries or meat are a crime should just be ignored, that's all."

"It's just a matter of a reality check," Feather put in with a chuckle.

Kay flushed, feeling acutely embarrassed now. "It's ok," he repeated. "I don't really want it. I will have some butter and Worchester sauce. That will do nicely."

Senka smiled softly from behind her glass of coffee. She was another one who made Kay feel uneasy. Her pretty and angular face was obscurely inscrutable and her mild language barrier only made her more so.

"That is a very English luxury," she said quietly. "Such fussing – fussy attitude over food. Where I come from no one will understand it. We the Serbians are the meat kings of the world."

"Really?" Feather asked.

"Mmm – nobody can cook meat as a Serb can. You English . . ." She shrugged, too polite to say what she was obviously thinking. "I miss it," she murmured after a moment.

"I'm not like that," Shirley said a little snappishly.

Feather made pacifying gestures. "We know, we know," she said. Shirley subsided scowling.

"Those dipweeds," she muttered. "Do you think I like saying all the time 'I can't eat this, I can't eat that'. Then it's 'Hey – here's Shell's plate – don't worry, I made you some special mash without butter in.' Or 'Hey – that looks delicious. Um – what's in it? Oh – sorry, I can't have that. No no – I'm fine with this cabbage and carrots – honest." She gave an expressive noise and hunched over her plate. "I'm a nuisance to everyone, nobody wants me to visit them for dinner and I just want to crawl away, like the fragile, sickly lump I am . . ."

Feather grinned. Shirley didn't look very sickly. Quite the opposite, being more of a chubby, rosy cheeked sort of character.

"And then those dipweeds decide to spin some dodgy thou shalt not philosophy and then expect everyone to bend over backwards to them and their high-flown fucking ideas without even the grace to be even a little embarrassed."

"Calm down Shell," Cal put in, grinning. "Don't waste your precious fragile, sickly energy . . . Senka? Tell me more. You got any recipes?"

"But of course," Shirley muttered, "*they* have a philosophy – *they* have principals – *they* are the fucking elite, only they just happen to have sent their fucking haloes to the fucking laundrette . . ."

Cal and Feather stared at her slightly bemused. Then Feather gave a dazzling grin.

"Oh dear," Cal murmured in anticipation.

Feather aimed a snort at him, then leaned forward intimately. "Well," she said. "Speaking as one who is not a complete stranger to the taste of fresh, living blood – I have to agree with you of course."

Shirley gave her a blank look.

"Life and death, life and death," Feather said in a singsong voice. "They always dance hand in hand. Every life with a million deaths to its foundation – everything kills something in order to live. You don't get far without learning that one."

There was a silence.

"How they do it – up to them. In my case," she grinned again, "bare hands and sneaks. It was warm. Liquid. Liquescent is perhaps the word."

"Really?" Shirley murmured faintly.

"It felt good," Feather said. "I was hungry – it satisfied. I felt alive. It felt decidedly dead. You don't need any equation beyond that one."

The silence stretched out. Cal gave a tiny grin. "Are you still annoyed about that Chicken?" he demanded. Feather gave him a defiant look.

"Senka?" he murmured.

"Hmm?"

"You were saying?"

"Yes," she said. "I can tell you about Ćevapčići . . . The – trick is to mix together both the meats, not just one . . . the beef and the pork – of good quality – with the right spices. Garlic. A little onion. All ground very finely. Like a small sausage – but not as bad as . . . joj, I mean it has the different texture – firmer than English sausage. It is pure meat. Very simple – but perfect. Served with a sauce which we call ajvar . . . made of roasted lantern pepper and the – melancana – what is it? Large and purple cucumber fruit? Jaje? Something to do with eggs?"

"Well – yes," Shirley said at last. "Ok – I don't know if I could go quite that far . . ."

Feather leaned forward, still grinning. "Oh but you have to," she said. "Otherwise your philosophy dies. Then you are no different from those who are so terrified of it they can't even touch it."

"I don't have a philosophy," Shirley cried. "I specifically avoid having a philosophy. I don't care two straws what people do. I'll eat what I damn well want to eat and I ain't a culinary evangelist. So Kay," she cried, rounding on him so suddenly that he jumped. "For gawd's sake, have some cheese."

Cal gave a snort of laughter.

"I like that phrase," he said. "A Culinary Evangelist. You should make a play called that."

"Only if I can be the food," Feather put in.

"Be the food?" Shirley said. "I thought you would prefer to eat it?"

Feather shrugged.

"Naah," Shirley said grumpily. "Eating people? We don't need any more 'My Friend Ana' performances here. They would just think you were making some crap protest of some kind. You know the sort of thing. Lie down in some giant plastic tray covered in shrink-wrapped plastic and try to shock people. As if we don't know what we are made of anyway."

"Depends how you do it, though," Feather replied. "Shrink-wrap? Sounds more appetising to me than anything else. I'll have mine medium rare, I think." She chuckled. "Peppered Protester served with fries and onion rings? I bet they taste good. Most of them would run a mile from junk food."

Cal gave another snort of laughter. "Or perhaps that's what we have been eating all along. If you call it chicken, and I call it chicken – then I guess . . . it's chicken."

"I wouldn't mind knowing what I taste like," Feather continued. "Or what you taste like," she added teasingly to Cal. "That would be interesting."

"Naaah," Shirley said. "That would be a bit of a waste. I suggest we eat Jenny. Not that there is much meat on her. Just threads and famine-fat on her arse because she refuses to eat properly."

Kay quietly cut open his potatoes and treated them to a knob of butter and a dusting of cumin, trying to keep out of the conversation, which seemed to be getting vicious.

"It would be an ultimate self-awareness though," Feather said, ignoring Shirley. "Not much to know about yourself after that."

"So who gets to eat you?" Shirley asked.

"Not me," Cal grunted. "Not in public anyway."

"No?" Feather teased, and suddenly flexed herself against him, shoving her arse vigorously against his crotch in a blunt gesture that made Kay flinch. Cal simply gave her a tolerant frown and twirled her away.

How could he just do that? Kay felt his skin prickling. There was a scuffle and a high-pitched giggle from Feather who fled across the room as Cal gave her a strong slap on the backside.

"Now then, you two," Shirley growled, while Senka just shuffled her chair away to a safe distance, smiling silently over her coffee.

Cal sat down, totally unruffled and took a sip from his mug.

"Of course," he said, "I am not that fond of cabbages. Mildly offensive things that they are. Perhaps we should protest against them."

"Huh?" Shirley demanded.

Just as Kay was putting his condiments back in his cupboard, the door opened and Catherine, the house warden, looked in. She was a woman somewhat older than most of the students – though like many wardens here, she was an ex-student who had never quite managed to escape from the place. She was quite blunt and no-nonsense but Kay had always got on with her quite well.

"Hi," she called. "Have you seen Elizabeth?"

Kay froze.

"No," Feather said after a moment. "Not today. What's the matter?"

Catherine looked fretful. "I can't find her anywhere – and her room is wrecked. If you see her tell her to come and find me, will you?"

Kay stared at her glassily. Room wrecked?

"Ok," Cal said casually.

Then Catherine was gone and Kay sat down quickly at the table again. The conversation continued – something about launching an anti-cabbage protest march and moral awareness campaign – but Kay hardly heard it. Senka also looked a little restive, and after a moment she excused herself and glided out of the room.

Kay watched Feather, Cal and Shirley still bickering and chattering and he felt something screw up ever so slightly inside him. Shell he didn't care about – even Cal he preferred to ignore. But Feather, sitting there and occasionally injecting a comment, was making him feel uncomfortable. He had listened to her talk of warm blood and bare hands with a strange shivery feeling that wasn't really unpleasant. Something about that image seemed very pure and simple in this world of too-complex emotions and fear, all of which only felt stifling. But now the conversation seemed to have gone banal.

"And of course," Cal said, "when you think of the disgusting ways that cabbages are treated, I think it is only right that we should all avoid them. It's the only thing to do of course. The only way to fight. Nothing whatever to do with the fact that I can't stand them, of course . . ."

"Where do you think she is?" Kay put in.

"Who?" Shirley demanded, but both Cal and Feather gave him a brief thoughtful look.

"I don't know," Cal said. "At Archers, students come and students go – and sometimes the rhyme, reason or notice isn't very apparent."

So that was it, was it? Nobody was particularly worried, then? In spite of Catherine's mention of a wrecked room? He drew a deep breath. What was going on here? His chest felt tight with what felt almost like terror.

Something was very wrong somewhere.

Calvin stood up then. "Right," he said with an acceptingly weary sigh. "I have to go and get some work ready for tomorrow," he said. "Don't eat anybody without telling me first, will you."

Shirley gave a giggle and also stood up. "Me too," she said. "Kay, please eat some cheese. You will leave me feeling guilty now."

Kay smiled. "Ok," he said, lying. "A cheese and apple dessert perhaps?"

She gave a satisfied nod and the two were gone. Kay felt as though some faint impairment to his sight and thoughts had suddenly faded away and he sighed.

It was a very articulate wish right now – that Cal was far far away from here. How could you really talk to someone when a third person was hanging around? The one to one was the ideal. Nobody to get in the way. Why was that so rare?

A twinge of salt sea in the air?

These thoughts hurt a little, and he returned to his potatoes with a sigh. But then, this was a different sphere and what difference did it make? It was Elizabeth he should be worrying about – her absent figure sitting inside him like a missing tooth, wreathed in dread. That feeling you get when you know something is wrong but neither analysis or observations really provide anything to support it. Where was she? He swallowed potato heavily.

The door opened again then, interrupting his downward-sliding thoughts, but it was only Bel hurrying to her cupboard. Kay gave her a brief nod and smile, but paid no real heed. It was Feather that he was watching, sitting opposite him idly swinging her feet. Watching her staring into space with a vacant look on her face. Feather was not a conspirator against him. Was she? He ought to be saying something to her. Something – anything. A sound to cut through the deadly silence. Everyone hated silence. You always had to have something to say to fill that and banish it from the fireside.

But then the silence was broken – interrupted by a noise he had never heard before in his life. A high-pitched wandering note ending in an exclamation mark.

What music was that?

It took a moment before he realised that it was a sound of protest. A strangled wail. And that Bel was stepping sharply away from her fridge in a curious walk, eyes and mouth open.

He caught a flash of red and was aware of Feather looking round sharply. The chair scraped on the floor. Bel's hand banged against the wall.

"Fuck," she cried.

Kay felt a wash of annoyance at the abrupt return of the normal. The equation flashed through his head: Bel + red = squeal, without general sympathy on his part. For a second, Kay thought strong language.

"Oh my – gawd . . ." Bel gasped, stricken.

More noises breaking the silence: Feather's chair finished its painful scraping across the floor. Her jeans-clad knee contacted a table leg with a dull bang. The fridge also sounded then as well in a jangle of jars and bottles, as the door Bel had knocked away drifted into the wall.

"What the hell?" Feather demanded, and there was a note in her voice that made him pause.

The fridge was spattered with red. Red – Bel's phobia. Blood? Was it? Drips of it had trickled through the shelves and through the food on then before pooling at the bottom in a distinct small puddle. Kay scrambled up as well and stared closer, trying to work out what he was seeing and quickly following it back to its source – a sodden plastic bag on the shelf at the top, belonging to the Indian student Inderjit.

How could it be blood?

"Fuck," Feather muttered in surprise.

Kay stepped over to look closer. A smell radiated out of the fridge that made him cringe – but that was nothing unusual. Salty, fishy plus rotten vegetable essence. Student fridges always smelled bad to one degree or another. Kay forced himself to ignore that though and gingerly pulled the bag open – inadvertently releasing another spill of whatever it was as he did so. Inside was just a tightly wrapped and wet foil package. Kay stared a moment, then picked the bag up by the handles and rushed it across to the sink, leaving a trail of drips, while Bel shrank away. Kay was startled at the genuine extremity of the reaction that could be read on her face.

"Oh gawd," she said again, actually looking slightly faint. "That is so disgusting! What the fuck is going on?"

Feather jumped up and to his side, watching curiously as he dropped the mess onto the draining board, trying not to think about the stacks of unwashed dishes. The liquid felt thin, smooth and claggy – very much like blood, in fact – splashing in alarming spots on the shiny metal of the sink. He upended it. The foil came open easily enough and he stared in surprise.

Feather gave a snort of laughter.

"It's only a steak," she cried.

Kay wasn't sure weather to feel shocked or relieved and he tried to push the tension out of his shoulders. A steak? He glanced sideways at Feather, who was poking it curiously with her finger.

"Nope," she said. "Not a fresh human heart – left bleeding and dripping by the crazed Indian man-eater from the music block. I think we should christen today the Day of Meat. We can't seem to escape from it."

"It must have heard you talking about it," Kay said with a smile.

Kay glanced round at Bel anxiously and found her huddling against the fridge as though trying to hide behind it.

"How," she said miserably, "can a steak possibly . . ."

"What's the matter with you?" Feather demanded, not unkindly.

"That – that stuff. I just have to . . . Look, please – clean it up – get it away from . . ."

Kay gazed after her in astonishment as she shook her head sharply, then crisply walked out of the room, fists clenched.

"Bloody nuisance, isn't it?" Feather said brightly, pulling him back to earth with a bump. She giggled. "I can't see her getting very far on bare hands and sneaks," she said, lowering her voice. "What do you think, Kay? The therapy available for confronting phobias can be quite interesting, actually. Should one be brutal or pampering? What are the merits of the two approaches? Or would you advocate a sort of nice cop nasty cop method?"

"I dunno," he muttered. "I'm not a doctor."

"I am," she said with a grin. "Trust me."

He stared at the trail of drips he had left across the floor to the sink, then snorted and tramped back to the fridge. It wasn't that bad a mess. That plate of pasta foolishly left uncovered was done for – though Feather might disagree. But apart from that . . .

It was not his job to sort this out. It was not even his fridge. But he watched himself begin to take things out of shelves and stand them on the table.

Feather sat back in her chair, her head flopping over backwards so she could watch him upside-down.

"Oh Kay," she murmured, smiling, and mimed a spanking gesture. Kay wasn't sure if it was aimed at him, the absent Bel, Inderjit or everyone in general.

"Well," he muttered. "Not as if I have anything better to do. Some people have these enigmatic things called 'lives' – I always wondered what they were."

Feather grinned cheekily.

"Well," she said, "I ain't helping you."

He grunted, rinsing jars under the tap and arranging them into a neat line.

"Nope, nope" he said. "Not your problem."

Then Feather's phone rang, interrupting. She sighed and jerked it out of her pocket.

"Yes?" she barked, still leaning back over her chair. Kay finished washing up, listening with half an ear.

"What?" She gave a tiny laugh. "Hi – I know. What can I do for you? Well – I don't see why not. When?" she demanded. She glanced at her watch. "Ok. That's one hour, fifteen minutes to get there? What have you got for me? Something comfortable I hope."

Kay methodically began mopping out the fridge. There was a faint scent of blood – the characteristic pleasant smell of fresh beef. But it was mixed with all the many other smells that go with a student fridge, and they weren't so nice.

"Ok – I can handle that," Feather was saying. "But tomorrow morning by seven, ok? Good."

Kay glanced at her over his shoulder.

"Ok," she said. "Bye."

She gave a yawn and flipped herself back upright.

"I have to work tonight," she said, and he gave her a surprised look.

"At this time?"

She nodded. "I'll be back for tomorrow morning," she said.

"What are you doing?" he demanded, puzzled. He couldn't read anything in her face. She looked slightly fretful at having to shift, but that was all.

Feather gave him a mischievous grin.

"Emergency therapy," she said. "Didn't I tell you? I am a doctor."

He slid a shelf back into the fridge and gave her a puzzled look. He was about to ask more when Bel put her head round the door.

"Have you – er – have you . . ."

"Yes," Feather cried gaily, dancing across the room. "He's mopped and manned the pots and pans – cleaned the yoghurt and dried the cans. Swept the dishes and cleaned the place – and done all this so you can show your face . . ."

She gave her a tiny bow. "Yes," she said. "It's safe to come in again. Goodbye goodnight." She waved to Kay and hurried out, leaving Bel scowling after her.

"Manned the pots and hopped the tans," came drifting back. "Kept the kisses and cleaned his face – and all so the pretty girl can show him her place . . ."

"I cleaned it out as best I can for the moment," he said, trying not to laugh. "It should be alright since most of it was wrapped up."

"Thank you," Bel murmured, stepping over and peering into the fridge like an inspector and then doubtfully at the row of jars and packets taken from it. Then, with a sigh, she began gathering her own stuff. Thank you, Kay thought, then watched in puzzlement as she dropped it all in the bin before returning for a second load.

"You're not throwing all that away surely," he cried as she crossed to the bin with a second armful of yoghurt drinks and quorn burgers.

She nodded.

"But it's all wrapped and sealed," he protested. "I just washed it for you."

Bel looked miserable.

"I'm sorry," she snapped. "There's no way I can touch this food now." She dumped the load in the bin with a clatter and stared back at the fridge. "Err – thanks for cleaning it all though," she muttered and hurried from the room again.

Kay stared after her in silence, then turned away with a grunt. He stepped to the sink and looked in. The scent of blood was strong, mingling with the salty smell of the dishes, and he stared in bewilderment. The steak had already formed quite a pool of watery blood around it even here and it was dripping depressingly down into the stinking crockery in the sink. That in itself wasn't a problem – the blood was, if anything, cleaner than what it was landing in. But how could a simple steak have made such a mess, he wondered. Must have been very fresh. Or more likely frozen and thawing out all over the place. He gave a grunt of anger.

It must indeed have heard Feather talking.

Then there was a sliding crash behind him and he jumped round, for a moment feeling a shock of fear that was quite out of proportion. A jar lay smashed on the floor in a pool of black pepper sauce. He stared at it, dimly remembering putting it on the table. Ok – must have rolled. Ok – must have put it on its side without noticing and it rolled . . .

The smell of blood and sauce hung in the air. A smell that was salty and sickly. It seemed to be overlaid by something faintly rotten – but that was no surprise here so close to the sink.

"Fuck it!!" he snarled, slamming out of the room and stamping upstairs. With Feather gone and Elizabeth missing, room trashed, what point was there in staying awake?

He flung open his door, trying to ignore the waft of salty smell that still seemed to cling to him.

As he settled down, fully clothed, into bed, the lights of the Brockden Centre on their aging electrical circuits flickered off and on once.

* * *

When he found himself surrounded by salt water again, Kay felt an instant shock of fear, expecting people, hands, music – all for him. But now all there was around him was the quiet sea and green islands of sea grass. The storm of people seemed to have passed, the sun was higher and there was nothing left but bleak loneliness.

The piano was still there as well and that sent a small prickle across his skin. Of memories. It looked like a sodden wooden and metal corpse, lying slanting in the mud, its lid up and leaning tall like a fin, its keys like broken teeth and the wires hanging flaccid in the heavy metal framework. The whole thing was now a dull brown, stained with green algae and crusted with sea life.

Kay stared at it, feeling cold. Then he reluctantly pulled his eyes away and continued looking round the bleak scene. This place seemed to suggest something of southern East Anglia, where he had grown up. Only more so. Estuarine mudflats surrounded him almost as far along the coast as he could see in an endless landscape of sand bars, salt marsh islands of succulent samphire and coarse eel grass – home to a myriad tiny snails and flies. The terrain was as flat as any ground could be – a patchwork of tiny islands filled with the piping of birds – with what might have been a hint of trees on an equally flat land off in the distance in one direction – and the flat, shimmering expanse of the sea spread out in the other.

Kay began to relax a bit and take the opportunity to enjoy the scene a bit. Kay liked the sea, after all. He had spent his life not far away from it and the ever-changing landscape of the coastline where sea met land had always been a fascination for him. These flat salt-marsh lands especially were extraordinary. Surprisingly well-defined islands of green that vanished twice a day. The channels between them, muddy and bottomless looking. These were places where a vast sky of loneliness rested gently on your shoulders and where the endless piping of birds and buffeting winds was still not enough to break the silence. The haunting wandering of the first of Britten's *Six Metamorphoses after Ovid* came back to him – *Pan, who played upon the reed pipe which was Syrinx, his beloved.* It wasn't so hard to associate Pan with this lonely seashore, whatever his traditions said – especially in Britten's very English evocation. For a moment, he wished his dream had brought him his oboe as well. Or perhaps that little wooden flute. Both would fit here in this incarnation of loneliness – and, on this cold spring day, the marsh seemed to sing.

It didn't last though, for soon there was an interruption. Dark. A clamour of voices waking him up. From somewhere in the corridor. Someone was crying, though he had no idea who. It was hard to identify a person from their sobs.

"What the hell?" someone demanded – sounding unusually breathy and agitated.

"I don't know . . ."

"Something . . ."

". . . computer . . ."

"Mia has . . ."

". . . it was gone – I couldn't find . . ."

"She's . . ."

". . . like Jenny is . . ."

". . . I don't like . . ."

Kay rolled over and tried to go to sleep again, but something about the tone of the voices had made him uneasy.

The next day Kay woke late and remained in his room playing the oboe until late afternoon. He was trying to play Birtwistle's *Pulse Sampler* now – the Britten made him feel melancholy and the wild intensity of this piece was much more appropriate. Even cathartic. Something enthralling, but requiring such dedication, discipline and skill that it also almost equated to a human sacrifice.

It was strangely soothing.

Finally though, his hands exhausted and his lips hurting slightly, he put it aside and went downstairs, grabbed himself a carton of fruit juice and took it outside, settling in the Brockden Centre's large front courtyard. It was cold and already beginning to settle towards evening, but the air was refreshing after the day's work.

Brockden seemed quiet. Unusually quiet. The few people he passed seemed subdued and nervous. The end of the academic year was always a tense and pressuring time – a time for unease and bustups – for relationships to end and for the college counsellor to claim overtime. But even so, the atmosphere seemed unusual.

Kay was not paying much attention though. Other people were starting to seem less and less a part of his life. What was there to do except eat, sleep, play music and count pennies? He felt leaden – not just about Elizabeth now but about the whole sphere of existence. Why pick on one thing, after all, when the whole world stank to high heaven. Where depression was concerned, it was good to be generous. When this bubble of college life was over, for instance – what then? Just him and his oboe alone against a hostile world of rock musicians, crass music videos and job centre staff. What was the point of even trying?

From inside the entranceway came the sound of a whistle. He recognised it quickly enough. That was Jim, one of the music students – the one who had so gallantly sacrificed his teaspoons and the workshop's drill bits for the gold and silver party. He always whistled the same simple phrase. Day in day out – month in month out – it hadn't changed. Kay had wondered to himself how any music student could go through college with a single phrase lodged in his head – just a simple cadence of six notes. He didn't know what it was from and didn't want to know. The thought of that only served to bring Elizabeth crashing back into his head, simply by force of contrast. Elizabeth Ise was subtle and exploratory – not even close to whistlable. He remembered one concert of hers that he had attended – a couple of new piano pieces. The first thing she had played had been an extraordinarily quiet and static texture – as tranquil and restful as anything he had heard. But watching her play it had left a strange feeling in his stomach, because then it could be seen that what had gone into that tranquillity was actually the most intense activity, her hands lashing about the keyboard in what looked like a barely controlled scramble to catch all the notes, all across the keys, at the correct times – but a scramble where the fingers landed on each key with the softness of a caress.

You could have said it was irrelevant – especially if you were used to listening to recorded music. But Kay wasn't sure. It had lingered in his mind as seeming to sum her up somehow. Elizabeth Eyes, smooth surfaced but complex and intricate in foundation.

However profound that was . . .

And now as invisible as the silence left behind after the last note had faded into the dark . . .

One of the scariest silences you can ever hear.

Where was she?

Absently he finished his fruit juice and watched the willowy figure of Senka come in from the distance and make her way towards the front door.

"Who needs it?" Kay muttered aloud, deliberately slurring his voice as though drunk. Then he noticed that Jim had come up behind him, glass in hand, and he jumped slightly.

"Are you OK?" Jim asked.

"Yes," Kay said heavily. "Sorry, it is just a very strange world."

"Well," Jim murmured doubtfully, "This place is, that's for certain." He sat down and regarded Kay with tired eyes.

"Hey – you think this place is haunted?" he asked bluntly. Kay jumped.

"Eh?" he said.

"Mia told me that she felt someone touch her in her room last night. Scared her out of her wits."

"Really?"

"And things have been falling off shelves and rolling around by themselves. Perhaps we have a poltergeist."

"Perhaps," Kay said woodenly. "We also have a Mousehole filled with cheap beer, which is also well known for generating supernatural phenomena."

"And Elizabeth?" Jim demanded, causing Kay's stomach to contract. "You know, there's a rumour going round that her room wasn't just trashed – it was totally wrecked and soaked with water. They say that her clothes were found lying on the floor in a perfect human shape. You know . . . her underwear still, sort of, inside – where it should be . . ."

"Yes?" Kay confirmed dully. To the best of his knowledge, nobody had seen inside her room except Catherine the warden. "And remember what Matt came up with last term – how the whole Brokden centre we live in was just the visible tip of a vast wrecked alien craft that was still intact below us and sending out these special rays that were turning us all into brain-dead freaks? He really believed it."

"Yes . . . well . . ."

Kay snorted. "You don't need an alien craft to turn us all into brain-dead freaks in this place," he muttered.

"Yes," Jim cried. "But can't you feel the atmosphere in this place? Can't you feel that something is really fucked up somewhere?"

"Oh I can feel that," Kay agreed sourly.

Jim stared round. "It is so quiet here these days. Everyone either in their rooms or gone home or out of here at a safe distance."

That at least was true. It was unusually quiet for a Brockden evening, with the night closing in now, dark and featureless. The quiet somehow brought it home how isolated this place really was – this lonely monster of a building sprawled among woods and fields, well over half a mile from the nearest off-campus life in Archers. It was not hard to imagine cabin fever and spontaneous fears and stories sweeping through this place when the darkness had closed over it – with or without a source.

Jim reached for an abandoned wine bottle, uncorked it and poured himself a glass of dregs. It was probably sour, but he drank it quickly anyway and slammed the glass down again.

"I thought there was a crack in the ceiling in my room when I woke up this morning," he said quietly. "This huge crack that just widened and widened. I actually reached out and touched it – felt the broken edges of the plaster. But then – a few minutes later, when I woke up a bit more, it was gone again. Weird huh?"

"Mm."

"And what did happen to Elizabeth? And why does everywhere smell of salt?"

Salt? Kay stared at him sharply. "Perhaps she just got fed up with us and went home," he said, trying to sound casual. It was still almost impossible to talk about Elizabeth without feeling an agonising blast of something like panic inside.

"But – her phone is off – and what about her room?"

He had her phone number?

That gave Kay pause for a moment.

"If there was anything weird about her room, the police would have been here," Kay said bluntly. That was something that had been going through his head a lot in the last few days. If anything odd had happened to Elizabeth then surely there would have been some fuss. But as yet – except for an increasingly impatient Catherine – there had been nothing.

Abruptly he rose to his feet, watching his hand carefully to prevent it twitching.

"I have to do some practicing," he said. "I had better go."

"College is finished now though, isn't it?" Jim asked. "Just waiting for the next batch of results. That's one reason we are all so on edge."

Kay sighed. "I don't have to be doing college work to practice," he said. "I just need to play, ok?"

"Sure," Jim said with a shrug. "Take it easy."

Kay entered the building and drew a deep breath, his heart beating unexpectedly hard. What the hell was this rubbish? All Jim's talk about spooks and weird stuff shouldn't get under his skin. But, somehow, it was. It was nonsense – of course. Just a bit of hysteria that was building up. Cabin fever. Classic end-of-yearitis. And if it wasn't for Elizabeth nagging and worrying at him, he wouldn't care.

He could not shake off the feeling that he had driven her away somehow.

He glanced back into the dark courtyard and at the wine-drinking figure of Jim and felt a wash of annoyance. How dare he make up dumb stories about this? About her. He swore to himself and forced himself to start walking again. Somewhere down the corridor was Feather's room and he hesitated. That friendly hug of hers and her pragmatic common sense filled his mind. Feather? Feather was great. Clever and sensible and the antithesis of everything that was clustering around him right now. He didn't like tapping on doors and disturbing people, but Feather was different. He found a strange kind of trust for her. The feeling that you could actually relax with her. Something he felt very rarely.

Finally, he stepped forward again towards her room. Perhaps just for once the over-familiar Cal would be somewhere else and they could talk a bit before bed.

There was no light shining through the crack at the bottom of her door though. Perhaps she was asleep. It was getting quite late after all. He drew a disappointed breath.

But then, from within, came what sounded like a sob.

Feather? Crying? Kay paused and gazed in shock at nothing. An unexpectedly violent shock of feeling. Of many different feelings that there wasn't time to analyse. But prominent among them was a weird flash of delight. Feather unhappy? Crying just as he sometimes wanted to cry in the nights whilst trying to sleep. Oh, the envy of one who could actually cry! What glory was that? And what else was there here? A fellow feeling in misery? Perhaps together they could find some comfort. Comfort was a mutual activity after all. Like all the big things seemed to be.

Feather's eyes had always revealed the haunting things that lived inside her. Kay hesitated a last moment, then tapped on the door.

"Hey? Feather? Are you alright?" he called softly. Then he pushed the door open.

Later, that was what went round and round in his head. Why had he opened the door? It nagged at him because it was so totally out of character. A rare bit of bravado or trust indeed. But at any rate, he peered in – taking a long moment to work out what he was seeing, because the room was very dark. What was on the bed only revealed itself as two figures when Cal raised himself on his arms and looked at him.

"Awww," Feather cried, slightly muffled and, for some mysterious reason, putting on an American accent. "This ain't a spectator sport, y'know. You'll embarrass him."

She was on her back, bare thighs up almost precisely vertically and angled apart at a very nice ninety degrees. She gave her hips a quirky heave and stared at him with a comical but challenging expression on her face.

"Damn," Kay muttered. "I just . . . I mean, I was only . . ."

But that was pointless babble. His feet were already dragging him out of that room and he found himself in the corridor, the door closing with a bang behind him. He stared at the dull painted wood blankly, then caught a distinct giggle from inside and jerked away. Turned crisply and tramped up the stairs to his room without looking back.

* * *

A crack in glass.

What can you say? What can you do? Kay felt smothered in thick brine, which closed over his eyes, breaking up the sky into blurred ripples. He sat up sharply, gazing round. In the salt marsh, the tide was coming in. Birds howled. A million tiny sea snails started their lives for the day. Wires swept to and fro in the waves that surged in. Wires draped with seaweed and human hair. Wires trailing over him – the broken metal ends tickling his skin. He was sitting against the piano, leaning against one of its rough and harsh wooden legs. He stared round the land and sighed. It was a desert. Filled with salty crisp samphire, but a desert none the less. It was a vast world of flatness with only the shaggy form of the piano visible for miles in any direction.

A touch to a piano key brought nothing but silence, so Kay felt in the water around him, found a pebble and tossed it quietly.

It landed with the tiny click of wet stone on wet stone. And somehow that sound it made seemed just about the most disturbing sound possible. It reverberated out across the miles like a form of echolocation . . . and the sonar only proved what he already knew.

There was nothing here.

He was alone.

Kay screamed – but the sound seemed feeble and pointless compared to that tiny click that had gone before . . .

It was a few hours later that Feather found him on the stairs, his face feeling strange and that almost microscopic click still ringing in his ears. He tramped down and made to pass her. But she intercepted him.

"Hey," she said, her cheerfulness sounding a little forced for once. "Are you all right?"

"Yes, yes," Kay murmured casually, again making to pass her – but she stopped him.

"Hey," she said again. "Look – what happened . . . not a big deal. You know?"

"What?"

Feather frowned and uncharacteristically struggled with words. "You looked so dismayed, that's all," she said.

"Yeah yeah," he muttered. "I actually thought – well, that you were crying or something. So I I I looked in. It's ok."

Feather stared at him, looking puzzled and Kay realised that he must be wearing an expression on his face – though he wasn't sure what it was. Every muscle seemed to be fighting with every other muscle, so who knows? Kay felt a twitch hovering hopefully somewhere in the background as well, but he stamped on that firmly.

"Well yeah," she muttered uncertainly. "The mighty and wonderful sex act. Centre of life and the world – and – and all that . . . Kay? What's wrong? I don't understand."

He tried to get control of his rigid face.

"Hey," she said. "You looked as though you were afraid I was going to come after you and steal your eyes in payment for that brief glimpse of my . . . but, it's nothing."

"I know," he managed. "Yes – yes – it's fine. Look, sorry – I have to . . . to . . ."

Gesturing urgent appointments in far away places, he gave her an odd ducking nod and smile and hurried on down the stairs. He could feel her staring after him with a dismayed look on her face, her eyes burning into his back like a stubbed cigarette. It twisted at him – but he clutched down on that tightly, his jaw and shoulders aching from the tension. Just get away from that stare. That's all.

Finally he heard her shoes continuing away upstairs and he stopped. Seven. Eight. Then a pause – round the corner. She was out of sight. One, two, three . . . He tuned his ears to the building and took in the sounds. Four, five, six. Count them. Up up up – brief silence of carpet. The door opens – a clank against the fire extinguisher. Soft padding footsteps now – fading away down the carpeted corridor. Three, four, five. He counted them – but then the door swung to again, cutting off everything. A second distant bang as a room door shut. Was that her?

Who knows? But anyway – she was gone.

Kay relaxed and leaned against the wall. Hey-ho. And wha'do ya'know? Feather was right of course. It was indeed nothing. Call it – yes – call it a little extra bonus in daily life – that brief glimpse of her dot dot dot. A little touch of paprika in a day that was mostly just dull stock. But then, why did these corridors seem so very bleak now? In contrast to the rooms, the walls out here were minimally decorated and severe – and why did they suddenly seem so dark and clinical as he slowly allowed his awareness to enter the muscles of his own face and try and find relaxation. The Brockden Centre brooded. A big building that suddenly felt very heavy above him. Kay felt empty and silent – as though all thoughts had thought themselves out a long time ago. Silent maybe – but the pain without the thoughts was as fresh as dew. Now he relaxed, there it was, waiting for him with a friendly smile – roiling and prickling inside.

Cal and Feather . . .

Of course. Why not?

shrug

How easy was it for a pure emotion to be perverted? As easy as it was for it to lose any coherence – and flap about like a severed fanbelt in some impossible engine. Lashing anyone it came in contact with to shreds. Was there even such a thing as a pure emotion, or was everything that anyone had ever said on the subject, wrong? Where was the difference between love and friendship? Or was everything that anyone had ever said on that subject, also wrong?

Probably.

It just wasn't fair, he thought, starting to walk towards the kitchen again. Really. Was it. Why did this have to happen? For a nothing and a why-not, it seeded a very sharp hurt inside. Bickering – silly – petty little pains, they were. Of course. Pains that should be swatted like fireflies. Get rid of them. They were unworthy. But of course, the other side said, they wouldn't go. He wished that Elizabeth was dead – wherever she had gone. He wished Cal was as well. The world would be a much better place without both of them. Then he and Feather could just wander and talk . . . but who cares? Jealousy? With/without reason? Oh but there's always a reason and anyone who doesn't believe it is a liar. In Kay's head, an aching hollow place bled a stream of red and black. That was the reason – you didn't need a reason beyond that.

Kay grinned and tripped a little dance step down the corridor. It was a step that, had he noticed, mimicked the one in his dream almost perfectly. The pantomime villain, with a cape and top hat. The dancing demon. Aaah but there are reasons, he thought, dancing. All the reasons that anyone needs. They are sitting there in that hollow place inside – a four-pointed tetrahedral thorn suppurating in blood. Dancing. A prancing, jerking walk as he strutted down the corridor, twirling sharply and jutting his hips under a big thin grin. The points buried deep in flesh. So what does this mean? It means that the hollow must be emptied. Purged. And that requires flesh to be torn. Squeezed. Squeezed. Squeezed. Squeezed out. And in again. The thin, claggy feel of blood running free. The smell of salt. Of sex. Then empty that hole – and purge the thorns forever.

When he reached the kitchen door, he paused a moment. He punched the wall hard and cheerful, bringing the dance to a close. Please – let there be nobody in the kitchen.

No joy. Shirley looked up sharply from her pasta as he peered in. Kay saw her eyes flinch in something like fear and he clenched his teeth. Afraid? Well, why not? What else could he expect?

"What's up with you?" she asked.

"Nothing!" Kay snapped brightly. Then "I just wish I was dead, that's all," slipped out before he could stop it.

"Yeah?"

To hide his embarrassment, he crossed the room, his feet still following the rhythm of the dance. What did it matter? He felt as though he was floating. It felt good. He slammed open the door of his fridge with a rattle of bottles and peered in with a flourish. Shirley watched as he glared for a moment, then he grabbed a packet of cheese and slung it into the rubbish bin with a crash. He swore to himself.

"Nope. I will refrain." he sang. "You are allergic to it." He rummaged again.

"Huh?" Shirley stared at him. He grabbed a packet of sausages.

"Can't eat that either," he said, singsong and weary. "Not while Jenny is living here." The sausages went into the bin in a neat pass backwards and he twirled round again. "Mushrooms?" he asked picking one up by its stalk and regarding it like a college professor. "Oh sorry – Bel can't stand them. My apologies." The mushroom bounced off the bin lid and rolled behind the freezer. "Fuck it all!" he cried, suddenly loosing the dance and grabbing a carton of apple juice before hurling the door closed again with savage force.

"Hey – er . . . calm down!" Shirley murmured.

"Huh? What?"

"What's got into you?"

He glared at her. The pressure was suddenly intense. His head was starting to hurt.

"Nothing has got into me!" he cried banging the carton down on the table, releasing a small tossing splash. "I just hate this place and everyone in it." His voice was rising and becoming shrill and Shirley shrank back into her chair. "That's all," he cried. "Nothing to worry about! It doesn't matter, of course. Who cares? I just . . ."

His words were cut clean by a splitting crash. A jar of lemon curd, one of several assorted jars standing in a line on the worktop beside him, had burst into shards, spraying yellow curd and pieces of glass across the work surface at him.

The silence was icy.

Shirley's mouth opened in a questioning O.

There was a small pain blossoming and Kay tasted lemon on his lips. He slowly raised a hand to his face, then stared vaguely at the small smear of blood, his expression blank. Then he looked down at his shirt, which was also plastered with the yellow spray. It was warm, he realised. Almost hot. Warm = heat = expansion = pressure = rupture . . .

He hauled himself away from the worktop, staring blankly. He felt like ice – but the rage still continued somewhere. It had to, because a second jar exploded and he hastily shielded his eyes while Shirley fled to a corner and continued staring. Something was flowing through the kitchen. A third glass jar burst – spraying its contents across the work surface. And a fourth. Kay just stood and stared as the explosions worked their way through the line of jars. One after another they detonated until the room was thick with a heavy scent of fruit and lemon and salt and marmite and chilli sauce. Then it was over. The whole thing had taken barely half a minute.

Shirley came forward cautiously and Kay looked at her, shaking. He felt as though he had been squeezed like a handful of melting snow inside a giant fist.

"What the hell?" Shirley gasped, her face white. She shook her head and snapped. "Right – that is it! I am getting out of here! This building is – is . . ."

She sniffed.

"Oh for fuck's sake," she quavered. "I can smell salt – sea – whatever."

Kay drew a sobbing breath.

"What?" he managed.

"This whole fucking building smells of the sea," she cried, her voice shrill. "You telling me you haven't noticed?" A moment later Kay was alone.

Kay was in the bathroom cleaning up his face when Jim came bursting in. It wasn't that badly cut really – the worst being an inch long scratch on his cheek.

"What the hell is going on?" Jim cried. "Hey – what's happened to your face?"

"Just a cut," he said tightly. "Or two. What do you mean what is going on?"

"Shirley is having hysterics upstairs, babbling about ghosts in the kitchen," Jim said excitedly. "She says you were there. What the fuck happened?"

Kay nodded slowly. "I don't know," he heard himself say. "A few jars got broken and I cleaned them up. But I didn't see any ghosts."

"Then what . . . what's going on here?"

"Shirley," Kay said quietly, "is just a stupid girly girl. She yells the place down when a bee gets into her room. 'Oh – sorry to bother you – but – but – it's so big . . .'" he mimicked savagely. "She is just over-reacting."

Jim looked at him doubtfully. "Oh whatever," he grunted – and sniffed. "Do you smell of salt?" he asked.

"Marmite perhaps," Kay said tightly. "One got broke. Horrible smell."

"No – I mean . . ."

He broke off and shrugged. "Damm, I can't wait for this term to end so I can get out of here. You know Jenny moved out this morning? I am so thinking to follow her."

"Did she?" Kay murmured without much interest. He had to think for a moment to remember what she looked like. All he could really remember about her was that she sang indifferent pop songs, lived on vegetarian Indian food, was a devotee of Pro-Ana websites and was terrified of spiders to the point of mania. Died her hair streaked with carmine and usually wore ersatz walking boots and mirror glasses. What she was actually like – no idea.

"No great loss," he muttered, half to himself.

"This place is truly fucked up," Jim said absently. "The energy here . . . the vibrations . . ."

Kay's fist contacted the white porcelain sink with a bang.

"What vibrations?" he yelled, making Jim flinch. He slammed a hand against the wall and cocked his head in an exaggerated listening pose. "I don't feel anything," he snarled.

"But –"

"This is just a building – filled with artistic idiots, marijuana and too much fucking cheap booze. That's all I can feel."

Kay dabbed one last time at his face and hurried from the room and back upstairs, leaving Jim staring after him, shocked. But what did that matter? Must get out of here – somewhere private. His chest now felt like his face had before – as though every muscle in there was struggling to pull itself away from every other. His heart was thudding conspicuously. He passed Senka on the stairs, who stopped and stared after him with those intense and soft southern European eyes. She said nothing.

He swept into his room and stared round quickly, trying not to tremble. Then his foot kicked at something on the floor – there was a small sliding sound.

It was a penny.

Kay came to a complete stop and stared at it, all the rage knocked out of him in an instant.

A small gleaming disk of copper resting on the dark worn wood floorboards. A beautiful sight. The rich lustre of one of the loveliest of metals – far more beautiful than gold. A perfect disk of light, staring up at him . . .

What was he doing? What was coming over him?

He made a half-step towards the door, yanked for a moment by the almost irresistible urge to go and find Feather – but he halted himself sharply. Who knows where Feather was or what she was doing – but chances are she would be out of reach. Instead, he grabbed the jar of pennies and stared at it. This thing alone seemed to cut through the clouds that surrounded him. They were a hint that there was something out there that went beyond the horrors and misery that he could see and feel and understand of the world and the people in it. They said that someone, somewhere was watching him. Someone who didn't hate – didn't fear. Someone who was just . . . interested. Who was it? he wondered desperately. Someone – somewhere . . .

It seemed a hopeless puzzle.

He slumped into bed, clutching the jar to him as though it were a source of heat. He curled up, huddling the covers around him and froze, staring at nothing. Instantly, he felt suffocated – drowned. Water flowing into his mouth and nose. The tide was obviously high now. He was trying to breathe, but there was something above that was trying to keep him under the water. Not much to see – just dark shapes blurred by salt. But the waves were breaking round three sturdy pillars that surrounded him. Above, it was flat and pressing down – the water slopping against it, leaving him only an occasional gap between water and wood to catch a breath.

It was the mouldering form of the old piano, he realised. He was actually sitting under the instrument again and he struggled out, spitting sea water and blinking in the new light. The sea was all round – the marsh had almost vanished. The islands of samphire, eel grass and tiny marsh snails were just vague swirling shapes in the rolling sea – an endless pattern of blotches. Even though this was a familiar place – a place with a hint of home about it – there was a feeling of agoraphobia here now. The shore seemed a long way away and he was sitting surrounded by sea. Far off in the distance he could see the protruding shape of what might have been another wreck – a boat perhaps? Or something else? He wasn't sure. Some other absurd musical instrument maybe? It looked as though it was made of metal, the twisted, rusting sheets clawing at the grey sky. The forlorn remains of some previous visitor here, long since smashed and torn apart – as he had been . . .

In some surreal way, the rusty metal seemed to be shaped like the gigantic bell of a brass instrument. A dead super-tuba lost in the wilds – the sound it would make, low beyond hearing.

Kay sighed and pulled himself up onto his knees. And it was then that he realised that he wasn't alone. Now, Feather was there, white naked and plastered with mud. She was down on her hands and knees, crawling among the submerged marsh plants, and she looked surprisingly at home here as she gathered samphire and stuffed it into a string bag slung round her shoulders – looking like some obscure sea mammal, her naked skin built for the water. She squatted on her heels in the mud, washing the succulent plants in one of the channels before stashing them in her bag. Then she actually went down, head first, nose up – like a water reptile – and half swam, half wriggled through the deeper water and bottomless looking soft mud across to the next grassy islet. She scrambled up onto all fours with a splash and shook her hair violently, then hauled herself out onto the new island and stood up, staring round her.

Kay watched her. In a culture that attempts to hide the naked body, when it is visible, it instantly draws attention. Kay recognised that and sighed fretfully. Why was the human body so beautiful? It didn't make much sense when you thought about it. A strange gangling, inefficient creature – that's what people were. A little white naked rat squirming and thronging through the world. An evolutionary quirk that made no sense. After all – what was the point of the human body? Feather's smooth white fragile skin? It gleamed helplessly in the dull sea light, looking as though he could wreck it with a single touch. It was soft. Fragile. Nothing to help it or protect it. No fur. No scales. Not even any pigment really. So what was going on? Why – just why – was Feather naked? Anyone have a clue? Why was she exposed to the sun and the thorns without a nice covering of fur? Animals only went naked when there was a reason. Water? Underground?

So – Feather was a water animal?

Maybe. She looked the part.

Kay wasn't a scientist – and the fact of Feather's nakedness meant more than just scientific speculation. Sense or not, the world works in its certain ways. The body is more powerful than the mind – the cock and the cunt ranks higher than the cranium. Kay couldn't help latching onto her as she stood there, though he fought a lost battle against it every inch of the way.

"Feather," he grated. "Why don't you give over?"

She paid him no attention. Indeed, from the way she moved and acted, he might as well have not been there. She just sniffed about unconcernedly as he knelt in the swirling sea, staring after her, eyes on her small and neatly round buttocks. However, none of this was real. Must remember that. He just stared desolately after her as she dropped onto her hands and knees again and carried on collecting samphire. The electrical connection of her naked body shaking him with amps and volts.

"Feather, please," he begged, even lost in his dream. "It's not you . . ."

Why was the human body so beautiful?

"Not – you . . ."

Kay clutched at his face and made a long low sound that was half groan, half laugh.

"Not you, fuck it."

Then he realised that he was in his own bed and familiarity came back to him with a wince and a twinge of guilt.

How many times did this need saying?

Elizabeth was the important thing . . .

Missing Elizabeth.

Vanished Elizabeth.

Elizabeth the room-wrecker. Elizabeth the runaway. Elizabeth Eyes, the safely boyfriendless, smooth-surfaced girl in room 18.

The sense of dread came back immediately, however. A sense of guilt and terror that coiled around the long-haired composer and bound her tight inside him. Where was she? He stared up into the dark ceiling and tried to find Elizabeth's face. The lines of her body. Tried to conjure her up in her so-loved flesh and blood. But somehow it seemed vague – and that hurt. Had he ever known quite what she looked like? Looking back, he suddenly wasn't sure. But if not, then what exactly was it that he had fallen in love with?

Just an idea?

A concept?

Something in his own head?

Feather at least seemed more real and familiar. But then, there was something about Feather that was almost universally real and familiar.

Kay sighed and stared round the room, mentally resigning from the problem. How long had he been asleep? It was deep dark now – the middle of the night. And the dream was gone. Goodbye Elizabeth. Goodbye Feather. Goodbye familiar salt marsh. Time to wake up – to where reality waits. He felt exhausted but also restless and there was only one thing that seemed to make complete sense now. He needed music. It was the only voice left when all the others had failed you. However, it was not the pristine complexity of his oboe that drew him. That seemed almost impotent in its precision. Instead he turned to the new flute, picked it up and put it to his lips. Time to explore this thing a bit more and find out what it could do.

Even as he played the first note, he realised that it seemed to be taking him somewhere new. Somewhere he had never visited before. The rawness and simplicity of this instrument was as different to what he was used to as it was possible to be. Whatever traditions and culture were behind it were completely unknown, and Kay was pleased with that. The interaction of himself and this unknown pipe was producing a sound with almost no reference to external music at all. This was something personal. The music was as delicate and atonal as anything he had played, but this time it was his own and what flowed out now felt like a part of his own deepest places.

Kay played, letting the music happen. He was able to apply simple structures and patterns – able to direct the music to a certain extent. After about five minutes he brought it to a close with a neat fade-out and sat staring at the wall . . .

And, right across the Brockden Centre, the lights flickered off and on again. The TVs staggered. CD players went blissfully silent.

The computers shut down and students swore in exasperation and kicked the furniture.

Kay lowered the flute, startled out of his daze by the flicker, wondering to himself what his neighbours would be thinking of this unusual evening recital.

A minute later, the lights flickered again. Somewhere down the corridor a male voice yelled out to fucking hell, no doubt as his computer shut down for a second time. Kay winced. These flickers were not unusual in the shaky electricals of the old building, but they pricked at him. He felt the last wisp of the recent music fade away to nothing and he clutched at it. That music had said something important and he didn't want to loose it. That would be a tragedy.

Then, from somewhere in the distance, revealed by the silence, there came a growing whisper of disquiet. Raised voices. Banging. There was a call of shock from below. Sounds of question. Hey – come here. Open the door. More banging. Footsteps descending the stairs.

Kay listened, prickling. What the hell was going on? There was an edge to the sound that seemed more than just the usual student fuss. He gazed hugely at the door, trying to hear through it, right to the heart of the building. But then his listening ears were assaulted by a tremendous crash right there in his room that sent him twitching back in stark terror – before he realised that it was his music stand, which had collapsed, the screw giving way and sending it telescoping down, shedding a strew of sonatas and *avant-guard* musical jitterings across the floor. He stared at it dumbly, shocked at how violently his heart was pounding. Then he gave a wail and hauled himself up, tangling in bedclothes that almost seemed to make a grab for his legs. He hurled himself at the door and dragged it open. The scent of salt seemed to be pricking at his nostrils and he groaned. That wasn't possible – that wasn't the stench of the sea he could smell. No way. No fucking way . . .

The sea was miles away . . .

Outside, there was the sound of movement – of people stirring and approaching – of an alarmed Jade Halls hauled from their beds or their late night toil by the commotion.

"What is . . ."

" . . . to . . . Feather?"

"... I don't ..."

Feather?

He hurried downstairs to where a small crowd was thronging round Feather's door. But they couldn't hide the great wet stain that flooded the corridor outside – and the almost suffocating rank smell of the sea. He gave a small sob and collapsed against the wall.

"I heard her scream," Shirley was saying over and over to anyone who would listen. Someone was banging again.

"Feather?" that someone called urgently.

Kay approached the door, but all he could do was lean against the frame, exhausted. He couldn't thump on it. Other people were still arriving. Jim. Senka, looking frightened. Inderjit appearing by his side dressed in his pyjamas.

"Kay?" Senka asked, worried. But Kay ignored her. Then Cal came storming from nowhere, his face frowning and his lips tight. Kay looked at him, stricken.

"What happened?"

"Is she alright?"

"What's going on?"

"I heard her ..."

"Oh fuck ..."

"All right – all right! What's going on?" That voice was Catherine. He turned sharply. Yes – she was here too. There was an immediate babble answering her, but he couldn't hear it.

"All right, keep clear," she snapped. "Kay – will you get out of the way?"

He felt himself gently tugged to one side and Catherine stamped past him.

"Feather ...",

"The Sea?"

" ... please not –"

"Where ...?"

"Surely –"

"... must be ..."

Catherine slammed the key into the lock and flung open the door, her face grim. Silence fell instantly as everyone craned forward to see. Kay also suddenly woke up again. He pulled away from whoever was holding his arm, shoved viciously through the crowd, ignoring the angry protests, and stared in, his skin crawling.

The room was empty . . . and it was soaked from floor to ceiling.

The stench here was suffocating – the same rank decaying salty smell that was becoming so horribly familiar. Drips pattered in a wild rhythm among the chaos of papers, sodden clothes and books. Feather's small computer lay forlornly on the floor, the screen shattered and filled with water. Kay stared in, his eyes desperately trying to absorb all the details. On the floor lay sodden books – art, novels, nature guides, op art, a book on Banksi, another about the Son of Sam, a guide to Japanese sex techniques and Shibari and, most unexpected, something ironically entitled 'The Prostitute's Survival Handbook' in big urban-comic letters. Kay blinked at that dumbly.

And something else. Lying sodden and spilled on the floor, horribly insignificant among the ruin, was a plastic money bag full of gleaming pennies. Kay stared at that as well and his trembling increased.

A murmuring ran through the crowd. Catherine just stood and stared, her face blank. Then she spun round and hauled the door to again and pocketed the key. For a moment Kay met her eyes – eyes that looked heavy and dull. Then she turned away and, without a word, marched down the stairs.

The crowd showed no signs of dispersing – but Kay found himself being led away. He stared round in bewilderment, then froze in horror when he saw who it was.

"Come on," Cal said quietly. He didn't say anything else. He never did say more than he had to, damn him. He just gently tugged him along, ignoring Kay's feeble attempts to pull away. It should never have been Cal. Not the terrifying Cal. That was the worst thing possible.

After a moment, he found himself back in his room and he sat down heavily on the bed, feeling too drained to do anything other than wait for whatever was going to happen next. Was Cal going to kill him? That would be appropriate, perhaps. This was the end. The war was over and his throat was going to be cut. But instead Cal just stepped cautiously over the strewn music and lent against the wall quietly watching him as he sat hunched and silent. He felt like a tiny child, caught up in something so big that he cannot possibly grasp the scope of the flashing lights and clamouring rescue workers – but knowing that there was going to be one hell of an unpleasant punishment for it following sometime soon.

"You ok?" Cal asked at last.

"Yes," he managed coldly. "Fine." He glanced at him for a split second, but could read nothing. Cal was always inscrutable. He was just staring at the window now, out into the countryside dark beyond.

He seemed to be trying to smell the place – and smell Kay himself. To try and read it all like a dictionary entry.

"Gone," he murmured, as much to fill the silence as anything.

"Is she?" Cal said.

Kay jumped. "What?"

"What happened?"

Kay drew a deep breath.

"I heard people yelling," he said. "I went down there – and she had – gone. How?"

Cal made no reply to that. Just remained standing and watching him.

"Whatever," Kay said. "I am the piper – but I don't know."

"Piper?" Cal demanded, with a puzzled frown.

Kay gave him a smile. "Dance," he said in a sing-song voice. "That's all. Dance the villain dance and follow me. Far and away – to call the sea . . ."

Cal was staring at him so piercingly that he collected himself and stopped talking. Finally Cal sighed and shifted.

"I'll tell you something Feather said to me once," he said at last. "About you. She said that you need a touch of something – a sign – that goes a little beyond the normal. Perhaps because you can't quite read the normal. You need the world to prove itself to you."

Kay gave him an uncomprehending look. Cal glanced at the jar of pennies, still lying in the bed beside the huddled figure there – then back round the room. "Feather is a very isolated character," he said at last. "Like you perhaps. She seems outgoing . . . but you cannot really get close. She has a huge wall around herself. It's not an aggressive wall – you can see in if you bother to look. But what goes on inside that wall – well, you can't touch it. Can't change it. You just have to sort of accept that."

Kay glanced at him again. Why was he telling him all this now? Kay wasn't interested. What did Cal know about it, anyway? Kay was the original. The foundation. He had been watching Feather since the day she arrived here. No one else watched like that.

Cal peered at him and sighed.

"Everyone is scared now, Kay," he said softly – a little grimly – turning towards the door. "The building stinks. People are leaving. People are sleeping with friends and boyfriends in other houses."

Silence.

"They say the building is haunted . . ."

Cal looked at Kay for half a minute longer, but Kay made no response. Please, Kay thought. Just get out of here . . .

Finally he did so, leaving Kay alone.

A murmur of uneasy voices – outside. The front door slammed.

"Through to . . ."

"I am . . . out . . ."

" . . . a quartz too . . . Feather was . . ."

". . . haunted . . ."

"I thought that . . ."

" . . . killed. I wanted to . . ."

" . . . this term . . ."

Kay could hear no music anywhere in the building . . .

Waves.

About an hour after the events in Feather's room, Kay quietly entered the kitchen and grabbed for the carton of apple juice he kept in the fridge.

It was a sombre party of students who sat around the table. Bel was quietly cooking pasta, but she was the only one on her feet. No one seemed to be talking. Kay felt glassy and numbed, but he glanced around suspiciously. Nobody met his eyes.

Cal heavily reached out to the bottle of wine and poured himself another glass.

"Anyone?" he asked, looking round.

"Here," Someone said, pushing her mug (with the slogan 'Mad Cows' written on it in big childish pink letters) across to him. Cal already looked a little drunk, Kay realised darkly – not the happy sort of drunk but a heavy bitter kind. But he sipped anyway. Kay sank into a chair in the corner and stared into space.

This was what you did at college. You sat in the kitchen. With a bottle of wine perhaps. Making conversation.

"What are you doing when you go home," someone asked someone else abruptly.

"Just getting totally wasted," that someone else replied with feeling. "Then sleep for a few days. I need it."

"I am going back to Poland," someone else put in. "See all my friends again in Poznan . . . will be nice."

"Not me," Senka said. "I shall be staying here. I can't go home yet."

That brought the uncomfortable conversation to a halt. Kay just sat there watching – waiting for it to continue. Finally, Senka sighed and poured herself another glassful. "Quite a lot of people are staying in the area," she said. "Even when the course is over in a few weeks. I don't think they know what to do next. What to do out there in the – well – the real world."

"Well – I shall be singing with my band in Glasgow," someone said. "I have it all sorted."

"You studied Theatre though, didn't you?" Senka murmured.

There was a silence again. No one seemed really talkative. Bel dumped a wobbling mass of yellow pasta into a bowl and sat down to eat. It smelt strongly of burnt cheese and Kay almost subconsciously wrinkled his nose slightly. With some people, food almost becomes a Pavlovian event.

"The world is an – unfriendly place," Senka said at last. "Where do we go? What do we do?"

"Hmm?"

"A small theatre company in Germany? A job looking after owls? Into modelling? Working in the local fish and chips?"

Cal sighed.

"I think," Senka murmured, "we have so many luxuries now. Of thought. And fears. I think we are all – will be very surprised by the next few times."

Kay nodded in agreement. Still normal. Nobody was looking at him.

Cal grunted. "We'll find that the real world makes much less fucking sense – and is actually much less fucking real," he said at last. "What I am going to remember is being a creative eccentric surrounded for the first (and possibly last) time by other creative eccentrics – and that we jostled like colliding dimensions in M-Theory. And what universes we created as a result?"

He glanced round at the blank faces and smiled. Kay downed another mouthful of juice.

"I remember 'art' – in inverted commas," Cal continued. "And depression and bust-ups and rows and tears and illicit substances and more 'art' and lots and lots of sex – at least everyone seemed convinced that lots and lots of sex was happening to other people. Even the strange stuff – miseries, despairs and rages – are going to seem more real than anything – out there." He laughed softly. "Study? What study?" He rubbed his chin and subsided over his mug of wine. "Oh – that study," he murmured dryly. "Yeah – I suppose there must have been some of that involved . . . somewhere."

"I am glad we are leaving though," Shirley muttered, her voice heavy. "Whatever. I don't like this. I swear it's haunted. We should get out now. I don't fancy another night . . ."

"Well," Cal said. "Term's nearly over now anyway – and where would we go? Home? Everyone who can go home, has."

"I don't want to vanish like Feather," Shirley said, then broke off as the room froze silent. Cal frowned and turned away.

Jim made an uncomfortable noise. "You think that was . . ."

He shut up. Kay glanced round the room, sharply aware that something had changed. Everyone seemed to be looking at him now. Furtively.

Dully, he took another drink, his heart beating fast.

"What do you think, Cal?" Jim asked. There was a silence for a moment and Cal frowned uncomfortably. "I –" he began. Then he hesitated, as though wondering what language he was supposed to be speaking in. "I don't know," he grunted at last. Jim subsided doubtfully. Kay stared in increasing panic.

What authority did Cal have to pronounce on these things? Why was everyone asking him? Ask me, Kay wanted to shriek. I can tell you that nothing is happening.

"Can you still smell it?" Senka asked at last. "All I can smell now is cooking."

There was some cautious sniffing. Kay included. Smells were strange things – sometimes there, sometimes not. Sometimes detectable, sometimes not. Faint but pervasive.

Salt.

Sea.

Strange.

"Has it gone?" Shirley demanded.

There was a shaking of heads.

"Well," Senka muttered. "If I never smell the smell of the sea again I shall be very happy. I am glad I live many miles from the sea at home in Serbia."

Again there was a silence and Cal gazed moodily into his empty glass. A hint of wine cloudieness in his eyes.

"She must have just . . . gone," he said at last. "All nonsense."

"Oh come on," Shirley growled. "Can't you feel that . . ."

Cal gave her a dark look.

"No," he said bluntly. "There are no ghosts here. It's something else."

But what? Kay thought urgently.

"Then what do you think happened?" she demanded. "Do you have any idea what has been . . .

"No ghosts," Cal growled darkly.

"Well what then? You think it was someone who . . ."

Kay stared blankly as she broke off again, censoring herself. Someone who what? There was an uncomfortable silence full of eyes. Kay felt his stomach dropping like an elevator with leaden terror.

Suspicion. That's what it was, Kay decided. The wary eyes of the British trying to make up their mind to burn you at the stake. Eyes who were trying to tell you something that the owners didn't dare to.

They knew, those eyes said. They actually knew. Knew and condemned.

Kay the piper.

"Look, can't we just – just not now," someone else muttered awkwardly. "I don't think anyone has a fucking clue what happened."

He wanted to stand up briskly. *Ok – I had better get back to work. Goodnight folks.* Not that any work needed doing these days. Or maybe he should stand up and take a farewell bow and raise his imaginary top hat to everyone gathered here before dancing out with a flourish. That would be more appropriate. Braver. More truthful. But that was impossible. Instead he simply fumbled the carton onto the nearest work surface and abruptly made for the door, his chair shifting with a clatter that sounded like a train wreck.

Everyone was staring after him and his feet caught. He corrected his step, then froze in shock, realising that he was dancing after all. One arm out. The attempt at concealment had failed and would now become a flight in panic. And everyone could see it.

Bring down the curtain now, please . . .

He clenched his hands, deliberately scraping his nails hard into his palms so hard that one of his nails split. Then he was finally out of the room and staring, numbed and dead, at the corridor. His head empty. This was the end. This was no longer home. It was time to go. Time to start walking.

With a light sigh, he floated quickly up the stairs towards his room. He paid no heed to the occasional figure who passed by on that long migration. Not even when they stopped and stared at him. The audience that was following his dance all the time, with its critical but acceptingly earnest eyes. Was that Senka, sitting her pretty arse on a step, staring up after him? How could it be? She was in the kitchen. But now here? He blinked at her a moment then passed her. It didn't matter. The staircase turned then anyway, so out of sight out of mind.

Then Cal came suddenly out of the distance (un-definable) and stared at him sharply.

"Hey," he called, frowning. "Are you alright?"

Kay shook his head and frowned, not in answer to the question, but in a general negation of his presence. Cal didn't matter now either. Somewhere in the future was his door – a door that seemed bent like a ship's sail, but he scrabbled at it and, after much keys and wrenching, he got it open.

Cal was still following him. Why would he not just go away?

"Kay," he called after him, but Kay ignored him and almost fell in, shovelling it closed behind him and making for the only solid thing he could see – his bed. And, by it, the penny jar. He collapsed on the first, clawing at the sheets, then hugged the second to himself, closing his eyes. Was a bed the only refuge? The only home?

No doubt.

There was banging in the distance . . .

"Kay . . ?"

The sea was washing nearby. He could smell it – there was a sea fog rolling in across the East Anglian marshes. Home. And somewhere off in the distance, he could hear the waves breaking. Somewhere off where edges didn't meet like edges should. Only vague hints of his old room could be seen in the dark. Just a room. As small and miserable as any student room. There was his oboe case – the oboe lying on the table nearby, fully assembled – his black coat hanging on a peg – a music stand full of Britten and Birtwistle . . .

And there was the antique flute.

He picked up the instrument and turned it over in his hands. It was just an unobtrusive piece of wood. And what? He was the piper. He had played that instrument – and Feather and Elizabeth had joined his dance. It was impossible of course – but everything was impossible in this world. Love was impossible. People were impossible. Sex was impossible. He himself was impossible. Compared to that – why not?

Then there was only one thing to do now. In this calm and crystalline place, there was only one person left that Kay hated now – only one left that he loved. Calm – sea, sky, Kay. Clear. So do your work. Please? One last play, he thought. One last piping. One last dance.

Where previously he had faltered his way with the unfamiliar mouthpiece, at least trying to make music, now he just launched himself at it – dived straight into the sound. The flute produced a dull, whistling, droning sound at first as his breath sighed into it, but he didn't care. It was music – whatever it was, it was music. Who the hell had any right to define what music was and what it wasn't? Air streamed out of him harder and harder, quavering and breaking around hidden sobs and replenished with huge gasping breaths. All his carefully developed breath control had gone to another place now and he just huffed and puffed, blowing harder and harder, the sound squealing higher and higher – louder and louder – in a slow crescendo that any composer would have been proud of.

And as he played, the world changed. The light glimmering in from the dark beyond the windows and under the door was becoming flushed with pink and more alive. Sunset pink. Subtle changes of air pressure and temperature seemed to be following his music – as his breath changed, so did the world around him. Kay was dimly aware of the feel of crisp, cold sea air. But he wasn't really thinking, only playing. Playing music that would never be equalled on the planet – not ever. Music that finally expressed something.

The flute piped him on towards the sea, lying serene among the marsh islands, as a waking dream. Towards a huddled figure. Then he watched her eyes opened sharply and everything changed again. Shock. Bleak grey – pink – daylight. The sound of birds screaming. Sea Birds. Cold . . .

Feather sat up sharply, her sodden clothes squelching around her – sat up, her eyes wide and mad with terror, gazing around her at the bleak mud she was sitting in – at the shallow water lapping round her arse and legs – the bitter cold wind prickling at her skin – and howled in panic.

Kay stopped playing abruptly and the silence crashed in. The quiet pink sun and the total silence filled with birdsong left Kay swimming and uncertain – frozen solid. He stared down at the terrified figure in the mud, but she didn't look at him. In her seeming shock and terror, she looked even more like an animal, flinching left, then right, trying to work out which way to react. But still somehow at home in her natural habitat. And perhaps she was. What was it she had once told him? *. . . was a wild girl – not a silly farm lass but a wild girl with seaweed in my hair . . .*

Like him. If only he had been able to tell her that . . .

"Feather?" he called desperately. "I didn't love you – Feather?" There had to be some way to amend this mess – but she made no reaction to him. He reached out towards the floundering figure. "Feather?" He wailed. "I didn't love you, ok – it was all just a mistake. I was confused. It's ok, fuck it. It doesn't matter. When did it ever matter?"

He was losing the ability to talk though as his feelings coiled round him like a strangling rope. So instead Kay danced. Again he found his feet moving in that prancing, jerking walk as he strutted through the mud towards her, twirling sharply, sending water everywhere. Again he danced with his cape and top hat. "No way," he managed. "My blood – you . . . I didn't . . . on the piano . . . they tore me to pieces. What was I supposed to think? The ladymusic is gone. But you weren't a musician at all."

Off in the distance, clutching shapes of ancient wood and wire were silhouetted against the pink. The rough leaning fin of the piano lid. Somewhere, the twisted bell-shaped remains of the metal boat were also visible. It looked like an absurd grave. It was cold – the wind cutting across the marshes . . . the water rippled . . .

"Feather?" he called again, shrill.

But she couldn't see him.

Kay sighed. There was only one exit now. There was only one responsibility. And, with that, he found himself feeling strangely calm and crystal clear. Somehow . . . beyond. Where did love stop being love and become hate? Was there ever any real difference? Perhaps not. Both were emotions that sought to consume their subject.

Feather hauled herself to her feet and stared around, dizzy and dripping. She even looked slightly transparent – as though she had been artlessly copy/pasted on top of this scene, though why that should be, he had no idea. Finally she began to walk away tentatively across the mud, treading carefully but seemingly able to progress well enough. He stared round at the washing water.

The sun was setting, he realised – not rising. He could see that it was lower in the pinkish haze. That seemed important. Better an ending than a beginning. Nothing else happened. Just still air and the scent of salt. Pure, complete, tranquil stillness.

This is not death.

"What?" he asked, still blank.

Kay stared round, realising that he could see his room again, mixed in with the seascape. The sea was fading away?

That was not an answer that he wanted.

"But I played the flute," he wailed plaintively – like a reproachful child stating what should have been obvious. Flinging the words wide across the flat land. He staggered to his knees. "For god's sake," he screamed.

Silence. He stared round in horror, unsure if he was really here. If this was a dream or if everything before this had been a dream and he had finally woken up – now only to fall asleep again. He was in an agony of terror lest this marsh fade away. This was where Elizabeth and Feather were – somewhere. Beyond the door of his room, the lights went out, but Kay hardly noticed, just sat there, penny jar in his lap and instrument in hand. They flashed once then cut completely again and Brockden was dropped into complete early-year darkness. Voices murmured in the distance. A knock on the door. It opening in a crack of torchlight. Cal staring in anxiously. Senka with an arm round his shoulders.

Kay?

So what was there to do? There was nothing left now. Feather was just walking away across the flats towards the shore – and with her walked an entire life. His own life. It was finished. And the only thing to do now was walk as well. Walk – a long long long way . . .

He quietly poured fruit juice into a cup.

"Say when," he said with a smile.

"When," Feather said at last, and took up the glass for a tranquil sip. "Nice," she said, and settled down against the window frame, staring out at the flat green fields and hint of the sea in the distance. "You have a nice place to live, Kay. I feel very relaxed here."

He nodded. "I can never leave the sea," he said. "Not for long. There is something about that sound – the waves in the shingle – that has me prisoner."

"I can imagine," she said. "You must show it to me."

"I should like that. I'm glad you are here, Feather."

She leaned back languorously. Kay realised that he was still holding the penny jar and he put it down on the table. Feather's eyes found it and twinkled.

"You still have that thing? I am touched."

He smiled. "It means a lot to me, in its own way." He rose to his feet. "Look – I have this as well." He produced a coil of copper wire from a shelf and she stared at it in surprise. "Remember this?" he asked. "Remember that evening at college – the TV cable?"

She grinned and nodded. "It's been a while," she said. "I have missed you."

He reached out to her hand and stroked it gently – but then flinched at the touch of her skin. It was as cold and as smooth as glass. As his fingers contacted it, there was a flash of blue that blossomed there and trickled across her body. She gave a gentle laugh.

"Kay," she murmured. "You know me – I am always moving. Never still. I am also the sea . . . I was a wild beach-girl with seaweed in my hair. Remember? I am what crashes in out there against the shingle – didn't you know?"

He swallowed hard. "Home," he muttered.

She stood up and spread her arms. "I have been for years."

"Then why do you want me to show it to you?"

She smiled. "Because I want to see it through your eyes," she said. She turned and opened the window. "Look," she said. "It is blowing up a storm – tonight will be wild. Shall we go out? And taste the salt?"

He nodded in silence.

Outside, the wind raced past his face and flung Feather's hair up in a spiral. There was no rain, but the air was wet and salty with spray from the sea. Spray that intensified as they walked slowly through the fields towards the beach. Tasting the salt indeed. The sounds of the storm boomed unimpeded over the flat east-Anglican landscape. Here, the fields were almost at the level of the sea, which was only kept from raging through here by the high shingly bank, which they tramped up with an effort. And beyond, in the lowering evening, there was just a world of water. Huge waves rolling and curling and breaking on the shingle. Sea. Close – scarily close and scarily there. The shingle swirled back and fourth with a sound almost like screaming.

He wished he had his oboe with him. The sound of Benjamin Britten rang in his head here. East Anglia was Britten country after all. Feather stared down the shingle slope and flung up her arms.

"I can feel it," she cried. "The tides and waves. I am rising – I am falling . . ."

A flickering flash of blue on her skin.

Suddenly, unexpectedly, Feather grabbed him and snaked round him. Suddenly her face was against his and he flinched in shock.

"Kay," she murmured. "From me – to you . . ."

It was a very intense kiss, her tongue gently probing between his lips and finding his. Her breath whispering over his cheek.

Her lips tasted of salt.

For almost a minute she hugged him tight, then slipped away.

"I . . ."

She hushed him. Words were not needed here.

Then there was a rising shriek and a vivid flash and bang out over the water. Feather stared round sharply. A rolling light in the middle distance. A boat was swamping out there under the massive waves of the North Sea. He could see it, leaning heavily into the water, haloed in white spray. And rolling in towards the shore.

A flat hooting, ringing through the bleakness. Over the flat lands and flat beaches.

"Feather?" he murmured. She gave him an excited-looking smile, shifting in a crunch of shingle.

"Hey Kay," she said. "Got any tools?"

"Tools? Why?"

She pointed at the foundering boat. "There," she said. "Plenty of pickings when the tide goes out. Have you got tools?"

"What do you . . ."

He blinked in amazement as she tramped heavily down almost to the surf zone and stared out into the waves that were taller than she was. Her body seeming almost to glow in the low light and moving in the rhythm of the sea.

"Wait a moment," he cried.

A second flare went up from the doomed boat – a wailing shriek and a violent flash bang.

Suddenly, irrationally, Feather seemed as though she was two miles away – nothing more than a speck in the distance. It was a desolate feeling. He stood on the shingle forlornly, staring out, trying to find a spot of familiarity in this lonely flat beach that was supposed to be home. But all there was here was alien. A glance revealed strange masts and towers and fences lying abandoned and ruined and forgotten in the shingle. Wires everywhere, whipping and clanging in the wind. The boat was almost on its side, heaving and foaming, side on to the waves. It was finished, he knew.

Kay slowly tramped down after her, until the spray was blowing in his face like rain. Feather's face was alive with excitement and he drew a deep breath.

"Low tide," he murmured, stepping to her side. "Twenty to six in the morning."

Feather, flickering and blue, glanced at him briefly, then turned her hungry eyes back towards the sinking boat.

"Ok," she said.

It was hardly even visible here, the sea was too high as wave after wave came barrelling in. But it didn't matter. It was the sea that Kay was looking at. There was something about the sea that represented the ultimate purity – the sea that could wash away everything human – could cleanse all emotion. And when the sea rose up like this, nothing mattered any more. Fragile naked humanity was helpless and insignificant against the water.

"Kay?" Feather murmured. "Look."

A huddled heap on the strand line, just above the waves. Kay registered it with a prickling feeling, then Feather was tugging at it, trying to separate the twigs and seaweed.

Then a familiar face – familiar long smooth hair. Kay dropped to his knees, feeling as though the waves were breaking, not on the shingle, but within his own body. But Feather only sighed.

"This is not death," she said cryptically. Kay just stared at her, then back down at the huddled form.

It was impossible for tears not to stream down his cheeks.

"Wake up," she whispered, shaking Elizabeth's shoulder. "Wake up – the dream's over now."

"Feather, no," he managed heavily, trying to say what was the point? When did the dream ever end? But Feather ignored him. Her skin was flashing blue, brighter than anything he had seen before. Gleaming almost transparent in the dark. Seeming somehow infinitely removed. As removed as Elizabeth was, maybe. More so.

"*Kay*?"

He stared blearily up at the dark. The glimmering dark of a small room maybe – the feel of a strange bed underneath him. The murmur of voices in the distance.

"Yes?" he murmured, briefly distracted. "Feather?"

He stared round the fading shingle bank.

Nothing.

He reached out and the penny jar dashed against the shingle and exploded. Exploded in a rain of gold and silver that sprinkled the beach like spilled jewels. Kay stared at them, lying among the stranded samphire and sea grass, glimmering in the wet, catching glints of the faint light, unsure himself why he had done that. But it felt right, as far as it felt of anything. The pennies could now remain here, a mysterious and unknown offering to the sea.

The Whispering Girl

Slovene Pronunciation Guide:

C	= ts	as in Tsunami
Č	= ch	as in Chapter
J	= y	as in Yellow
K	= k(c)	as in Kill
S	= s	as in Severe
Š	= sh	as in Shoe
U	= oo	as in Room
Z	= z	as in Zoo
Ž	= s	as in Measure

Night

The music was Toru Takemitsu. Small orchestra. Sounds shifting and changing, as sweet and as elegant as cherry blossom on a dark night.

And it was dark. The lights in the flat were switched off, reducing the room to a black cave lit only by a pale glow creeping in from the windows.

Tallis leaned on the sill quietly, seated comfortably on a small stool. Dressed uniformly in black, he was almost invisible and he knew it and took comfort from it. But the dim light picked out his face like a shadow picture, leeched of colour, making his eyes into deep holes, his downturned mouth barely visible and his nose unexpectedly sharp and pointed – all under a vaguely straggling black mop of unwashed hair. There was a gleam of the same dark light off the lenses of the pair of binoculars as he picked them up and gazed through out into the night – studying the vast illuminated wall that rose before him.

Tallis was looking in the mirror.

This wall was covered with patterns that changed endlessly – lines, criss-crosses, shapes – perhaps even letters and diagrams if you looked closely enough. The lights from this readout shone out across to him in an unending stream of messages. There were stories here, he knew. Countless tales acted out, both by the lights and by the people within the lights. Stories that could be read and savoured with aesthetic appreciation – or learned from like fables. And at times like this, with modern classical music trickling soothingly from the CD player and an endless stream of information entering his eyes, Tallis felt more relaxed than at any other time of the day or night.

This wall was the Drugi building, a vast tower looming from the ground to the sky before him. Drugi – the Second – was the great apartment block that sat opposite, across the road. The exact twin – or mirror – of the place he lived in himself. Two great towers facing each other – known together as the Dvojčka or Twins. They rose together high above the city of Ljubljana, two giant standing stones of formal concrete and glass. Sometimes it almost seemed to Tallis that he could lean out and touch the other wall.

And then what? Would his mirror twin lean out and touch him?

Maybe – but it was somehow obscurely apt that the flat directly opposite him was empty – it had been dark for as long as he had been there.

Tallis twitched the binoculars downwards as a pedestrian passed below, his shadow moving around him in a slow dance under the lamps. The two buildings sat in a small area of park – paths, slightly scruffy lawns and small bushes and trees – through which the access road flowed like a black river. The lawns were sterile and the trees were city trees – small and faintly embarrassed looking and unsure why they were there. The street lamps studded the world below in constellations that enveloped the whole area in an orb of dingy light. In the distance, he could just make out the moving lights and hear the unending roar of the motorway that bordered the complex. The streaming cars and lorries bridged the Dvojčka access road on a flyover, a big dark bridge of cold concrete.

Directly below him, twelve floors down, was the most forbidding feature of the Twins. Two dark mouths opened up facing each other – the gaping jaws of two underground car parks, fed by the road that ran between the two buildings. From up here, all that could be seen of his own was the shallow concrete rim glowing in the orange light. But if there was any doubt then all that was needed was to check in the mirror – everything here was mirrored and Drugi's flat, slot-black hole sat there like some obscure sex organ. Two lanes each served these mouths – one in and one out – and they were separated by a narrow concrete ridge. Cars would vanish down into the depths like fertilising sperm, or immerge from below him like obscene eggs laid into the dark city.

"Well, Clair," he murmured, almost under his breath. "Not much is happening through the looking glass tonight. The lights just seem random."

Clair, as usual said nothing and the binoculars swept on across the wall.

"Lines," he murmured. "Circles, squares . . . yes." He smiled and let the binoculars fall to the end of their strap. "You know what, Clair? It really is like a digital readout – like pixels on a screen. Perhaps if I was far enough away then I would be able to see the picture . . ."

A last glance up at the night sky above the building – black and overcast.

"Do you love me?" he whispered. "Ali me ljubiš?"

You what?

"No – not you, Clair," he said with a sigh. "Don't worry." He gave her a sharp look.

No stars, he thought with a sigh, leaning back against nothing on his stool. Then he hauled himself to his feet and transferred himself to his bed. He groaned heavily, placing his hands over his eyes.

"Clair," he murmured unhappily. "I will never sleep tonight. This is the third night in a row. What shall I do?"

Silence.

"I cannot just go out again," he said plaintively. "There are too many reflections out there."

I like reflections, Clair said.

"I know you fucking do," he snapped, then shook his head. "They freak me out."

He rose to his feet and paced across the room, switching on the first small light that the flat had seen. "Fuck it," he muttered crossly. What was there to do in life except eat and gaze out of the window?

And right now the thought of food revolted him.

". . . so tired . . ." he murmured heavily. His eyes felt prickly, his lids ached.

Back at the window, he peered down one more time. A glare of light washed across the road, cutting through the orange haze and lighting up the opposite wall. It swelled and turned and the building he lived in laid another egg, momentarily sending a whole new pattern flashing across the wall before it swerved away and made its escape.

It caught speed and moved away, accelerating as it finally dived into the darkness of the flyover and vanished, leaving just his own faintly reflected face.

In the glass, Clair looked at him, and shrugged.

He sighed again and turned away.

"Shall we?" he asked.

Maybe the night beyond the doors was better – slipping through the dark streets of Ljubljana where he would neither have to see or be seen by anyone or anything. That was comforting somehow. Ljubljana seemed quiet and good-natured, unlike some places – even on its night side.

He grabbed his long black raincoat and black shoes and dressed quickly, then went out, slamming the door behind him, passing down the hall, the lift and out into the quiet night. It was pleasantly cool and the air was fresh with a hint of fog.

Clair peered at him from a window and he paused glancing at her.

"Hmm?" he said. "Now what, my dear English Phantom? Kaj zdaj? Where shall we go?"

Silence. Clair ducked her head. He shrugged.

"Then," he murmured, "we shall just wander, yes?"

Yes, Clair said.

He strode off down the path, walking under the streetlights and watching his shadows revolve around him. At this time of night, there was almost nobody about at all. Unlike some cities, Ljubljana had a quiet time out here in the suburbs. And, in this isolation, the grim and functional suburban architecture that surrounded him seemed more ghostly in this light mist than any ruined old mansion or forgotten cottage and he drew his coat about him tightly, keeping to the road. One could almost imagine that humanity no longer existed here. Not an unpleasant thought but even so, he walked faster, keeping an eye out for Clair following him. Then he was approaching the flyover, which cast its shadows as black as pitch across the road.

He sighed.

The bridge was the old boundary stone of his world. It reared overhead, its anatomy somehow connected to the buildings and the car park – as though a part of the circulatory and reproductive system of this complex organism. Passing into its black space, he tasted the familiar stale and dead smell – no rain fell here to wash it clear and nothing grew. It was deep dark cave darkness now – could have been peopled with ghostly figures for all he knew. Eyes were useless here and so the other senses woke up. The sounds coming in – sifted and analysed. He could hear the traffic passing overhead – cars and lorries – keeping up a continuous whispering, echoing din. Then a car moving somewhere else – further away. A voice a few blocks away. A laugh. A door closing. A shifting sound somewhere close by. All so quiet that he was unsure if they were really there. The shifting came again. Was there someone there in the dark with him? What was that noise?

"Clair?" he whispered, but she gave no response.

Then, like an opera singer yelling out at just the right moment, the dismal cry of a cat came through the darkness and he prickled with shock. It was so close and unexpectedly loud that it went through him like a knife and his foot slipped off the curb, sending him stumbling into the road. He caught himself and forced himself to calm down. But ghosts of that sound remained in his ears as he strode impatiently onwards out of the dark and back into the normal orange streets.

He tramped on, following his promise of just wandering at random – his feet barely consciously leading him to darker and darker and quieter and quieter ways. These streets were barely more than narrow lanes somewhere in Ljubljana's suburbia. They were lined with pretty houses now with steep roofs and wide eaves – and simple gardens, sometimes planted with rows of vegetables. In the near distance, the howl of a train sounded and he paused. A two-tone hoot and the rumble of an engine. What was it? An intercity heading northwards bound for the forlorn old ironworking town of Jesenice and the cooler and wild Alps? Or one of the many goods trains that slowly crossed this city, eager for sleep in the stinking mass of here?

Train, Clair said beside him, with a nod. He jumped slightly and glanced round at her. Nodded back. "Yeah," he murmured. Then he clutched his long coat around himself and started walking again, his feet drawing him in the direction of the vanishing noise. It wasn't far away and crossing a road and a small parking area quickly brought him to the unfenced tracks. A lot of the railway tracks in Ljubljana were unfenced, something that Tallis rather liked. What were fences, save for a pointless line on the map?

Train, Clair said again, insistently.

"Yes yes."

He slipped through the masses of maple bushes that clustered alongside the rails and floundered through into the open again, the Ljubljana lights suddenly seeming much more remote now. A quick step upwards, slithering on tumbled ballast and his foot touched something that looked cold. Metal cold.

He pulled himself up and stared at the scene. The rails passed – faintly gleaming threads curving and fading into the dark. Above him, the electrical wires hummed – lines of black against a black sky. He stared at them uneasily. This was a wasteland if anything was. The railways were a place where the desolation said as clearly as if it had a voice that it was not a place for people.

Clair sat down, gingerly dropping her arse onto a gleaming rail and regarding him questioningly – and even as she did so, he became aware of a thrumming sound. She jerked her hand down to the rail beneath here and gave him a comical look

Train, she said excitedly, looking like a child about to go on a trip to somewhere that only a child could find exciting.

"Yes, train," Tallis said aloud, patiently, stepping across the tracks.

Below him the rails quivered like a cello string as a glow of light approached from round a bend in the track, carried on a crescendo of sound that rose to a dramatic roar.

Clair stared sharply and gave a whoop, jumping to her feet again. He watched her face split into a huge theatrical scream that became a laugh, then became a scream again – all silent. She pointed into the glare of light as though it was all a big joke that he would easily get if he just thought hard enough. Tallis stared forward blankly as the light grew and suddenly appeared blazing out as three glaring white eyes. What was happening here? Somewhere, there was someone behind that light – driving it. Presumably. Could that someone see him? Could anyone? Or was he just another reflection in the glass?

A deafening tone filled the air. There was a yell of metal against metal as the breaks came on, which answered that question at least.

The train was moving with the slow lumbering care of all trains passing through Ljubljana, but even so, there was no time to stop. Clare capered wildly out of the way, still laughing.

Tallis spread his arms to the light in a half-shrug, almost as though asking for approval for what was about to happen . . .

And just before the train quietly hit and spread him down the track like butter on bread, he watched her fade suddenly into twin plumes of mist, which coiled and dissipated as though they had never been.

Flat no. 18. Floor 7. That was where Tallis lived. The flat itself was small but it contained everything he needed – and it was quite pleasant by and large. Surprisingly so, considering the bleak concrete that housed it. That seemed characteristic of Slovenia in some ways, and Ljubljana especially. Individual people cared enough to keep the apartments unusually pleasant by English standards – but the buildings they had to work with could be grim, oppressive and aging. Outside his flat, in the corridors and entranceway, a different story came to the fore – almost a more correct and expected one. A tale of bleak and functional spaces – of weathered paint and old floor tiles. Something that spoke of a different world completely. Slovenia had joined the recent war for just a few days before luckily getting out of it again – but even so, these modernist buildings left over from before that time seemed massive and exhausted from the political mess of the old Yugoslavia that had spawned them.

Tallis didn't mind though. This bleak world outside almost seemed to fit like a glove. It was the part of the country that he felt closest to – rather than the sweet tourist-ready city centre or the gentle countryside of traditional hayracks and scattered, wide-eaved, steep-roofed buildings.

Tallis passed outside and strode off down the path through the grounds, walking under the streetlights and watching his shadows revolve around him. It was late now and deserted and, in the mist, these concrete buildings and the bland green spaces between them were more ghostly than any ruined old mansion or forgotten cottage. He drew his coat about him tightly, keeping to the road as he passed around the vast corner of the Drugi building. He felt as though something was tying his insides into a knot – a tension – and he walked as fast as he could towards where the flyover loomed, casting shadows as black as pitch. He looked at it heavily and felt in his pocket, though he knew he had forgotten his torch. The roar of the road above was continuous, though muted and it seemed to be having an effect on all his senses, as though the sound was a blindfold and breathing mask at the same time. He could neither hear nor see anything else in that dark place, but he sighed and pressed on. Beyond, there would be light and even activity with the late night people wending their way home from the street-side cafés and burek kiosks.

The architecture of the bridge was massive, like some great hall, and he passed into its echoing space, hearing his footsteps amplified and reverberating. Had orchestras ever given concerts in places like this, he wondered. He tried to imagine musicians blaring out the contents of his CD player in this echoing space – Fitkin or Birtwistle or Takemitsu – and shivered at the imagined sound. Under here, it smelt stale and dead – no rain fell to wash away the faint smell of piss and rubbish and nothing grew here in the shadow. He could hear the traffic passing overhead, the cars and the lorries keeping up a continuous whispering, echoing noise that smothered his senses. Around him, in the shadows of the bridge, he could see nothing, hear nothing, smell nothing. Perhaps it was peopled with silent figures watching him – it could have been. What sounds were hidden beneath those whispering engines?

From the middle distance, the dismal cry of a cat came through the darkness and he prickled slightly. There is no sound quite like the howl of a cat and Tallis felt full of a sensation that felt as though it had been around for millions of years. The cry turned the night a different colour – imposed a pattern over the world and he came to a complete stop for a second. Then stamped a foot forward again impatiently, only to walk right off the curb and stumble clumsily into the road. The stumble came with a twist and a turn and, when he found his feet, he realised he wasn't sure which way to move. Which vague lighted world had he come from and which was he going to? It was a momentary disorientation, but for the moment it existed, it left him completely unable to move.

He swore quietly. The dark was his friend. The cats were everywhere and their noise was normal.

Then, from the distance, came the sound of a car and an accompanying glare of light. Two white eyes and a brittle white glow that crept into the darkness like an invading fungus. Tallis turned to glance into the glare – then turned hastily away again, hunching into his coat. Too bright. But at least it lit his way back to the nearby pavement and at least he could see into the dark spaces that surrounded him now. At least two dark questions could be answered. He glanced around quickly for the cat – simply because it was there. Somewhere. Or two cats maybe, since it had been howling. The white flood swept round and up, flowing among the dark pillars and crannies of the bridge. But there was no small furry shape running from the glare in resentment. Instead, in a flash of dull white, it swept across a seated figure. Seeming little more than a pair of piercing eyes staring straight at him out of a pile of rough fabric.

Tallis' hair prickled at the realisation – his skin seemed to shrink on his body, a shaking chill playing in the tiny hairs of his skin. She was only visible for a few seconds before the light passed on and escaped out into the open air again – but that was long enough for Tallis to build an impression of hair like a white explosion in the dark, of ragged clothes that hung and trailed about her looking more like dead leaves than cloth – of that pair of huge black eyes that gazed straight at him unblinking out of a startlingly small, round face. All that before the darkness came swirling in again like water and left him blind.

Now there was nothing except shifting afterimages that seemed to dance there and form into almost recognisable shapes. Patterns.

Had it been real? Aside from the fading car engine, the silence seemed absolute. There was only the sound of his heart, which was hammering urgently, and his breathing. Save for the sound his clothes made as they brushed his skin. Save for the whispering from overhead.

The silence was like oil.

He felt frozen. The shock he felt was irrational, he knew. It was just a figure standing there in the dark. No doubt some homeless girl keeping away from the misty night. One of Ljubljana's few but surprisingly dignified and calm people of the streets.

When Tallis took a tentative step forward again, it sounded deafening and he flinched. There was a small knot of trembling taken root inside him. And even as he added his own sound of walking to the general symphony – as he stepped slowly towards the outside world again – he was still trying to listen.

Until the bridge was far behind him.

After a few minutes of walking, he entered one of the many small parks – patches of green grass and bushes – that filled the city. Here he felt better and he remained there for a while, strolling around gently and sitting on benches. As he watched the occasional passers by, he became aware that the alien sensations were fading and the dark was comfortable again. Again the feeling of being at home here in the city night. It was almost as if the passers by were putting on a performance for him. Couples strolled by, arm in arm, and Tallis watched them with head cocked. So many couples – so many people paired off. So many reflections. Where did that leave them? Did they take this mirror world for granted? Or did they also understand what came with isolation? Or was that just a discovery for the future? Which came first? He sighed grimly. "I am the original, Clair," he said under his breath. "Everything that people celebrate so much – it is just little flashes of encounter in an eternal darkness." He grinned and slowly caressed the concrete wall beside him. "Behind every encounter there exists an un-plumbable world of non-encounter." His tone of voice was quiet, almost chanting. "And what is love without the night and its emptiness to frame it?"

The figure he had seen under the motorway lingered in his mind and he twisted his lips slightly. That scene – those few seconds of touch from another soul – that stood as a perfect microcosm. A representative of all human contact. Just a sweep of light through the darkness. Just as distant and just as enigmatic – it didn't really ever become much more than that. But even so, there were questions, even if unwelcome. What had she been doing there? Stray people wandering the streets were not something you saw much of in Ljubljana. She had looked so unreal – so still and unmoving. Almost like a ghost. Like a story. Something that went beyond any concepts of culture and location. You just didn't expect people to sit like that – in the dark – so still. Watching you.

But he chased her away. He did not want to think about her now. He hadn't thought about anyone except Clair for a very long time, and that was fine. Eventually he rose to his feet and turned away, his feet barely consciously leading him away from the park and into the smaller streets of the city. Away into the back ways of Ljubljana, passed closed shops, pizzerias, cafes still serving red wine or the local beer to the night people, burek stands still open with sleepy and dour looking men leaning on the counter. He glanced at them speculatively. "En mesni burek, prosim."

"What do you say, Clair?" he murmured. "Hungry?"

Silence.

It didn't matter.

This night was full of ghosts. Nights often were, if you looked for them. He saw another a few minutes later as he approached the Ljubljanica river, the relative noise and activity fading behind him to a distant suburban murmur. For a moment he felt a thrill run through him at the glimpse of a small seated figure – piercing eyes watching him. Could it be the same person? Those eyes were the same – but no. No no no no. This was a different character entirely – different clothes, different face, different body, everything. She was seated in a corner gazing up at him, tears trickling intermittently down her cheek; but the thing that caught Tallis' attention straight away was what had happened to her hair. It was disfigured by a giant burn mark. Somehow she had set herself on fire. No doubt drunk and wretched, and he came to a complete stop and looked at her carefully, making no effort to conceal himself. She was wearing tatty jeans and a cold looking T-shirt. Hey, he thought with a ghost of a smile. I'm looking at you – don't you see me? Don't you care? But she gave him no response – just sat there and wept and watched. The scene appeared to him from without, almost like a picture – just two figures looking at each other – the one standing like a tall and indistinct black column in the dark – the other hunched and ruined, like a wounded animal. He moved closer a step, but then she opened her mouth. He clenched his fists and froze as still as a statue.

"Who are you?" she gasped and Tallis flinched in a second shock. She was English. Not just an English speaker – she was English. Her voice was surprisingly clear and light as well. Not slurred or broken. She gazed up at him tensely for a few more seconds, then she suddenly scrambled to her feet and stepped quickly forward. He backed away, his heart racing. She was considerably shorter than he was – in fact, she seemed tiny – and she had to stare up to look into his face, her eyes still moist and streaming. They were huge in the darkness and, along with her angular white face and slightly snubbed nose, gave her a kind of strange alien attractiveness.

She reached out and touched his coat. "Do you love me?" she demanded and he stared at her in horror. "Is that right? Is that it?" Tallis slowly drew a deep breath and stepped back, then turned and began to move off down the street. Her hands trailed after him, then flopped to her side and she stood there gazing in silence. This was the second time this night that a small shiver had taken root inside him. The second time that a ghost had planted a seed in his mind like a parasitic wasp. He glanced back several times as he walked – her bright wild eyes and desperate face gazing up at him from his memory. That single phrase, deranged though it was, burned in his mind. Love? Love her? It had formed a connection somehow – a wire that gleamed with white heat between them – a wire that was his awareness of her despairing soul. In those four words she had opened herself up to him completely. He hesitated more than once, half inclined to turn back – but finally he strode away, heading for home. He paced back up the road into the suburbs again, watching the dark houses and apartments. Lighted windows were few and far between here and now and he walked quickly, comfortably conscious that, away from the streetlights, he was practically invisible in his black clothes. Again it came to him how much he felt at home out here, not involved in the night-life but still a part of it – still watching. The sky was glowing a grim orange as the low-hanging haze reflected the Ljubljana lights and he felt for a moment as if he wasn't walking through the city's gracefully curving roads at all, but through a quiet spot in the middle of a vast fire. A fire that turned the sky light and burned the world to a cinder.

At last he arrived back at the Dvojčka but of coursed the bridge was still there as one last obstacle. He felt heavy with sleep now – melancholy and depressed. And the bridge seemed to talk to him. A faint deep voice lost in the sounds of traffic, its words muffled beyond understanding. But it was talking of staring eyes and dripping tears. It made him shiver as he finally passed into the dark. Ahead, beyond the concrete ceiling of the bridge, Drugi and Prvi loomed huge and tall and home, rising into the sky. The sight of them increased his tiredness. Perhaps he would even sleep tonight.

Of course, he peered around in the dark, looking for the figure he had seen. But he could make out nothing. There was no car to help him this time. He pulled his coat round him tightly, listening to his footsteps as they filled the night with more messages. Was she still there somewhere? But even as he wondered, he called himself a fool. It didn't matter if that apparition was there or not. She was nothing more than some junkie lost in the dark and what interest could that possibly be? She would be sitting there behind him, eyes half-closed and head nodding, pupils maybe hugely distended – mouth slack and an expression of nothing. Generally moving in slow motion, even her thoughts. As though dead in her skin, feeling the white cold of the concrete radiating up through her arse like a deep pool of water and little more than that.

But even so, he found his feet slowing as he stepped out into the light. And when the sound came from behind him, he stopped instantly, glancing back without surprise. As though she was inevitable. The shadow peeled off her like a shed skin as she stepped out from the dark. It flowed and folded down her body, revealing her – first a disembodied head, then her shoulders and chest, then her hips – then she stopped, still legless, staring at him in silence. He flinched sharply – a thousand messages exchanged in a moment. Reality and imagination were the same now – indivisible. She gazed at him with those piercing eyes and absently shook her damp hair away. Her tattered white top and thin trousers. A tiny gesture with her hips. Her lips twitched. Her arms held tightly to her sides, almost as though she was hiding them behind her back. But they were already covered with loose fabric that hid everything except for her fingers. All this seen in astonishing detail – almost as though in a moment of hyper-awareness – as he stood like a statue. Her eyes were on him curiously, burning out of her round white face. Black eyes like coal. Large against her pale skin. The motionless centre of a kaleidoscope.

Then she swung away. As her body moved, her face remained strangely still and expressionless.

"Ne ne," she whispered.

Tallis felt an almost overwhelming urge to call out after her. Make a sound. Hoot like a bird. Anything to break the silence. But he couldn't. The ice wouldn't leave him, even after she was gone among the bushes. It was a long minute of silence before he finally managed to move. Then he walked slowly up to the main doors of the Prvi building and passed within, his head down. Must get inside, he thought. Must get inside. Then you can think . . .

Tallis lay in bed unable to sleep. He had arranged the bed against the low window, so that from where he lay, he could see the vast shape of the Drugi building, studded with lights. That was ok. That was how the hours passed. The building was block-like, the surface disturbed by small balconies of concrete and railings. In shape, it was like lying before a huge standing stone, though a standing stone that blazed with changing light. As usual, he found himself searching for patterns in the lights that gleamed like constellations. There was a precise T shape of darkened windows that slowly began to stand out and draw his eyes. The left end of the crossbar was the uninhabited flat directly opposite him – at least, presumably it was uninhabited. It was an eternal dark area in the ever-changing pattern of light with no sign of life. Had it ever been occupied? Would it ever be occupied? Or was this something eternal? Some eternal blank spot in the mirror, just for him? The windows gleamed slightly in the light from the street lamps and he thoughtfully reached over for the pair of binoculars that he kept there precisely for this purpose. He sat up and focused them carefully, first sweeping across the face of the Drugi building with its occasional moving figure, then settled on that dark emptiness. He moved the glasses along the three windows but all were blank, save for a few shadowy suggestions of shapes inside – chaotic looking shapes like disordered furniture or hanging fabric.

As he lay there, it occurred to him with a twinge of regret that he had never seen every window on that expanse lit up together. There were always dark spaces somewhere, for nobody had all their lights on at once. It must be quite a sight though. The mighty Drugi would blaze like a lantern. In contrast, he had seen it all dark once, when a power failure had put both buildings out for half an hour one night – though that was also rare, for even in the small hours there would be a light on somewhere. The trace or tale of some nocturnal story of wakefulness as the person behind did – what? Whiled away the sleepless night hours? Worked? A night of illuminated sex with no time for sleep?

The power failure hadn't lasted for long though. As he sat at his window watching the weird sight of the dead building, even that ghostly darkness had soon been interrupted by the flickering light of torches and candles – an odd dim spectre of its former brilliance.

Finally he shrugged and lay down again. He felt tired but not sleepy? And he made a heavy sound.

"Clair?" he moaned.

The music was Morton Feldman. Crippled Symmetry. It was an apt soundscape for these twin towers in its endlessly repeating, reflecting melodic lines.

Day

Day was . . . what?

Piercing.

Hurtful.

Tallis didn't like it. It turned the great tower opposite from a blazing readout into a dreary building in brownish concrete. This was why Tallis liked to spend the day asleep if he could. Now though, he walked past shop windows and paused to stare in. On the other side of the glass were trendy displays of merchandise. Within the glass, there was a looking-glass world that was no longer surprising. A world where his own face could never be found and where the faces that could never seemed the same as the scattered passers by. A place where nothing could be pinned down.

Reflections.

Except for Clair at least, he reminded himself. Her reflection always showed up sooner or later.

This was the centre of the city, and it was a world away from the concrete suburb he lived in. Not far away, the Ljubljanica river flowed under the Three Bridges – Tromostovje – and here the buildings were either new, clean and polished from top to bottom, or old and tatty in a picturesque sort of way. In the more secluded places, graffiti was scribbled in profusion – grotesque images and words that Tallis couldn't quite read – adding a touch of something else to the mix. In this world of amiable stone, people seemed more amiable as well. There was a friendly atmosphere – an atmosphere of tourists and young Slovenians out enjoying their city, eating burek or pizza or sipping coffee and wine at tables that filled the street. Sweet, cheerful Ljubljana.

He peered at a display of colourful mugs and tins of tea in one window – Šipkov čaj, Kamilični čaj, Planinski čaj and Metin čaj – but out of the corner of his eye, he still tried to catch the elusive reflections. They were harder to see in the daylight, and that unnerved him. He knew they were there – but could only make out glimpses.

"Clair?" he whispered under his breath.

The next shop was a kind of delicatessen. The window was filled with cuts of cured meat – pršut, all bright improbable red flesh and white lines of fat. There were little portions of pâté, jars of preserved boletus mushrooms and hard white-dusted sausages. It looked good. But behind it, there was just confusion and a capering figure. He was sure of it. He passed on to a small restaurant, with menus filled with kalamari and grilled meat – the familiar čevapčiči and pleskavica. Refošk wine and medica. Then there was a clothes shop, filled with mannequins dressed in elegant clothes that, however fine they were, Tallis could never imagine actually wearing – especially outdoors.

"Clair?" he barked again – then gave up with a sigh. There was no reason to be out under the sun anyway. Instead, after pausing to buy a few bags of supplies, Tallis rode a quick bus ride back to the suburbs and the Dvojčka with some relief and tramped quickly through the streets towards home. There, he could curl up and doze until dark.

Then he turned a corner and found his way blocked.

The cat raised its head and looked at him and Tallis stared back curiously. It didn't run out of the way, as he approached. Instead it just stood there, looking at him and even forcing him to a halt. Either that or step right over it. It was like nothing he had ever seen before – very large and greyish in colour, with big eyes and a long scruffy coat. There was a thick collar round its neck as well and he could make out something written on it.

Mačka.

There was something familiar about that grand sounding name, but it took a moment for him to remember that it just meant 'Cat'. Someone's pragmatic choice of name? Or a label? Why should you label a cat? He smiled briefly – but not for long, for the cat was still staring at him with a calculating look, as if it was carefully memorising his face and picking through his thoughts for useful information. Tallis stood feeling a little at a loss, as though they were in some kind of stand-off. He was reluctant to just step over the animal or walk out into the road, in spite of an increasing feeling of self-consciousness.

The memory of a baleful howl creeping through the darkness of the underpass flickered through his mind then and that brought a slight irrational prickle. Fortunately though, the cat did not make him wait much longer. After one last intense stare, Mačka turned away, sliding off into the bushes.

Tallis was left to press on, a little slower than before. He felt an unexpected touch of the dreamlike and dazed – the sleepy shock of an unreal feeling that encompassed everything around him. The feeling that the whole city of Ljubljana was just not quite real, any more than it was quite home.

It was not until he noticed a movement away across the grassy area in front of the Dvojčka that he woke up suddenly. The movement turned into a small figure coming in his direction – a small and slight looking girl in jeans, her head incongruously decked with a large woolly hat that hid her hair . . .

She seemed to be watching him.

Tallis stared back blankly for a moment, then quickly stepped to the door of the Prvi building and let himself in.

Now Tallis lay in bed restlessly. He wasn't particularly tired, but lying in bed seemed the best way to pass the daylight hours. It was a chance to think – though there was really only one thing in his head today. Sometimes, just the merest glimpse of a person can be enough to haunt the mind for ages afterwards. It is something everyone has experienced. A face and figure is glimpsed in the crowd who you will never see again – but still a connection is formed. A ghost seeded in the mind with a shock that you never quite forget for the rest of your life.

Is that love?

With a furious snort he rolled over. By this time, the bedclothes were in a hopeless tangle and he kicked at them, sending them billowing over his legs. The white figure under the bridge, in her loose white top and thin trousers, was just such a ghost. Some lost character wandering the night – but even so, Tallis couldn't get her out of his head. She came with questions – perhaps that was it. Not many people came with questions. Who was she – and why was she? With a hint of bitterness, he found himself wondering what it would be like if she was here – right there, next to him. Her strange floppy clothes left in a heap on the floor. She would be dirty, her hair damp and tangled. Her body pale and smooth – pungently smelling. She would be surprisingly strong for her thin size – gripping at him and clutching sharply with grimy fingernails.

"Ah joj," she said, her voice grating. "Moj Tallis. Seks seks seks do konca. Pofukaj me do rdečega in belega – white heat. Moja pička je vsa v ognju. Daj me, da bom kričala . . ."

His hand wandered down and he began to masturbate gently – a little reluctantly.

Her naked legs slid against each other and spread. There seemed nothing clumsy or sluttish about it – she was serenely self-confident and beautiful as she lay, back arched, mouth open, eyes huge and dark. He looked at her skin, tracing the flesh of her legs. It looked, in his dream, as if it were made of a material like leaves – as if she herself was more vegetable than meat – and for some reason he didn't understand, that thought was almost unbearably exciting.

"Tallis – moja pička je vsa v ognju – pofukaj me do rdečega in belega – I will . . . fire burn and howl – joj – joj – joj – daj me, da bom kričala . . ."

His own hands now seemed like stems – fingers extending like twining vine and they flowed across her skin, round, through, under, over – tracing the shape of her and losing her in it. A vegetable symbiosis of leaves and hills and valleys of flesh. Landscape. Growth. And in this thicket of them, her vagina seemed like a flower – the petals opening – lots of colourful petals in many layers, fold after fold until it bloomed. There was sweetness to taste here – a slightly rank and musky nectar that made his head swim – the soft petals caressing his face, the feel of her body soft and strong . . .

"Tallis? Uh uh," Clair piped plaintively, tugging at him. Tallis rolled over with a growl.

"Go away," he snapped.

She stared at him, head on one side, a dumb but wounded look on her face. He sighed – feelings of sex fading. For a moment he was furious, but then he shrugged. He didn't want to start thinking about a total stranger, anyway. What was the point?

"Whatever rights you had once, you forfeited them long ago," he said darkly.

Clair tried to snuggle up beside him, but he pushed her away. She rolled over sulkily.

"I'm hungry," she said. He sighed.

"Yeah?"

"Food," she demanded emphatically.

Tallis lay there for a last few moments, letting the feeling of the girl in white finally fade. Then he pulled himself to his feet and through to the kitchen.

"Ok ok," he said, spreading his hands dramatically. "Food is coming."

Clair gave a nod of satisfaction.

He switched on a hob and set a heavy pan there to heat up. A knob of butter went in and slowly melted. Clair was clustering around him like a cat at feeding time, and Tallis waved her away in annoyance.

"Food," she cried eagerly.

"Yes yes," he said, producing a large kitchen knife and studying it, first one side, then the other. "Just wait a bit, ok?"

The knife went in easily, but it took a lot of effort to finish the cut – to the bone of his upper arm, then down, until a big slice hung free.

He sighed and set his teeth. One last cut and the meat fell straight into the pan. It was still quite cool though – too cool. Bad mistake. The sizzling was muted. He tended it vaguely with a plastic spatula as it slowly heated. Began to brown and sear. At the same time, nursing his increasingly streaming arm. With a growl of exasperation, he turned on Clair, who was crooning happily over the sizzling pan, and hit her hard with the spatula, leaving a small smudge of oil on the seat of her jeans. She gave a yelp and backed off.

"Sit down," he snapped. "It won't be long."

He leaned against the cooker, suddenly hit by a wash of dizziness. He glanced down gloomily at his arm, which was trickling blood everywhere. Was it worth it? Some splashed on the hot hob as he tried to stir the pan, and instantly the room was hit by a pungent smell of burning.

"Food," she cried again.

He picked up a bottle of wine and sloshed some in over the meat. It exploded in sizzling and a great cloud of steam arose. A good dash of salt and pepper followed it, as well as a pinch of the salty local vegetable stock and a bay leaf.

He sighed and pulled up a chair. His head was spinning and the pain from his arm was starting to make him loose co-ordination. His clothes felt drenched. But it was ok – the meal was nearly ready.

"Plate – please," he muttered and Clair dived face-first into the cupboard to fetch one, oiled arse bobbing in the air. He reached up and tossed a slosh of corn flour water into the pan, stirring it in quick, then he grabbed it and lurched across to the table.

The meat went on the plate – looking very appetising. Well-cooked actually. Then the rich salty wine sauce was poured over it. A fine meal, he thought, if rather lacking in vegetables.

Clair sat down with a happy noise. He stumbled backwards until he hit something, then slid down until he was sitting with his back against the warm stove and stared at her glassily, mouth open, his head slowly nodding.

Clair liberally applied yet more salt and glanced down at him with an exaggerated wink.

Night

It was dark when he stirred from his bed and reached out to put some music on. The music was Messiaen – the Visions of the Celestial City – and, as he sat listening to the complex beauty of it, he found himself linking it in his mind with the towering shape of the Drugi building, the lights of which were just beginning to shine out in the gloom. That was a celestial city if anything was, with its weird constellations of lights.

Sometimes, he knew, the sun would rise directly above the roof of Drugi – the Dvojčka solstice. He even knew precisely when that was, and on these days Tallis would do little other than lie there and watch. But the sun spoke of daytime. What was more interesting was the moon. At night, he would follow that body's progress in relation to the apartment block with interest – watching how it moved in relation to the building, to the lighted windows, and especially waiting for the nights when the moon sat directly on the topmost point of the tower.

It was almost a sort of very localised and personal astrology, though one with neither predictions nor warnings tied to it. An astrology that existed simply for its own sake.

Now though, the moon was hidden. There was only the wall and its lighted windows to read. The dark space of the uninhabited flat was still dark of course. It still attracted his binoculars, for he was increasingly certain that the empty flat was the exact mirror of his. It might even have the same number. In a way, it was his flat. He had never actually been inside Drugi, but perhaps he should change that. Perhaps he should go across, climb up and break into the empty flat. Switch it on. Wake it up. Then look out of the window, across to his own. Be his own reflection.

Then, somewhere in the dark window or in the lens against his eye, something moved.

Every muscle ceased to function – freezing solid. He struggled for a moment, then drew a deep breath with an audible grunt. If the whole building had started walking towards him, it could hardly have been more of a shock. In the darkness of the window, there had been a swish of white. A face appeared and looked out. A small and round face covered by straggling hair. Two arms covered by bulky flowing fabric . . .

There was an irrationally huge burst of feeling as he recognised her . . .

The duality of this world of towerblocks always suggested a duality of the soul – something that Tallis had never really found. The duality was easy to see. The mirror – the reflection – the pair. That was the usual state of things. A reflection to complete the mirror, in fact. Tallis had always just been the one side though – alone. Reflectionless in a world of reflections. Therefore it had always been a bitter if maybe unimportant symbolism that the room of his mirror twin should be empty. But now? Her? There, as his mirror twin? What was she doing there? Had she just broken in? Why? Was it even possible that she lived there? In a strange world without lights? The thought was almost too exciting to bear and he dropped the binoculars from jittering fingers and let his head fall against the glass with a bump. Was that why she had made such an impression in that dark moment under the bridge? Was that why he couldn't get her out of her head?

When he looked again though, the window was blank. As it always was. It looked so mundane that he was suddenly unsure of his memories, but his fast-beating heart and sweat-slimed skin were enough to ground him in reality. Twanging with confusion, Tallis screwed up his eyes a moment, wanting to shout out at the top of his voice. In frustration, delight, terror.

What should he do now?

But then he happened to glance down and realised that the view was still not quite deserted. This was a night of more than one ghost, it seemed. A second figure was standing on the grass in the garden. Refocusing his binoculars, he could catch a glimpse of her up-turned face, her hair concealed by a large woolly hat.

Were either of these real?

He couldn't make out much from almost directly above, but she looked lost and forlorn in the sodium light desert. She was just standing there, staring first at the door that let into his building, then up at the wall above her. In spite of the top view, it seemed he knew who it was. He knew that slight body, looking worn and exhausted by the world. It was the English girl with the burnt hair and the huge tear-stained eyes. It had to be. And the whispered phrase 'do you love me' came drifting back through his mind. What was she doing there? Had she followed him home? After just one brief meeting? There was a logic to it – but it was a strange logic. It was a long trip, part of it by bus. And now she was just staring at the door. It was locked, he knew and, unless anyone came in and opened it in the process, there was nothing she could do. He sighed. Eventually she just moved away, slowly, looking behind her and up – towards him. The glimpse of her face in the binoculars, with her huge forlorn eyes made him finally drop the glasses and retreat into his room.

Day

Around the lovelorn Tallis, everything had disintegrated into a bright blur. People moved arm in arm, their bodies shimmering like something molten. There was a scream somewhere inside him – it flitted around, trying to find a way out of him, but he kept the doors closed to it and it had to be content with its own echoes. Why – why did it hurt so much to have no reflection? To be betrayed by every window? The pain of loneliness and isolation that he felt was so sharp it was almost beyond believing. In his head was a cry for oblivion that was constant. Anything to reach an ending. Imaginary tears trickling down his cheeks where there were none in real life. He wanted to be crying – even here on this bench in the middle of the small Miklošičev park. But he couldn't. His face felt like a mask. Perhaps that was for the best – but at the same time he wished that his eyes could indeed be a window to his soul. He wished he could send everyone running away screaming at the sheer horror of what he was. Reflections all of it – of each other. Every person who walked past him seemed to be a reflection that he could never reach. A reflection of somewhere – someone. Other.

Finally he rose from the bench, quite startled to find that he was physically trembling. Only slight, but it was there. He was remembering very clearly why he hated the daytime. Everything seemed so much worse when the sun was shining.

He left the park, Slovenians streaming round him like water. People walking. People walking past in pairs or groups – complex reflections. Reflections as they lived their lives – worked – ate – as they had sex in their beds – as they created and dreamed. The glare of the sun twisted and churned – and even that seemed to form symmetrical patterns – greedy, hungry patterns. The whole world was full of patterns of one sort or another – patterns and mirrors that were trying to guide him in a direction, but he didn't know which.

He walked past shop windows and paused to stare in. At the familiar unmatchable faces and the confusion where nothing was as expected. Except for Clair at least, he reminded himself. Her reflection always showed up. For all that this confusion – or his own absence from it – twisted him, maybe there was something comforting about it. Comforting about not existing – and he sometimes wished he could enter that world and stay there and live there. It was a world where being a reflection meant nothing. Not everything.

More windows. Dummies posed in the window of a clothes shop – contorted female figures with glazed eyes and dead hair. They beckoned to him as he passed, and even their plastic bodies seemed more real, in their manufactured solidity, than the Slovenian flesh that walked past behind him. He paused and gazed into the shop curiously. The window display was protected from the lights within by a screen, so he could still see the mirror world. Clair spread her lips in a sort of grin and the mannequins watched him.

"Well well," he said, peering into their big eyes. "So what can you tell me?"

Tight jeans and a black lace top. Hair: golden and flowing.

A denim skirt with a jumper and a scarf. Hair: brown and short.

Black leather trousers with heavy cuffs and a metal-studded belt with a metallic blue short-sleeved top. Hair: black and straight.

Tallis grinned at them.

The patterns ghosting in the real world behind him – the sunlight, the human mirrors – seemed to have solidified or crystallised in the reflection, for everything was overlaid by a tracing of black geometric lines, among which the mannequins and Clair nestled like spiders in an untidy web. But no spider makes its web of intersecting squares and regular triangles, and Clair shrugged. These shapes seemed to fragment the world like broken glass – as though the window had cracked into a dozen pieces of sharp silver rain.

Clair twisted the shoulder of one of the mannequins, giving it a rough shrug.

Tallis eyed them one by one. Black leather trousers were sexy, though the jumper and scarf looked the most realistic. Their eyes glittered at him in the well-lit gloom.

Clair had gently turned their heads to look at him now. Like a window dresser, she stepped behind one of the mannequins and began to strip it. It was she of the leather trousers and, as he watched, they slid to the floor, exposing white plastic that gleamed in startling contrast to the shining black.

The black lines tangled and changed.

It seemed that mannequins were not given underwear to wear.

Tallis looked at the plastic hips and crotch with a downwards pointing smile, while Clair spread her hands to fanfare her achievement. There was nothing under the leather but a rough mound of plastic and Tallis shrugged. If that was what women were, then why embellish it, he thought and chuckled.

Then the black leather girl beckoned to him.

Amid a sea of shifting reflections, Tallis wasn't quite sure and he looked over his shoulder quickly to check it was none of the shadows walking the street behind him that had somehow crept in and done it. Nobody was paying any attention though and his eyes slunk back to the glass again.

The figure waved, then knocked on the window. Her hair was shifting under Clair's hands – becoming more untidy and straggly, which plucked at his awareness with a cruel nip.

"Ok," Tallis said aloud, hands on hips. "You have my attention."

Clair also leaned against the glass, on the inside, to watch the performance as the Black Leather Girl kicked away her black leather and her blue top and leaned forward, her lips spreading in a straight grin. She waved her arms awkwardly and then actually reached through the glass towards him, causing him to step back sharply. But she wasn't after him. She clutched about and grabbed at something. Something on his side of the reflection. Outside nothing of it was visible, but when she hauled it back inside again it turned out to be a white top. Simple – loose – tattered. Familiar.

Clair applauded briefly and nodded, gesturing Tallis to watch.

Black Hair lewdly cupped her featureless, plastic crotch for a moment. It was a silly movement, like something out of a porn movie, and Tallis frowned reluctantly. But then she abandoned that and quickly put the top on. Her thin arms thrust into the sleeves and the folds of it tumbled down, hiding her hips.

Tallis sighed and leaned forward, feeling a sudden shot of pain. The tattered top – a whisk of white in the dark – the yowl of a cat. He stared suddenly rapt at the figure in front of him as she leaned down, resting her forehead against the glass, nearly against his own. Her head leaned on one side, her arm circled in an awkward but inviting gesture.

Clair drummed on the glass, rubbing at it – pointing – and Black Hair again reached through.

It was like reaching into a pool to clutch at your reflection, he thought – and he was the reflection. None of this out here was real, but there, inside, was a person who was inviting him in. Somewhere he knew that it was all an illusion. That whatever unreality possessed him was not something that could be broken through so simply. But even so, he made no effort to pull away as Black Hair's hands slipped round his neck and shoulders, cold and hard.

They slipped – and then grabbed tight.

Tallis found himself hauled forwards sharply, his face driving against the cold glass. The pressure was painful, but he only struggled briefly out of instinct. Somehow it felt like a step in the right direction – even when, with a violent jerk, he was pulled right through in a scream of pain. The glass shattered and sliced at him, and then a second tug dislodged the entire window. Tallis screamed aloud as the whole pane collapsed, cracked into a myriad pieces of sharp silver rain – vicious white edges that descended on his neck like knives.

And then the mirror was broken – for Tallis came apart. He had a brief image of his body still leaning there against the remains of the window frame, a grotesque splash of red where his head should be contrasting sharply with his black clothes, before he tumbled helplessly and his vision was filled with nothing more than tattered white fabric.

"Hm – oprostite?"

The voice came cutting through him, as painful as the glass, and he looked round sharply at the smartly suited young woman who was regarding him with a hint of nervousness.

"Mmm… je vse v redu?"

"Sorry?" he begged.

"Err – you – are . . . ok?" she repeated in English.

He glanced into the shop again, taking in the mannequins in their contorted poses and the real people beyond them, gazing out curiously, both within and in reflection.

"Yes," he said heavily. "Sorry."

"Then please – move away?" she asked. "You disturb the customers and the workers."

He winced in embarrassment and set his teeth. "Sorry," he said hastily, trying to stand up straight and look smart – trying to talk fast and crisp so perhaps she wouldn't quite understand what he was saying. "I didn't mean to cause trouble. Just tired. I will go . . ."

He glanced briefly into the window again – at the mirroring streets that it still showed. Clair had also gone, he saw and he set his lips and hurried onwards, head low, leaving the shop manager staring after him curiously.

"Clair," he growled, peering furtively in shop windows as he passed them. She had to be around somewhere.

"What are you trying to do?" he demanded. "Are you trying to kill me?"

Occasionally a flicker of movement that might have been her would be visible at the edge of a pane of glass – but she would always slip out of sight. "Clair?" he snapped. "Don't mess me around."

He stopped by another window. This shop was closed and the darkness within offered no barrier to the reflections he wanted.

"Clair?"

He peered in.

"Show yourself."

He groaned and rubbed his eyes. Behind his eyelids there flashed brief ghosts of the sun-patterns that had haunted him earlier. He had never before realised the patterns that fill the world – the intersecting lines and plains of a geometrical universe. And for some reason they filled him with unease. Why did everything have to be so well-ordered and precise? Chaos and pointlessness seemed so much more comfortable.

When he found himself at the bus stop he gave up looking for her. There was no point. She would always be back again sometime – somewhere – as soon as he forgot about her.

The sun had gone now anyway. The light was fading. So that was ok.

A few minutes later, a bus with the right number stopped and sprung its doors open hungrily. Tallis hopped aboard, tossing a bus token into the slot and stepping sharply on into the vehicle. It was articulated in the middle with a flexible, concertina-like section that allowed the bus to navigate the narrow and tangled city streets. Tallis settled right in the centre of the concertina as the bus swung away and down the road, leaning against the rail there and staring out at the passing city.

Ljubljana was a city of contrasts and no mistake. Outside, gleaming glass-fronted blocks passed by. Tall and progressive looking with daring and innovative architecture. Hotels. Shops. Offices perhaps. But cross a junction and things change with startling suddenness. Then gloomy and artless apartment blocks frown down, obviously unchanged for years and dating from a time when rigorous functionality was the only thing that mattered. Then cross another junction and there would be smaller, alpine looking houses, complete with their steeply pointed roofs and huge eaves. Everything in Slovenia seemed just a little more extreme than what was familiar from England. What was bright and cheerful was very bright and cheerful – and what was gloomy and dark was very gloomy and dark. What is modern is new and exciting – and what was old is crumbling and dreary. The same contrast is there in the people as well. Even Tallis, who spent most of his time alone, could see that, for all their friendliness and attractive natures, there was a huge core of melancholy in the Slovenes who filled the bus around him. Whether it was grimly-tenacious looking businessmen, older women who looked as though they had come straight and exhausted from a southern vineyard – or the young girls, their pretty faces with the characteristic prominent cheekbones of this part of Europe, but still haunted and slender. Still with a fracture somewhere deep down – right through the middle.

Clair's English face, when it finally appeared, was in a marked contrast to this.

"Clair?" he growled under his breath. "Why are you here? I came here to get away from the English. I'm fed up with the English and I am fed up with you . . ."

She waved urgently.

"Yes yes," he said. "I know."

The bus paused at some traffic lights, then swept on over a sparsely populated dual carriageway. Tallis stirred. Even from here he could see the tall form of the Dvojčka in the distance – already with a few lights gleaming.

"Nearly home."

Clair nodded. She looked exhausted, but she was still keeping up, running hard. Tallis made himself stop looking for her among the flickering reflections, raised his head and set his chin determinedly.

The bus twisted its way for a while through a precise grid of suburban streets – featureless apartments and houses broken by the occasional illuminated pizzeria, café or counter advertising Burek or Čevapčiči, then Tallis jabbed the button to stop it.

Nearly home.

Night

He walked onwards, crossing the last few blocks towards the Dvojčka. After the movement of the bus, the streets looked like a painting to him – enough to make him wonder why he wasn't walking through a sea of statues, like the mannequins in the window, instead of the few moving figures in evidence here. He passed a bitter-faced old woman with a bag – a young girl in jeans – a tall young man with an unshaven chin. But then there was nothing. Just stillness. He turned right then left then right again – crossing roads full of stationary cars – walking on – until he saw one more thing that moved.

A low grey shape slipped across the path some distance in front of him. Big and ragged looking.

Then it was gone into an alleyway.

Tallis came to a halt and stared after it.

"Mačka?" he whispered.

Could it have been?

As his eyes followed the retreating shadow, the last light gleamed off something wet lying by the side of the road. He stepped up to it and peered closer at the twisted mass of blood and feathers. It had been a pigeon, he realised. He could see its beaked head lying inert and twisted back.

He regarded it for a moment, feeling unexpectedly grim. There was nothing unusual about cats hunting birds, he knew that. But this savaged mess only seemed to put an exclamation mark under the strange feeling that grey cat gave him. He glanced around again, looking for a returning low grey shape. But the road was deserted. Too deserted. Ljubljana could be remarkably still and silent at certain times of the day.

Slowly, Tallis made his way towards home. Glancing around the severe grounds of the Dvojčka, he caught himself hoping to catch a glimpse of a white figure. But he didn't see a single living thing as he approached Prvi and let himself in. The world could have been empty as far as he could know.

Then it was up an empty lift and into an empty stairwell. It was pitch dark and he fumbled for the light switch, then swung through into the corridor.

There was a dark shape on the floor by his door – and he hesitated, wishing he had switched on more lights. He wasn't sure what it was at first. Too big to be an animal. Maybe a sack of something?

But then she shifted and unfolded – and he stopped abruptly. The dim light from the stairwell caught a flicker of her wild, gleaming gaze. She was sitting against his door, her ragged jeans-clad knees drawn up and her head on one side. Perhaps as a bizarre form of introduction she reached up and grabbed off her hat, revealing the great burn mark and she tossed the remainder of her hair with a sigh.

Tallis drew a deep breath and stepped forward, wondering how to get past. Wondering what she wanted. She slowly and heavily scrambled to her feet and reached out to him with two fingers. He felt the touch on his chest that lingered there for a moment, then fell away – and she repeated her familiar question.

"Who are you?"

He hesitated – and drew a deep breath.

"I am Tallis," he said reluctantly – and she nodded briefly.

"Black-Coat Tallis," she murmured, brushing again at the fabric and smiling slightly. He looked at her suspiciously, but she looked neither drunk or stoned. Her eyes were wide and she gazed at him with an intensity that made him feel deeply uncomfortable.

"My name's Peresce," she said softly. "I mean – Feather. Yes – I can be Feather again for you. Can I come in?"

He hesitated, then slowly unlocked the door.

"OK –" he said. He held the door for her and she slipped in looking round with eager glances. Tallis followed her.

She looked like a cat, he thought. Sniffing curiously around a new space.

"Excuse the mess," he said flatly, not really apologising.

She shrugged as though that was utterly irrelevant, brushing at abandoned crockery and unopened post with a sensitive finger. He crossed to his chair and she stared round uneasily, not sure what to do.

"Sit," he offered. "Anything to drink?"

She sat gingerly opposite and regarded him thoughtfully.

"I can bring you food," she said earnestly. "I can – I can I can feed you."

The 'I can's came out in a dull sequence. It wasn't a stammer.

"Sorry?"

"Hungry," she said. "But I don't understand."

"What don't you understand?"

He stared at her in bewilderment. The tone of her voice was of one who repeats something parrot-like. She nodded.

"You – home safe," she said. "My friend. Getting late. Yes. Drink. Yes please, Black-Coat Tallis."

Frowning, he rose to his feet and crossed to the cupboard.

"I haven't much," he said. "But I have a little grappa, or some orange juice. Or both."

"Sorry," she said, trying to sit up straight. "I didn't mean to cause trouble. Just tired."

"Eh?"

"No? Please. Some orange juice?" she said, pointing carefully at the carton. "And you my dear? Do you wish for a drink?"

"What did you come here for?" he asked carefully, pouring her a glassful. She flinched.

"Should I not?" she said.

He floundered. "No – yes – I mean –"

"I came to see you," she said.

"Ah," he murmured. He stared round restlessly and the silence stretched out.

She took the glass and sipped. "Drink," she said. "Ok, Tallis – do you love me?"

He froze. What did she mean by that? Was she just desperate and lonely? It could mean anything from a yearning for companionship to an offer of sex in return for somewhere to sleep. He wasn't sure, and none of the possibilities seemed appealing.

"Tallis – I want you to live a long time," she said.

"Well –"

She shook her head. "Don't die so much," she said. "I hate it when that happens. I can hear you, Tallis," she said, clutching at his hand. "I can hear you dying all the time. Over and Over. Right across the city. Please don't."

Tallis gazed at her, stunned.

"But –"

"I also am dying all the time. Over and over. It's all a dream. Train," she said abruptly. "Remember? Train?"

That brought a prickle to the back of his neck.

"Hungry," she said. "I can bring food. Are you hungry Tallis?"

Abruptly he rose to his feet.

"Come on," he muttered, heading for the door. Still holding her orange juice, she followed him unquestioning. He marched out of the flat and down the hall towards the lift.

"Tallis," she murmured as he pressed the call button. "I need to know."

"Know what?"

"Know if you love me. I love you. I love everyone."

"That's nice," he said grimly, as the doors slid open.

"Tallis," she said, as they began to descend. "The cat is hungry."

"Which cat."

"Big grey cat. Meow. Will you feed it?"

In his memory, Mačka again slunk across his path.

"Um – if I get the chance, yes" he said, placatingly.

The doors opened again and he led her through the foyer to the door.

"Now you – go home safe," he said as it slid open. But even as he said it, a shock of complete déjà vu and artificiality hit him as he realised that he had repeated her own earlier words almost exactly, even down to the tone of voice. "It is getting late," he stammered.

"I don't have a home to go home safe," she said sadly.

He stared at her. For a brief moment, Tallis was tempted to take her back upstairs again, to let her stay with him. But then he stamped on that. He did not want anyone near him. That would not be a good idea. "Are you – ok?" he murmured.

“Mm,” she said. “Yes thankyou, I haven’t much. But a little grappa, and some orange juice. Or both – at home. Somewhere. Thankyou.”

She stepped outside, looking back forlornly.

“It’s all mirrors, Tallis,” she said finally. “Reflections. Everything. Even you. Me.”

“Mirrors?”

“Us,” she said, then she shrugged and stepped away, pacing off down the path, still holding his empty glass.

He stared after her for a long moment.

Dying over and over?

That was how it worked.

Reflections? Patterns? Loops? Cycles?

After a moment, he found a huge sigh escaping – a sigh that made him sag slowly against the doorframe, bewildering emotions roiling inside him.

Then he glanced up – at the immense standing stone of Drugi – and closed his eyes for a second. The amazing, incredible memory of the face at the window had never left him and now, in his confusion, he opened himself to it. That face . . . inside him, it was like a cello string vibrating as an endless bow played an endless tone. That face was like a pile of concrete suddenly shifting slightly. Like a hand that squeezed his tongue with a constant steady pressure.

He felt as though Feather had subtly broken something inside him – some flash of reality had been extinguished. And, as he stared up at Drugi, he felt his chest tighten. It was a fantasy of course – a dream perception. But he glanced about nervously and found himself getting into motion and walking the short distance to the Drugi entranceway. There was no sign of a low grey shape haunting the grounds however, and no painful yowl came through the night. What was it Feather had said about feeding him? Why on earth should that be anything to do with Tallis? Judging by the dead pigeons and other animals, Mačka was quite capable of looking after herself.

He tried to shrug away the memory of Feather and all the incomprehensible things she had said. But it was hard.

Climbing the steps up to the Drugi entranceway, he paused. The doorway into the mirror twin was propped open invitingly, held ajar by a box of junk mail awaiting recycling. He couldn’t remember ever seeing that before. Not in the country of the careful and precise Slovenes. But the meaning and implication was obvious. Still not really thinking or allowing himself to think, he stepped inside and stood staring at the lift in front of him. Everything here seemed an exact mirror of his own Prvi. Even down to the shabby foyer. The rack of mail boxes, some bent and forced open by impatient tenants who had lost their keys. The same dents? The official looking notices in Slovene. The very same creases and folds? The chipped paint on the doors. The same maps and constellations? Tallis stared round feeling quite spooked. He hesitated to even look too closely at the mail boxes, in case his own name should stare back at him. Spelt backwards. He cast his mind back to all the times he had lain in bed, gazing out of the window at this rising mirror tower. The moon dancing above the roof and all the things that went on inside the gleaming lights of it. All the people moving through their lives. Perhaps they really were a mirror. Perhaps the detail was there. His neighbour, a young woman he had never talked to. Had he also been watching her each evening across the way? As she sat at her computer and studied or watched TV or lay in bed masturbating. Were they the same? The man upstairs, whose dull thumps of activity could occasionally be heard through the ceiling? Who lived opposite him? Their faces seemed blanks to him and he wasn't sure. But if all this was true, then why was his own mirror room always dark? Who lived as the mirror of himself? It had always been no one. But then . . . this figure? White? Loose top. Thin trousers. Impossibly there. How did all this work?

Tallis found his heart beating fast in almost painful discomfort. If the world had gone into reverse around him, with everyone walking and driving backwards, it could hardly have been more disorienting than this mirror world. This was Alice going through the looking glass. Only in the process, in some obscure way, Alice was going home. A totally modern day version of the old story set in a world of old communist plaster and gleaming florescent lights.

Slowly he crossed to the lift and summoned it. Lights counted downwards and at last the doors opened and he stepped within. He was moving. When the doors of the lift closed, there would be no turning back. He shivered slightly at the thought, feeling unaccountably afraid of this journey, and it was a moment before he reached out and pressed the button for floor 7 and felt the lift begin to rise. It even sounded the same as the lifts in Prvi and again it seemed as though he was just going home. He wondered again to himself if it could possibly be that the dark flat was the same number as his own, as well as in the same place.

Soon to find out.

When the lift stopped and he emerged, the disorientation increased. Everything was reversed and he stood still a moment to collect his sense of direction, working it out in his head. Prvi must be to his left and he looked that way, scanning the doors and trying to remember the layout of the wall. At last he picked his way along – and arrived at flat 18. For a long moment he stood looking at the door, his face creasing into a grimace that was almost wry. It was a plain wood door like all the others throughout the building – like his own. The number hung there – just two pieces of metal screwed on. His own number. And very slowly he reached out and knocked.

Maybe it would just be opened by an enquiring man in a striped shirt and no English – or a harassed looking woman in an apron, whereupon he would stammer an *oprostite* and crawl home again with no little relief.

But there was no answer.

Nobody home?

He pushed at the door – locked – then leaned his head against it with a grunt of humour. If this was an anti-climax, it was one that left him feeling relieved. Relieved beyond his ability to analyse. He drew a deep breath and turned away. Only to freeze sharply, realizing that he was not as alone as he thought. A small figure. In the hallway. With eyes. Staring at him. He stopped moving so sharply that he rocked forward on his toes.

"Mačka?" he managed?

The grey cat made no reaction. Just stood and watched.

"What are you doing here?" he said shakily, before pulling himself up sharply. He drew a deep breath, all sorts of complex emotions swirling through his head, then stalked violently forward. Mačka turned to watch him keenly as he circled past then spun away and hurried to the lift, trying not to run. All the while he stood their waiting for the lift to arrive, Mačka was staring at him until he felt as though he was going to crack and shriek. It was an irrationally huge relief when the doors of the lift closed and cut out those unmoving cat-eyes.

The music was *Music in Contrary Motion* – Philip Glass. The rigid and harsh repeating minimalism like the glass and concrete fronts of skyscrapers and apartment blocks. Endless, formal and hypnotising. A little painful but obscurely soothing.

Tallis lay on his back on the bed and stared at the ceiling.

"What do you make of it, Clair?"

The lights of his CD player winked like a tower block in miniature.

"It's only a cat," he muttered.

Day

Sunlight.
Bright.
Birds singing.
He would not go out today.

Night

The music was dark like the night. *Secret Theatre* by Harrison Birtwistle. Eerily clicking patterns and a terror that brought a breath swirling through the city mist that spoke of things far away and cold and granite-bound. The lights were switched off, reducing the room to a black cave lit only by the pale orange glow from the window. Tallis leaned on the sill, motionless – almost invisible in the gloom, but the light picked out his face like a picture – making his eyes look deep, his downturned mouth thin and his nose long and pointed – all under untidy and unwashed hair. Around his neck, the binoculars hung on a strap and he gazed through them intently at the vast illuminated wall that rose before him. The lights shone out across to him in an unending stream of messages. Countless tales acted out by the lights and the people within the lights.

"Lines," he murmured. "Circles, squares . . ."

These stories were ancient ones. Stories of love and dreams. All encapsulated in the strange world of the tower. And all reflections.

No stars, he thought.

"Love me?" he whispered – and smiled. "Do you love me?"

Clair cocked an eyebrow.

"No no – I don't know who I am talking about. Not you."

He sighed and dropped the binoculars to the end of their strap. He hauled himself off the stool and reached for his coat, dressed quickly and tramped out the door. Down the hall, the lift, and out into the quiet night. He drew in a relieved sigh. It was pleasantly cool and the air was fresh.

"Now what, Clair?" he demanded, glancing in a nearby window. "My dear English Phantom? Am I crazy? Think she'll be waiting for me?"

Tallis smiled, uncaring what Clair thought. His expression was unusually serene as he walked. Even the glimpse of something red in the path didn't have much of an impact. He peered closer. A rat – torn almost in half in a mess of bloody organs.

The brittle clanking music of *Secret Theatre* rang through his head.

Feed the cat?

He sighed and walked on. Only to pass another pigeon a few yards later. Headless and ripped open. These little corpses rang with a puzzling eeriness here in the urban darkness – a darkness lit by sodium lamps that somehow made things far stranger than the darkness itself. There was no mist – not after the previous day's sun. But still the precise, sharp images of concrete and roadway were there to haunt him. Stained with blood. He wondered to himself what it would be like to live in the country. A dead bird would mean nothing there. It was only here that it seemed alien. But this cityscape seemed like home to him, at least at night. In the country, there was nothing ghostly – just the dark hanging over everything. But here the sight of the concrete and roads filled him with a wild emotion that was almost of love.

"Where are you?" he whispered aloud.

He walked among the bushes, the vast bulk of the motorway beginning to make its presence felt as an edge to the environment. He was making for the bridge again – just in case. But in the mean time the concrete soared through the sky like a dragon – a dragon that roared and breathed and stank of burning petrol. Grass and bushes – formally laid out city green. It was strange but out here he felt happier than he had for days. Happier and filled with a sense of expectation, leaving him open to the night air, and he drank it eagerly, city air though it was.

"Where are you?" he whispered again.

And there she was.

It was as though she was waiting, as he came up on her from behind, her ragged clothing hanging limply and familiarly around her as ever. He stopped still – he couldn't help it – and gazed at her. She was so beautiful, he thought. Dirty and ragged, her hair a tangled, straggling thing, but she was so beautiful. In this place. In this night. Her body both slight and oddly, comfortingly solid and real, her arms slender shapes hidden under the covering fabric. In the dark, the vision he had

had of her as a plant came back to him. It was there in the way she walked, in the flow of her hair and neck. In her loose leaf-like clothes. He stood still. He felt frightened and paralysed – conscious that he was standing here gaping, but unable to break out of it.

Then he moved again, and she turned sharply. For a moment it seemed that she would just walk away. Tallis froze, filled with a sense of the desperate fragility of an encounter. How easy it would be for her to just go, right now – and end the world.

For a moment there was nothing but the most perfect stillness. Then her head tipped to one side, regarding him. Her eyes seemed to be looking him up and down, rising and falling over the length of him without moving the rest of her head – from his white face to his black shoes. It was strange how these precise details came to him so clearly. Her tattered white top and thin trousers. A tiny gesture with her hips. A curl of her hair suddenly tumbled over one eye and almost made him jump. He wanted to speak – ask who she was, hoot like a bird or something – but it was she who broke the silence.

"Kdo si?" She asked – and her voice was nothing more than a whisper.

He stared at her.

"Od kod prihajaš? Živiš tu? Si osamljen? Si lačen? Si utrujen?"

"Sorry?" he managed at last, desperately – his grasp of the Slovene language giving out in confusion at those whispered questions.

She paused, staring at him. Then she smiled a small smile.

"You – come with me?" she asked haltingly.

Tallis stared blankly. Come? What? Where? Why? But she said no more. She had left the invitation – though what it meant he couldn't fathom – and now she simply turned away and walked softly in the direction of Drugi. Her feet seemed almost silent on the concrete path.

He gazed after her – then found himself following. Fear filled him and his chest felt like lead, but he walked anyway. He had to. Ahead, her pale form vanished among the bushes, but that didn't matter because he knew where to find her. Knew the way into the looking glass. The path cut straight across to the access road – straight for the open area in front of Drugi and at last he stood at the foot of the vast wall. He leaned back and looked up, feeling a sudden wash of dizziness for it seemed to go up and up forever. The lights shone out amid the black in an unending column to the sky and he shivered heavily, then set out walking along the wall towards the entrance.

As he rounded a corner though, he came face to face with someone else. Feather. Woolly hat.

He murmured "oprostite" almost under his breath, speaking Slovene almost automatically, and made to slip past her, but she put out a hand and grabbed his shoulder.

"Where are you going," she gasped, and he pointed up at the bulk of the Drugi building.

"Up there," he said. "I – have to see someone."

She shook her head pleadingly. "No," she said. "Don't go. Don't leave me now."

That phrase . . . it seemed such a strange cliché in such a strange environment that for a moment he was speechless. He tried to walk on, gently disentangling himself, but she hung on, her feet dragging and scuffing against the path.

"I must," he said intensely, feeling more and more frightened.

"Tallis," she murmured and suddenly pulled herself close to him, her arms squirming around him, her body rubbing against him, her lips looking for his neck. He shrank away but she wouldn't let go. "Tallis," she moaned. "Don't be afraid of me. I really – really . . ."

"Feather . . ."

"Really – really . . ."

"Let me – go."

"Really – don't want you to die any more."

Tallis gave a groan of confusion and despair and she shook her head.

"Do you love me?" she cried into his shoulder. He gasped and tried again to pull away, but her hands fastened onto his coat.

"I just need to know," she cried. "Just – fucking tell me."

"But I . . ."

"Please, don't die Black-Coat – Tallis" she wailed – her voice grating and hoarse. "I love you," she cried. "I don't want you to go –"

"Let go of me please," he said tightly, pulling at her hands.

"Tallis –"

He got a hand loose, but it immediately fastened in his hair. He tried to back away, but again only managed to drag her with him. He tried to push her away . . .

Then she shouted out, her fingernails clawing painfully down his cheek. “No,” she yelled, at the top of her voice. “I won’t let you. You can’t. Don’t you fucking dare . . .”

Lights were flickering on above them on the lower stories of the two buildings and Tallis gazed up at them in despair.

“Love,” she cried, the word sounding like a curse. He gripped her hard and hurled her away from him. “Love,” she spat again, staggering to regain her balance. “Love – the walls – the windows . . .” She howled as though physically wounded. “The train – the cat, Tallis – the knife – the window – the . . .”

She hurled herself at him again, her arms spread wide – embracingly. But before she could clutch him, his fist struck her a blow beside her left eye.

She flew backwards with a grunt, almost seeming to lift off the ground for an instant. Her hat came off and the remains of her hair tumbled free.

“Train,” she muttered, staring up at the sky. “Yes – trains. Window. Cat. Break. Drink. Sorry – I didn’t mean to cause trouble. Just tired. I will go . . .”

She drew a deep breath and sat up sleepily.

“I’m . . . sorry,” Tallis murmured, reluctantly relaxing his fist.

“Any rights I had once,” she said under her breath, “I forfeited them. Long ago. Do you know?”

“What?”

“What do you think? Forfeit?” Then “eat,” she gasped abruptly. “Eat. Wink? Love you . . .”

He gaped at her. “Feather . . ?”

“I can bring food. Mačka . . . hungry. Oh dear, but you don’t like it.”

Slowly Tallis began to back away, his face setting into a frown.

“Hurt. I don’t understand. Tallis,” she wailed, lifting her head and gazing after him. “Please don’t go . . . I need you . . . I can bring food.”

"Feather, please," he said coldly. "I have to go." He turned away, ignoring her anguished wail after him.

"Tallis," she cried. "Don't forget the mirror . . ."

He glanced over his shoulder. She had rolled onto her front and was trying to pick herself up onto her hands and knees. She gazed at him for a moment, her eyes huge. Then she suddenly arched her back downwards, lifted her head and yowled like a cat.

It was a terrible noise – half meow, half scream – and Tallis gazed at her, his heart racing. She looked like an animal now – tensed and ready to spring at him. She hissed through clenched teeth, then yowled again, her hands clawing at the ground.

Tallis turned away sharply and almost ran down the path in the direction of Drugi as the sound echoed after him among the buildings with the booming resonance of a concert hall. Glancing urgently over his shoulder, he stumbled into the entranceway. He reached out and pushed at the door – and was not particularly surprised when it swung open, letting him into the dark hallway. His foot kicked over the junk mail box in a strew of paper, but he ignored it. He ignored the light switch as well, though he knew where it would be in this mirror world. The light of the street lamps outside that came drifting in was enough to light his way to the lift.

The apartment was barer than he expected, now that he finally found himself looking into it. There was always something unexpected about an unfurnished home. It was not like a naked person – a person stripped of a covering that wasn't really a part of them. Instead, a room was left somehow incomplete and thus disturbing. No chairs, no tables – nowhere to sleep. And a faint stale and sickly smell in the air. Worst of all, it was still an exact mirror of his own apartment – and the creeping feeling began to grow that this side of the mirror could perhaps be the more real. This was the ultimate – the original. Perhaps it was him and the life he spun round himself that was the dream. The ghost. Perhaps that was what all these reflections and absence of reflections were telling him.

He fumbled for the light switch, but it was dead. He peered into the small hallway, leading off into the dark, feeling very uncertain. Ok – perhaps he had it all wrong after all. No one could live in this bleak and empty space.

"Hello?" he called softly.

Carefully he stepped in. He glanced round, looking for something to prop the door open with, but there was nothing so he let it close behind him with a sigh. That cut out the last light drifting down the corridor, but in exchange another faint light shone from somewhere. Sodium orange – pale and wan. Presumably from the windows in the rooms the hall let into.

There was one other thing visible he saw – and that was a piece of shit on the ground. It didn't look human though, he thought. Whatever arsehole had produced that was much smaller. The mental connections quickly brought a memory, first of a slinking grey shape and then of Feather's parting cat-cry, both accompanied by a sick feeling in his stomach that he tried to chase away as irrelevant now.

He realised that he had come to a halt again. Standing still as a statue wasn't going to achieve much. Better to have a quick look round here and then get out – back home, to think. He forced himself to move, tramped down the hall to the two doorways there and peered into one of the rooms. It was the small kitchen – without any way to eat or cook a meal. Just bare fitted cupboards and a gas connection on the wall. The light of the city drifted in from outside and told him that the room was empty, so he turned away and tried the one opposite. This was the bedroom – his bedroom. The curtains were closed, making the dark almost impenetrable – but he could just make out that his bed was not there. No wardrobe or cabinet. The smell seemed stronger here though.

It wasn't completely bare though. In the corner was a heap of something – his eyes showed him what looked like old clothes, blankets and newspapers – pages from *Delo* and *Večer* – as well as the glossy Slovene-language junk mail that arrived regularly. This was the first sign of something other than emptiness and he stepped forward a pace or two. But as he did so, something moved.

To his straining nerves and senses, a flash bulb couldn't have been more of a shock. He felt a jump go through every inch of his body and he slammed against the doorframe. His hand fumbled hopefully for the light switch, but even as he did so, a low shape slid across the floor, catching a single stray sheet of paper with a tiny sound.

"Odvil sem vse žarnice."

The voice was no more than a whisper.

"Sorry," she said. ". . . I took the . . . žarnice . . . the lights – out."

Tallis leaned against the door, feeling blank. The low shape had stopped and was staring at him – he could just make out two eyes.

"Mačka?" he managed, barely audible. A second, larger figure was moving now – there was a shifting in the heap and he caught the glimmer of a face. She absently brushed her damp hair away and looked up at him.

"It is . . . ok," she said. "I am able to see you."

"Why?" Tallis gasped, whispering in return and realising as he said it that it was the first word he had ever addressed to her. The sound of that whisper, ringing around outside his head, was like a bell and he wondered just how many questions he was asking with this simple word.

The figure made a movement like a shrug.

"I do not like the light," she said. "Like you. I think?"

Still her voice hadn't risen above a whisper – but there was no need to. Here, in this place, any louder sound would ring out like a trumpet. Here was a place where you could hear everything. A finger resting against the plaster. Your clothes moving against you as you breathed. Tallis could hear it all.

He stepped forward another step and was finally able to make out her long garments falling loosely over her arms – her thin trousers, legs crossed. She was sitting in what looked now like a nest of fabric and paper. Was this her bed? There were also a few clothes lying about. Woman's clothes. Underwear in fabric puddles on the floor – a second but identical pair of trousers in a double circle – just as it had slid off the legs it covered. It was all worn and dirty looking.

"Very good," she said. "I am . . . welcome you. It is nice that you came."

"Hvala," he muttered uncertainly.

"What is your name?"

"Tallis," he whispered, feeling completely bewildered. "Er – who are you?"

"Me?" She hesitated. "Ime… Ne uporabljam ga več. Čemu? I . . . do not . . . use a name."

"Oh?"

"But my cat is called Mačka."

Mačka? He thought. 'Cat'?

And even as he was introduced, Mačka came into view again. He strolled out of the shadows, regarding Tallis with a long look and then jumped into the girl's lap. She welcomed it awkwardly, without using her arms, leaning down and touching her face to the cat's head and letting it settle down comfortably. Tallis began to wonder if there was something wrong with her. Were her arms crippled?

He gingerly stepped across to the window and tweaked the curtains open, letting a bit more light in, which showed up the room better. He peered out – and there was Prvi. It was another monolith studded with lights – and directly across from him was a dark flat. Just a couple of windows amid the wide expanse – nothing more than a dot almost.

Tallis drew a deep breath – thinking of mirrors and reflections. Then she was beside him and his skin prickled. She walked strangely, he realised again. Without moving her arms and with a curious swaying gate. She leaned her head against the window frame and followed his eyes.

"Home?" she asked. He nodded. "You live alone?" A second nod. "Here?" Nod. "Why?"

Tallis sighed. "I came here – see the world. To get away from the sinking ship . . ."

All that sounded trite though. "I was looking for something," he said.

"You find it?"

Tallis smiled.

"I don't know. Maybe I was looking for nothing at all."

She was standing very close. He could smell her very strongly at this range – but he didn't mind that. Whatever smells were caught up in this room, there was something very raw and real. Her eyes just stared at him – soft and immense and dark. Tallis gave up trying to talk.

Just those eyes were enough to last forever.

She didn't reach out to touch him. She kept her arms behind her. Instead it was her nose that softly touched his cheek as she leaned in. That was all. Just the feel of her nose brushing his skin – travelling from cheek to ear and down to his neck. Then it was her teeth – he could feel them against his skin – they took a small fold of his cheek and nipped sharply. Tallis gave a small wince but did not pull away. Then her lips were there, fastening on his neck and sucking sharply, creating a prickly shock of feeling all down his back.

"Tallis?" she whispered.

Then there came a small pain at his chest that he didn't recognise. It made him flinch and he glanced down at the source. What was she doing now?

The knife handle protruded from his ribs, somewhere below his heart.

It was the first time he had really seen her hands. Her fingers – her nails were dirty, he realised. Caked with dark matter. But even so – very delicate fingers. On a hand smeared with clear fluid – and an arm that disappeared immediately under its covering of fabric. Why were her arms always covered?

"Tallis," she whispered. "Oprosti."

He just stared down blankly. Red was trickling down his skin now. The knife shifted slightly in his flesh and pain flickered – growing like little alpine flowers beside a stream.

He made a small sound – even unaware of its emotion himself. She pushed at him gently and he found he couldn't resist. His body wasn't functioning as it should and he sat down abruptly with a jar that made more pain bloom. Pain inside – not outside. It was a bad stomach ache and a scratch – that was all. He flopped down on his back, hands clutching at the carpet.

"Look," she said, pointing towards the kitchen with an arm that she seemed hardly able to lift.

He didn't look round. "What?" he asked.

"No food," she commented simply. "Hungry cat." She shrugged.

Tallis stared at the ceiling. Whatever he felt, it was still too big to see properly. There was a lot of water though. Swirling. Heavy.

"Why did you . . ."

He gave up – he didn't understand – either the answers or the questions. He reached out and clutched at her arm. She flinched away.

"O hudiča, to pa boli," she exclaimed sharply. She stared at him heavily. "Pain," she said softly. "Don't touch there . . ."

Tallis wanted to laugh.

"Pain?" he croaked. What was pain?

"Mačka is hungry," she said.

Tallis sighed. A chill was beginning to creep in, and with it a shivering and numbness.

"I could have fed you," he said lamely. "I can – I can, I can feed you. Why did . . ."

What was the point of that question? There seemed no questions left now.

"I don't eat much," she said. "But I must feed my cat." She looked at him in silence for a moment, then sighed. She sat back, reached out her frail, draped arms and stroked Mačka softly.

"I don't understand,"

"It hurts," she murmured vaguely.

She sadly sat back and began undoing the buttons on her shapeless top garment. She pulled it open, revealing a small vest, then shook it off with a wince, showing him her bare arms.

"Bolje, da vse veš," she said sadly.

Tallis gave a grunt of shock. The best he could do at the moment. He tried to sit up, but the effort only brought a small howl of pain and he flopped down again with a bump. Her flesh was ruined. Meat from her upper arms was missing – torn away in shreds leaving a mess of running scar tissue and fluid. The marks of teeth.

"Oh – joj," he exclaimed – and turned away, closing his eyes.

"It hurts," she whispered. "Too much. No more."

Tallis gave a sobbing groan. He began to understand what she was saying.

"Are you hurting, Tallis?" she asked softly. He hardly knew what to say to that. She leaned over him, peering at the wound, and Tallis cringed away. He didn't want to feel those ruined arms, but she considerately kept them folded tight behind her back. Instead her head came forward and she kissed the skin near where the knife protruded, then rested her cheek on his chest, which was rising and falling rapidly as he panted for air.

"Res mi je hudo zaradi tega – ampak moram to storiti," she said sadly. "Delaj kar moreš in naredi kar moreš na tem svetu. To pomeni, da je povsod žalost."

Tallis gazed down at her uncomprehendingly – not understanding most of her words but feeling the slithery and sad touch of her hair on his chest. There was pain in her eyes. And regret.

"Moraš sprejeti žalost – ali umreti. Jaz še nočem umreti."

Umreti? Tallis knew that word. It meant death. Nočem umreti – that was 'I don't want to die'. He stared up at her, trying to chase away the clouds that filled his head.

Don't want to die?

"You are dying though," he said. "Ti . . . boš kmalu umrl. No – you are dead. Are we all dead?" He stared again at her ruined arms. The stench from them had only increased now they were exposed – and what was left of her looked stick-like and starved. Her skin almost transparent. How was she even alive now?

She gave him a wooden look.

"Ne," she said.

He didn't bother to argue.

"I need . . . eat," she said. "Mačka." She leaned down again. Vendar bo kmalu dovolj hrane – Tallis." She made a biting gesture at his wound, then stroked her cheek against his shoulder again. Tallis closed his eyes.

"What's your name," he wailed loudly, the effort bringing a blast of pain. It was the first time that either of them had spoken above a whisper, and the shock was profound. He saw her flinch and back away.

He could feel the knife in him – something hard and inflexible where there should be nothing inflexible. He could feel that hardness twisting at him with each breath – and with each breath a new flower of pain bloomed. He gave an exhausted wail.

"Tallis," she soothed, brushing him with her face. Her skin was soft – just like a bag of water. Whatever flesh there was, it had dissolved into tears . . .

The room was darker now, anyway – he was sure of it. He couldn't see much at all now, save for the white of her face and hands. He was left in a world of touch. Her skin. The floor. The liquid flowing out of him. The occasional touch of fur as Mačka sniffed round excitedly. He wouldn't have been surprised if the feel of teeth had come out of the darkness – but there was none of that. He wanted to cry. He felt he should be crying. But he couldn't. He wanted to clutch at his face, to claw his nails into his flesh – to reach out and tear her ruined arms off her body. But he couldn't do that either. It didn't matter though. None of this mattered. At the end of the day, there was no such thing as a reflection. That's what all experience told him. The mirrors were empty – the darkness was total. That was the original –

And down below in the gardens, Feather, still on her knees, clutched at her head and screamed and screamed, madly beating at the ground till her hands were bleeding.

Endword

The Sea Train

"Feather is on this train," I said suddenly. My sister stared at me.

"Is that a fact?" she murmured. I fiddled nervously with the papers on the table in front of me.

"Yes," I said, trying to sound decisive.

Around me, the train plunged smoothly through a night full of snow. This, just about the only train ever to stop now at the station we were bound for. This was a classic intercity 125 – flat pointed nose, comfortable enough and smooth running. There was barely a sway or a jerk as it drove onwards, the ever more occasional snow-bound lights flashing past outside. The carriages were quite crowded – though not painfully so. There was room to move. But the mundane world of the train surrounded us and could not be ignored – bored children, sleepy students, elderly ladies trying to pretend they were comfortably at home. There was a constant low murmur of conversation interspersed with the occasional bleep of a phone or the miniature engine-noise of a portable music player. My sister sat opposite me, staring out of the window and looking gloomy – trying to ignore both me and the chaos. I didn't blame her.

Nevertheless, Feather was on this train. I had to say it.

The great intercity had passed through station after station, heading away from London and towards the wild lands – stopping at some stations, racing through most in a blur of lights. Large main-line stations – pretty little country stops – run-down halts – all sitting under a weight of white. They all looked familiar – as though seen again after a long interval. Or as though remnants of mostly forgotten dreams. And all were quiet and empty, save for the sometime scattering of people that the train spat out.

And between the stations, there was just darkness. You can never make out much detail of the surroundings from a night train – not even when the landscape is painted white with snow. No matter how much you stare. The wild lands were hidden. As perhaps they should be.

They smelled sweet though. It felt like going home.

I leaned back and studied the papers again, carefully putting them into order. *To Call the Sea, The Angels, Yellow Eyes, The Book of Tides . . .*

And now what? All stories come to an end eventually. As the soldiers used to mutter in the darkness of World War Two, this is a dirty business. A mug's game. A filthy rotten mug's game . . .

"The city was no home," I read aloud. "No safe place. It was only back here in the wilds that she felt any kind of relaxation. Wilds where the sea pounded eternally and was called home . . ."

"The sea?" she murmured.

"We are riding towards the sea," I said dreamily. Just the mention of the word brought a strange feeling – both of some form of terror and of home. The sea – the one place that bears the illusion of resisting peoples' efforts to chain it. The sea – that can wash away every fence ever made. The sea where emotions and yearning suddenly seem belittled.

. . . and when she fled in panic from the city, she knew not which way to run. Only that she must find a quiet place where her scars of measuring might be healed and where the measuring men could not find her. But that place was still far off. This was still the maze - the maze of reaching hands and gleaming red lights . . . each about a centimetre and 1 foot 4 inches above the ground. The running girl ran and was broken and ruined by it. But the running had been eternal. Had been always. The eternal fugitive . . .

This place, this maze, was just a landscape of sea and sea grass. And finally, exhausted, she sat down on a patch of soft wet shingle. It was peaceful here. Samphire was growing in the mud an arm's length away and she plucked a few shoots and chewed them. Crisp and salty. It was cold here as well – a sharp, clear cold that was not unpleasant. Whatever direction this journey was going – out, in, back, towards – she tried to put that out of her head. It was better to ignore that which was clustering round her.

Feather, the running girl.

As she let herself relax, she became aware that the sound of the sea had a definite pitch. A definite note. Unsure what was hearing this – her ears or her arse – she remained still and listened and, now that she had noticed it, it was impossible to lose it again. The air shook and shimmered with the onslaught of the water. Then she slowly turned over and lay down, pressing her face into the shingle, heedless of the damp. Without sight, the drone came loudly then – like a musical note played on a base clarinet. The distant trees joined it, whispering words that soothed and calmed and spoke of things a world away from measurement. She lay there motionless and was refreshed for a while.

"You are harsh," my sister said softly, and I gave her a hollow look. Not disagreeing. It would be nice to think that stories come from somewhere else and that mine is not the responsibility. But I suspect that is a false comfort.

"I wonder where she is," I murmured.

"What?"

"Perhaps she's in the quiet carriage," I said, gloomily registering the expression on my sister's face. "Yes – where you are safe from those twin great horrors, the mobile phone and the chuff chuff of the mp3 player. Sitting there, staring out into the dark and tasting the sea hidden in that blackness. That same sense of terror and home . . ."

I broke off. Nothing I could say seemed adequate. Or even to make sense. But then, it never did. Even though mine was the job to work this little magic. This strange mug's game.

"Maybe you should have forgotten her years ago," my sister said. "And relax – stop fretting. It's just a story. And we will be home soon."

I gave a tense sigh. "Stop trying to be reasonable," I snapped harshly. "I shouldn't be here at all."

She flinched and I regretted it the moment I said it. She settled against the window looking even glummer and I sighed. She was a small woman – looked and felt rather retiring and shy. Always wore a long coat that reminded me, surreally, of some kind of US private detective.

"Sorry," I murmured, though unhappily aware of the pointlessness of that word. She shrugged.

Somewhere down the line was our station. I could visualise it in my mind. A small, worn out little place of cracked concrete and shabby buildings. Broken, boarded windows and locked doors. A memory. One of those ghostly platforms that you occasionally glimpse going past the train window, blurred and indistinct. Ghost stations, like ghost towns, where life has moved away from them and just left them in the wilderness. With wherever they are, and whatever they were once for, seemingly long pushed aside – the concrete and slabs of the platform left to succumb to the horsetails and grasses that force their way through. And that was it. That was our station. In its ruin, it even seemed to pay homage to the sea echoing in the distance – to speak of the pointlessness of most built things in the face of that.

The dark outside though gave no clues to where we were – or how far away home was. So instead, I stared at the jumbled confusion of unglamorous pages in front of me.

. . . and it wasn't a ruler any more. A measuring instrument yes, but it was a metal rod – long and smooth and rounded, with finely machined calibration engraved into it. There were dials and screws and adjustable position markers. It also looked as though the whole thing could open out in three expanding, measurable blades, though she couldn't imagine for what purpose . . .

"Where you belong, Feather. Oh yes? Sit at his feet . . . suck his cock . . . perhaps? Why not?"

I sighed at that.

"Are you ok?" my sister murmured.

"Why the fuck am I on this train?" I found myself wailing. So loud that the lady sitting across the carriage looked round at me nervously. "I should be at home," I muttered. "And Feather should be . . . somewhere far away."

"Hey . . ."

"And happy." I sighed. "Why could I never make her happy?"

There was a clatter and jerk. The train was on points again. These seemed somewhat familiar and I glanced round. The landscape outside changed – withdrew, creating a strip of snow alongside us, the white ghost of an old siding. Flat snow with a double undulation of rails – and the occasional dead twig sticking up through it. I drew a deep breath.

"Nearly there," she said quietly.

. . . and, here on the outcrop, the running girl could run no further. The chase was over now. The epic was closed – the circle full. The story finished. And somewhere, in the distance, still more measurement was coming – inevitable. The world demanded. What

would be measured, she had no idea. The measurement of running out – of outgrowing – the measurement of your progress through the maze. And of the end of all stories . . .

The running girl slid into the water beyond the outcrop – into the crashing sea. But still she wasn't sure if this was forwards or backwards. Was this the end of the maze – or the beginning? The loop of grey water that held her like a swing, breathless and happy. The old cliffs where the sea sucked and drew . . .

"The train will shortly be arriving at," the generic voice intoned somewhere in the general train murmur, waking me up sharply.

I gave a groan. Time to go. I felt a throb of excitement. Who was Feather? I hardly knew. She was a stranger – a total stranger. All metaphors about parents and offspring – creators and created – came to nothing really. And there wasn't time to think anyway as the train was already slowing. Outside was still dark, but we wearily hauled ourselves to our feet. Leaving the carriage was a gloomy business of stepping gingerly over outstretched feet, pushing past the shoulders of people you would never touch under ordinary circumstances – cutting through the middle of conversations and shoving strangers' luggage out of the way. But we eventually made it to the vestibule, where the train was louder, the air was cooler and a few stray travellers hung around seatlessly.

I leaned against the doorframe and shut my eyes for a moment. The motion of the train seemed much stronger here as well. I could feel it swaying and plunging and it fitted with the vivid image that was playing in my head over and over . . . of swirling water – plunging – plunging . . .

I drew in a deep breath and suddenly had to blink away tears. My sister grabbed me by the shoulder and I looked at her heavily.

"It's ok," I said. "It doesn't matter. Just where is this fucking station?"

Leaning out of the window, I could just make out dark hedges, then a few dim lights haloed in flurrying snow. The platform was there, passing by, slower and slower. The tall, stained railway sign – one of the few still attached to its poles – read home. A deserted, badly lit, empty platform that was somehow called home.

Then the train hauled itself to a halt with a small twitch and sat still and thrumming, as though exhausted by the effort of deceleration.

And I was hanging out of the window and struggling to open the door. For a moment I thought it wouldn't – that it had been locked for some mysterious reason. That this place was more ghostly than I had ever imagined and that nobody could ever really disembark here. But then it gave way with a plunge and I almost fell out into the snow. My sister behind me. I quickly collected myself though and stood, staring round hopefully. She tugged her coat round herself tightly and made for the footbridge, but I stopped her.

"We have to wait," I said.

"Huh?" she demanded.

"Feather," I said woodenly, uncomfortably aware that this was going to be a battle.

She drew a sharp breath. "Oh for fuck's sake," she snapped. "It's cold. Come on."

I stood firm. "So how else can I end this? I may be confused, but even so . . . if I have to end it, I want to do it this way."

"It's just a fucking story," she cried. "So what if it's the last one. Have you forgotten what fantasy and reality are?"

I gave her a look that dug my heels in firmly. "Of course I know," I said dryly. "That's why we are waiting."

Whatever she might have said to that was cut off when, without fanfare, a door opened further up the train and a figure hastily stepped out. The only other person to disembark. My sister frowned and I stared hopefully as she approached.

I should be writing this down, I thought. But how? What is there to say? Like an unrequited love returning from a long trip as you stand and wait to greet her with a nervous swirl in your stomach, I stood there as she approached. She glanced at me sharply, nervous at my intense stare.

"Feather?" I asked. She flinched violently, a dawn of something like panic in her eyes. She stepped back and looked as though she was about to run. Something was singing in my head and I said the only thing I could think of that could possibly validate this connection.

"The city was no home," I murmured. "No safe place. It was only back here in the wilds that you felt any kind of relaxation. Wilds where the sea pounded eternally and was called home . . . yes?"

There was a sudden thrum from the train and I flinched and

glanced past her. Inside it all looked very bright and busy. Very normal. People were still sitting there dozing or chatting – whiling away the night journey and this brief and instantly forgotten halt in the middle of it. Then the train began to move. Feather stood there like a statue as the carriages slid past, picking up speed and gliding away from the ruined platform. The ear-piercing shriek of the rear engine came and went and then there was just lights slowly fading off and vanishing down the track. I sighed. There was a sense of loss in the lingering darkness that replaced the train.

Then even the noise was gone as well – the thrumming of the tracks finally making way for the other sounds of the world. The faint susurration of the wind and snow and, for the first time, the wash of the distant sea.

"Who are you," she murmured at last – still suspicious.

I stared in silence – unable to talk as my stomach swirled with something that was almost agony – even beginning to wish I hadn't done this crazy thing. I was aware of my sister standing there behind me looking rigid, but I had to ignore her. All I could do was hold up the papers in my hand and she stared at them blankly.

"Do you want to read?" I asked. "Maybe you can take control of this. In the same way that, if you wake up into a dream, you can take control of that. Would you like to rewrite the last chapter?"

> *. . . and in the pitch dark there was nothing to do except follow the wave as it smashed down, and the running girl smashed down with it into a pitch dark sea. That same drone rang out. Only this time it was thunder. Not one bass clarinet, but a whole orchestra of them, playing in monotone in this seaworld. They piped her onwards as she drifted – filled with the sense of dissolution. Limbs hanging useless in the water, bones shattered. The sea was flowing and singing, but who could know where? The running girl was carried – directionless – through this maze of tiled watery corridors and whispering musical instruments – where hands wanted to touch and flesh brushed cold and familiar. Then the dark took her hand and lead her away from the world. Where there was only black water – to awaken to cold and dark reality . . .*

She was naked, I read aloud – *and she found that she was shivering*. And that was it. The story was finished. A story of escape and ruination – the only thing I could possibly think of. The only possible ending. Feather backed away, still with eyes full of terror. She didn't trust me – and why should she? I was only a stranger. But she was also not quite able to turn and run. The sight of her confusion hurt, but I tried to keep calm. I knew that she could see it though – knew everything that was going through her mind. Her fear and her eternal running. Her confusion at my eyes that beseeched something she couldn't understand.

I finally dropped the pages to my side. "Perhaps we are parallel," I said dizzily. "Perhaps it's my own future that I am creating. What do you think?"

Finally she stepped backwards sharply.

"I have to go," she muttered.

I watched her with resignation as, falling over her feet slightly, she fled for the footbridge. Pattering footsteps muffled by snow, and then she was gone with barely a change to this dark evening. I sighed and rubbed at my face, papers crumpling in my hands.

My sister just stood there staring dumbly, not able to do anything as I slowly collected my wits. But even so, it was her blank eyes that finally woke me up and forced me to collect my wits.

"David?" she asked uneasily. "What is –"

But I looked away and cut her off with a gesture. I couldn't find it in me to answer questions. So instead, after a moment, we started walking through the trampled snow up the steps of the footbridge and over the gleaming threads of the railway line. The view here was wide, but the darkness was complete – not a gleam of light anywhere other than a few cold stars shining in the gaps in the clouds. But the snowy landscape itself seemed to have a faint glow now and I could just make out the tracks fading into the distance. I followed them with my eyes. The train we had ridden was long gone, but I could still imagine it racing onwards – carrying familiar people to familiar destinations.

I could have been eloquent of course – I could have worked out long speeches filled with violins and trumpets. What sentimental or philosophical self-indulgences could I have allowed myself here? But no. I was that honest at least. Maybe it was all a waste of time – you can't change the world after all. Or maybe it wasn't. One thing at least was true. The continual measurement of life did seem at a safe distance now – finally left behind. Maybe, in that sense at least, my own phrase was not so unreal. Ruination and escape.

The sound of the sea was stronger up here as well.

"I don't understand," my sister stammered, almost inaudibly.

I smiled slightly. "Maybe it's all a story. Maybe I even made you up?"

"Please," she murmured uneasily.

"It's a mug's game," I said. "Really."

Outside the station there were dark lanes waiting – lanes unbroken by any hint of light. And great bushes and trees of ivy hung heavy and white. A dark through which Feather had already passed, running to the stormy Ocean. And into that darkness we headed also.

(David Rix does not have a sister)